Two Days in Caracas

A Titus Ray Thriller

a novel by

LUANA EHRLICH

Visit the author's website at www.luanaehrlich.com

ISBN-10: 1511628650
ISBN-13: 978-1511628655

To Ray Allan Pollock,
for giving an eleven-year-old girl
permission to read adult spy novels.

PART ONE

Chapter 1

Monday, June 4

I needed to move. I needed to do it soon. I was standing inside the doorway of an apartment building on *Calle Alturas*, just a few blocks from downtown San José, Costa Rica. It was an ideal location, but I knew my presence was going to start drawing attention any minute.

Right now, the torrential downpour made it appear as if I were simply seeking shelter from the rain. However, such tropical afternoon showers usually gave way to sunny skies very rapidly in this part of the world.

Once that happened, I would need to move quickly.

I studied the house on the corner. Then, I scanned my surroundings for a building public enough for me to monitor the residence from a distance.

The overall construction of the house, with its concrete-block walls and iron bars across the windows, appeared typical for the neighborhood.

I could see nothing unusual about it.

However, its innocuous look didn't mean anything. In fact, the normality of the place made it easy for me to believe it might be Ahmed Al-Amin's safe house in San José.

On the other hand, I wasn't totally convinced Ahmed was even in

Costa Rica in the first place.

When I'd arrived at the CIA's Operations Center in Langley, Virginia, Douglas Carlton, my operations officer, had briefed me on the status of Ahmed Al-Amin, the Hezbollah assassin I was tracking. Afterward, I'd questioned one of the Agency's logistics analysts on the authenticity of the San José address he'd given me.

"How can you be certain Ahmed is at this location?" I'd asked him.

"Because we're getting pings from all the texting."

I shook my head. "I can't believe Ahmed is using an unencrypted cell phone. He's one of Hezbollah's top operatives, and if he's using his cell phone, he certainly knows our satellites can track him."

"Oh, it's not Ahmed who's doing the texting. It's the Venezuelan kid who's with him. Every night he sends a text message back to his girlfriend in Austin. Ahmed might not even know the guy is using his cell phone."

Would Ahmed really be that oblivious to what his traveling companion was doing? Somehow, I doubted it, but I didn't argue with the impossibly young analyst.

Instead, I turned my attention to Josh Kellerman, a briefer from Support Services, who spent the next thirty minutes going over my legend, explaining the myriad of details involved in the cover identity I would be using in Costa Rica.

My business card indicated I was Rafael Arroyo, Vice President of Sales for Global Resources. Kellerman gave me a brief overview of the industrial refrigeration units I was supposed to be selling, along with several boring, but very colorful brochures.

The Rafael Arroyo legend was one I'd used on previous trips to the Middle East, although then I'd been given an Arabic name. Strangely enough, I felt very comfortable in the skin of a refrigeration salesman.

Following my briefing with Kellerman, I went over to meet with Sandy Afton. She was in the southwest wing of the Agency's New Headquarters Building, where Support Services had an area the size of a department store solely devoted to men and women's clothing. Although the women's section was twice as large as the men's section, I'd never questioned the need for this.

As soon as I arrived, Sandy showed me the clothing choices she'd made for me. I approved most of them, and after that, while my suitcase was being packed by one of Sandy's assistants, I changed into a *guayabera* and a pair of dark slacks for my flight to Costa Rica.

When I'd come out of the dressing room—looking like a refrigeration salesman—Sandy had deposited the clothes and shoes I'd just removed—along with my wallet and any other items identifying me as Titus Ray—inside a metal box about the size of a small footlocker.

The last thing I did was hand over the keys to my Range Rover. I did so reluctantly, because, although I'd just purchased the car two months before, I'd already fallen in love with it—or, maybe I'd simply fallen in love with the idea of owning my own vehicle.

I said, "My car is parked over by the west gate in the parking lot used by Security."

"Why is it parked over there?"

"Because there's a handgun underneath the front seat, plus a spare in the glove compartment, and I have extra magazines in the side pocket of the duffel bag in the back."

She smiled. "I can see why they wouldn't let you drive inside the complex. Speaking of weapons, I know you don't want me to issue you a firearm before you leave, so I've instructed the embassy in San José to provide you with whatever you need when you get there."

I seldom requested the necessary credentials permitting me to get on a plane with a gun. Doing so was too much of a hassle and only served to draw attention to me.

I never wanted to draw attention to myself.

Never.

Sandy said, "I've already spoken with Ben Mitchell about the type of weapon you'll need."

Carlton had set me up with Ben Mitchell, the "Economics Officer" assigned to the American Embassy in Costa Rica. He was my contact while I was in country. In reality, like me, he was a covert intelligence officer.

Carlton had told me Mitchell had been with the Agency for five years and was classified as a Level 2 officer. While I was a Level 1 officer, I didn't think Mitchell's lower status would be a problem for me on this particular mission.

I wasn't acquainted with Ben Mitchell, but that didn't surprise me. I'd been in Iran and Afghanistan for the past seven years, and I hadn't traveled south of the border during that time.

Mitchell was scheduled to meet my flight from Miami. Meeting a refrigeration salesman from Global Resources was a natural thing for him to do in his role as the American Embassy's Economics Officer.

I was sure he would think Rafael Arroyo was a great guy.

However, as it turned out, Mitchell didn't come to the airport in San José to meet Rafael Arroyo, because, after leaving Agency's headquarters in Langley, Virginia, I had decided to change my plane ticket and take an earlier flight.

After landing in San José, I'd rented a car and arrived at my present location without having had any contact with Ben Mitchell.

That's the way I preferred to work.

Completely alone. Solo.

Now though, as I observed the boxy concrete house from the shelter of the apartment building, I was beginning to regret my decision to ditch Mitchell.

Having another set of eyes at the rear of the house might prove beneficial, and since I'd come to the address directly from the airport, I didn't have a weapon on me.

Knowing what I knew about Ahmed, I had no intention of confronting him without some kind of firepower.

When I'd entered the *Calle Alturas* neighborhood earlier, I'd spotted a man and a woman inside a Toyota Highlander parked about a block away from the safe house. I knew they had to be members of the surveillance team Mitchell had brought in to keep an eye on the house until I arrived. They were clearly amateurs, and if Ahmed were in the house, it wouldn't be long before he would notice them as well.

If he hadn't already spotted them.

The rain finally let up, and I stepped out of the doorway and walked over to a small pastry shop located next door to a video store. Three small café tables had been placed on the patio in front of the pastry shop, and when a waiter had finished drying off one of the wrought-iron chairs, I sat down and ordered *un café sin leche*.

Once the waiter had gone inside to get my coffee, I felt inside my pants pocket for my satellite phone and punched in the numbers I'd memorized before leaving Langley.

When Ben Mitchell came on the line, I told him my location and asked him to meet me. He said he would be driving a late model Jeep, and then he hung up on me.

He sounded ticked off.

♦♦♦♦

I was savoring the last drops of my second cup of Costa Rica's finest beverage when I spotted Mitchell driving down *Calle Alturas*.

He followed my instructions and parked one block south of my location. As he made his way up the busy street carrying a hard-shelled briefcase at his side, I had plenty of time to observe him.

The first thing I noticed was that he was about my height—six feet—but, unlike me, he appeared very young. He had a round, boyish face, and his thick, dark hair was disheveled, as if he'd recently been caught up in a windstorm. However, since there was no wind to speak of, I suspected this was simply the type of modern hairstyle adopted by guys under forty these days.

Although he wasn't obvious about it, I saw him carefully assessing his surroundings, including me. However, he barely gave the faded green house on the corner a cursory glance.

When he reached the pastry shop, he extended his hand, put a smile on his face, and said, "Mr. Arroyo, I'm Ben Mitchell."

We shook hands, and as he seated himself, he signaled the waiter he wanted what I was drinking. While the waiter was getting his coffee, we chatted about Global Resources.

For any interested observers, I took out one of the company's brochures and made a big show of unfolding it and pointing out the features of an expensive refrigeration unit.

Once the waiter had placed his coffee on the table and left, Mitchell leaned in toward me and asked, "What exactly do you think you're doing?"

His smile had disappeared.

"I'm tracking a terrorist who killed one of our covert operatives in Dallas last month. Weren't you briefed in on this?"

"Of course, I was briefed in."

Mitchell picked up a spoon and studied it.

He appeared to scrutinize it so intently, someone might have thought he collected spoons for a hobby. After a few seconds, he laid it back down on the table and looked up at me.

I noticed his eyes were slightly dilated, and I saw a muscle on the left side of his face begin to twitch. I immediately recognized these as signs Ben Mitchell was having trouble controlling his temper.

I recognized the symptoms because I had often exhibited them myself.

He said, "I was told to meet you at the airport later today. Mind telling me what you're doing here now?"

I was amused by his anger, and until a few months ago, I would have enjoyed seeing just how much I could have harassed him before he finally exploded. Now, though, I resisted that temptation and explained myself—sort of.

"I took an earlier flight."

He nodded his head but kept looking at me, as if he expected me to continue giving him an explanation.

I thought about the nonchalant way he'd done the recon on the cement house while appearing not to do so, and I decided to give him what he wanted.

"Look, I came in earlier than expected, because I've been doing this long enough to know my chances of staying alive are always better if I do the unexpected. Being predictable gets you killed."

He shifted his eyes over to a couple of kids riding their bikes down the sidewalk and gave them his full attention for a few seconds.

I sensed his anger was dissipating, and it made me wonder if Ben Mitchell was a short fuse but quick recovery kind of guy.

He turned and looked at me once again. "How long have you been with the Agency?"

I knew that old trick—gain control of your emotions by changing the subject—and he had just executed it perfectly.

"I was recruited back in the late '80s."

"An old-timer, huh?"

"I prefer the word seasoned."

He gave a short laugh. "Okay, how do you want to play this?"

I suggested he move his surveillance team in the Toyota Highlander further down the street and then have them point the vehicle in the opposite direction. I also told him I wanted a specific description of anyone they saw entering or leaving the house.

He called and gave Josué, the driver of the Toyota, my instructions. Then, I explained about the exfiltration procedure Carlton and I had worked out at Langley. The plan's endpoint culminated when we had Ahmed safely tucked away in a luxury cell at the Jihadi Prison Camp at Gitmo. Before that happened, though, Mitchell and I still needed to give the details some fine-tuning.

He glanced down at his watch. "I'm due back at the embassy in fifteen minutes. Will you be sticking around here?"

"Looks like Josué and his partner have this covered for now. I'll go check into my hotel and meet you back here in a couple of hours. Let's meet at the restaurant on the corner."

He agreed, and then he headed back to his Jeep. Once I saw him drive off, I picked up the black briefcase he'd left behind and made my way over to my rental car.

Just to make sure I wasn't under surveillance, though, I made several stops along the way—once to select a CD from a sidewalk display, once to purchase some fresh pineapple from a fruit vendor, and once to buy a lottery ticket from a kid with a dirty face.

As far as I could tell, no one appeared to be the least bit interested in me, and when I drove away from the neighborhood, I felt certain my prospects for capturing Ahmed were excellent.

Later though, I wondered if I'd stayed around the neighborhood a little longer, if I could have prevented what happened next.

Chapter 2

The hotel I'd booked in San José was located near the center of town. Hotel Plaza Real wasn't much to look at on the outside, but my room was clean and located near the stairwell—perfect accommodations, as far as I was concerned.

After hanging out the "Do Not Disturb" sign, I locked the door and opened the briefcase Mitchell had left me. Nestled inside, I found a semi-automatic pistol, along with a holster and some ammo.

When my satphone vibrated a few minutes later, I'd just finished checking out the weapon.

The call was from Mitchell.

"There's a package for you here at the embassy," he said. "My instructions were to give it to you when you arrived at the airport *later* this afternoon."

Unlike earlier, he sounded more amused than angry with me.

"I'll meet you at the embassy within the hour."

"Why don't I just bring it by your hotel? It's only a few blocks from here."

"No, that won't be necessary. I'll come over to the embassy."

I heard him sigh. "I don't suppose you're staying at the Hotel Sabana where you're booked, are you?"

"No."

"Of course not."

I asked, "What's the protocol once I get to the embassy?"

"Go to the lobby reception area; give your name to the security officer in the last cubicle on your right, and he'll escort you to my office."

He hung up without saying goodbye.

♦♦♦♦

The American Embassy in San José was located near the downtown plaza on a quiet side street. Compared with other American embassies, it wasn't a very impressive building, but, when I arrived, the reception area was bustling with activity.

I quickly scanned the crowd.

Most of the faces were Hispanic, but there were a few Caucasians interspersed among the double lines. I made note of two men with Arabic features sitting side-by-side. They were filling out some paperwork, and one of them appeared to give me some extra attention.

Following Mitchell's instructions, I walked over to the last cubicle on my right. To my surprise, Mitchell himself appeared and buzzed me in the locked gate and through to an adjacent door.

Once inside, he motioned for me to follow him down a short hallway toward an elevator.

"Is the embassy shorthanded or is there some other reason why you're moonlighting as a security guard?"

He smiled. "I was *asked* to escort you."

Once we entered the elevator and it started its descent, I said, "Okay, I'm curious. Asked by whom?"

"The COS wants to meet with you downstairs."

I could tell he was enjoying the fact I was on the receiving end of something unexpected. It never occurred to me I'd be meeting with Toby Bledsoe, the CIA's chief of station in Costa Rica.

Of course, Mitchell knew that.

Although I'd spent a few years in the early part of my career assigned to the Latin American desk, I was—strictly speaking—a Middle Eastern operative. My mission inside Costa Rica was being run by Douglas Carlton, my operations officer and head of the Middle Eastern division at the Agency. The two of us had worked together for a long time, and I could think of no reason I needed to meet with Toby Bledsoe while I was in Costa Rica.

I moved over to the elevator's control panel and hit the emergency stop button.

The elevator came to an abrupt halt.

Mitchell immediately placed his hand on his firearm. "What's going on?"

"Take it easy," I said, raising my hands to show him I wasn't a threat. "That's what I want you to tell me. What's going on?"

His shoulders relaxed, and then he laughed. "Oh, so that's it. You don't mind giving surprises, but you hate receiving them?"

"That's it."

"We can't talk here."

He reached over and punched the button for the basement level once again. "If the elevator stalls, security will sound the alarm."

When the doors opened on the basement level, I followed Mitchell down a narrow hallway to an unmarked door. He used his keycard to get us in, and motion-sensor lights came on as soon as we entered the room.

I immediately recognized the room as The Bubble. All embassies are required to have them. It's a soundproof unit lined with acoustical tiles and used for meetings of a sensitive nature or sometimes for interrogating people with sensitive information.

It's a sensitive kind of place.

I took a seat at one end of a long conference table.

"So why does Bledsoe want to see me?"

Mitchell held a finger to his lips and removed a small, gray device from his pocket. It was an electronic debugger, about the size of a cell phone, and he used it to sweep the room for any electronic listening devices.

It never beeped.

Once he'd determined the room was clean, Mitchell slipped the device back inside his pants pocket and sat down at the conference table across from me.

He said, "Toby Bledsoe doesn't believe you're here tracking down a terrorist. He thinks you're here doing an internal investigation on him."

I thought he might be joking, but I could read nothing in his facial expression indicating that.

I doubted Mitchell's disclosure, but I didn't doubt he believed it.

While I knew the Agency's Office of Inspector General (OIG) was responsible for internal investigations inside the CIA, I'd never heard of an intelligence officer being used to conduct such an investigation.

"Why would Bledsoe think such a thing?"

"He has sources inside the Agency who told him the Deputy Director put you on a year's medical leave a few months ago. Now you've shown up here in Costa Rica in pursuit of a Hezbollah terrorist. Costa Rica is not a hotbed of terrorism. The facts just don't add up, and believe me, if the facts don't add up, Toby gets paranoid."

"Well, good for him. Paranoia should be mandatory for all station chiefs."

Mitchell grabbed a bottle of water from a credenza behind him.

"Want one?"

I nodded, and after he'd tossed it over, I asked, "Is Bledsoe involved in something that might initiate an internal investigation from the OIG?"

Mitchell unscrewed the bottle cap and took a long drink.

He shook his head. "Not that I know of. However, a few months ago, San José's leading newspaper wrote an exposé on a special unit within Costa Rica's own intelligence service. The article claimed the unit was funded by outside sources, and the agents involved had been conducting illegal wiretapping activities against drug traffickers. There were allegations the unit had been recruited, trained, and funded by the CIA. If that was our operation, Bledsoe never told me anything about it."

I smiled at his disclosure. "Getting caught in a foreign country doing nefarious deeds is always regrettable, but it's not likely to trigger an internal investigation by the OIG."

Mitchell shrugged. "Well, all I know is, Toby got pretty upset when he heard you were coming here."

Moments later, the door to The Bubble swung open and Toby Bledsoe entered the room. He was carrying a bulging black briefcase at his side, and the moment he crossed the threshold, he stopped in his tracks and stared at me.

I returned the favor.

If Bledsoe's lined face and sparse gray hair were any indication, he was close to the Agency's mandatory retirement age. I immediately thought he looked more like a beneficent grandfather than an intelligence operative.

As he continued looking me over, I had a hard time defining the expression on his face. Finally, I decided it was either mild amusement or great displeasure.

Mitchell broke the silence. "Toby, this is—"

Bledsoe stepped forward and grabbed my outstretched hand. "Titus Ray. I know. I know."

"You're looking good, Toby."

Bledsoe turned and addressed Mitchell, who seemed surprised to discover Bledsoe and I knew each other.

"I'll take it from here, Ben. When I'm finished talking to Titus, I'll send him up to your office."

Looking embarrassed, Mitchell mumbled something about checking in on the surveillance team and headed out the door.

After he left, Bledsoe took a seat in the chair opposite me and hoisted his overstuffed briefcase up to the table after him.

Neither of us spoke for a moment.

Finally, I said, "It's really great to see you again, Toby."

He peered at me over the tops of his glasses. "You mean you've finally forgiven me?"

"Almost."

♦♦♦♦

For the next twenty minutes, Bledsoe and I talked about the time we'd spent working together in Nicaragua helping organize the oppositional forces against the socialist Sandinista government.

I was fresh out of the CIA's training school at Camp Peary then, whereas Bledsoe had already racked up years of field experience. We'd often butted heads because I was arrogant and self-centered. Like a young teenager relating to a parent, I thought I knew everything and Bledsoe knew nothing.

"Ben Mitchell reminds me of a young Titus Ray," I said.

Bledsoe picked up a bottle cap from the table and flicked it across the room toward a wastebasket.

He missed.

"Yeah, except he doesn't question everything I tell him."

I knew Bledsoe had to be referring to the time I'd almost gotten both of us killed because I'd refused to believe his intel about a Sandinista general.

I ignored his pointed remark and asked, "You mean like the story you told him about the OIG investigating you?"

Bledsoe's craggy face morphed into an expression some might describe as a smile. Others might identify it as a grimace.

"He told you that, huh?"

I nodded. "He also thinks you're too paranoid."

Bledsoe slapped his hand down on the wooden table. "That kid. I was just messing with him about the OIG. He takes things way too seriously."

"So I've noticed."

He shook his head. "Don't get me wrong, though. He's got excellent tradecraft and great surveillance skills. I'm sure he's going to be a superb operative. He could probably teach you a thing or two."

"Toby, why am I here? I'm sure you didn't drag me in The Bubble to talk about Ben Mitchell."

He unsnapped his briefcase. "No, I didn't."

After removing several file folders and a laptop computer from the briefcase, Bledsoe pulled the only red-tagged folder from among the stack and laid it down in the space between us.

"Before I show you this, Titus," he said, tapping his forefinger on the red folder, "tell me why the DDO is allowing Carlton's office to run a Middle Eastern operative down here in Costa Rica."

I tried to deflect Bledsoe's question. "Haven't you read the DDO's brief on—"

"Oh, don't give me that," he said, brushing aside my remark with a wave of his hand. "I want the real story. Why did they pull you off a medical to go after this Ahmed Al-Amin?"

I smiled at him. "Okay, Toby, I'll give you the real story, but you realize I'm breaking the DDO's rules about sharing operational intel across divisional lines?"

Bledsoe leaned back in his chair and clasped his hands behind his head. "And since when has breaking the rules ever bothered you?"

Chapter 3

I decided to give Bledsoe the full background on Ahmed Al-Amin. For one thing, I'd learned early in my career that withholding information from a station chief wasn't a very smart idea.

Another reason I went ahead and gave him a complete rundown on Ahmed was that I suspected he already knew the story anyway. If that were the case, and I didn't tell him everything, he might decide not to give me his full cooperation.

Less than full cooperation from Toby Bledsoe was like having no cooperation at all.

I began by telling him what had happened to me six months ago in Tehran.

"After spending two years running an operation inside Iran, I lost my entire network. Five of my six assets were either murdered or tortured to death."

Bledsoe asked, "Did VEVAK kill them?"

He was referring to Iran's secret police, and I suddenly remembered Bledsoe's intense hatred for Nicaragua's elite security force, the DGSE, and his obsession with any country using a secret police force to terrorize its people. When I'd worked with Bledsoe before, he had the names of all the organizations engaging in such atrocities memorized, and he would tell anyone who would listen to him about the number of people they'd killed each year.

"Yes, it was VEVAK."

"Thought so."

"You'll be happy to know when they came after me, I managed to kill two of their agents."

"How did you escape arrest after killing them?"

"The only way I could. I jumped off a three-story roof. I survived—I guess that's pretty obvious—but when I jumped, I shattered my left leg. I wouldn't be here today without the help of our Israeli friends."

"Mossad showed up?"

"Just when I needed them."

"You were very lucky, Titus."

"I believe God was looking out for me, Toby."

Bledsoe raised his bushy eyebrows and chuckled. "Really?"

I ignored his skepticism and continued. "Mossad put me in a safe house while my leg healed, but the whole time I was there I had both VEVAK and the Iranian Revolutionary Guard scouring the countryside looking for me. I finally made it across the border into Turkey and back home to the States, but, like I said, I wouldn't have done so without the help of Mossad."

"So what happened? Did VEVAK want revenge for the agents you'd killed?"

"You guessed it. A few weeks after I got back to Langley, Carlton showed me the NSA intercepts indicating VEVAK had hired an assassin from Hezbollah to track me down in the States."

"That would be Ahmed Al-Amin?"

I nodded. "While I was on medical leave in Oklahoma, I got a flash priority email from Simon Wassermann asking me to meet him in Dallas. He was just coming—"

"Why would he contact you directly? Why wouldn't he go through Carlton?"

"He had his reasons, and no, I'm not going to tell you what they were."

Bledsoe shrugged. "Suit yourself."

"He was just coming in from an assignment in Syria where he'd been running assets inside one of Hezbollah's affiliate groups. When we met in Dallas, he told me his agent knew Ahmed was already in the States and had crossed the border with the help of one of the Mexican drug cartels."

"Simon was always one of the best at working an asset."

Since he'd used the past tense when speaking about Wassermann, I suspected Bledsoe already knew what I was about to tell him.

"After we talked, Simon left the room to get something out of his car, and that's when he was shot by a high-powered rifle. He never even had a chance to defend himself."

I paused when I remembered standing over Wassermann's dead body in the parking lot.

A wave of sadness washed over me, but I shook it off and continued. "The rain had been coming down pretty hard, and since Simon was wearing my baseball cap, I'm pretty sure Ahmed thought he was taking me out when he shot him."

"And you're positive the shooter was Ahmed?"

"Yes. He shot Simon from a van on the far side of the hotel's parking lot. The hotel's security cameras showed the van leaving the area immediately after the shooting."

"I'm assuming he ditched it immediately."

I nodded. "The FBI found the van abandoned in Waco. It was registered to a student at the University of Texas in Austin, a Venezuelan. There was no sign of the Venezuelan in Austin, though, and his friends told the feds he had left school and gone back to Caracas. This was later verified by his girlfriend."

"So is this Venezuelan student the kid who's traveling with Ahmed?"

I nodded. "Carlton got a positive ID on him from a car dealer in San Marcos, Texas, about two weeks ago when he paid cash for a brand-new Dodge Durango. His name is Ernesto Montilla."

"So Ahmed and this Ernesto kid have been traveling through Central America for the past two weeks?"

"That's right."

Bledsoe removed his glasses and started massaging the bridge of his nose. "What does Carlton think they're doing here in San José?"

Although Bledsoe's question sounded innocent enough, answering it could get me in some hot water back at the Agency.

After 9/11, many of the restrictions governing intra-Agency

communications had been lifted. However, one rule affecting station chiefs had been left in place. Specifically, all product produced by one division had to undergo clearance by the Deputy Director of Operations before being passed along to another division.

This was as crazy as it sounded.

Since I was operating under the Middle Eastern division and Bledsoe was a Latin American station chief, we weren't supposed to share information with each other—at least not without contacting our division heads first. If I decided to answer his question, I'd be violating an Agency rule about sharing intel with field officers who hadn't been briefed into the mission.

However, if the files Bledsoe had taken out of his briefcase were any indication, he seemed poised to bypass certain procedural rules and share some of his intel with me.

For that to happen, though, I knew I would have to do the same.

It took me all of five seconds to decide to tell him everything.

"After Simon Wassermann's death, our analysts believed Ahmed would immediately return to Syria. However, when he started his cross-country trek through Central America, the analysts revised their opinion. Now, they believe he's been given another assignment, probably another contract kill, and since he's got the Venezuelan kid with him, it could mean he's headed there."

"Have they identified his target yet?"

"No, not yet, but I believe it's someone Iran considers either a threat or a detriment to their plans in Latin America." I shook my head. "But it doesn't really matter, because I'm authorized to take Ahmed into custody and dispatch him off to Gitmo immediately. Maybe his interrogators at Gitmo will get that information from him."

Bledsoe looked at me as if he didn't quite believe I was being forthcoming with him.

"Does the Agency know how Ahmed arrived in the States in the first place?"

"Carlton said he flew to Mexico City from Damascus on a Lebanese passport. Once he got to Mexico, he disappeared. But since Hezbollah has ties with the Zeta drug cartel, our analysts believe the cartel helped him make his way up to Nuevo Laredo, over the U.S. border, and then on to Dallas. They're still pulling the data threads on that connection though."

Bledsoe said, "I know the cartel must be involved in this, and I'll tell you why."

He opened the red folder and removed a single sheet of paper. "About a year ago, after I made several unsuccessful attempts to obtain any intel on the drug cartels operating here, I finally recruited an asset inside the Zeta ring. His name is Hernando, and although he's a very low-level employee, he's a solid source of information.

"Right now, all he does is take care of administrative details and run errands. I've been very cautious about using him because I want his bosses to trust him completely. That way he can work his way up the ranks and be privy to the kind of information we can use to bring down the cartel's entire network. I've been carefully grooming him for over a year now. It's been a slow process, but I'm certain we're going to get some results soon."

"I haven't forgotten your cautious nature, Toby."

He stared at me for several seconds, probably trying to decide if my remark was meant as a compliment or a criticism.

I tried to look noncommittal.

He went on. "For the past six months, the cartel's been ferrying drugs into the States using couriers who pose as tourists from San José. Since my asset arranges visas and airline tickets for them, I asked him to photocopy the passports of the mules they were using to move their product north. Here's the list I made after he gave me the passport copies."

He handed me the sheet of paper he'd been holding in his hand.

As I scanned the contents, he asked, "Anything jump out at you?"

My eyes ran down the list of Hispanic names and countries of origin gleaned from the passports of the people working for the cartel.

"More than half of them are from Venezuela."

"Move to the head of the class."

He opened a second folder and pushed several sheets of paper across the table toward me. "I know these aren't the best quality photos, but tell me what you think."

I flipped through several pages of passport photos. There were no names identifying the faces, but it didn't take me long to draw a conclusion.

"As a group, I'd say all these men and women appear to be of Middle Eastern descent, probably from Syria."

"My thoughts exactly," he said. "However, all the Venezuelans on this list," he held up the first document he'd given me, "belong to these people." He held up the pages containing the passport photos of the Syrians.

"So you think Venezuela is supplying false passports to various Syrian men and women, and then letting the cartel use them as drug runners?"

He nodded his head. "That's exactly what I think."

He gathered up the documents he'd shown me and shoved them back inside his briefcase. "You can see why your operation linking a Hezbollah operative from Syria and a Venezuelan student got my attention. That's why I wanted— "

Mitchell suddenly opened the door and entered The Bubble.

"I'm sorry to interrupt, but Titus said to let him know the minute there was any activity at the house on *Alturas*."

"What happened?"

"A man just walked out the front door."

Chapter 4

I rode with Mitchell back over to the *Calle Alturas* neighborhood. Along the way, he called in a second surveillance team, so we could meet up with Josué and his partner in the parking lot of *El Supermercado,* a grocery store located a block away from Ahmed's safe house.

Within five minutes of our arrival, Mitchell's first surveillance team pulled in and parked beside us. Josué stayed inside the SUV while his partner, a young woman with a long black ponytail, emerged from the passenger side.

After she slipped in the backseat of the Jeep, Mitchell introduced her as Sonya. She gave me a curt nod, and then she handed Mitchell an expensive-looking camera with a telephoto lens on it. He clicked through several shots on the camera's LCD monitor.

As I waited for him to finish, I noticed Sonya was staring at me from the backseat. When I glanced back at her, she smiled and looked away.

Mitchell shook his head as he handed the camera over to me. "Not much there. The next to the last shot is the best one."

As we were leaving the embassy, Mitchell had told me his watchers hadn't noticed any activity at the house until an old man was seen coming out the front door. He'd walked the short distance down the block to a bus stop—using a cane for support—and then boarded the next bus pulling up to the curb a few seconds later.

I looked at the camera's monitor while scrolling through the photos.

Sonya had managed to snap several frames, but the one showing the old man's face was only a profile of him. It was taken at the moment he was boarding the bus. However, with his beard and sunglasses, it was hard to note any distinguishing characteristics.

Mitchell asked, "Is it possible that old man is Ahmed?"

"Possible? Sure, it's possible, but I can't be positive from these shots."

I turned around and addressed Sonya in Spanish. "What impression did you have of the man in the photographs?"

Costa Rican women are called *ticas*. They're known throughout Latin America for their extraordinary beauty, and Sonya was a true *tica* in that sense. In fact, I found it hard not to be distracted by her expressive brown eyes as she answered my questions.

"Well, . . ." she said, pausing as she gave some thought to my question, "he was walking to the bus very slowly."

"Could you tell if he needed the cane for balance or do you think it was just a prop?"

"I couldn't say for sure, but it looked as if he were leaning on the cane as he walked."

"Where was the bus headed?"

"It was *El Central*, so it was going downtown."

Mitchell interjected. "From there, he could have caught a taxi or taken another bus to almost any place in Costa Rica. However, if the old man were really Ahmed, why would he be taking the bus? He's got the kid's Durango parked right outside the house."

I said, "Perhaps he wanted to arrive at his destination in the guise of a harmless old man who takes the bus."

I handed the camera back to Sonya. "Thanks for your help. You did the right thing by continuing your surveillance on the house and not following him. If he suspected someone was watching the house, getting on the bus might have been a ploy to draw you away."

She looked over at Mitchell and nodded. "That's what Ben instructed us to do."

Mitchell glanced back at her and smiled.

I couldn't help but notice their eye contact continued for several seconds longer than necessary.

As Sonya started to get out of the car, she turned back to Mitchell. "Didn't you say there were at least two people inside the house?"

He nodded. "That's right."

"So why did he lock the front door when he left?"

Both of us considered her question for a moment, and I waited to see if Mitchell might work it out for himself.

A few seconds later, he looked over at me and asked, "Why would he lock the front door from the outside if there were still people inside the house?"

"Let's go find out."

♦♦♦♦

Sonya got out of the Jeep and walked back over to the Toyota after Mitchell had instructed her to tell Josué to stay in place until he called them.

Once Mitchell had pulled out of the parking lot and into traffic, I asked what he'd learned about the owners of the house on *Alturas*.

"Property ownership here is not as transparent as it is in the States. The owner of record is listed as *Banco Nacional*, but that doesn't mean an individual doesn't own it. I've asked one of the property analysts at the Agency to access the bank records and find out who really owns it."

"That may take awhile, but I'm betting someone from one of the cartels is the real owner, and it's one of their safe houses."

When Mitchell turned onto *Calle Alturas*, he parked the Jeep across the street from the pastry shop, near the spot where I'd purchased the CD earlier in the day. As we sat there observing the house, he used his cell phone to check in with his second surveillance team, and I decided it was a good time to phone Carlton and get an update on Ahmed.

After I'd verified my code with Communication Services, Carlton came on the line.

"Did your flight arrive early?" he asked.

"About five hours early."

I knew Support had already told him I'd changed my ticket, and that he wasn't really surprised to hear from me so soon.

But, Carlton was Carlton, and playing mind games was a specialty with him.

He also had control issues and micromanaged his office down to the last detail, requiring all staff—from data analysts to support technicians—to give him hourly updates whenever his operatives were in the field.

I never took exception to my handler being a control freak—except when he decided to delve into my personal life.

He asked, "What's your assessment? Have you seen any activity?"

"Nothing definitive yet. No clear sightings of either Ahmed or Ernesto. An elderly male was seen leaving the house and boarding a bus about an hour ago, but he hasn't been identified yet."

"What about the vehicle?"

"It's parked outside the house. I'm looking at it right now."

He asked me some additional questions about the location, specifically wanting more details on the neighborhood around Ahmed's house. Finally, he asked if I thought there needed to be any changes in the number of team members on the extraction team.

When I'd answered everything to his satisfaction, he said, "What's going on with you?"

Was it something in my voice?

Did I give off a certain vibe when something was bugging me?

I asked, "Did Ernesto text his girlfriend in Austin last night?"

I heard papers rustling as Carlton shifted through the printouts. I knew he could immediately lay his hands on the reports, because, even though he was simultaneously running several covert officers, he had his oversized desk arranged in what he called his stacks.

"I have the information right here."

There was dead air between us for a few seconds.

I knew he wanted me to make some observation about how efficient he was in finding the information so quickly.

I kept quiet.

After a beat or two, he continued. "Yes, he contacted her last night around midnight, but he also texted her earlier today. He was texting her about an hour ago."

"An hour ago?"

"That's right," he said. "An hour and twenty minutes ago, he texted her again. What bothers you about—"

"I need to go. I'll get back to you soon."

♦♦♦♦

After Mitchell finished talking to his surveillance team, I asked if he had any binoculars in the car. He pointed to the floorboard behind my seat.

"Did Carlton give you anything?"

"Not exactly," I said, pulling out the binoculars.

I slowly scanned the three windows facing the street. Venetians blinds were covering all three windows, but I still tried to see if I could detect any shadows or signs of movement behind them.

It was an exercise in futility.

I said, "Call Josué and Sonya and get them over here. I want to send Sonya up to the front door and see who answers it. She can pretend to be a neighbor who needs to borrow something."

"I don't think she—"

"Scratch that. Have her grab some advertisements from *El Supermercado* and tell her to look as if she's delivering them around the neighborhood. We'll see if she gets a response when she delivers one to Ahmed's door."

Mitchell sounded hesitant. "She's strictly surveillance, Titus. Nothing more. She's had no training for anything like that."

"Call her. I think she'll do it."

Mitchell hit the speed dial on his phone, and after, listening to his conversation with her, I could tell Sonya had agreed to do it.

The moment he hung up, he said, "She'll do it, but I think you're putting her at risk. What happens if Ahmed answers the door?"

"Ahmed is not going to answer the door, Ben."

"How can you be certain of that?"

"Because he dressed up as an old man and left the house an hour ago."

Chapter 5

While I made my way down *Calle Alturas* toward the alley running behind the safe house, Mitchell and the other members of his surveillance teams positioned themselves at various locations at the front of the house.

Although I wasn't particularly worried about Sonya's safety, I still kept an eye on her as she walked down the street, holding some kind of flyer in her hand. Playing the role I'd assigned her, she stopped at a residence along the busy street and tucked one of the flyers inside the front door.

I watched her for any signs of nervousness.

I didn't see any. Not one.

Although Mitchell had indicated she wasn't a trained agent, she nonetheless followed prescribed tradecraft. She even acted as if she didn't know me when we passed each other on the narrow sidewalk.

Once she'd turned the corner and headed toward the safe house, I disappeared down the alley running behind it. Barely thirty feet in, I came across a shed at the back of the property and crouched down behind it, waiting to hear from Mitchell.

From this position, it was easy to observe the rear of the house. It looked almost identical to the front, with iron bars running across three sets of windows. The only difference appeared to be the back door. There were no iron bars protecting it, but it looked to be a solid piece of wood protected by a single deadbolt.

Five minutes went by, and then I received a call from Mitchell.

He sounded relieved.

"Sonya's leaving. No one answered the door."

"Just as I expected."

"Shall I meet you at my car?"

"No, hold your position. I want to check something out."

While waiting for Mitchell's phone call, I'd noticed the blinds covering one of the back windows were either broken or hadn't been closed properly. Either way, there was an opening about an inch wide at the bottom of one of the windows.

Abandoning my position near the shed, I covered the backyard in a few quick strides. Then, I cautiously moved along the side of the house in order to take a look inside.

Suddenly, I heard a dog growling.

I immediately looked around for any sign of the animal, but no pooch appeared.

After a beat or two, I approached the window. The opening I had observed was low to the ground, so I squatted down in a half-crouch and attempted to look inside.

That's when I heard the growl again.

This time, I realized the noise was coming from inside the house.

However, peering through the opening in the blinds proved useless; it was simply too dark inside to be able to see anything.

Within a few seconds, though, I realized the sound I'd heard wasn't the sound of a dog growling.

It was the sound a human being, someone who was dealing with an intense amount of pain.

♦♦♦♦

I immediately called Mitchell and had him meet me at the back of the house. While waiting for him to show up, I called Toby Bledsoe.

He quickly agreed to do everything I asked of him.

When Mitchell arrived in the Jeep, he pulled a crowbar out of his trunk and ordered the other members of his surveillance crew to watch the front of the house while we approached the rear.

I withdrew my firearm and covered Mitchell, while he used the crowbar to breach the back door. As soon as we were inside, he set the crowbar down and pulled out his handgun.

We had entered the house through the kitchen. It was in shambles, but there was no one in there to greet us.

However, the smell of unwashed dishes and rotting food was almost a presence in itself. The odor permeated everything. Flies hovered over food-encrusted plates and cockroaches scurried across the countertop.

Mitchell and I moved from the kitchen into a narrow hallway. From there, I could hear the distressful sounds I'd heard earlier. I quickly determined the noise was coming from a room at the end of the hallway.

The door was closed, but, if the Disney poster covering the doorway were any indication, the room must have been a child's bedroom at one time.

I used hand signals to let Mitchell know I wanted to check out the rest of the house before entering the bedroom. He nodded his agreement, and in less than a minute, we'd cleared a sparsely furnished living area, a bathroom, and a second bedroom.

All were unoccupied.

As soon as we'd regrouped in the hallway, I gave Mitchell a nod, and he slammed his foot into the Disney poster. His heel hit the spot right above Mickey's head, and the flimsy wooden door shattered.

♦♦♦♦

Once inside, we discovered a man writhing in pain. He was curled up in a fetal position on a blood-soaked mattress, holding his abdomen.

That area appeared to be the source of all the blood.

When we came through the door, his eyes popped open. Seconds later, he raised his arm as if he were beckoning us to his side or trying to fend us off—I wasn't sure.

I knelt down beside him and felt his pulse.

It was weak.

"We need to get him out to your Jeep," I told Mitchell.

When he didn't answer, I turned around and saw him staring down at the body, seemingly paralyzed by the ghastly sight.

I realized he hadn't seen a lot of wounded men before.

When I repeated the order, he immediately grabbed his phone and told Sonya to get the Jeep ready.

After he hung up, I said, "See if you can find some towels or a bed sheet, anything we could wrap around his middle and stop the bleeding."

Mitchell went across the hallway to the bathroom and returned with a couple of dirty towels. I pressed them against the man's wound and helped him sit up.

He groaned and mumbled something in Spanish.

"What's your name?" I asked.

"Ernesto," he muttered. "Ernesto Montilla."

Seconds later, he passed out.

♦♦♦♦

Before entering the house, I'd called Bledsoe and asked him to find a medical facility where no one would ask too many questions.

Once we got Ernesto inside the car, I called Bledsoe again, and he gave Mitchell directions to a clinic in Heredia, a small village located on the outskirts of the city.

Mitchell drove the Jeep through the crowded streets of San José at breakneck speed; perhaps trying to compensate for his momentary freeze at the sight of Ernesto's wound. However, I was grateful he did it without getting us killed, or even worse, stopped by the local authorities.

I sat in the backseat with Ernesto and applied pressure to his wound. After examining his abdomen, I determined someone had taken a knife and slashed him numerous times.

When we were almost to the clinic, he regained consciousness, and that's when I noticed his lips were moving.

I whispered in his ear, "Where's Ahmed?"

His speech came in short, breathy gasps. "Tried to . . . kill me."

"Where is he, Ernesto?" I asked. "Where's Ahmed?"

When he didn't reply, I thumped his face a couple of times.

He didn't respond, and I thought he'd passed out again.

However, a few seconds later, I heard him say, "Venezuela."

I realized the boy might simply be delirious about his home in Venezuela, so I pressed him. "Venezuela? Has Ahmed gone to Venezuela?"

He didn't slur his words this time. "Soon. Going . . . soon."

"What's Ahmed doing in Costa Rica?"

"Pasa . . . pasa . . ."

Since we were speaking Spanish, when I heard him say *pasa*, I thought Ernesto was trying to say they were just passing through Costa Rica the same way they'd been passing through other Central American countries.

However, that didn't make sense because he and Ahmed had been living in the safe house for over a week. I started to press him on this, but, after struggling to get his breath, he finally completed the word.

"Pasa . . . Pasaportes."

Passports.

Ahmed was in need of a passport. That made sense.

The moment I started to question Ernesto further about the passport, his head lolled to one side. Although I could tell he was still breathing, he was out cold once again.

Two men pushing a gurney were waiting for us when we pulled up to the clinic's emergency room. Mitchell handled everything with the staff, and I found an isolated spot in the waiting room where I could call Bledsoe.

After updating him, I requested he put a surveillance team at the airport and have them report any sightings of an old man with a cane trying to get on a flight to Venezuela.

"Carlton will have to do a rewrite of the mission now," I told Bledsoe, "and I want you to be briefed in on the operation."

"That only makes sense."

"Well, I'm not going to use that as my argument."

He laughed. "I'll start making some inquiries about the passport angle from some of my sources."

"We also need to get Ernesto's vehicle off the street and have Carlton send some of our forensic guys down here to look it over."

"I'll see what I can do. What about the house?"

"Ben and I will head back over there in a few minutes and see what we can turn up."

I spotted Mitchell wandering around the lobby and waved him over.

Bledsoe asked, "Anything else I can do?"

"Yes. Notify your communications officer I'll need a video hookup with Carlton's office later today. Set it up for three hours from now."

"Done."

As I was about to hang up, he added. "Be careful when you and Ben go back to the safe house. Remember the cartel has eyes everywhere."

"Roger that."

Just as I hung up, Mitchell walked over.

"That was Toby," I said. "I told him we're headed back to the house now."

He shook his head. "He didn't make it. Ernesto is dead."

Chapter 6

Mitchell was quiet as we drove back into the city, and I wondered if the bravado I'd seen in him earlier in the day had been tamped down by the stark realities of death.

Death, especially a gruesome one, can shock the human organism into a kind of lethargic depression. In Afghanistan, I'd observed this behavior in operatives arriving in country straight from the Agency's training facility at Camp Peary.

Since I knew Mitchell didn't have much experience in the field, I regretted the arrogance I'd displayed toward him earlier in the day.

Regret wasn't a familiar emotion to me, and after a moment's reflection, I wondered if such remorse had anything to do with my recent conversion to Christianity.

My experience of faith had come about when I was forced to live with some Iranian Christians in a safe house in Tehran for three months. However, in my line of work, I wasn't exactly sure what living out my faith was supposed to look like.

Now, as difficult as it was for me, I decided I needed to try and connect with Mitchell on a more personal level.

I said, "The first time I was sent to the field, Toby Bledsoe was my operations officer. This was way back before the Agency was restructured. All our handlers were on-site then, running operations from an office building or a hotel room, sometimes even a jungle hut. Toby had already been on the ground in Nicaragua for almost a year when I arrived. That's how we knew each other this morning."

Mitchell sounded both intrigued and surprised at my revelation. "You were with Toby in Nicaragua?"

"For a short while," I said. "We were trying to get support for the Contras. The President hoped to use them as an oppositional force against the Sandinista regime."

Mitchell pulled up to a stoplight and looked over at me. "I've heard plenty of stories about those days. One of my trainers at The Farm spent a couple of years in Nicaragua. He claimed some of the money used to train the rebel forces came from selling cocaine to the Colombian drug traffickers. Is that true?"

"Not while I was there. At that time, Congress was willing to allocate plenty of money, and our job was to spread it around. But Toby and I weren't operating in the jungles of southern Nicaragua or Honduras, and we weren't involved in training anti-government forces. We were stationed in the capital city of Managua. Our mission was to bribe the judges and politicians, along with some Sandinista generals. By doing so, we were hoping they would start supporting the rebel forces."

"Sounds better than living in a tropical jungle for weeks."

"It might sound that way, but compared to maneuvering around the bureaucracy of the capital, traipsing around the jungle was a cake walk. I was a greenhorn, so I wasn't exactly sure how to identify the real enemy. I made an enormous error in judgment along those lines. Consequently, Toby got me kicked out of the country."

Mitchell raised his eyebrows at my admission. "Toby refused to work with you?"

I nodded. "I'd gone against his instructions by striking up a friendship with a Sandinista general. My foolishness nearly got both of us killed, and in fact, Toby lost one of his assets when the whole episode blew up in my face."

"Did he file a formal complaint against you?"

"No, nothing as mild as that. He pulled some strings at the Agency, and before I knew what hit me, I found myself stuck in Barranquilla, Columbia, trying to stay one step ahead of a couple of drug kingpins. There were times I didn't think I would survive the night. It's taken me a long time to forgive Toby for that."

"Yet, here you are, a Level 1 agent. Somewhere back there you managed to redeem yourself."

"The Agency pulled me out of Latin America in the early 90s when they needed personnel with language abilities. They were desperate for operatives who could learn Arabic or Farsi after the first Gulf war, and I was one of them."

"So I'm guessing you've been in the center of some Middle Eastern hot spots since then."

"Pretty much."

"Ever been to Iran?"

I hesitated, suddenly conscious of his Level 2 status. Nevertheless, I said, "That was my last assignment."

He was passing a slow vehicle on a winding mountain curve, but he still took his eyes off the road a second and glanced over at me. There was an expression of unbelief on his face.

After he'd pulled back into his lane, he asked, "How long were you there?"

"I ran a team of six assets for almost two years."

"By yourself?"

I had noticed his sense of excitement building with each question, and although I knew he'd just been confronted with Ernesto's death, I decided not to spare him the awful reality of my botched mission in Tehran.

"Yeah, I was alone, but don't get me wrong, this was no James Bond adventure. The mission was totally blown, and all my assets ended up dead, except for one."

He stared straight ahead, nodding his head up and down as he digested this information. After a few minutes, he asked, "Was it your fault?"

I decided not to tell him what really happened; that I'd lost my assets because a division head and the DDO had been playing head games with each other. Such information might make me look good, but it might also cause him to question the reliability of the very people who would be sending him on some dangerous mission in the future.

He didn't need that—at least not so early in his career.

"The whole situation was very complicated," I said, "and whenever anyone dies on my watch, I always feel responsible."

Mitchell shook his head. "That was a horrible way for Ernesto to die."

"A knife wound to the stomach is something taught at Jihadi training camps. If it's done correctly, a major blood vessel won't be hit, and the victim can live for several hours, sometimes even a whole day. However, the pain becomes so excruciating, when death finally comes, the victim will open his arms and embrace it."

"So you think Ahmed meant for Ernesto to suffer?"

"I do."

"Why?"

"I'm guessing he caught Ernesto sending a text message to his girlfriend. When I talked to Carlton earlier, he told me they'd gotten a ping on the cell phone about two hours before we found Ernesto. I believe when Ahmed discovered what Ernesto had been doing, he saw him as a traitor—at least according to Hezbollah's code of justice—and administered his own punishment. Under a different set of circumstances, Ernesto would have been tortured for several days in a very public forum. He could have even been beheaded. Instead, Ahmed chose to inflict a slow death on him as the next best thing."

"Ahmed must have left the house immediately after killing him."

I nodded. "I believe when Ahmed discovered the cell phone, he knew there was a possibility he was under surveillance, and that's why he decided to change his appearance, take public transportation, and get away from the house as quickly as possible."

After Mitchell had parked the car on *Calle Alturas*, he turned toward me and asked, "Why do you think he was traveling with Ernesto in the first place?"

I pointed toward the house where Ahmed had been staying. "I'm not sure, but maybe we'll find some answers in there."

♦♦♦♦

Before entering the house, Mitchell told his surveillance team to notify him immediately if they saw anyone approaching the house or poking around the Durango.

Once again, Mitchell and I entered the house through the back door. This time, though, we took our time.

I assigned Mitchell the room where we'd discovered Ernesto, and I did a thorough search of the other bedroom, because I just assumed it was the one used by Ahmed.

It didn't take me long to verify this.

In the top drawer of an ornate bureau, I found a Lebanese passport in the name of Adnan Chehab. However, the photo inside was of Ahmed Al-Amin.

Along with the passport, I found a couple of prepaid cell phones and a man's wallet. The only item inside the wallet was a credit card issued by a bank in Beirut. It also bore the name of Adnan Chehab.

Although there were a couple of shirts hanging in the closet, most of Ahmed's clothes were either on the floor, on the bed, or piled in a corner of the room. After searching through them and finding nothing of interest, I pocketed the passport and the credit card and left the room to check on Mitchell.

I found him standing in the center of Ernesto's bedroom in front of the bloodied mattress. For a moment, I thought he'd frozen up again, but, when he saw me, he turned and said, "You know, I believe you're right about what happened here."

He pointed to the broken parts of a cell phone lying on the floor opposite the bed where we'd found Ernesto. It appeared as if someone had flung it against the wall. The force of the impact had caused it to break apart, and the pieces were scattered along the baseboard.

When I bent down to take a look, Mitchell said, "Don't bother. I've already searched. There's no SIM card. Ahmed must have destroyed it or taken it with him to dispose of it later."

"What else did you find?"

"That gym bag over there," he said, pointing to a blue, nylon bag on the closet floor. "Inside it were Ernesto's clothes, a bunch of paperback books, and some restaurant menus from the Austin area. But, this was in the bag's side pocket along with his wallet."

Mitchell handed me a Lebanese passport identifying Ernesto Montilla as Fadi Chehab.

"Ahmed was also traveling under a Lebanese passport."

I showed him what I'd found in the other room.

Mitchell said, "They were using the same last name. Maybe they were passing themselves off as brothers or cousins."

"Was there anything else in the wallet?"

"There was no money; only a credit card in his Lebanese name. However, I did find this."

Mitchell handed me a folded newspaper clipping.

The one-column clipping from a Venezuelan newspaper contained no date. However, since the folds were still crisp, I figured Ernesto couldn't have been carrying the snippet of paper around with him for any length of time.

The newspaper headline read, "President Recognizes Work of Trade Minister." The story had a photo attached to it showing the president of Venezuela presenting a man with a certificate of some sort. The caption underneath the photo identified the man as Roberto Enrique Montilla.

My first impression of the award winner was that he looked a lot like Ernesto Montilla and could possibly be his father.

The article itself described an occasion when the Venezuelan president had recognized Montilla for his work as an assistant secretary in the international trade division of the Ministry of Trade and Commerce. At the event, Montilla had received a commendation for the markets he'd opened up in Syria for Venezuelan businesses. The article went on to explain how such markets benefitted Venezuela's mining industry.

I smiled as I handed Mitchell back the newspaper clipping. "Most likely, this article is about Ernesto's father."

"Why does that make you smile?"

"If this guy is Ernesto's father, then we know the Montilla family has ties to the Venezuelan government as well as ties to Syria. Remember those connect-the-dot puzzles you used to do when you were a kid? The ones that had you connect all the dots, so you could see the outline of a picture?"

Mitchell looked at me as if I were crazy. "Yeah, but what's that got to do with anything?"

I pointed at the newspaper article in his hand. "That clipping provides me with two dots in our puzzle. In the case of Ahmed, he's from Syria, but for some reason, he wants to go to Venezuela. That's our first dot. This article tells me that Montilla, who's from Venezuela, has spent some time in Syria. That's another dot. If we can connect these two dots, then maybe we'll begin to see the bigger picture of why Ahmed is headed to Venezuela."

"It almost sounds as if you want him to make that trip."

I decided Mitchell was much more intelligent than he looked.

Chapter 7

After arriving back at the embassy, Mitchell and I went down to The Bubble. Five minutes later, Bledsoe lumbered through the door with his big, black briefcase.

Once we'd given him our findings from the safe house, he called in Marlow, their communications officer, who set up a video conference link for me with Carlton back at the Agency.

Bledsoe and Mitchell left the room when Marlow arrived, and once he'd completed all the hocus pocus to link me up, I also told him goodbye.

After that, I initiated the call.

When Carlton came on the line, I noticed he was using the small conference room adjacent to his office.

If he'd chosen to involve more personnel—as most division heads often did—he would have been forced to use the larger conference room on the fourth floor. However, true to his minimalist management style, only two other people were present for my Operational Field Update (OFU).

As expected, Carlton was seated at the head of the small, rectangular table. To his right sat Katherine Broward, one of the Agency's top counterterrorism analysts. On Carlton's left was C. J. Salazar, chief of the Latin American desk at the Agency.

Salazar and I had never worked together before, but his reputation was often the subject of gossip around the Agency. On the other hand, Katherine and I had frequently worked together, even attempting a personal relationship at one time, but nothing had ever occurred between us to generate any gossip around the Agency.

As often happened between the opposite sex and me, my extended trips around the globe served as a hindrance when it came to establishing a long-term connection. Not surprisingly, Katherine had moved on after we'd dated a few times.

I'd recently talked with Katherine, though, because she'd been on my debriefing team following my failed mission to Iran. She'd also been one of the people to witness my confrontation with the Deputy Director of Operations, Robert Ira, after I'd discovered he was the person responsible for the loss of my network in Tehran. When the DDO had forced me to go on a year's medical leave—his way of punishing me for my hostile public exchange with him—Katherine had been very sympathetic to my plight.

In truth, Ira had wanted to fire me, but Carlton had intervened and negotiated a medical leave for me instead. However, my year off was cut short when Ahmed Al-Amin had murdered Simon Wassermann in a parking lot in Dallas.

Having one of his own intelligence officers killed on American soil had caused the DDO to bring me back to active status.

Whether I was being allowed to pursue Simon's killer as part of my continuing punishment, or whether the DDO really felt I was the best person for the job, wasn't all that clear to me yet.

But, I intended to find out.

♦♦♦♦

Carlton acknowledged my presence on camera and requested the code numbers Marlow had given me when he'd set up the video link.

The moment I supplied them, Carlton touched the recording button on an electronic console in front of him and said, *"Titus Alan Ray, Level 1 Covert Intelligence Officer, initiating the OFU on Operation Clear Signal; Code 56415."*

Carlton glanced down at the stack of papers in front of him and adjusted the corners of the pile, making sure they were perfectly aligned with each other.

Once they appeared satisfactory to him, he looked up at me and said, "Proceed with your update."

Although I knew operational updates were a necessity, I still hated doing them. To me it was like being asked to describe a living human being, but then being restricted to describing only the skeletal frame.

An OFU was like that; all bones and no flesh.

I gave the group my OFU on Operation Clear Signal.

"Approximately five hours ago, an elderly man was observed leaving the safe house and getting on a downtown bus. I have reason to believe that man was Ahmed Al-Amin. About two hours later, after hearing someone in distress inside the house, I made the decision to breach the back door. Ben Mitchell, along with his surveillance team, provided me with backup.

"Once inside, I discovered Ernesto Montilla in a back bedroom. He was bleeding from a knife wound to his abdomen, and Mitchell and I drove him to a clinic in Heredia. On our way there, I managed to ask him a few questions before he passed out. He admitted Ahmed had stabbed him and left him to die. He also said Ahmed was headed to Venezuela and was in San José to pick up a passport. That's all the intel I was able to get from him. He died shortly after we arrived at the clinic.

"When Mitchell and I returned to the safe house, we retrieved several personal items, plus the passports the men had been using. We determined Ernesto was most likely murdered by Ahmed because he'd been using a cell phone without his knowledge. The cell phone itself was broken into several pieces, but no SIM card was recovered.

"An additional piece of intel was discovered in Ernesto's wallet. It was a newspaper clipping showing a photograph of Roberto Montilla. There's a family resemblance in the photo, which leads me to believe Roberto could be Ernesto's father, and the age difference would seem to indicate that possibility. The caption underneath the photograph identified Roberto as an assistant secretary in Venezuela's Ministry of Trade and Commerce. The article noted he had recently received a commendation from the Venezuelan president for the work he's done opening up markets in Syria.

"The Dodge Durango remains parked at the safe house. However,

I'm making plans to move it later today, so our forensics guys can examine it. My priority now is locating Ahmed."

Because Carlton always required it, I added, "End of update."

However, knowing I'd provided him with a clean copy of the OFU, I decided to take the opportunity to make a request of Carlton and have it on the official record.

"Douglas, I know it's going to be difficult for Ahmed to leave Costa Rica without obtaining another passport, so I'm asking for authorization to read Toby Bledsoe into this operation. He's sure to know the passport players in this region, and we're going to need him to represent the embassy when decisions have to be made about Ernesto's body. He can also coordinate with the Agency's forensics team on Ernesto's vehicle."

Carlton didn't say anything.

The only sound I heard was the low hum of the noise-masking devices inside The Bubble.

Since Carlton was a person who thoroughly processed things before making a decision, his lack of response didn't surprise me.

I didn't necessarily like it though.

Carlton turned to Katherine and said, "Proceed with your report."

Katherine tucked a strand of her long, honey-blond hair behind her ear and smiled at me.

"Titus," she said, tilting her head slightly toward the camera, "it's good to see you again."

She glanced down at her laptop. "You're right about Roberto Montilla. The data we've turned up on Ernesto shows Roberto is his father. As you read in the newspaper clipping, he holds one of the top positions in the Venezuelan Ministry of Trade and Commerce and handles their international trade division. On a more personal level, Roberto is married and has another child, a daughter, who's living at home. We're in the process of pulling up his financial records right now. What we have—"

"See what you can find out about his travel itineraries," Carlton said, interrupting her. "I'd be especially interested in knowing when and where he's traveled outside of Venezuela."

Katherine nodded and continued. "At Ben Mitchell's request, we initiated a data dig into *Banco Nacional's* records trying to pin down the ownership of the house on *Calle Alturas*. In the end, there were no surprises. We discovered two brothers own it, and both have strong ties to the Zeta cartel."

Katherine looked up from her computer. "We believe this is further evidence Al-Amin has been under the cartel's protection from the moment he landed in Mexico. What we haven't been able to determine is the connection the cartel has . . ." she paused and corrected herself, "or rather had to Ernesto."

She returned to her laptop. "Ernesto was enrolled at the University of Texas for two years, and his time there had been without incident. The FBI conducted a full background check on his girlfriend also. Her name is Charlotte Tedesco, but she goes by the name of Charlie. Nothing out of the ordinary turned up on her. There was no connection to the cartel there either. We still don't have any idea why the cartel put Ahmed and Ernesto together as traveling companions. The data points just aren't there right now, but we're continuing to work on it."

When Katherine finished her report, Carlton turned to me and asked, "Do you have any questions for Katherine?"

"Maybe we're looking at Ernesto from the wrong angle," I said. "Forget the cartel. See if you can find a connection between Ernesto and Hezbollah or Ernesto and Ahmed. We know Roberto Montilla has been traveling to Syria, and we know Damascus is Ahmed's home base. Did Ernesto accompany his father on those trips to Syria? Did he get recruited by Hezbollah when he was over there? I'm fairly certain we'll find some connection between Ahmed and Ernesto through Roberto's visits to Syria."

"You're wrong," Salazar said.

Both Carlton and Katherine looked startled at Salazar's comment, but I knew it probably wasn't what he'd said that surprised them. Instead, it was the fact he'd just violated Carlton's strict protocol regarding meetings being documented for the official record.

The rule he'd broken—participants must maintain silence at all times unless information is requested—was a rule Carlton strictly enforced. It didn't matter who was seated around the conference table, everyone was required to obey The Rule.

However, I was more concerned about Salazar's negative comment than I was about maintaining Carlton's protocol games.

Before Carlton had a chance to cut him off, I asked, "Do you have another theory?"

"It has to be the cartel," Salazar said, "They have their tentacles everywhere, even in places you wouldn't imagine."

Although C. J. Salazar used his initials as his first name, his first name was Carlos. Unbeknownst to him, everyone at the Agency called him Cartel Carlos. He'd been tagged with the nickname because he had a tendency to blame the drug cartels for any disreputable activity south of the border.

"You heard Katherine," I said. "There's no obvious cartel connection with Ernesto."

Salazar looked at me as though he thought I needed a good scolding. He even pointed his finger at me. "The cartels have connections everywhere. They probably had something on this Montilla kid and threatened to harm his family unless he cooperated with them. It happens all the time."

"If Ernesto came in contact with Muslim extremists, he could have become radicalized. That happens all the time too."

"Latin America isn't the Middle East, Titus."

His patronizing tone flew all over me.

"There's plenty of evidence Iran is pouring millions of dollars into Latin America. Why do you think they're setting up cultural centers and mosques all over the place? They're trying to establish a Muslim presence in our backyard, and the hopelessness of young Hispanics caught up in the endless cycle of poverty leaves the door wide open for their jihadist mentality."

"Ernesto Montilla wasn't some poverty-stricken young person. His rich father was giving him a university education in America. Check his father out. He's probably getting his money from the cartels too."

"It's not a question of—"

"Let's save this discussion for another day," Carlton said, cutting me off.

He never tolerated arguments around his conference table for very long. I thought it was probably because he detested any disagreements being recorded on the official transcript, and I wondered if that's why he had established The Rule in the first place.

Carlton turned to Salazar, "I asked you here to give Titus a report on the rifle used to kill Simon Wassermann. You may proceed with that report now."

Salazar went into a tedious account of how his office—with the help of the Mexican government—had recovered the high-powered rifle used to murder Simon Wassermann. They'd done so after a shootout between two rival drug lords in Nuevo Laredo.

I stopped listening after a few minutes.

I didn't care about the weapon. All I cared about was the man who'd used that weapon to kill Wassermann.

Once the video conference was over and Salazar and Katherine had left the room, Carlton said, "I've decided to have you brief Toby Bledsoe into the operation. I'll call him when I get the authorization from the DDO's office, and I'll be sending you down a forensics team to have a look at the Durango."

"Thanks. Douglas. Having Toby as one of the principals should make things easier for me."

"Am I right in thinking the two of you have a history together?"

Carlton never missed an opportunity to let me know how much he knew about me.

"That won't be a factor."

"Make sure it isn't," he said. "We can't let personal feelings get in the way of grabbing Ahmed before he leaves Costa Rica. The last thing we want is for him to make his way to Venezuela."

It didn't happen often, but there were times when I disagreed with Carlton about operational objectives.

I was beginning to wonder if this might be one of them.

♦♦♦♦

After leaving The Bubble, I found Bledsoe and Mitchell waiting for me in the station chief's office. I wasn't surprised to find the cramped workplace piled high with books and file folders. Bledsoe had never been a fastidious kind of guy, and his office reflected that aspect of his personality.

As soon as I entered the room, Bledsoe gestured toward a wooden tea trolley in a corner of his office. It was reminiscent of an oxcart, and I immediately recognized it as a miniature version of the *carreta*, one of the symbols of the Costa Rican coffee trade. There were replicas of *carretas* in the marketplaces around the city and tourists snatched them up as souvenirs.

On top of the *carreta* was a coffeemaker with an assortment of mugs beside it.

"There's coffee," Bledsoe said. "Make yourself at home." When I headed over to the coffeemaker, he added, "Use the Dallas Cowboys mug. I'm sure it's cleaner than the rest of them."

Knowing he was setting me up, I still asked the question. "Why is that, Toby?"

"Nobody ever uses it."

"Right."

When we'd worked together in Nicaragua, Bledsoe had continually harassed me about being a Dallas Cowboys football fan. I'd always admitted to being a fan, but never a fanatic. This was a term I had reserved for Bledsoe, who had an undying love for the Washington Redskins.

Both Bledsoe and Mitchell were seated on a well-worn, brown leather sofa. Spread out on the coffee table in front of them were several documents with the word CLASSIFIED printed across the top. While Bledsoe was studying the classified papers, Mitchell was looking at a video on his iPad.

I told Bledsoe, "Carlton said to read you into the operation. You'll get official confirmation later tonight."

"Did you tell him I'd discussed the passport angle with you?"

It bothered me that Bledsoe thought I might betray him to anyone at the Agency, but then I remembered my history with him and understood why he might have thought that.

"I told you I wouldn't say anything, didn't I?"

Even before I saw the look on his face, I realized my answer had come out sounding harsher than I had intended it to be.

No one said anything.

Mitchell kept his eyes on the video he was watching, and Bledsoe suddenly became interested in one of the classified documents on the coffee table. The strained silence went on for several seconds, and I tried to think of a way to diffuse it.

I finally said, "Cartel Carlos sat in on the video conference with me just now."

"Oh, no," they both said in unison.

Bledsoe laughed and then shook his head back and forth. "Better you than me, my friend."

I grinned at him, taking his remark to mean we were both on the same page now, and the difficulties we'd had in the past were behind us.

At least, that's what I told myself he meant.

Hoping to sustain the camaraderie, I spent the next several minutes telling the two of them about my discussion with Salazar.

As I wrapped it up, Bledsoe admitted Salazar had been very supportive when he'd requested supplemental funding to recruit additional assets inside the drug ring, but he said the division chief had not been so helpful when he'd suggested the Zeta drug ring might be in league with some of the Middle Eastern terrorist groups.

"He was extremely skeptical," Bledsoe said, "and that's putting it mildly."

"I'm convinced they're working together, and once we've grabbed Ahmed, we can grill him on how Hezbollah is using the cartel to further its own interests."

Mitchell finally looked up from his iPad. "I think we may have caught a break with one of the surveillance cameras at the bus stop."

He turned his iPad around so I could take a look at the screen. "It could help us grab Ahmed before he takes off for Venezuela."

I tried to look happy about that.

Chapter 8

Mitchell pointed to the video on his iPad, which showed passengers getting off an *El Central* bus. The old man from Sonya's photo shoot was the fifth passenger to disembark, and as he slowly made his way across the plaza to another bus, he was using the halting gait of a feeble old man.

I asked, "Where did you get this?"

"One of our tech guys here at the embassy hacked into a CCTV camera at a bank across the street from the bus hub."

"I can't make out the name on the bus."

Mitchell said, "It's *La Periferica.* It runs around the city's outer perimeter."

Bledsoe said, "It's unfortunate he took that particular bus because there are at least fifty stops along the way. Finding where he got off will take some time."

I said. "We believe the cartel is helping him get a passport, so you should narrow the search down to the neighborhoods where they operate." I looked over at Bledsoe. "What about your contact inside the cartel?"

"I've already left a message for Hernando, but sometimes it takes a few days before he's able to get back to me."

I walked over to the coffeepot and refilled my mug. "I want to get Ernesto's vehicle off the street and have a look inside. His car keys didn't turn up at the house, so I'm assuming Ahmed took them with him. It shouldn't be too hard for one of us to break inside and hotwire it, though. After that, we can move it to a location where our forensics guys can take a look at it. Carlton said they should be here by tomorrow."

Mitchell spoke up. "I'll do it. I need to check in with my surveillance team anyway."

Bledsoe said, "Take the Durango over to the garage on *Avenida Santa Cecilia*. I'll call Franco and tell him you're coming."

Before Mitchell walked out the door, he turned around and addressed Bledsoe, "What's going to happen to Ernesto's body? I mean . . . well . . . he's at that clinic all alone now."

The sadness in Mitchell's voice surprised me, and I figured Bledsoe had heard it too, because he sounded empathetic when he answered him.

"Yeah, son, that's a tough one. And I'm sure it wasn't easy seeing him tortured like that. I'll get someone at the Venezuelan embassy to let his family know and—"

"How difficult would it be for you to keep his death quiet for a few days?" I asked. "Most likely, Ahmed thought he would be out of the country before anyone discovered the body, so I'd like to see what he's up to before someone contacts Ernesto's family."

Bledsoe grunted as he got off the couch. "Good idea. That shouldn't be too difficult."

Mitchell left the room without saying anything.

Bledsoe shook his head. "That boy's difficult to read sometimes. One minute, he's wise beyond his years, and then, the next thing you know, he's throwing a temper tantrum just like a three-year-old. Did you notice how emotional he was just now?"

"Give him a few more years with you, and he'll be as hard-nosed as the rest of us."

He rolled his eyes. "Yeah, right."

"I think I'll head back to the hotel now."

He drained the last dregs from his coffee mug. "There's nothing more you can do here until we locate Ahmed. Why don't the two of us grab a bite to eat later this evening."

"Sure, I'd like that."

He glanced at his watch. "I have to make some phone calls first, but

I should be able to get away from here around eight o'clock. Do you think you can find *La Argentina?* It's a restaurant about a mile south of *Avenida Central.*"

"I'm sure I can manage it. Will I be able to order something there besides beans and rice?"

"They serve only the finest Argentinean beef at this restaurant," he assured me. "I expect their steaks will even meet *your* standards."

He picked up the desk phone, but then he quickly put it back down. "I'm also expecting you to reveal the identity of the person Ahmed plans to assassinate if he should make it to Venezuela."

Bledsoe was expecting a lot from me—maybe a little too much.

◆◆◆◆

As I drove away from the embassy, I thought about Toby Bledsoe and his implication I already knew the identity of the person Ahmed planned to assassinate in Venezuela.

I didn't.

But that didn't mean I didn't want to get inside his head and discover who was on his hit list.

The DDO's office referred to an unidentified assassination target as a UAT, and the more I thought about it, the more I saw the benefits of trying to discover the identity of the UAT.

For one thing, there was a good chance Iran's Revolutionary Guard Corps had targeted the UAT because they considered that person to be an enemy of the Iranian regime. And, in my mind, anyone who was an enemy of Iran might be convinced to work for Uncle Sam, particularly if they were told they were on Ahmed's hit list.

The benefits of discovering the identity of the UAT were just as compelling when I considered the possibility that Ahmed's target could be an American, someone like John Luckenbill, our Head of Mission at the American Embassy in Venezuela. There was even a remote chance the IRGC planned to take out the Venezuelan president and then blame it on the CIA.

Even if I managed to grab Ahmed before he left for Venezuela and prevent him from making the hit, most likely, the IRGC would send another assassin to finish the job. Next time, though, the Agency might not have the intel available to prevent the shooter from fulfilling his contract.

When I returned to my hotel room, I continued mulling over my options. My gut instinct told me following Ahmed to Venezuela and pinpointing his target was a better choice than grabbing him while he was in Costa Rica.

However, I knew it wouldn't be easy to convince Carlton to revise the operational objective—it never was.

Was such a fight worth having?

I found myself vacillating back and forth, and all of a sudden, it occurred to me it might be a good idea to pray about my decision.

Praying was a new idea for me, and like a baby learning to walk, I still needed a lot of practice to gain any confidence in the concept.

I sat down on the edge of the bed and talked to God about my desire to bring Ahmed to justice for the murder of Simon Wassermann. I also told him I needed his guidance in order to make the right decision about pursuing Ahmed.

When I finished, I hadn't made up my mind about what I should do yet, but I felt certain, when the time came for me to make that decision, I would know what to do.

♦♦♦♦

It was just getting dark when I left the hotel to meet Bledsoe at the restaurant. As I maneuvered through the traffic on *Avenida Central*, my satphone rang.

It was Mitchell, and he sounded anxious.

"We have a situation."

"What kind of situation?"

"I was on my way over to pick up the Durango when Sonya called. She and Josué had been watching the safe house, and she said when Josué left her to go down the street and grab some sandwiches, a black Chevy Suburban with four men inside showed up. They—"

"I'm on my way now. It will probably take me about ten minutes to get there."

"No, listen. They didn't go inside the house. When they pulled up, two guys jumped out of the Suburban, and then they got inside the Durango and drove off. Sonya said it all happened in less than thirty seconds."

"How did they manage to get inside the Durango so quickly?"

"One of them had a key fob. He used it to unlock the doors remotely."

"Which direction did they go? Maybe we can locate them."

He hesitated a moment. "Sonya's following them now."

"Is Josué with her?"

"No. As I said, he was down the street getting something to eat when this went down. She didn't have time to pick him up."

"She shouldn't be doing this alone, Ben."

"I know. I know," he said. "I'm tracking her location now. I'll get back to you."

I drove toward downtown San José, and when I turned off the main highway, Mitchell phoned me back.

"She followed them to the *Zapote* District. They took the Durango to a warehouse on *Calle Pacifica.* She's parked there on the street waiting for us."

"Send me the directions."

"I just did."

I phoned Bledsoe—who was just entering the restaurant where we'd agreed to meet—and told him we had an emergency. I gave him a moment to return to his car, and then I called him back.

After hearing about the crisis, he said, "Ahmed must have sent someone after the car."

"It looks that way."

"That doesn't make a lot of sense, though. He can't be driving to Venezuela."

"Perhaps he wants the SUV for some other reason. Maybe the cartel is taking it in payment for services rendered."

"Send me the address of the warehouse. I'll meet you there."

"No, you're not operational yet. I promise I'll call you if we run into a problem."

I hung up when I heard him start to protest.

The moment I turned on *Calle Pacifica*, I started searching the dashboard GPS for an alternate route. Traffic was moving at a snail's pace, and within a minute, both lanes were at a standstill.

My phone rang.

"Where are you?" Mitchell asked.

"I just turned on *Calle Pacifica*. I can't move, though; both lanes are completely blocked."

"I'm ahead of you. It's the same here. A garbage truck is stalled at an intersection."

"Did you tell Sonya about our delay?"

"She's not answering her phone."

"Since when?"

"Since I called you twenty minutes ago."

"Did you tell her to stay in the car?"

Mitchell sounded panicky. "Yes, of course I did. I specifically told her to stay in the car, but she's not the cautious type. I'm sure you noticed that this afternoon. Ever since you sent her to knock on Ahmed's door, she hasn't stopped bugging me to let her do more than just sit in a car. Now, she's probably done something really foolish."

"Ben, calm down. I'm sure there's a simple explanation. Maybe the battery on her phone is dead."

"Traffic's moving now."

"Park on the street where I can see you, but don't go near Sonya's car."

"If something happens to her, it's all your fault."

♦♦♦♦

A few minutes later, I spotted Mitchell's Jeep. He'd parked it in front of an automobile salvage yard. Down the block, about one hundred yards away, I saw the Toyota Highlander.

I continued driving west on *Calle Pacifica*. As I drove past the Toyota, I glanced inside.

There was no sign of Sonya in the vehicle.

I left my car in the parking lot of a bar—where the loud salsa music inside was also entertaining the patrons on the patio outside—and walked back up the street.

When I passed by the warehouse where Sonya said she had last seen the Durango, I realized her idea of a warehouse was vastly different from my own. True, the building might have once been used to store something, but now the dilapidated structure hardly seemed to qualify as a warehouse.

The one-story building, constructed from cinder blocks and covered over with a tin roof, looked abandoned. Wooden planks had been nailed across the windows, and the wood was dark and weathered, as if it had already withstood a dozen rainy seasons.

Such neglect made the recent addition of a new overhead garage door, in the center of the building, look out of place. The opening was big enough to accommodate a large truck or, at the very least, a Dodge Durango.

There was no activity around the warehouse, though, and the graveled parking lot was completely deserted.

I crossed the street and headed back toward my car. When I was passing Sonya's vehicle, I took out my cell phone, and once I was opposite the back door, I slowed down and pretended to punch in a phone number.

At the same time, I did a careful sweep of the vehicle's interior.

Sonya wasn't hunkered down inside, and I couldn't spot her cell phone or the camera she'd had with her earlier in the day—no purse there either.

As I continued walking back toward my car, I called Mitchell.

"She's not in her car."

"What now?"

"Drive up the street. On your right, there's a bar called . . ." I looked around for a sign, ". . . *Los Mojitos*. I'll meet you outside on the patio."

Once I'd entered the restaurant, I chose a patio table with a good view of the warehouse. A few minutes later, after I'd ordered a glass of lemonade, Mitchell walked in. When the waitress brought my drink, he ordered a Diet Coke.

Although Mitchell started pelting me with questions, I put him off while I studied the warehouse.

The front of the building faced the graveled parking lot, and I could see a chain link fence running along the rear of the property. However, I noticed the grass between the fence and the back of the building wasn't as overgrown as the area at the side of the building.

I pulled out my Agency phone and keyed in the coordinates of the warehouse, hoping to get a satellite image of the area. Within seconds, I was able to study the terrain around the warehouse.

As soon as the waitress left Mitchell's drink, he started questioning me again.

"What's the plan? How many guys will we need to get in there? Should we call Bledsoe for backup?"

"Hold on, Ben."

I handed him my phone. "Describe what you see between the chain link fence and the back of the warehouse."

He stared at the screen. "Has it been cleared off?"

I waited.

He used the zoom feature to get a better look, and I noticed he was taking his time and analyzing the possibilities before drawing a conclusion.

Very good, Ben.

He looked up from the screen and stared over at the warehouse. Then, he looked down at the screen again.

He said, "There might be a back exit. Although from this angle, it's really hard to tell. If there's a door there, then a vehicle could possibly drive out along that chain link fence and exit onto *Avenida Doral* instead of exiting here onto *Pacifica*."

"Exactly."

"Whoever took the Durango could have driven in the front door and then gone out the back way."

I nodded. "They probably had a forty-minute lead on us. So if—"

Mitchell's phone chirped.

When he looked down at the caller ID, I knew who it was just by the look on his face.

"Where are you?" he asked, gesturing toward the door to let me know we should leave the restaurant.

I threw some money on the table and followed Mitchell out to the parking lot. He tapped me on the shoulder and pointed up the street.

Sonya was at the intersection across from the bar.

"Yes, I see you," he said, disconnecting the call.

Sonya came toward us with a big smile on her face. Swinging from her neck was the camera with the big telephoto lens, and she looked excited, as if she'd just been to a really fun party.

"You won't believe—"

"Get inside the car before you say another word," I said, opening the back door of the Jeep.

Once Mitchell and I had gotten in the front seats, Sonya pointed toward her camera and said, "You won't believe what I'm about to show you."

Chapter 9

I told Mitchell to move the Jeep over to an unlit corner of the parking lot, but I had him park the car, so we could still keep an eye on the warehouse.

As soon as we were in the shadows, Mitchell turned around and asked Sonya. "Where were you? Why weren't you answering your cell phone?"

Sonya's face was still flushed with excitement, but her breathing had evened out now, and I had the sense she was very good at calming herself down in a stressful situation.

"I followed the Durango to that warehouse," she said, gesturing at the building in front of us. "When the men drove up to the door, it opened automatically, and they just drove right in. I knew the building used to be a bakery warehouse, because my cousin Armando grew up here in the *Zapote* district. We used to go around to the side entrance just before closing time, and the workers would give the kids in the neighborhood the pastries they couldn't sell that day."

I said, "So there's another entrance on the opposite side of the warehouse?"

She nodded. "It's just a single door. It was the employee entrance, the one the workers had to use."

I asked, "So you went around to the back of the warehouse?"

Before Sonya could answer me, Mitchell said, "I explicitly told you to wait in your car until I arrived."

All the concern he'd shown for her earlier in the evening had vanished. Now, the only thing left in him was anger at her freewheeling actions.

She ignored him and continued, "I went around the block, so I could approach the building from *Avenida Doral*. The employee door wasn't boarded up, so I picked the lock."

She cut her eyes over toward Mitchell, but he was staring out at the warehouse.

"Who taught you how to do that?" I asked.

She gave me a mischievous grin.

"A friend."

"Come on, Sonya," Mitchell said, looking at her now. "Get on with your story. What happened when you got inside?"

Her smile disappeared. "I'm getting to that."

The emotional underpinnings of their relationship were beginning to trouble me, and even though I knew why I felt uneasy, I decided not to say anything—at least for now.

Sonya said, "It was dark inside, so I used the light from my cell phone to make my way from the employee area down the hallway to the manager's office. As I got near the office, I heard voices coming from the main area of the warehouse where the trucks used to be loaded. By the time I made it to the office, I was able to shut off my phone because both the vehicles inside the warehouse had their headlights on. It was—"

"Wait a second," I said. "There were two cars inside the building?"

She nodded. "Besides the Durango, the Chevy Suburban was there. I think it was the same one I saw at the safe house, but I'm not sure. The Chevy's headlights were illuminating the Durango while the men were unloading it."

"Could you see what they were unloading?"

Sonya handed me her camera. "See for yourself."

I quickly scanned through the images on the camera's monitor.

The bright headlights in the darkened warehouse, coupled with Sonya shooting through the glass partition in the office, gave each shot a dreamlike quality. In fact, the scenes almost seemed surreal.

However, the reality of what was going on was real enough.

The camera had caught the four men removing an array of

weaponry from the floorboard and side panels of Ernesto's car. After that, they were transferring them over to the trunk of the Chevy.

I passed the camera over to Mitchell.

After looking through the images, he gave the camera back to her. "You took an awful chance getting these."

There was a note of giddiness in her voice. "It was worth it though, wasn't it?"

Mitchell didn't reply, and she directed her attention to me. "I was afraid the shots might not turn out since I was taking them through the office window."

"They're great," I assured her. "Once we identify these men, we'll be one step closer to finding Ahmed. You did an excellent job."

Perhaps taking his cue from me, Mitchell finally smiled at her and said, "Yeah, good job, Sonya."

She smiled back at him. "I guess I should have called you first, but I didn't stop to think about it. I just did it."

I asked, "What happened after the men unloaded the weapons?"

"They got in the Chevy and drove out the other side of the warehouse. I gave them several minutes to clear the area, and then I left the building. That's when I called you."

I tried to clarify what she'd said. "Did you say all four men left in the Chevy?"

"Yes."

Mitchell sounded excited. "So the Durango's still inside the warehouse?"

"Yes," she said, looking back and forth between us. "They left the Durango there. Is that important?"

I said, "We'll know for sure when we take a look inside."

♦♦♦♦

Mitchell and I retraced Sonya's steps, making our way around the block to *Avenida Doral,* where we entered the warehouse by using the employee's service entrance. Sonya had relocked the door, but, within a couple of minutes, I was able to get us inside.

It was pitch black.

After Mitchell switched on the flashlight he'd brought along, I realized we were in the employee break room Sonya had mentioned. Although we didn't think anyone else had entered the building since Sonya had left, we drew our weapons and moved cautiously down the hallway toward the main warehouse area, stopping every few minutes to listen for anyone moving around inside.

The building was hot and stuffy and smelled like a combination of sweaty gym clothes and sourdough. The condition of the building didn't seem to bother the rats, who scattered in every direction once the light hit them.

When we entered the manager's office, the first thing I noticed was Sonya's handprints in the layers of dust covering the heavy wooden desk. I grabbed some newspaper off the floor and smeared the prints. Then, I laid the crumpled newspaper back on top of the desk in an attempt to cover up anything I'd missed.

"Really?" Mitchell commented in a half-whisper. "You're also a neat freak?"

I was.

But, that wasn't why I'd cleaned the prints off the desk.

I whispered back, "If they decide to come back for the Durango, I'd rather no one notice someone's been in here recently."

I took one last look around the office and then signaled for Mitchell to open the office door leading out to the main area of the warehouse. We moved along the interior walls, skirting around a bunch of wooden shelves, which, despite their rickety condition, were still standing.

When a couple of large, slick rats surprised Mitchell by scurrying across the path in front of him, he readied his weapon as if to shoot, but then, when he recognized the rodents weren't a threat, he started breathing again.

It was soon evident no one had been left behind to stand guard, so, once we reached the warehouse floor, I had Mitchell switch his flashlight to full mode.

For a few seconds, both of us stood there in the silence looking at what the men had taken out of the car's interior in order to get at the weapons inside.

On the floor in front of us were the SUV's backseats and most of the floorboards, along with whatever remained of the side panels. Scattered among the various parts were food wrappers, water bottles, and soda cans—residual remains of Ahmed and Ernesto's cross-country trek.

"See what's left in the trunk," I told Mitchell. "I'll take the front seat."

As I slid in the passenger seat, I took out my phone and used the light from the screen to examine the interior.

I spotted a can of Mountain Dew sitting in a cup holder.

But, that was it. There was nothing else in the front seats.

I searched beneath the seats.

Still, nothing.

However, when I opened the glove box, I saw it contained several maps, and I took them out and spread them across my lap.

At that moment, Mitchell stuck his head through the driver's side window. He was holding a Smith & Wesson revolver.

"They missed this."

"Sloppy."

"Also these."

He showed me two boxes of .50-caliber cartridges.

"Obviously, we're not dealing with the brightest bulbs in the chandelier."

"Heavy duty stuff," Mitchell said, hefting the boxes of ammo in his hand, "but I didn't see a .50-caliber weapon in Sonya's photos."

"Put those back exactly where you found them. If Ahmed carried some type of inventory list, someone will show up here looking for them, and like I said, I don't want them to know anyone was here."

I continued to sift through the maps, looking for any markings or notations on them. However, it didn't take me long to realize I needed to do a more thorough examination in a location with better lighting.

The moment I walked around to the back of the vehicle, Mitchell's phone started vibrating. He listened for only a few seconds, and then he immediately hung up.

"Let's go," he said, moving toward the manager's office. "Sonya said a car just pulled into the parking lot."

♦♦♦♦

When we arrived back at Mitchell's Jeep, Sonya said the older model black Mercedes she'd seen had never even pulled up to the warehouse doors. It had simply turned around in the parking lot and exited onto *Avenida Pacifica.*

"Sorry," she said, "I guess I blew that."

"No," I said, "alerting us was the right thing to do."

Sonya pointed to the maps in my hand. "Did you find something?"

"I'm not sure. Right now, I'm convinced our best chance of locating Ahmed is to identify the men in the pictures you took."

Mitchell said, "I'll upload the images and send them to the Ops Center as soon as I get back to the embassy."

"While you're at it, send Toby a copy, and I'll let him know what happened here tonight. Make sure you maintain surveillance on this place and the safe house for at least the next forty-eight hours."

As I pulled away from *Los Mojitos*, I phoned Bledsoe. After I'd summarized the evening's events, I asked, "Can we still meet for dinner? I'm starving."

"Come out to the house. I'll fix us an omelet."

"Are you sure? It's almost midnight."

"I'm sure. My wife's in California, and except for George, I'm all alone out here. The address is 222 *San Rafael*. That's about seven miles due west of the embassy."

"I'm on my way." Just before hanging up, I added, "Check your computer. Ben is sending you some photographs, and I'm sure they'll keep you awake tonight."

"Why should tonight be any different? I haven't had a good night's sleep since I heard you were coming to Costa Rica."

Chapter 10

When I located the address Bledsoe had given me, I wasn't surprised to see he lived in a gated complex behind a concrete brick wall. In fact, I expected it.

Bledsoe was an American Embassy employee, and he looked like a rich American, which made him the perfect target for terrorists and kidnappers.

What I didn't expect, however, was the massive house and gardens behind the wall. It appeared as if the Bledsoes were living the good life in Costa Rica.

As soon as I parked in the circle drive, Bledsoe appeared at the front door holding the collar of very large, black Doberman.

He must have noticed my hesitation when I got out of the car.

"Don't worry," he said. "As long as you're not threatening me, he's a very friendly dog."

"Should I say something like 'I come in peace' so Fido can be assured of my true intentions?"

"Like any good bodyguard, he can read your true intentions."

When I crossed the threshold, I carefully eased my way past man and beast in what I hoped was a non-threatening manner.

After entering the house without incident, I followed Bledsoe through the marbled-floor vestibule and down some steps to a sunken living room, where a contemporary L-shaped sofa took up the majority of the space. The couch faced a big-screen television set, and just before Bledsoe picked up the remote control and turned it off, I saw a late-night comedian smiling at the audience and scratching his head.

"You're free to make yourself comfortable here," he said, "or you can come out to the kitchen with me."

I pointed at the dog sniffing at my leg and asked, "Where's your friend going to be?"

"George, come here."

The dog immediately walked over and stood beside Bledsoe.

"Get in your bed."

George headed toward an overstuffed pillow in a corner of the room. After making a couple of tight circles—as if he were chasing his tail—he plopped down on the bed with his head between his paws. While the dog no longer appeared menacing, his eyes continued to track me.

"George? You named your dog George?"

Bledsoe shrugged. "Margaret named him. When she and the trainer went to pick him up from the breeder, he was fighting with all the other puppies in the litter, so she named him George after George Foreman. He's never lost his aggressiveness, especially when he's crossed."

"In that case, I'll come out to the kitchen and watch you cook."

I followed Bledsoe through an archway into a very large and very white kitchen.

Bledsoe picked up a half-filled wine glass, and after taking a sip, he pointed over to a wine bottle and said, "Pour yourself a glass, and I'll finish up our omelets."

As he started to take a drink, he stopped himself. "I just remembered. You don't drink, do you?"

I shook my head. "Not really. But I'd love a cup of coffee."

"Help yourself."

I walked over to a black coffeemaker sitting all by itself on the white countertop and brewed myself a cup of coffee.

Then, I took a look around the ample kitchen.

The simplicity of its design appealed to me.

The cabinets were white, and against the backdrop of the black appliances, looked especially stark. Besides the coffeepot, no other small appliances, containers, or utensils were on the gleaming white countertop. The color palette, plus the uncluttered look, was futuristic, minimalist, and seemed out of sync with Bledsoe, who was wearing a stained knit shirt, lounge pants, and looked worn out.

I slid onto a barstool. "I have to admit, Toby, I never would have pictured you living in this type of house."

He chuckled. "Me neither. We bought this place from the owner of a coffee plantation who went bankrupt. When Margaret's father passed away three years ago, she kept his houses in New York and Los Angeles, but, even so, she decided she wanted a much grander house for us here in Costa Rica." He shrugged. "What can I say? It's her money."

He glanced over at me, as if he thought I might like to make some comment about his wife or her money.

I didn't.

He shook his head. "The funny thing is, now that she's been trying to run her father's businesses in the States, she's seldom here."

He transferred the omelet onto a plate. "Her father would be so proud of her now. She's finally become the son he always wanted."

When we'd worked together in Nicaragua, Bledsoe had never had many kind words to say about his wealthy father-in-law, who, according to him, seldom missed a chance to berate his only daughter for marrying a government employee and rejecting the kind of life he'd always planned for her.

Bledsoe laid a plate in front of me. It was filled with a large omelet covered in salsa, along with a couple of fresh pineapple slices dripping in juice. He brought an identical plate over to the kitchen bar for himself and sat down beside me.

"What about your father?" Bledsoe asked. "Are you still estranged from him?"

The question stunned me for a moment.

I seldom talked about my father now, but, when I'd first gone to work for the Agency, the childhood memories were still painful, and I wasn't as hesitant to share them. Since Bledsoe and I had been stuck together for long stretches of time, my relationship with my father had made it into many of our conversations back then.

My father, Gerald, had been an alcoholic, and even though he hadn't been physically abusive toward my mother, my sister Carla, or even me, I had always felt his emotional detachment was a form of cruelty.

He had worked on an assembly line at a GM plant in Flint, Michigan, where I'd grown up, and he'd provided a good living for us. However, on his way home from work each evening, he would always stop off at a neighborhood bar. When he got home a couple of hours later, he would have a few more drinks, and then he'd finish off the evening by drinking himself to sleep.

My mother blamed his drinking on the three years he'd spent with the Army in Vietnam.

Growing up, I'd desperately wanted my father to pay attention to me, and I'd often wondered if I was the one responsible for his aloofness. Later, I realized drowning his memories in booze was his own choice, and it had absolutely nothing to do with me.

In my late teens, my father and I had stopped speaking to each other altogether. By the time I'd joined the CIA, we were completely estranged.

I answered Bledsoe's question. "He passed away in '92 of liver cancer."

"Oh, I'm sorry to hear that," he said. "Where were you? Were you able to attend his funeral?"

"I was in Iraq. It happened during the first Gulf war, and Douglas had just been named to head the Middle Eastern desk. He brought me home when he got the notification. He didn't know me very well then, and at the time, he didn't explain why I was being pulled out. If he had, I would have insisted on staying and finishing the operation. There was no need for me to be at my father's funeral."

Bledsoe surprised me by reaching over and placing his hand on my shoulder. "No, Titus, you would have regretted not saying goodbye. I'm glad you had closure."

"Maybe you're right."

I didn't really agree with him, though.

Determined to change the subject, I said, "This is a great omelet. Not as good as the steak you promised me, though."

Bledsoe started to reply, but then, his computer beeped, and he immediately got off the bar stool and walked across the room to read the flashing red alert message.

"Time to get to work," he said. "Ben just sent me the photographs from Sonya's camera."

♦♦♦♦

While Bledsoe pulled up the images on his computer screen, I brewed myself another cup of coffee. Then, I sat down beside him and viewed the photographs for the second time.

Looking at the images on his computer screen—instead of the tiny monitor on Sonya's camera—gave me a better feel of how the men had worked together to strip down the Durango and unload the weapons. I suspected this wasn't the first time the men had engaged in such an activity.

Each one appeared to have an assigned task, with the oldest guy in the group inspecting the guns as they were hauled from the vehicle's secret compartments. I noticed he was also the one who appeared to be giving the orders.

After we viewed the last frame, I asked Bledsoe, "Recognize any of those guys?"

"No, but the tat on the big guy's bicep is a Zeta symbol."

"So the drug cartel has expanded its operations into gun smuggling now?"

"Well, sorta. I knew they were supplying arms to the FARC guerillas in Colombia in exchange for a cut of the drug trade—that's probably where those weapons are headed—but, I didn't know San José was one of their transfer points. The smugglers usually stay away from the big cities and stick to the countryside."

"Hezbollah might have made them a special deal because of Ahmed."

"Or maybe this shipment is the first of many more to come."

"That's possible. It didn't look like the warehouse had been used for a long time, yet, someone had installed new entry and exit doors just recently. That should tell you something."

Bledsoe took off his glasses and rubbed his eyes. "When Salazar hears the cartel is running guns through Costa Rica, I may get the extra personnel I've been requesting."

I took my empty coffee mug over to the sink and rinsed it out. "Look, Toby, as much as I'd like to help you put these drug traffickers out of business for good, I'm only here to find Ahmed. My only interest in the cartel is their connection to him. The analysts at the Agency believe Hezbollah made an agreement with the cartel to get Ahmed into the States, and now, it would appear Ahmed's part of the bargain was to pick up a load of weapons and transport them here for the cartel's operations in South America."

"It's a typical exchange of service contract and a cartel trademark. Unfortunately, they've been having lots of success building their illegal enterprises this way."

"Ahmed didn't come down here for the sole purpose of making a weapons' delivery. Ernesto specifically said Ahmed was here to pick up a new passport."

"Like I told you earlier, someone in the Venezuela government is supplying either the Syrians or the Iranians with illegal passports, and this could be how Ahmed is getting his new one."

"Maybe there's a problem with Ahmed's new passport, and he refused to release the weapons shipment until he had it in hand. That may be the reason he's been here for over a week now."

Bledsoe nodded. "So you think he has his new passport now?"

"That's certainly possible, but my gut says no. Ernesto's death messed things up for him, so he may have given up the weapons in exchange for another safe house. When Ernesto talked about the passport, the impression I got was that Ahmed was still waiting for it to arrive."

I gestured at the images on Bledsoe's computer. "Either way, Toby, I believe the key to finding Ahmed is for you to meet with your cartel asset. You need to show him Sonya's photographs and see if he recognizes any of the men in them. Ask him if he knows where they're staying. And be sure to show him a photo of Ahmed. Tell him—"

"I know how to run my own asset, Titus."

Whether it was Bledsoe's angry voice or the sudden movement he made when he got up from his chair, the Doberman in the next room suddenly lunged from his bed and headed toward me.

Bledsoe rushed over to the archway and ordered the dog to stand down, and George immediately turned and headed back to his bed.

"I apologize, Titus," Bledsoe said, "He thought I was being threatened."

"I'm the one who should apologize. I've been operating solo for a long time now, and I'm used to running my own show."

"And giving orders."

"Well, that too."

"No harm done. Besides, I always get cranky when I haven't had enough sleep." He shrugged. "Anyway, I've already signaled Hernando I need to meet with him, and I can't do more than that without putting him at risk. In the meantime, the Agency analysts may turn up something on the men in those photographs. It could take a few days, but I'm sure we'll find Ahmed eventually."

I nodded. "Thanks for the omelet, Toby. I should get out of your hair now and let you get some sleep."

He didn't bother arguing with me. "I'll walk you out."

"I've made plans with Ben to meet him at the warehouse in the morning, and I'll call you when we get there."

Sadly, none of those statements proved true, and I never saw Toby Bledsoe again.

Chapter 11

Tuesday, June 5

It was after two o'clock in the morning when I returned to my hotel. Although I was tempted to take a more thorough look at the maps I'd found in the glove box of the Durango, I thought better of it and opted for sleep instead.

When I was awakened by my satphone a few hours later, I was dreaming about a dogfight. The dream included George, the black Doberman. He was snarling and charging at a yellow Lab.

In the seconds before the phone's vibration penetrated my consciousness, I recognized the yellow Lab was Stormy, a stray dog I'd adopted while living in Norman, Oklahoma.

Stormy wasn't backing down from George's aggressiveness, but I had the feeling he felt vulnerable and unsure of himself, even though he was managing to stand his ground.

I grabbed the phone off the nightstand.

"Yeah."

"Sorry, Titus, I know it's early."

"It's okay."

It was Carlton.

"Do you have something for me?" I asked. "Did you get a hit from the warehouse photographs? Please tell me you've pinpointed Ahmed's location. Toby is working on the passport angle. I found some maps in the Durango that could be useful."

I'd never been accused of talking too much—unless I was suddenly awakened out of a deep sleep.

When that happened, whatever my sub-consciousness was processing at that exact moment would come spewing out of my mouth before I could stop it.

It had happened to me several times in Afghanistan when Skip Coleman, Art Jernigan, and I were hunting the Taliban. At that time, we were within hearing distance of the enemy, and after a couple of close calls, both guys had learned to cover my mouth before shaking me awake so my jabbering wouldn't give away our position.

Carlton said, "I'm not calling about Ahmed. Are you awake? Do you need a minute?"

"No, no, I'm fine. What's up?"

"There's no way to say this except just to say it. Communications received a call through your CIS contact number. It was your sister. Your mother passed away a couple of hours ago."

"My mother?"

Suddenly, I couldn't find my voice.

"Yes. I'm so sorry, Titus."

"Oh . . . well, thanks. Ah . . . I guess I should call Carla."

"I'm sure she's waiting to hear from you."

"What . . . ah . . . What exactly did she say?"

"As to be expected, she thought she was leaving a message on your home voice mail. The call came in about an hour ago. If you want to hear the message for yourself, your clearance code is 4976."

"4976. Got it."

"Travel has you on a flight through Houston to Detroit using your cover name. It leaves San José in a couple of hours. Follow the usual procedure when you arrive."

"Okay, sure."

"I've already spoken to Toby Bledsoe. He said you're in a waiting mode there, and you're just passing time until he hears back from one of his assets. He also said it wouldn't make that much difference if you were gone for a few days. I suggested bringing in another operative, but he didn't see the need for it."

Fully awake now, I paced back and forth across the tiny room trying to sort out my priorities, not to mention my emotions.

"No, Douglas, there's absolutely no need to read anyone else into this operation. No need whatsoever. I can get regular updates from you and Toby while I'm gone."

"I'll have to do what's best for the operation."

Alarm bells went off inside of me when I heard him hinting at pulling me from the mission.

I tried my best to reassure him. "I won't need to be gone for more than a couple of days, three at the most. The last time I talked to Carla, she said my mother had already planned her funeral."

"I have you cleared for a week. That's the usual allowance, unless circumstances warrant otherwise."

"I won't need that much time."

"Again, please accept my condolences."

The moment I disconnected the call, I felt as if a fifty-pound weight had suddenly been placed on my chest.

Without warning, the remnants of my dream came bubbling to the surface, and I immediately found myself identifying with Stormy's emotions when he was fighting off the black dog.

Like him, I felt vulnerable and a little unsure of myself.

♦♦♦♦

A few hours later, as I sat in a departure lounge at the San José airport waiting for my flight to be called, I tried to focus in on the operation and the best means of locating Ahmed.

The synapses simply wouldn't fire, however, and I couldn't concentrate on the mission. Instead, my mind was flooded with memories of my mother.

She had been the exact opposite of my father. Whereas he had been totally disconnected from the family, she had engaged with her children on every level.

My mother, Sharon, was a high school science teacher, and she had taught at the same school for thirty years, retiring a few years before my father's death. Although I knew it couldn't possibly be true, I couldn't remember her ever taking a sick day.

She would get up before dawn, grade some papers, do a load of laundry, and put dinner in a yellow crock-pot before heading out for work. After school, she ran errands, drove Carla and me to our after-school activities, and returned home every evening to deal with an alcoholic husband.

She made sure we did our homework, met with our teachers, and taught us how to drive. She even attended all my high school football games, and she cheered so loudly all the guys on the playing field could hear her.

However, her biggest contribution to my life was instilling in me a love for my country. She was barely a year old when her parents got out of Poland and came to America—just weeks ahead of the Nazi invasion—and they loved their new home with an intense passion and ingrained that same kind of fierce loyalty in their daughter.

The Vietnam War took her brother's life and her husband came home from it a broken man, but my mother always believed America's desire to bring freedom and democracy to any nation, even Vietnam, was the right thing to do.

After leaving home to attend the University of Michigan, I didn't go back home very often, especially after I met Laura Hudson, a girl in my freshman biology class, whose parents I quickly adopted as my own.

When Laura and I got married a year after we met, my parents attended the wedding in Ann Arbor. However, I never took Laura home to Flint to spend any time with my family.

Since my father and I were barely able to be in the same room together, my mother never complained to me about my absence. Later, I realized she must have preferred peace in her household, instead of the turmoil my presence seemed to bring.

The month after I graduated from the university was the same month Laura had divorced me. It was a mutually agreeable decision after we both realized I hadn't married her because I loved her, but because I had loved being a member of her family. Immediately after that, I went to work for the CIA. However, I told my family and friends I worked at the Consortium for International Studies, where I was a research analyst.

Even though my sister, Carla, and I had a close relationship during our childhood, when I left home, we grew apart. For one thing, I felt she resented the fact I'd broken ties with the family and moved out of the area, while she had married her high school sweetheart and settled down a few miles from where we grew up.

Immediately after my father's funeral, Carla had cornered me in my old bedroom.

"Have you seen the changes in our mother?" she had asked me. "I think she may have suffered a small stroke last year."

"She seems fine," I said. "In fact, she's in the kitchen right now making me a big breakfast, even though I told her I'm leaving in a few minutes."

"But, Titus, that's my point. She loses track of time easily. She's very forgetful, and sometimes, she even calls me by a different name."

"Have you taken her to see a doctor?"

"No, of course not. You know she's never sick, and for the past six months, she's been busy taking care of Dad."

The moment Carla mentioned my dad, I exploded. "So what do you expect me to do about it?"

"I've given up expecting you to do anything in this family," she said. "Obviously, your precious consulting job is far more important than what's happening to us back here. Forget I said anything. I'll take care of her."

"I'm a research analyst, not a consultant, and I'm not asking you to take care of her."

"Well, someone has to see about her now that Dad's gone."

At that point, I completely lost it.

"Dad never took care of her, Carla. You know that as well as I do. It was always the other way around. He was the one needing someone to take care of him."

Before she could answer me, I grabbed my luggage and headed out the door.

My guilty conscience went with me.

Later that week, before returning to Iraq, I sent Carla a big check and told her to use it to get our mother some medical attention.

The process of getting any kind of diagnosis on my mother took almost a year, and once it was confirmed she had Alzheimer's disease, several years passed before she had to be placed in a nursing home.

Once that happened, I had the nursing home draft her medical expenses from my bank account once a month.

A few years after that, while I was in the States for a few weeks, Carla urged me to come for a visit, and I returned to Flint for a few days.

Although she seemed to be in good health physically, I was amazed at how much her mind had deteriorated since being moved to a nursing home. Even though I spent several hours a day with her, she never seemed to recognize me as her son.

Sometimes, she thought I was her husband. At other times, she acted as if I were one of her former students. Once, she even thought I was Uncle Harold, my father's brother.

In our conversations, she often struggled to complete her sentences or to maintain coherent reasoning, but, despite that, she always wanted to talk. The topic she wanted to discuss was religion—particularly faith.

When we were growing up, she had never discussed spiritual matters with me, and I had no basis for understanding what she was trying to articulate. After a while, I became so frustrated with her efforts to get me to understand what she wanted to say, I finally gave up listening to her altogether.

Until recently, I hadn't given those conversations with my mother much thought. However, a few months ago, in a safe house in Tehran, I'd made my decision to follow the teachings of Christ, and the first person I'd thought of afterward was my mother and her spiritual needs. That's when I wondered if her incoherent efforts to talk about God had been an attempt to ask forgiveness for her sins, just as I had done.

I despaired for my mother's soul in those hours after making my decision, because I knew she was already in the latter stages of the disease and could no longer communicate with anyone around her.

I had discussed this with Javad, the Iranian Christian who had led me to faith in Christ. "I think it's too late to talk with my mother about Christ. Perhaps she was trying to get through to me the last time I saw her, but now, I'm afraid she's doomed for all eternity because I couldn't help her then."

"Hammid," he said, calling me by my cover name, "Jesus said, 'I am the light of the world. He who follows me shall not walk in darkness, but have the light of life.' If your mother was truly seeking Jesus, you can be assured he is even now shining in her soul. He is the light, and while he always wants us to share that light, he never asks us to be that light."

Now, as I was preparing to bury my mother, those words were a great comfort to me.

♦♦♦♦

A dark-skinned man, wheeling a blue canvas suitcase, suddenly caught my attention.

He was moving from the security area toward the boarding lounge where I was seated. His profile reminded me of the photographs I'd seen of Ahmed back at Langley.

I started to leave my seat and follow him, when a young girl suddenly ran toward him from the opposite direction. When he turned to greet her, I was able see his features more clearly.

It was not Ahmed Al-Amin.

I felt relieved, because I'd finally decided the benefits of allowing Ahmed to leave Costa Rica far outweighed any intel the Agency might glean from snatching him up in San José and dropping him into Gitmo. I now believed the interrogation methods there wouldn't yield the kind of information I might discover by letting him get to his destination and his target.

For this risky method to succeed, however, I needed to be able to track him once he arrived in Venezuela. For that to happen, I needed Bledsoe's cartel contact to get me the name on Ahmed's new passport.

As if on cue, my satphone vibrated, and I saw Bledsoe's name pop up on my caller ID.

I said, "I hope you got some sleep last night."

"Don't worry about me; I'm fine, but I wanted to express my condolences before you left."

"Thanks, Toby. I appreciate that. I'm sorry Carlton had to disturb you last night. He said you discouraged him from assigning another officer to this operation, and I'm grateful for that. I owe you one."

"I've got people on the ground here who can run down any leads on those photographs. And, here's some good news. Hernando contacted me this morning. He can meet me tonight."

"That was quick."

Bledsoe sighed. "I know what you're thinking, but don't worry. Hernando hasn't been compromised. He sounded completely normal. In fact, he let me pick the place for us to meet."

"Do me a favor, Toby. No matter what time it is, call me and let me know what went down."

"I'll do that. Best of luck on your trip."

When I hung up, Ben Mitchell entered the boarding area and walked over to where I was seated.

He addressed me by my cover name, "Mr. Arroyo, I was sorry to hear about your mother."

"Thanks."

I pointed at the black briefcase containing the weapon he'd given me less than twenty-four hours ago and said, "And thanks for coming all the way out here to get these materials. I didn't want to leave them with the hotel desk clerk, and I didn't have time to drop them off at the embassy."

I lowered my voice and handed him a large envelope. "These are the maps I found inside the Durango. Get them off in the diplomatic pouch to Langley today, and we'll see if our analysts can make sense out of the markings I found on several of them. Maybe Ahmed left us some bread crumbs to follow."

"We should have more intel on Ahmed's location by the time you get back. I have a team watching the warehouse, plus Sonya and Josué will be back at the safe house today. We're bound to get a break soon."

I saw Mitchell continually scanned the crowds. Yet, to any outside observer, I'm sure he appeared to be engaged in conversation with me. As I watched his behavior, I decided Bledsoe was right; Ben Mitchell had all the makings of a superb covert officer.

To make sure that actually happened, I decided to confront him.

♦♦♦♦

"Sit down, Ben. We need to talk before they call my flight."

Earlier, when I'd arrived in the boarding area, I'd chosen a four-plex of seats away from the main seating area. While waiting for Mitchell to arrive, I'd placed my carry-on bag on one of the seats and a copy of the current edition of *La Nación* on the other.

By doing this, I'd hoped to discourage any travelers from sitting near me, so Mitchell and I could talk. Now, Mitchell moved my bag to the floor and sat down in the plastic chair across from me.

"I'm not sure about the protocol while you're gone," he said. "Do you want me to send you updates by email?"

"No, Ben, what I want you to do is break off your relationship with Sonya."

He looked at me as if I'd just slapped him across the face.

"Sonya? What are you talking about?"

"You know what I'm talking about."

He broke off eye contact with me and shifted his gaze over to the bank of windows facing the airport tarmac.

After a few moments of silence, he asked, "Have you said anything to Toby?"

"No, and I don't plan to do so, but don't discount Toby because he's old. He knows how to read people, and you're not hiding your feelings very well."

He shifted his attention back to me. "My feelings are none of your business, and my relationship with Sonya has nothing to do with you."

His anger had hardened the contours of his face, and he no longer appeared as youthful as when I'd first seen him at the pastry shop.

"Ben, the rules against dating a foreign national under your supervision are in place for a reason. Your relationship is putting you both in danger, and you're jeopardizing your entire career by your behavior."

He crossed his arms in front of his chest in a classic gesture of defiance. "How do you figure that?" he asked.

"Sonya doesn't have any training when it comes to evading an attacker or dealing with an interrogator. Granted, she exhibited a lot of potential for fieldwork yesterday, but she was reckless and disregarded your orders because she thought it might impress you. Did you ever stop to think what might have happened to her if one of those cartel guys had seen her in the warehouse yesterday? Can you imagine what they would have done to her?"

He visibly flinched at the thought of Sonya in the hands of the cartel members.

"Yeah, that's right. You know exactly what I'm talking about, and that's why you were so worried about her."

He uncrossed his arms. "I had no idea she would go inside that warehouse."

"You showed her how to pick a lock, though, didn't you?"

He nodded his head. "She was always asking me to show her stuff like that."

"Encourage her to go back to school and take some law enforcement classes. Remove her from your watchers, Ben, and end the relationship before it ends your career."

He thought about my statement for a minute.

Then, like any good operative when cornered, he went on offense.

"You were involved with someone, weren't you? What happened? Did you get caught? Did something happen to her?"

Although he was closer to the truth than he probably imagined, I refused to answer his questions.

I said, "You need to date someone who works for the Agency. They encourage in-house relationships just to avoid this problem."

I heard the flight attendant announce the boarding process, so I picked up the newspaper from the adjoining chair and grabbed my luggage.

Mitchell said, "I have to assume all this advice you're dishing out means you're married. Does your wife also work for the Agency?"

"I'm not married, Ben, at least not anymore. But no, she didn't work for the Agency."

My admission brought a smile to his face. "It doesn't sound as if you're an expert on relationships then."

"I'm not," I said, as I turned and headed toward the boarding area, "but I learned an important lesson when I was married."

When Mitchell caught up with me, he asked, "What was that? Don't get married?"

I smiled. "No, I wouldn't mind getting married again one day, but I learned it's best to marry a woman because you've fallen in love with her. Don't marry a woman because you've fallen in love with her family."

He was quiet for a few moments. Finally, he asked, "Are you saying that little nugget of wisdom applies to Sonya and me?"

I stopped and faced him. "Sonya doesn't love you, Ben. She loves the work you do. She doesn't find *you* irresistible. She finds your career irresistible."

As I walked away, I wondered if my confrontation with Mitchell would have any lasting consequences.

It would, but not in the way I imagined.

PART TWO

Chapter 12

I had a two-hour layover in Houston, so I called Communication Services at the Agency and gave them clearance code 4976. Seconds later, I was listening to the painful voicemail left by my sister.

I was immediately struck by the sadness in Carla's voice, but I was also chastened by the frustration I heard there.

"Hi, Titus. It's Carla. I guess you must have turned off your cell phone. But, come to think of it, when have you ever picked up when I've called you at this number?"

For several minutes, all I heard were her sobs.

After a couple of attempts to speak, she finally said, "I'm sorry. I shouldn't have said that. What I'm calling to tell you is . . ." She stopped and started over again. "What I wanted you to know was . . ."

Finally, she said, "Titus, our mother passed away this morning."

Then, although there was a slight catch in her voice, she no longer sounded hesitant.

"The nurse said she died peacefully in her sleep, so I don't believe she suffered. It's early Tuesday morning here, and I haven't been able to talk to the funeral home yet, but Eddie and I think the service will probably be on Friday."

For several seconds, she said nothing, and I couldn't tell if she was crying again or just searching for the right words.

Maybe it was a little of both.

Then she said, "I know Mother would want for us to be together at a time like this, so I hope you can come home. Okay, that's it . . . goodbye."

I found a corner where I could have some privacy and after taking a couple of deep breaths, I called my sister.

"Hi, Carla, it's Titus."

"Oh, Titus, I'm so glad you called. You got my message?"

"I did. Are you okay?"

"Yes, I think so. I've been busy trying to take care of everything, but that's a good thing. I never knew there would be so much to do. It wasn't like this when Daddy passed away. Mother took care of everything then."

"I'm sure there's a lot to think about."

"You have no idea. My house needs cleaning, and there are phone calls to make, and meals to think about, and, well . . . it just seems pretty overwhelming to me right now."

"I'll be there tomorrow."

"Oh, thank God you're coming. Do you need Eddie to pick you up? Are you flying into Flint?"

"There's no need for him to do that. I'm flying into Detroit, and I'll rent a car and drive up to Flint. I should be at your house around ten o'clock tomorrow morning."

The PA system in the Houston airport announced the boarding of a Southwest flight, and Carla immediately asked, "Are you at the airport now?"

"Yes, I just flew in from Costa Rica. I was down there doing some research for CIS."

"I know you're a busy man, Titus. Thank you for coming."

"See you tomorrow."

When I hung up, I felt unsettled, and I couldn't tell if the cause of my discomfort were the lies I'd just told my sister, or the fact I was being forced to spend time with my family.

♦♦♦♦

After my plane landed in Detroit, I took my time disembarking from the aircraft. By doing so, I managed to be the last passenger off the airplane and the last one to arrive in the baggage claim area.

My fellow passengers were all bunched together around a motionless carousel, waiting to see if their luggage had been one of the lucky ones and had made it to Detroit. But, since that wasn't my problem, I focused my attention on the faces in the crowd.

Seconds after the carousel began moving, a heavyset man, wearing a dark blue suit, appeared on the scene. He had a lanyard around his neck with a badge attached to it. The badge itself was solid black with the name "Chuck" printed in large white letters.

Chuck was headed in the direction of the car rental counters, and he was wheeling a medium-sized gray suitcase behind him.

I left the baggage claim area and followed him.

Near the Hertz counter, Chuck sat down in a row of cushioned seats, and I took a seat in the same row, leaving a few spaces between us.

He placed the gray suitcase directly in front of the vacant seats.

As soon as I placed my copy of *La Nación* on the empty seat beside him, along with my bag, he slipped his hand inside his coat pocket and removed a brown manila envelope. He placed it next to the newspaper.

Then, without saying a word, he picked up the newspaper, grabbed my bag, and walked away, leaving the gray suitcase behind.

The Agency required a strict protocol when an intelligence officer returned to the States, especially while in the middle of an assignment. Resuming one's real identity in the States, with plans to return to an ongoing operation as a different person, was always a bit risky.

Although I doubted the exercise in tradecraft Chuck and I had just experienced was really necessary, Carlton's earlier instructions to "follow the usual procedure" indicated he expected me to adhere to these safety precautions.

Chuck had followed Agency protocol to the letter—unlike several couriers who could never resist attempting some kind of conversation with me. For whatever reason, I suspected Chuck enjoyed the small role he had just played in America's intelligence game.

After Courier Chuck had left the terminal, I moved to a different set of seats and opened the bulky manila envelope he'd left me. Inside, I found all the necessary documents for me to resume my life as Titus Alan Ray, an employee of CIS. There was a wallet full of cash, my current driver's license, two credit cards, and several CIS business cards.

The combination to the gray suitcase was attached to a memo—supposedly written by my secretary at CIS—informing me of the hotel reservations she'd made for me near my sister's home in Flint. Included in the memo was the name of the car rental agency holding my reservation for an SUV.

The last item inside the packet was my cell phone. It was the same iPhone I'd purchased for myself a few months before when I'd been forced to relocate to Norman, Oklahoma. It had some personal contact numbers on it, which I assumed was the reason Support Services had included it in the packet.

I was tempted to use the cell phone to cancel the hotel reservation the Agency had made for me in Flint. However, I could think of no valid reason—other than sheer operational paranoia—for doing so.

Besides that, I noticed the booking was for the Holiday Inn Express, and the thought of having their cinnamon rolls on my breakfast plate the next morning was enough to convince me to keep the reservation.

♦♦♦♦

After picking up my Lincoln Navigator, I programmed the GPS with the hotel's address, located on the outskirts of Flint in a suburb called Grand Blanc. If I remembered correctly, it was not far from Carla's house.

I made the trip from Detroit to Flint in about an hour, and I checked into the Holiday Inn at around eight o'clock in the evening. Then, I went across the street to an I-Hop, where I devoured a huge plate of pancakes and sausage.

As I was paying the check, one of my phones started vibrating.

It was the Agency sat phone, and the caller ID indicated Toby Bledsoe was on the line.

"Can you talk?" he asked.

"Give me a second," I said, and then I quickly walked out of the restaurant and over to a wooden bench facing the parking lot.

"I'm clear now."

"I called to give you an update on my meeting with Hernando."

"Did he know anything about Ahmed?"

"Not directly, but he said something big went down yesterday."

"Like what?"

"The cartel conducts its business at a seafood restaurant in the *San Rafael* district, and Hernando said his boss left the restaurant around three o'clock in the afternoon and didn't return until after closing at two this morning. He told me such behavior was unusual for Luca—that's his boss' name—because he always tries to be there for closing. Hernando said Luca didn't give him any kind of explanation for his absence when he returned."

"That's not much to go on, but his absence does fit the timeline of when Ahmed left the safe house and when Sonya saw the men unloading the weapons from the Durango. What about Sonya's photographs of the men in the warehouse?"

"Hernando was a big help there. He recognized all four of them. They all work for Luca. He didn't know their addresses, but he said he could probably find them."

"Did Hernando recognize Ahmed when you showed him his photograph?"

"Negative. He also said they hadn't received any passports from Venezuela in over a month. I told him to call me if anything unusual occurred, or if a passport arrived with Ahmed's picture on it."

"So the flow of passports from Venezuela has dried up?"

"It looks that way. That probably means Ahmed hasn't left Costa Rica yet."

"That's good. My job will be a whole lot easier if I know the name Ahmed will be using once he gets to Venezuela."

Bledsoe was quiet for a moment, and then I realized what I'd said.

Long-distance travel sometimes skewed my focus, and I knew if Bledsoe hadn't lost his edge, he'd catch my slip.

He asked, "Are you thinking of letting Ahmed leave Costa Rica and travel to Venezuela?"

Obviously, Bledsoe was still sharp. However, I detected only curiosity in his voice, no disapproval, so I just ran with it.

"I might as well confess, Toby. I've been giving it some thought. I realize it's going to be difficult to convince Carlton not to grab Ahmed while he's still in San José, but it could be beneficial to find out what he's up to."

A family had arrived at the I-Hop in a mini-van, and when they got out of the car, two of their four kids started chasing each other around the bench where I was seated.

"What's your rationale for letting him go?"

Before I could answer his question, one of the kids accidently ran into my bum leg, the one I'd shattered in Tehran. When I groaned, Bledsoe must have heard me.

"You don't want to discuss it?" he asked.

"No, that's not it. Just a second." I got up from the bench and started walking down the street toward the intersection.

"To put it simply, Toby. I'd like to know who's going to be Ahmed's next hit. It would be useful to identify the person Hezbollah considers to be an enemy, especially since I believe Ahmed has been hired to assassinate someone in Venezuela."

"I see your point. Why would Hezbollah send an expensive hit man halfway around the world to assassinate someone in Venezuela? His target would have to be someone important, someone the Agency might be interested in."

"Right, and if I'm hearing you correctly, you don't think it's a bad idea to follow Ahmed to Venezuela."

Bledsoe didn't say anything for a few seconds. Then he said, "Look, Titus, I don't think it's a particularly bad idea, but I'm not sure it's a particularly good idea either."

I crossed the intersection at the green light and turned into the hotel's parking lot. When I opened the door to the hotel lobby, I asked him, "Would you care to elaborate on that?"

"For starters, even if you knew the name Ahmed was using to get into Venezuela, you'd have no idea where he was headed once he got there. If you ran into trouble with the Venezuela authorities—who, by the way, are extremely hostile to the U.S. right now—they'd put you in prison and forget about you. I doubt the Agency would have much success in getting you out either."

"Something to consider."

"On the other hand, although Costa Rica would undoubtedly slap your hand if you got into trouble here, they would simply send you home. I think it might be far more prudent for you to capture Ahmed here in Costa Rica and then let the interrogators at Gitmo uncover the name on Ahmed's hit list."

I pushed the elevator for the second floor and replied, "You're not telling me—"

"Titus? Is that you?"

I turned around to see who'd called my name.

There was a note of alarm in Bledsoe's voice. "Did someone recognize you?"

"Yes, I just ran into someone I know here at the hotel. We'll talk later." Just before hanging up, though, I referenced the weather, an Agency code assuring him there was no danger. "I'm glad it's not raining there today."

As I ended the call, Uncle Harold encompassed me in a bear hug.

"Uncle Harold," I said, trying to extricate myself, "I had no idea you were staying here."

"We got in about an hour ago," he said, looking me over. "What kind of shirt is that? Are you living in the Bahamas now?"

Before heading over to the I-Hop earlier, I hadn't bothered to change out of the wardrobe, which Legends had chosen for me for the persona of Rafael Arroyo. Now, I realized I must have looked out of place this far north of the border.

"I've been down in Costa Rica doing some research for my job," I said.

"Are you still working for that consortium thing?"

I nodded. "Yes, I still work for the Consortium for International Studies. It's called CIS."

Even though I'd already pushed the elevator button once, Harold reached over and pushed it two more times in quick succession. "It's in Maryland, right?"

"College Park."

The elevator arrived, and we both got on.

"Which floor?" he asked.

"The second."

"Dorothy and I are up on the third floor," he said, pushing buttons two and three. "I believe that's the floor above you."

"You're right," I said. "The third floor is one floor above the second floor."

Uncle Harold had aged a lot since I'd last seen him, and I briefly wondered if his mental capacities had undergone some changes as well. While his hair was still full, it was now completely white, and multitudes of short white hairs were pushing their way out of his ears. He had probably put on at least thirty pounds.

After manning the elevator console, he turned towards me, and said, "I'm so sorry for your loss, Titus. I know Sharon's death didn't come as a shock, but it's still hard to lose your mother."

"Thank you."

When the elevator reached the second floor, I quickly stepped off.

Harold shouted after me. "Maybe Dorothy and I will see you downstairs at breakfast in the morning."

"Maybe," I said, waving goodbye.

Seconds later, when the elevator doors were just inches shy of closing, Harold stuck his hand between the narrow opening.

The doors immediately jerked opened again.

"You know," he said, holding the doors at bay, "I can't get over how much you remind me of your father. You look just like him. Same hair. Same features."

I mumbled an incoherent reply, and Uncle Harold nodded his head, as if my words made complete sense to him. Once the elevator doors finally closed, I escaped to my room and collapsed on the bed.

Right then, a Venezuelan prison cell didn't sound so bad.

Chapter 13

Wednesday, June 6

The next morning, after a few seconds of fiddling with the room's mini-coffeepot, I brewed myself a cup of coffee. Then, I took the Gideon Bible from the nightstand drawer and opened it to one of the Psalms.

Reading the Bible was a habit I'd developed after returning to the States from Tehran. Every morning, I'd go out to the sunroom in the house the Agency had rented for me in Norman, and I'd begin my day by reading a chapter from the book of Psalm and a chapter from the gospel of John.

When I'd been living with the Iranian Christians in Tehran, I'd noticed that reading the Bible had seemed to make a difference in their lives, and I believed it would make a difference in mine as well.

However, sitting in the claustrophobic hotel room made me wish I were back in the house in Norman. There, I'd always had a spectacular view of the sun shining through the forest of trees surrounding the property.

When Carlton had cancelled my medical leave and made me operational again, I'd ended up purchasing the farmhouse in Oklahoma, even though I'd only lived there for two months. Reflecting back on this impulsive decision a few days after signing the papers, I'd wondered if being cut off from the Agency had caused me to want to put roots down somewhere.

I'm sure any of the Agency psychiatrists would see it that way.

At the time I'd signed the papers, my rationale for buying the property was that I needed a place where Stormy could run free, or hunt squirrels, or do whatever dogs did in order to fulfill their purpose in life. But I didn't kid myself; I also knew having a permanent base in Norman would also make it a lot easier for me to become better acquainted with Nikki Saxon.

Nikki was a detective in the Norman Police Department. We'd met when she was assigned to investigate the homicide of a young Iranian woman. At the beginning of the investigation, I'd questioned whether Ahmed might have been involved in the murder.

Because that was a possibility, I'd been forced to reveal my true identity to Nikki, and after that, Nikki and I had developed a close friendship.

Such a relationship was foreign to me because I seldom allowed anyone to get very close to me. Nevertheless, when I'd been ordered back to Langley, I'd asked Nikki to be responsible for Stormy while I was gone, and she'd agreed to do so.

Now, as I put away the Gideon Bible, I considered giving Nikki a call. But the moment I picked up my iPhone, I noticed the time and remembered she was usually at work by seven.

I decided I would wait and call her later.

Or not at all.

Nikki knew I was away on an overseas assignment. I'd told her that much. I'd also told her I'd be returning to Norman between assignments.

In reality, I wasn't between assignments at the moment, and I wondered if calling her wouldn't simply complicate my already complicated life.

Besides that, I felt pretty conflicted about my feelings for her.

I decided to put off making a decision about calling her.

Instead, I pulled a toiletry kit out of my Agency suitcase and headed for the bathroom. As I cut the whiskers off my face, I remembered Uncle Harold's words from the previous evening. With my dark complexion and thick black hair, I knew I resembled my father, but I very much doubted I looked "just like him," as Uncle Harold had said.

I'd always thought of myself as a good-looking guy, but knowing

Uncle Harold, I didn't think he meant his remark as a compliment.

Uncle Harold was my father's brother, and when my father had been alive, the two men had never gotten along with each other, nor had they appeared to like each other all that much. Consequently, I'd always felt Harold viewed me as a younger version of my father and hadn't particularly cared for me either.

Carla believed the two brothers hadn't been able to stand each other because their personalities were so different. While my father had been aloof and unsociable, Harold had always been outgoing and talkative, engaging even strangers in long conversations.

Besides their opposing personalities, their careers had gone off in two different directions. Even though both had started out in manufacturing—my dad at GM and my uncle at the Knoll Furniture Company in Grand Rapids—Harold had retired as Vice President of Sales, whereas my dad had never been promoted above the level of assembly line foreman.

Although I felt Uncle Harold disliked me, he had a completely different relationship with my mother and Carla. He obviously adored both of them, and they had always returned his affection.

The last time I'd talked to Carla, she'd mentioned Harold had continued to visit our mother, even though she was no longer able to recognize him.

Now, as I stepped into the shower, I decided I would try and make a connection with Uncle Harold over the next couple of days. I wanted him to recognize that, unlike my father, I could be a friendly and winsome kind of guy.

At least friendly.

♦♦♦♦

Before leaving the room to get some breakfast, I picked up my iPhone and called Nikki.

"Hi, Nikki."

"Titus? I'm surprised to hear from you so soon!"

She sounded excited, and I realized I was smiling.

"I'm in the States for a couple of days, but I won't be able to make it back to Norman this trip. How's Stormy?"

I immediately regretted asking her the question.

Since I knew she was still recuperating from a gunshot wound, I should have at least inquired about her own welfare before asking about my dog's well-being.

"Stormy's just fine," she answered, seemingly unfazed by my insensitivity. "I love how happy he is to see me every day when I get in from work. I'm sure he misses you, though. Are you in Virginia?"

Before I could answer her, she quickly added, "Oh, I probably shouldn't have asked you that."

"You're in law enforcement. I'll make an exception."

She laughed.

It was a beautiful sound.

"I'm in Flint or, more precisely, Grand Blanc."

"Are you there to see your mother?"

Nikki Saxon was an excellent detective. Within days of our meeting, she'd managed to pull my entire life history out of me. And, even for a detective, that was not an easy task.

"In a way. My mother passed away yesterday morning. I was able to get away from my assignment to attend her funeral."

"Oh, Titus, I'm so sorry. She had Alzheimer's, didn't she?"

"Yes, but the doctors said she died peacefully in her sleep."

"And the funeral? When will it be?"

"Probably Friday. I just got in last night, but I'm headed over to my sister's house in a few minutes. I should know more after I talk to her."

"Are you okay?"

I suddenly found myself wanting to be open with her and not just give her a superficial answer. "To be honest, Nikki, I'm not looking forward to dealing with my family during the next couple of days."

She was quiet for a few minutes, and I pictured her running her fingers through her long brown hair, a gesture I'd seen her make before when she was on the phone and uncertain of what to say.

She finally said, "Families are never easy, are they?"

Nikki had grown up in a foster care environment. Her biological mother had been put in prison for armed robbery when she was three years old, but she'd never known her father. My family had been great compared with hers.

"I guess I should be more grateful for the family I've had."

"I know you loved your mother very much," she replied, "and I'm sure your sister is happy to have you there. Do you have many relatives in the area?"

"Not that many," I replied. "But you've asked enough questions about me, Detective. How are you? How's your shoulder?"

"I'm still doing some rehab on it, but it's healing up nicely. I'm back at work fulltime now. In fact, just before you called, I was on my way over to interview a witness in a robbery investigation."

"I won't keep you then."

"Hold on, Titus," she said, "don't hang up. I wasn't telling you about the investigation to get you off the phone. The witness can wait."

"Okay."

There was an awkward silence between us, and I couldn't think of anything to say.

She laughed and said, "You don't call many people just to chat with them, do you?"

"No," I admitted, "I never do."

"Well, there's a knack to it, and I hope you're not offended when I say you don't have that knack."

Now, I was the one laughing. "I'm not offended."

"Why don't you call me again before you leave, and we'll work on your technique."

"Okay, I might do that."

However, that phone call never happened, but something better did.

♦♦♦♦

There was no sign of Uncle Harold in the hotel's breakfast bar, but I chose a table for four just in case he and Aunt Dorothy decided to show up later.

While eating my scrambled eggs and cinnamon rolls, I surveyed the room—an occupational habit and totally unnecessary on a sunny morning in Michigan.

But, I did it anyway.

Two Hispanic men, seated on a couch in the center of the room, immediately got my attention.

They were drinking coffee and watching a newscast on the big screen television set. The younger of the two reminded me of Ernesto; not my last bloodied image of him when he was dying from the wound to his abdomen, but of the photograph I'd seen of him from the Fadi Chehab passport.

The guy triggered something in the subconscious part of my brain, and I stopped eating and tried to figure it out.

Ernesto. Photograph. Passport.

Suddenly, it came to me, and I immediately got up from the table, took out my satphone, and moved toward the doorway.

At that moment, Uncle Harold and Aunt Dorothy walked in the room.

"Titus, how are you this morning? You look a lot better than you did yesterday. I don't think travel agrees with you."

"Hi, Uncle Harold. I've saved us a table right over there." I pointed to my table in a corner of the room. "Aunt Dorothy, it's so nice to see you again. You haven't changed a bit. In fact, I think you're looking younger than the last time I saw you."

Aunt Dorothy, who seldom said a word, smiled at me; then, she reached up and patted my cheek.

They both seemed surprised when I excused myself and headed out the door.

When I reached the end of the hallway, I pushed opened the exit door and walked out onto the parking lot.

From there, I called Carlton.

After Communication Services put him on the line, he asked, "How's your family?"

"I'm going over to my sister's house in a few minutes. Right now, I'm out in the hotel's parking lot, so we're cleared to talk."

Sounding slightly exasperated with me, he said, "You've wasted a phone call. I don't have any new intel on Ahmed."

Carlton hated it when his operatives called him for updates.

He would call me if he had something new to report; I had been told this repeatedly.

He continued, "I believe Toby already informed you about his meeting with Hernando, but I still don't have anything on the identities of the four men in the photographs. Toby has the airport covered, so we're good there. I'll call you the minute I have something definitive to tell you."

"I wasn't calling for an update, Douglas. I just remembered something from our search of Ahmed's safe house. I didn't mention it the other day because I just now thought of it."

"Do I need to make this an official part of the record?"

"You can decide that later."

"I see."

Carlton hated having anything on the official record that even hinted at incompetence on his part, so he probably already knew where I was going with this.

"As I mentioned in the conference call yesterday, when Ben and I searched Ahmed's safe house, we discovered two passports. Ahmed had been using one, which identified him as Adnan Chehab, while Ernesto was using another one in the name of Fadi Chehab."

"Yes," he said, "Toby sent us all the information you collected from the safe house. We received it in the diplomatic pouch yesterday. Both passports were inside."

Since he still sounded like he was questioning the importance of my call, I hurried on. "When we searched the safe house, I only found Ernesto's phony passport."

I waited a few seconds to see if he might say something.

When he didn't, I asked, "So, where's his Venezuelan passport?"

Carlton didn't utter a word, but I did hear him sigh, and that usually meant he knew he'd missed an important detail, and he wasn't happy about it.

I couldn't resist rubbing it in. "I'm talking about the one he used to enter the United States, the same passport he used outside of Austin to buy the Durango; the one identifying him as Ernesto Montilla."

"Okay. Okay. You've made your point. His Venezuelan passport is missing. It wasn't in the safe house. Evidently, we both managed to overlook this important detail."

Shared responsibility for messing up—another one of Carlton's endearing managerial techniques.

I said, "I believe Ahmed took Ernesto's Venezuelan passport with him when he left the safe house."

"Why?"

"I'm not sure. I'll have to think about it."

"Look, Titus, right now, you need to be with your family. Let me toss this around with the analysts here and see what they think."

"Have Katherine's office take a look at it."

"That's where I'll start, of course. Now, quit stalling. Go see your family. I'll call you when we come up with something."

I went back inside the hotel and entered the breakfast area. However, my table had been cleared off, and Uncle Harold and Aunt Dorothy were nowhere in sight.

Maybe I should have been disappointed.

I wasn't.

Chapter 14

Carla and her family lived in a two-story red brick house with blue shutters about five miles west of my hotel. It was located at the end of a cul-de-sac in a subdivision called Chatham Hills.

There was a basketball goal at the side of the driveway, and near the corner of the front lawn, there was an aluminum flagpole flying an American flag.

As I looked at the recently mowed lawn and the petunias growing in the flowerbeds, the sight stirred something inside of me, and I parked on the street and stared at the picturesque setting for several seconds.

For some reason, I wanted this idyllic snapshot to be seared on the frontal lobe of my brain forever.

The longer I looked, the more I realized the scene could have been multiplied a million times over all across America. It represented the reason why I'd spent the best years of my life trying to make certain no jihadist, no drug lord, no maniac with access to nuclear weapons, no one, not one soul, would ever be able to destroy the land of the free and the home of the brave.

That philosophy gave form and substance to my ideals and was the motivation for everything I did as a servant of my country.

Granted, I didn't do it alone, but, just like every citizen sent out to protect American interests on foreign soil, sometimes I felt very alone when I did it.

♦♦♦♦

There were several cars parked in the driveway, but I pegged the older model Lexus as belonging to Harold and Dorothy, because it had also been in the parking lot at the hotel.

A Buick Enclave was parked in front of the Lexus, and as I walked past it, I noticed the back seat contained a variety of small boxes, brochures, and tinfoil packets. Carla's husband, Eddie, was a sales representative for some type of pharmaceutical company, and I quickly decided the Enclave probably belonged to him.

Next to the Enclave was a pickup truck with a University of Michigan decal prominently displayed in the back window. I knew Carla and Eddie's son, Brian, was attending the university on a full football scholarship, so I figured the truck was his.

Surveillance complete; I walked up to the front door and rang the doorbell.

It took a few minutes, but Carla finally answered it.

My sister had inherited my mother's fair skin and blond hair, but, unlike my mother, she was short and stocky and closely resembled pictures I'd seen of my Polish grandmother.

"Oh, Titus, I'm so glad you're here," she said, wiping her hands on a dishtowel. "Harold said he saw you at the hotel last night, but I thought you said you were flying in this morning."

It was more an observation than an accusation, and I mumbled something about not being sure of my plans and gave her a hug. As we embraced, she clung to me for a few minutes.

Moments later, she dried her eyes on the dishtowel and put a smile on her face. "Come on in. Everyone's in the back."

As we walked through the living room, Carla immediately began apologizing for the way everything looked. But, despite Carla's embarrassment, all I could see was the inevitable clutter caused by a very active family.

"Carla, don't worry about any of this," I said. "Your house looks great."

She looked back at me and grinned. "So you're not Mr. Clean anymore?"

"I didn't say that."

Carla paused at the doorway of the dining room. Then, as if she were announcing the next circus act appearing under the Big Top, she said, "Here's Titus, everyone."

All heads turned in my direction.

"Hi," I said in my best affable voice. "It's good to see everyone."

A chorus of greetings followed, and then Carla looked over at her daughter and said, "Kayla, would you and Aunt Dorothy come out to the kitchen and give me a hand?"

Kayla, Carla's second child, was sixteen years old and the only member of the family with auburn hair. She reacted to her mother's outrageous request by looking over at me and rolling her eyes.

Despite the drama, she grabbed her cell phone from the table and left the room. A few seconds later, Aunt Dorothy got up from the table and followed Kayla out. As she squeezed past my chair, she patted me on the shoulder.

Eddie grabbed a plate of raw hamburger patties from the kitchen bar. "Anyone care to come out to the deck and watch me burn these?"

Eddie and I had known each other since we'd played football together in high school, but we'd never been close. Other than sports, we seemed to have difficulty finding any shared interests. This was probably because I wasn't into sales conventions, the latest trends in pharmaceuticals, or discussing generic drugs.

By the time Eddie had entered college, his hairline had started receding, and now, his shiny top was bordered on both sides by a slight fringe of gray hair. He'd been a big guy in high school, but today he had less muscle and more fat on his large frame.

His son, Brian, who was built like him but had his mother's blond hair, followed his dad out to the redwood deck. I waited for Uncle Harold to maneuver himself out of his chair, and then both of us followed Brian outside and stood around Eddie's enormous gas grill.

The guys bantered about the nice sunny weather, the neighbor's new swimming pool, and the bad economy. About the time I'd exhausted my repertoire of banality, Carla opened the patio doors.

"Titus," she said, "the funeral home just called. They want to meet with us this afternoon, and I told them we'd be there at two o'clock."

No one spoke for several seconds, sobered by the reality of why we'd all been brought together in the first place.

"So the funeral will definitely be on Friday?" I asked.

Carla pushed the door all the way open and stepped out on the deck. "Yes, the funeral director confirmed everything last night. It's going to be at ten o'clock Friday morning in their chapel."

"Which funeral home are you using?" Uncle Harold asked. "I hope it's not Guthrie's. They didn't put out enough chairs at Scotty Welborn's funeral, and I had to stand for the entire service. I got so tired, I just knew I was gonna pass out."

"No, Uncle Harold," Carla said, "I told you yesterday we're using Brown's on East Hill Road. If you remember, they also did Dad's service."

I asked, "Why are we meeting with the funeral director this afternoon? I thought everything had already been planned."

"Mother just chose her casket and arranged for her burial plot to be next to Dad's. You and I will need to sit down with the director and decide about the music and who's going to speak at the service."

"I'll say a few words," Uncle Harold said.

"Titus and I will figure everything out this afternoon, Uncle Harold, but thank you for your offer."

When Carla turned to go back inside the house, I saw her give Eddie a knowing look. I wasn't exactly sure what that look meant, but, if I had to guess, I would say having Harold speak at the funeral was the last thing she wanted.

I asked Eddie, "How's your work going?"

I tried to think of the name of Eddie's pharmaceutical company, but it completely escaped me, and I wondered why I could remember an entire line of refrigeration units and not remember the name of the company where my brother-in-law had worked for the past fifteen years.

Eddie smiled. "It's been great. I was made district manager a couple of years ago. Now, I'm in charge of twenty sales reps, and I don't have to travel as much as I did before."

Brian said, "Dad won a trip to Las Vegas last year, and we all went with him." He leaned over and punched his dad's arm. "All the players on the team were totally jealous."

I said, "Good for you. I hadn't heard that."

Of course I hadn't heard that.

I'd been living in Iran at the time, and during the two years I'd been there, I hadn't spoken to Carla, although I'd arranged for the Agency to send gifts in my name at the appropriate times—a fruit basket at Easter and gift cards at Christmas.

After Eddie had finished flipping the burgers on the grill, he asked, "And you? Are you still working at that think tank in Maryland?"

"Yeah," Uncle Harold said, answering for me, "he's still doing research at some place called CIS."

Brian shook his head. "That's not right. That's not what Titus does."

My heart did a couple of cartwheels.

"Yes, it is," Harold insisted. "He told me so yesterday."

I tried to sound calm. "I'm still with CIS."

"Yeah, okay," Brian said, but he didn't sound convinced.

"It sounds like you don't think I work there anymore."

"Oh, I know you still work at CIS, but the last time I looked you up, their website listed you as a Senior Fellow instead of a Research Analyst."

I immediately relaxed. "You're right, Brian. I was recently promoted to Senior Fellow a few months ago. You've been checking up on me, huh?"

"I wouldn't say I was checking up on you, but since my major's in political science, I was hoping to do an internship in Washington this summer, and I thought you might know someone there. That's why I looked you up. You're listed under Middle Eastern Programs in the CIS directory. That's not my focus, and I decided you probably didn't know anyone important enough to help me find a job."

He was right.

I didn't know anyone important.

And what's more, no one important knew me.

I planned on keeping it that way.

"I can't think of anyone right now, but I'll certainly give it some thought."

Harold said, "Congratulations on your promotion."

My promotion to Senior Fellow had been engineered by Support Services at the Agency, because all senior fellows at CIS were required to publish scholarly works on a regular basis. To that end, I'd been teamed up with a professor at the University of Oklahoma to coauthor a book on the Middle East, thus giving me a plausible reason for my relocation to Norman during my medical leave.

Later, the Agency made sure that book never saw the light of day.

I said, "Thanks, Uncle Harold. I know you received your share of promotions while working for Knoll."

The moment Harold began describing how he'd been a top salesman for the company, my Agency phone started vibrating. I decided it was probably not the best time to answer it.

"I believe these puppies are done," Eddie said, transferring the grilled meat patties to a plate. "Brian, tell your mother lunch is served."

I crossed the deck and opened the patio doors. "I'm sorry. I can't stay for lunch. There's some work I need to get done back at the hotel."

When I showed up in the kitchen, Carla asked, "Can I get you something to drink? I've made some lemonade."

"Thanks, Carla, but I've got to get back to the hotel. I promise I'll meet you at the funeral home this afternoon at two."

"You're not staying for lunch?"

"I'm sorry. I can't."

As I walked out the front door, I heard Uncle Harold say, "I guess he didn't like his burgers burnt."

Chapter 15

As soon as I got inside the Navigator, I checked the caller ID on my phone. The screen indicated the call had come in from Bledsoe. Since he hadn't called me back immediately, I knew whatever he had to tell me wasn't red-flagged, so I drove the short distance back to my hotel before returning his phone call.

The moment I got inside my room, though, I sat down on the edge of the bed and punched in Bledsoe's number.

I told him, "I was with my family when you called. I'm clear now."

"You're sure?"

"Yeah. I'm good."

"We caught a break."

"What happened?"

"When Hernando arrived at the restaurant this morning, he was called into Luca's office and given a package to deliver. His instructions were to go down to the docks at Limón at six o'clock this evening and present the package to a Señor Montilla. He'll be aboard a yacht there."

"Montilla? Ernesto's last name? That can't be a coincidence."

"Not likely."

"Does the yacht ring any bells for you?"

"Yeah. It's *El Mano Fierro*, and it belongs to the cartel, but the port authorities have a hands-off attitude toward it."

"I'm assuming you had Hernando meet you somewhere before he delivered that package?"

"Yes, and when we opened the pack—"

Bledsoe stopped himself in mid-sentence and started speaking to someone.

"Who's with you, Toby?"

"Ben's here. We're driving to Limón now. We want to be in place before Hernando arrives at the yacht."

I felt frustrated I wasn't in the car with them and started pacing around the cramped room. "Don't keep me in suspense. What was in the package?"

"It contained a Venezuelan passport for Ahmed. The passport identified him as Alberto Estéban Montilla. Along with the passport, there was a substantial amount of Venezuelan currency—about fifty thousand in U.S. dollars—and a semi-automatic pistol."

"So it's confirmed Ahmed is headed for Venezuela."

"Unless the package is some sort of ruse, there's no doubt about it."

"It's no ruse. I'm certain Ahmed has a job to do in Venezuela."

"When I gave the Ops Center this information, they said I'd be hearing from them shortly. That makes me think Douglas is putting together a snatch and grab for tonight."

I sat down on the bed and took a deep breath.

"That can't happen, Toby. As much as I want Ahmed in custody for killing Simon Wassermann, I'm convinced the Agency would gain some valuable intel if he were allowed to make the trip to Venezuela."

"If that's what you believe, then you'd better get on the phone and make your case to Douglas right now."

"That's exactly what I plan to do."

"Good luck with that."

I heard him chuckle when he said goodbye.

♦♦♦♦

After I got off the phone with Bledsoe, I took a few minutes before getting in touch with Carlton. Even though I knew my time was short, I also knew I needed to make a few preparations before making the phone call.

Winning an argument with Carlton was never easy; however,

preparation was the key to doing so.

The first thing I did was boot up the computer Support Services had so thoughtfully nestled among the fresh shirts and underwear in the suitcase Chuck had left for me.

Then, after pulling up the Agency maps of the Caribbean, I located the city of Limón on Costa Rica's eastern coast and traced the route the yacht's captain might take if he were told to set a course for Venezuela.

Although I wasn't completely convinced Ahmed planned to use the yacht to get to Venezuela, I wanted to see what coastal cities were located along the way and where the boat might find safe harbor if he did.

The possibilities seemed endless.

Besides Venezuela's numerous coastal cities, there were several large islands belonging to Venezuela, and any one of them could be potential destinations for the yacht.

I didn't come to any conclusions from my search, but I definitely formulated some ideas about where Ahmed might be headed.

The next thing I did was use my Level 1 access to get into the Agency archives. I went back two years and did a search for field reports from Sam Wylie, the chief of station in Venezuela.

When Bledsoe and I had been reminiscing about our Nicaraguan days, he'd mentioned that Wylie, who had worked alongside the Sandinista rebels, was now the COS in Venezuela. If anyone had any insight about Ahmed's target in Venezuela, it might be Wylie.

There was no way for me to talk to Sam Wylie directly—at least not officially—because the Agency had strict rules regarding a covert officer from one division contacting a station chief from another division about operational matters. It could be done, but permission had to be granted first.

In my case, that permission would have to come from Carlton, who, in turn, would have to contact C. J. Salazar. The reason Salazar would have to be involved was because Sam Wylie was C. J.'s man in Venezuela.

Of course, the Sam Wylie I knew in Nicaragua would dispute that he was anybody's man.

I didn't have time to go up the chain of command, so I did the next best thing—I looked through Wylie's field reports for the past two years and scanned them for any references to Hezbollah.

There were plenty of notations.

This didn't surprise me, because I knew Iran had been fostering close ties with Venezuela for years, encouraging Hezbollah to build mosques, community centers, and neighborhood watch groups throughout the region. Refugees from Lebanon and Syria—all loyal to Hezbollah—had also been allowed to immigrate to Venezuela, and most of them had settled in areas where there was already a substantial Muslim population.

In several memos, Wylie appeared alarmed at how many people in high government positions were supportive of Hezbollah, professing hatred for both the U.S. and Israel. He described how Hezbollah had been increasing its money-laundering activities on behalf of Iran because of international sanctions imposed on them for their continuing nuclear program.

While all the reports were disturbing, Sam Wylie's main concern seemed to be a training camp Hezbollah had built. It was labeled a "youth camp" by a Venezuelan cabinet official and was located on Margarita Island, just off the northeastern coast of Venezuela.

When I picked up the phone to call Carlton, I noticed I had less than forty minutes before I was due to meet Carla at the funeral home.

I made the call anyway.

♦♦♦♦

The conversation with Carlton didn't get off to a good start.

First, I had to wait a long time before he came on the line. Then, there was a definite note of irritation in his voice when he greeted me.

"Why aren't you with your family?"

"I'm meeting my sister at the funeral home in a few minutes. What's wrong, Douglas?"

"Nothing's wrong, but you need to make this short. I was just about to start a briefing with the Clear Signal operations team when I had to excuse myself to take your call."

Not good.

Douglas Carlton hated to be interrupted.

The only thing he hated worse was keeping someone waiting.

Despite the odds of reaping a good harvest, I plowed ahead anyway. "That's why I called you, Douglas. I wanted to discuss the operation with you."

"Proceed."

Carlton always required facts before making a decision, so I began by reciting what we both knew.

"When Ahmed flew into Mexico City, the Zeta cartel immediately took charge of him. They provided him with a weapon and helped him enter the States. When he returned to Mexico after killing Wassermann, the cartel took care of him again. Then, when he and Ernesto headed to Costa Rica to pick up his new passport, he transported a carload of weapons for the cartel. When he—"

"Titus, why did you call me? I already know the cartel is helping Ahmed. What's going on?"

I reversed engines and switched over to a different track.

"When you go back to your briefing, I'd like for you to ask the team a question: Whose face will Ahmed be putting in the crosshairs of his rifle if he makes it to Venezuela?"

I paused a few seconds to see if he wanted to comment.

His silence indicated otherwise.

I hurried on. "The person he's after is either an enemy of Hezbollah or one of our own; perhaps even someone from our own embassy. If his target is Hezbollah's enemy, that person could potentially be our friend or, at the very least, an interesting contact for us. On the other hand, if Ahmed is after an American, then security procedures need to be put in place, because grabbing him tonight isn't going to stop Hezbollah from trying again, and the next time, we might not have the advantage of knowing the identity of the assassin."

"So you—"

"Or consider this: what if Ahmed has been hired to assassinate the president of Venezuela and then blame it on the U.S.? I know it's way above my pay grade to decide such things, but I believe it would be in our country's best interests to discover the identity of Ahmed's target as soon as possible."

Whenever Carlton disagreed with someone, he had the ability to make his eyes look twice their normal size. At the moment, I found myself praying for his eyes to be so small that tiny pinpricks of light would find it impossible to find their way inside.

I waited.

All I heard was silence.

I added, "I'm finished now."

"Let me see if I heard you correctly."

He recited the points I'd made in a slow, methodical voice. "Although we know exactly where Ahmed will be at six o'clock tonight, you're convinced it would be more expedient for us to let this terrorist go to Venezuela and make his hit. Is that correct?"

"Yes, except for the part about making the hit. I want to prevent Ahmed from carrying out his contract."

"So, if we let Ahmed leave Costa Rica, you want us to track him to his destination, identify his target, and—forgive me if I'm being too presumptuous here—send you in to save the day before he assassinates someone. Am I still correctly defining your wishes?"

"In a manner of speaking."

"I'll get back to you."

When he hung up, I barely had ten minutes left before I was to meet my sister at the funeral home.

Chapter 16

When I entered the lobby of Brown's Funeral Home at exactly two o'clock, my senses were immediately assaulted by the overwhelming smell of cut flowers.

They were everywhere.

A fresh bouquet—as tall as a fire hydrant—was positioned on an elaborately carved wooden table in the center of the foyer. Smaller arrangements were decorating end tables in the seating area.

Carla was seated all by herself on a small couch in a corner of the room, and I noticed she'd changed out of her jeans and frumpy shirt and put on a pair of black slacks and a flowery blue blouse.

"You're right on time," she said, scooting over and making room for me on the couch.

"You sound surprised."

She smiled at me. "Not really. You may be a busy man, but you've never broken a promise to me."

"What about the promise I made back in the third grade—the one about building a rocket ship to fly us to Mars?"

She laughed. "You were nine years old then. That one doesn't count."

"Give me some points, though. I did give it a try."

She suddenly had a faraway look in her eye. "You used to love astronomy. I remember how you saved for years to buy that huge telescope."

"Yeah, it took me six years to have enough."

"Whatever happened to it?"

"Would you believe I still have it?"

"Really? After all these years?" She shook her head. "You've always been a man full of surprises."

For years, I'd kept the telescope and a few other personal possessions in a storage locker near Langley, because I was seldom in the States long enough to have a permanent residence. However, when I'd been put on medical leave for a year, I'd retrieved the old telescope and taken it with me to Oklahoma.

Now, I pictured it sitting in the sunroom in Norman, and I had a sudden flashback of Nikki standing next to it while I explained all the focusing options to her.

"It's nice to see you smile, Titus," Carla said. "You look happier than the last time I saw you."

"Well, there's a reason for that. It's—"

I stopped in mid-sentence because an impeccably dressed man in a dark gray suit suddenly rounded the corner and came toward us. His attire put my Agency's clothes to shame. In fact, I felt downright shabby compared to him.

The man had sharp, chiseled features, and the square glasses he wore did little to soften the angles of his face.

He addressed Carla first. "Are you Carla Simpson?"

Both of us got up from the couch, and Carla said, "Yes, and this is my brother, Titus Ray."

"I'm the funeral director, Marvin Brown. I'm the person taking care of your mother."

We shook hands, and then he said, "I'm so sorry for your loss. Please follow me."

♦♦♦♦

The moment Carla and I were seated in his office, he gave each of us a packet of materials. The documents were placed inside a dark green folder with the name of the funeral home embossed across the front.

Brown spent the next thirty minutes explaining the items inside, going over the details of what kind of casket our mother had chosen, of where the burial plot was located, and of all the expenses associated with conducting the funeral.

After consulting a handwritten sheet of paper, he said. "When your mother planned her funeral fifteen years ago, she chose a non-denominational service." He set aside my mother's notes and picked up a second sheet of paper. "I'm assuming you don't want to make any changes in your mother's wishes."

Before either of us could answer him, he quickly ticked off a small checkbox on what appeared to be a funeral director's "to do" list.

"What is a non-denominational service?" I asked.

He looked up at me and smiled. "I'd be happy to explain that."

Carla said, "Dad had a non-denominational service, Titus. You were there."

"I hardly remember it."

Brown ignored Carla's remark and continued, "A non-denominational service is one that doesn't employ any religious rituals or religious music. There's no minister present. The deceased's life is celebrated through the recollections and stories of family members and friends."

"We don't want that kind of service."

Carla reached over and touched my arm. "Of course, we do. Mother wasn't religious." She looked over at Brown, "We won't need a minister."

I turned sideways in my chair so I could face her. "Are you sure about that?"

Brown quickly rose from his chair. "I'll give you two a few minutes to work this out."

When he left, he was careful to close the door very softly behind him.

♦♦♦♦

"Why would Mother want a religious service?" Carla asked. "You know she never went to church."

"The last time I was with her, she kept trying to talk to me about God."

Carla waved her hand dismissively. "That was just the Alzheimer's talking. She would say things like that to me too, but it never made any sense."

"Maybe it made sense to her," I suggested, "and because of her disease, she couldn't communicate those feelings to us."

Carla nodded her head and thought about what I'd said.

"Well, you could be right," she said. "A couple of church groups conducted services at the nursing home on a regular basis, and she always insisted on going to the one that met on Tuesday afternoons."

"That's what I'm talking about."

Carla laughed. "I always figured it was because their minister was so good-looking. Maybe that wasn't it at all."

"What's the name of his church?"

She gave me a strange look. "I have no idea."

"I'm sure the nursing home could tell us."

"Why is this so important to you? You've never cared about religion before."

"You're right, I've never cared about religion before and I still don't. But what I do care about is my relationship to Jesus Christ."

Carla giggled. "Are you kidding me?"

"I've never been more serious about anything in my life."

For the next several minutes, I attempted to share with Carla how I'd become a believer.

Since the circumstances and identities of the people who had led me to the Lord were classified, I simply told her I'd met some believers who, despite a difficult situation, were joyously happy. I also explained how committed they had been to studying the Bible and having regular times of prayer.

"That's incredible, Titus," Carla said, reaching out and squeezing my hand. "You sound very sincere about this."

"I want you to know God's love for yourself, Carla."

She withdrew her hand. "Are you trying to convert me?"

"I'm just asking you to think about it. That's all."

She nodded. "Okay, but what do your beliefs have to do with Mother babbling on about God?"

"When I made a commitment to Christ, I remembered my last visit with her and how she'd wanted to engage me in a discussion about God. I believe he may have been touching her heart in the same way he touched mine."

Tears suddenly welled up in Carla's eyes. She grabbed a tissue from her purse and dabbed at her face. "You could be right."

There was a knock on the door, and Brown opened it just wide enough to stick his head through the opening. "Have you been able to reach a decision on the type of service you'd prefer?"

Carla grabbed her purse. "My brother will talk to you about the service. Whatever he decides is fine with me." She got up from her chair and gave me a wave. "I'll call you later."

Once Carla had left, Brown settled himself behind his desk and asked, "And what have you decided?"

I made him wait a few more minutes while I made two phone calls.

The first one was to my mother's nursing home. The receptionist at the front desk gave me the name of the minister who conducted the Bible studies at the facility on Tuesday afternoons. The second call was to the minister of the Living Word Community Church.

He agreed to meet with me at eleven o'clock the next morning.

Although he sounded very pleasant over the phone, it was impossible to tell if he was as handsome as my sister seemed to think he was.

Somehow, I doubted it.

Chapter 17

As soon as I left the funeral home, all I could think about was calling Toby Bledsoe. I tried to stifle my impulse for two reasons.

First, I knew Bledsoe and Mitchell were still in the process of getting everything ready for Hernando's arrival at the dock by six. Since Bledsoe was the cautious type, finding a location where he could watch Hernando as he boarded the yacht to meet with Ahmed might take awhile.

The second reason I stopped myself from calling him was psychological.

I realized the unfamiliarity of being with my family and dealing with my mother's death had caused me to feel the need to touch base with something familiar to me. Running an operation represented that. I knew how to function easily in that environment, whereas I had no idea how to relate to a crying sister or a senile uncle.

Not to mention my own sense of loss.

For the first time, I was beginning to understand why Carlton kept asking me how I was doing.

♦♦♦♦

Since I'd skipped lunch at Carla's house, I pulled into the drive-thru of a fast-food restaurant and loaded up on burgers, fries, and lemonade. As I drove back to my hotel, my iPhone rang.

It was Carla.

"I'm sorry I had to run out on you like that," she said. "I know it must be hard for you to understand why I'm so emotional when Mother hasn't really been with us for several years now."

"There's no need to apologize. I took care of everything."

"Thanks so much for doing that."

"It wasn't a problem. I wanted to help."

"Listen, Titus, some of our friends from the old neighborhood just came by the house and brought us over tons of food. Could you come and eat with us around seven?"

"I'm sorry, Carla, I won't be able to do that. I need to spend this evening wrapping up some loose ends on a project I've been working on. I should finish it up by tonight, though, and I'll be free all day tomorrow. The funeral director said Mother's viewing would begin at two o'clock. Why don't you and I plan to meet at the funeral home then?"

"Okay. Don't work too hard tonight."

Working too hard was the least of my worries.

♦♦♦♦

After eating one of the burgers and half of the fries, I put the rest of my provisions in the small refrigerator in my hotel room and booted up my computer.

The moment I pulled up the NSA aerial satellite photos of Limón, Carlton called me.

He was using his stilted I'm-recording-this-so-don't-ask-me-any-questions voice.

"This call is your official notification. Operation Clear Signal has been revised."

I gave a fist pump and mouthed the word, "Yes."

But then, I adopted the more serious tone required for the official audio recording of our conversation.

"Understood."

"Further discussions are ongoing, and you will be informed of your status in a few hours."

I continued to hold the phone after Carlton had disconnected, and within two minutes, it was vibrating again.

"I know you have questions," he said, using the voice he normally used when he wasn't being recorded. "Ask me."

"Did you have a hard time convincing the team Ahmed should be allowed to leave Costa Rica and proceed to Venezuela?"

"Probably not as difficult as you imagined it would be. While your arguments were compelling, I had already decided we should let Ahmed continue on to Venezuela, especially after I heard what the analysts had turned up on Roberto Montilla. In fact, I'd made my decision to let him go before I ever received your phone call urging me to do so."

I didn't try to hide my frustration. "Why didn't you tell me about your decision when I called you?"

"I wanted to hear what you had to say. Besides, there wasn't time to explain things before you left for the funeral home. Speaking of which, did you get everything taken care of there?"

"Yes. Thanks for asking."

"Connecting with those from the past always has a way of giving us a new perspective on who we are in the present."

I wasn't sure how to respond to that, and for some reason, I knew Carlton wanted me to do so.

Instead, I asked, "So, tell me about Ernesto's father. What did they turn up on Roberto?"

"I won't give you a full briefing right now, but here's the gist of it. In his trade ministry position with the Venezuelan government, he's been overseeing construction of some very interesting buildings for a Syrian business enterprise. In reality, the whole enterprise seems to be a front for Hezbollah."

"What's so interesting about the buildings?"

"There are two of them, and both are located near port cities. One of them is in Maracaibo, west of Caracas, and the other is in Cumaná, east of Caracas. The buildings are storage units of some nature, but their construction is highly unusual because they're made of reinforced concrete. There's also a high wall around the perimeter with security barriers at each entrance. The refrigeration and heating systems being installed indicate the buildings have strict requirements for climate control."

"Have you been able to dig up any intel on them?"

"Security at the construction site is tight, so it's been impossible to ascertain much. Sam Wylie, the chief of station there, has been doing some preliminary investigation on the project though."

"Surely Katherine's office has come up with some possibilities for this type of construction."

"It's highly speculative right now, but one theory is these buildings could be used for storing chemical weapons."

It took me a few seconds to process this revelation.

"Are you still there?" Carlton asked.

"Yes. That's not good, Douglas. Not good at all."

Carlton's voice had a cautionary tone to it. "Because we have absolutely no confirmation of this right now, we have to be very careful when we start making assumptions. However, we're reasonably certain Hezbollah has recently acquired some of Syria's chemical weapons, and we know there's a close relationship between Hezbollah and Venezuela. That means even the hint of their sharing such weapons becomes problematic."

"Did you find a connection between Ahmed and these warehouses?"

"The analysts are still pulling the threads on that, but the fact that Ahmed is coming to Venezuela and he'll be using a passport with the same last name as the man who's overseeing this construction is definitely suspect."

"Did you discover anything about the yacht or its destination?"

"It's owned by members of the Zeta cartel, the same two brothers who provided the safe house for Ahmed in San José. Since Toby arrived at the port, he's been making some inquiries around the dock. So far, he's learned there's a five-member crew aboard, and they've been outfitting it with provisions for at least a week's cruise. I think we have to assume Ahmed will be on that cruise, and most likely, its destination is Venezuela. As soon as it leaves Limón, we'll be tracking it by satellite."

"Will you be monitoring Hernando's delivery of the package to Ahmed tonight or is C. J. Salazar running the show from Langley?"

"C. J. will be in attendance, but I will be at the helm and linked in to Toby and Ben."

Through the use of satellite and drone technology, most of the Agency's operations could be viewed in "real time" in one of the Agency's state-of-the-art Operations Centers. These facilities were identified as Real Time Management (RTM) centers. Observing the activities of intelligence operatives conducting an operation in a RTM center sounded exciting, but first-time team members often found the experience tedious, not to mention boring.

Most ops consisted of several hours of surveillance with only a few minutes, maybe even just a few seconds, of any kind of action.

However, when monitoring an event, I had never heard Carlton complain about his role as an RTM Operations Officer. In fact, I knew he relished the sense of control it offered him.

Carlton was big on control.

"Do you have any plans with your family tonight?"

"No, I begged off having a family dinner with them. I wanted to be available to take your call as soon as Hernando's drop occurred."

"I'll do better than a phone call. I've instructed one of the techs here to send the feed to your computer. You'll be able to observe everything happening in Costa Rica, as we're viewing it here from the Ops Center. You won't be able to comment, and I'm warning you; don't try to communicate with me. I won't take your call."

"Roger that."

"Your computer should connect automatically at 7:45. Can you secure your environment by then?"

"That's not a problem. I'm not expecting any company. Thanks for doing this, Douglas. I really appreciate it."

"I'm sure you do. I know control is very important to you."

Chapter 18

To kill time before my 7:45 deadline, I got on my computer and studied all the Agency files on Limón's port.

I discovered that while it was a busy cargo and cruise port, it was also being used by cartel and arms smugglers, who were bribing the port authorities with cash and drugs in order to use the facilities for their illicit trade.

As I read between the lines of the reports, I decided the Costa Rican government hadn't made much of an effort to crack down on these activities. Although one of Bledsoe's reports noted the national police had confiscated a boatload of weapons bound for the FARC rebels in Colombia the month before, it was obvious the shipment had only been detained because of intel Bledsoe had shared with the local authorities.

Satellite photos of the dock area showed there were two piers—one for container ships, located to the north, and a larger one for big cruise ships and private yachts, located at Limón itself.

Alongside the dock were restaurants, shops, and various kinds of businesses. And, in an apparent effort to grab the tourists' dollars, a variety of tents and booths had been set up at the end of the Limón pier.

Depending on where *El Mano Fierro* was docked, I suspected Bledsoe wouldn't encounter any difficulty locating a suitable observation post where he and Mitchell could keep an eye on Hernando's delivery of the package to Ahmed.

I'd just finished making myself a pot of coffee when my computer sent out a *ping, ping, ping.*

It was 7:45 in Flint, Michigan, and 5:45 in Limón, Costa Rica.

Showtime.

♦♦♦♦

I sat down at the desk, adjusted the height of the hotel's business chair, and studied the video feed coming in from the Operations Center in Langley, Virginia.

Although the sun was already dipping beyond the horizon in Flint, it was still high in the sky in Limón, and the first image I saw was an aerial shot of a beautiful yacht.

I knew the feed had to be coming from a drone flying overhead. Most likely, the drone's controller was working out of our base in Corpus Christi, Texas, one of several connected to the National Reconnaissance Office.

Although the boat appeared small at first, as the camera slowly zoomed in, I realized the yacht was much larger than I'd imagined it would be. It measured at least 130 feet in length.

The hull looked blazingly white in the bright sun, with dark tinted windows spaced at regular intervals along the main deck. Adjacent to the pilothouse was a Jacuzzi, and I spotted three figures standing alongside it.

The name, *El Mano Fierro,* was clearly written on her starboard bow.

Seconds later, the image on the screen changed, and I was viewing the ship from land.

A camera was pointed at the yacht, at the spot where I imagined Hernando would be coming aboard, and I had a pretty good idea this video feed was coming from a camera being held by either Bledsoe or Mitchell.

As if to confirm this, I began receiving audio, and the first sound I heard was Mitchell's voice.

"This will be the camera angle when he boards the yacht," he said.

Carlton responded, "Affirmative."

The video didn't change, and I heard nothing for a couple of minutes.

Then, the drone operator switched on the thermal infrared camera and captured the heat signatures of six people aboard the yacht. Two were on the lower deck; one was on the main deck and the other three were standing around the Jacuzzi, a short distance away from the pilothouse.

I remembered Bledsoe telling Carlton the yacht had five crewmen aboard, so I felt positive the sixth man must be Ahmed.

Bledsoe said, "The Messenger is approaching the pier."

Although Bledsoe was following Agency regulations by not identifying his asset by name, this old rule was a holdover from the decade when communications were not encrypted.

I realized Bledsoe's asset was about ten minutes early—not really a good idea when making a drop—but I was sure he was nervous and wanted to get the delivery over as quickly as possible.

The screen on my monitor changed as the drone operator switched off the thermal imaging.

Now, I could see a wide-angled view of the pier.

The camera began to follow an average built, young Hispanic male, wearing a blue baseball cap, who was sauntering along the pier and stopping at some of the outdoor kiosks along the way

I assumed this was Hernando.

I watched as he paused and talked with one of the vendors, eventually making a purchase and placing it in the small shopping bag he was carrying.

Maybe I'd been wrong about him.

He appeared to be killing time and didn't look as eager to make his rendezvous as I'd originally thought. If Bledsoe had schooled him on how to act relaxed, he'd done a good job.

I was guessing the shopping bag he carried also contained the package he was supposed to deliver to Ahmed. Bledsoe would have made sure of that detail.

Hernando stopped again. This time he purchased a carton of beer at a small *bodega*.

As he made his way toward the yacht's berth, he swung the carton easily at his side, looking very much like a young man on his way to a fun evening.

After a few minutes, Bledsoe said, "The Messenger is on board."

The image on my screen switched over to Mitchell's camera, which displayed a dockside view of the yacht.

Hernando walked up the gangplank.

He was immediately met by two crewmen.

One of them quickly frisked him, while the other one grabbed the beer from his hand. When Mr. Frisker also tried to take the shopping bag from him, Hernando refused, although he allowed him to look inside and view its contents.

The three of them stood around for several minutes, laughing and talking together, as if they might be good friends.

Finally, I saw another man emerge from the shadows underneath an awning.

Mitchell adjusted the camera to get a tighter shot.

It was Ahmed Al-Amin.

Previously, I'd only seen grainy photos of the assassin taken with a long-distance camera.

Now, with the video zoomed in within inches of his face, I was able to study the actual movements of the man—the man who'd been intent on killing me but had assassinated my fellow operative, Simon Wassermann, instead.

There was no doubt in my mind Al-Amin had murdered hundreds of others, including Ernesto Montilla.

Judging from the crewmen around him, Ahmed appeared to be of average height. He looked more Lebanese than Syrian to me, but it was also easy to see how he was able to pass himself off as a Latino.

His face was long and slender, almost oval in shape, with a scruffy two-day-old stubble and a darker moustache. The sunglasses he wore hid his eyes from view, but I was able to see his lips, and they were thin, barely discernible.

As I watched him, I noticed the expression on his face never changed. It made me wonder if he'd ever smiled, even once.

When he walked across the deck, he did so with authority. While the profile I'd read on him described him as a narcissist with a high degree of self-confidence, I also got the sense he had little empathy for others and didn't really care about what people thought of him.

Without greeting anyone, Ahmed joined the three men dockside. Almost immediately afterward, he began scrutinizing Hernando, looking him over for several long seconds.

I viewed this examination of Hernando as the type of caution required in Ahmed's line of work, but it still bothered me for some reason.

Ahmed turned and said a few words to Hernando. That's when Hernando handed him the shopping bag.

He took it without looking inside and then he turned to leave the deck. Without warning, Hernando put his hand out and grabbed Ahmed's shoulder.

The muscles in my neck tensed up immediately, and I heard Bledsoe utter something underneath his breath. It sounded like "watch it."

Ahmed turned and faced Hernando.

His body was perfectly still.

Perhaps sensing he'd made a mistake, Hernando quickly gestured at the Jacuzzi and started jabbering away. His face was animated. At one point in the conversation, he pointed over to the man who'd confiscated his beer.

The man in question smiled and raised the carton full of bottles over his head as if they were a trophy.

Everyone laughed—except Ahmed.

Almost as if he were thinking out loud, I heard Bledsoe say, "The Messenger may be asking The Subject for permission to stick around awhile and share a few beers."

Carlton asked, "Was he instructed to do so?"

"Of course not," Bledsoe said. "I told him to deliver the package and leave."

Mitchell chimed in. "He did offer to find out where the yacht was going."

Bledsoe defended himself. "I explicitly told him it wasn't necessary."

As the men disappeared underneath the awning, Carlton said, "Well, it looks as if he didn't hear you."

In a few seconds, the thermal imaging feed returned to the computer screen, and I watched as four bodies descended a staircase down to the main deck.

As I was trying to imagine the layout of the yacht, one of the Agency's techs manipulated the video feed, split it into two sections, and displayed a schematic drawing of the boat's interior on the left and the infrared figures on the right.

Now, I was able to tell immediately that all the men were in the forward section of the boat. The diagram identified the room as a salon and showed areas for seating as well as a section marked off for a wet bar. A galley was adjacent to the salon.

Unless the men ventured out onto the exposed deck area below the pilothouse, though, it would be impossible for anyone to observe their actions firsthand. At this point, everyone in the Ops Center was totally dependent on observing the individual heat signatures to figure things out.

Bledsoe said, "I don't like this."

I felt the same way.

"It's not ideal," Carlton said, "but, since he put himself in this situation, let's give him some time."

Bledsoe said, "If this situation starts to go south, I'll have to intervene. I'm not prepared to lose my asset."

Mitchell said, "I'm with you."

"I won't be responsible for losing two operatives," Carlton responded. "Ahmed is the Agency's priority here."

After a short pause, I heard Bledsoe say, "Understood."

His response didn't surprise me.

Although he occasionally bent the rules, Bledsoe wasn't one for defying his superiors. His longevity at the Agency bore that out.

A few minutes after the group entered the salon, one of the men entered the nearby galley. When he returned to the salon, he didn't join the other three but remained by himself near the galley entrance. It was only speculation on my part, but I believed the three men seated together were enjoying the beers provided by Hernando, and my instincts told me the person remaining aloof from the group was Ahmed.

As I sat in the hotel room, observing the scenario being played out on the yacht thousands of miles away, it occurred to me Hernando might not be in possession of a critical detail about Ahmed.

He didn't touch alcohol. As a Muslim, he was forbidden to do so.

Since Mitchell and I hadn't found any evidence of booze anywhere in the safe house, it was evident he was extremely disciplined about this restriction, even when he was on an assignment.

Such control might prove detrimental for Hernando, especially if Ahmed were the only clear-headed person in the room as the evening progressed.

Indeed, the results might be disastrous.

I picked up my cell phone, intending to alert Carlton, but then I remembered his last words to me.

I won't take your call.

As I considered what to do, someone knocked at the door.

"Titus, it's Harold. Are you there?"

♦♦♦♦

I closed the lid on my computer, and at the last minute, covered it with my blue sports jacket, thinking the military-grade computer might look suspicious to Harold.

I called out, "Coming, Uncle Harold."

I looked over and spotted the folder, which Carla and I had received from the funeral home, and I quickly scattered the pages around the bed, hoping Harold might think the loose sheets of paper represented the project I was supposed to be working on.

Moments later, I unlocked the door and ushered Harold inside.

I said, "Hey, it's good to see you."

"I'm not disturbing you?"

I motioned toward the bed. "No, I was just finishing up."

He seemed troubled about something and barely gave the documents I'd scattered across the bed a cursory glance.

"Tonight at dinner, Carla said you were in charge of planning Sharon's funeral service, and that's what I wanted to talk to you about. This won't take but a minute."

"Sure, come on in."

We'd been standing in the cramped space between the doorway and the bathroom, so Harold moved on into the room. There was a comfortable recliner next to the desk, and at first, I thought he was headed over there.

Instead, he plopped himself down in the desk chair with his arm resting just inches away from my sports coat. I found myself hoping Uncle Harold's hearing had deteriorated as much as the other parts of his body had. Otherwise, he might be able to hear the computer humming away beneath my jacket.

I took the recliner and tried to think of ways to get him to focus solely on me and nothing else. However, that wasn't necessary, because Harold had only one thing on his mind.

"I'd really like to do the eulogy at Sharon's service on Friday," he said. "I've known Sharon since high school, and I love her like a . . ." He paused. "Well, now that she's gone, I guess I should put that in the past tense. I loved her like a sister."

His eyes suddenly filled with tears.

"I didn't realize you and my mother had known each other that long."

He nodded. "We dated a few months during our freshman year in high school, but then, when I introduced her to Gerald, it was all over between us."

"You dated my mother?"

He laughed at my surprise. "Yes, I did."

He shook his head. "But we never talked about it. It didn't seem like a big deal to me because, not long after she dumped me, I met my sweet Dorothy. But your dad was the jealous type, so Sharon told me never to mention it. She said your dad thought we might get back together when he was stationed over in Vietnam. That was just crazy talk, because, by that time, I was in love with Dorothy."

I was amazed to hear this.

In fact, for the very first time in my life, this revelation made me wonder if the reason there'd been such animosity between the two brothers was because of Harold's past relationship with my mother.

However, I had no time to think about Harold's disclosure. My main objective was to get him out of the room as quickly as possible.

I asked, "Do you have an idea what you'd like to say at the service?"

Earlier in the day, I'd seen the look Carla had given Eddie when Harold had volunteered to speak at the service, and I knew my sister well enough to realize she didn't feel Harold should be given the chance to say anything at all.

"I haven't written it out, if that's what you mean. During our sales conventions, I never used notes, but everyone would always tell me I gave a great speech. I remember one time in Chicago when the sales—"

"Uncle Harold," I said, interrupting him, "I think it would be just fine for you to have a part in the service. Could you keep it under five minutes? I've asked a minister to be in charge of the service, and I want to give him plenty of time to speak. He was the one who visited my mother in the nursing home."

He grinned at me. "Sure, I can do that. A minister, huh? I remember she especially liked some good-looking guy who used to show up on Tuesdays."

Hoping he would take the hint, I stood up and said, "Well, it's settled then."

However, he remained seated and started in on a story I'd heard a hundred times before.

I resumed my seat.

As he was wrapping up his second anecdote, I glanced down at my watch and estimated that Hernando and Ahmed had been together for over an hour.

When Harold saw me look down at my watch, he finally took the hint. "Well, I'd better leave and let you get back to work."

As he pushed his overweight body out of the chair, he put his hand on the desk to steady himself, and that's when he partially brushed aside my sports coat. When that happened, the gray metallic surface of the computer was clearly exposed.

He stared down at the table.

"Titus, I must say I'm disappointed in you. At your age, you should know it's better to hang your clothes up the minute you take them off. That way, they'll last longer. I've had this jacket for thirty years now, and you can see how good it still looks on me."

I took his arm and steered him away from the desk.

"You're right, Uncle Harold. I should take better care of my stuff. Good clothes are hard to come by."

Suddenly, he pulled away from me, and there was a look of panic on his face.

"Do you remember my room number? Am I on this floor?"

"I don't know your room number, Uncle Harold, but you told me you and Dorothy were up on the third floor."

"Oh, wait," he said, reaching inside his pants pocket, "Dorothy wrote it down for me." He pulled a small slip of paper out of his pocket and waved it in the air. "I've got it now."

His memory lapse didn't bode well for Friday's eulogy, and I wondered how I was ever going to explain to Carla why I'd allowed him to speak in the first place.

What was I thinking?

I was thinking about Hernando. I was praying Ahmed wasn't going to kill him.

That's what I was thinking.

Harold paused when he came to the door.

"Titus, tell me. What's the one thing you need in this world in order to be happy?"

His question startled me, and I stammered around for a second.

He said, "It's important to know the answer to that question, son." He waved the little piece of paper containing his room number in front of me. "For me, the answer is Dorothy. I couldn't live without Dorothy. I need her to make my life complete."

"That's a good answer."

He reached over and squeezed my hand. "I think you've mellowed, Titus. You're a lot nicer than you used to be. Aging does that to a person you know."

I wasn't sure that was true.

I had met a lot of grumpy old people.

Chapter 19

When I went back inside the room and lifted the lid on my computer, it took a few minutes for the satellite to reacquire the signal from the Operations Center.

While I waited, I tried to put aside the visit from Uncle Harold and concentrate on the operation. Despite my efforts, I thought about his question.

What's the one thing you need in this world in order to be happy?

I realized it might be a good idea to give that question some more thought.

When the video began pixelating across the screen, I saw the sun had set in Limón. However, the lights on both the yacht and the pier made it possible for me to distinguish some features on the upper deck of the boat.

Then, the screen came into focus, and I immediately saw Hernando, plus the two crewmen he'd encountered when he'd first boarded the boat. They were descending the gangplank together, and Hernando looked unharmed.

When the audio came back on, I heard Bledsoe's voice. He sounded relieved. "There's The Messenger. He's about to leave the boat."

Mitchell said, "I don't think he's alone, though. His new friends are leaving with him."

As the men disappeared from view, Carlton said, "Could someone please move the camera?"

Mitchell began readjusting the camera for a wide-angled shot, and that's when I realized the drone was no longer providing video for the operation.

I didn't know whether the surveillance plane had run low on fuel or if something else had happened to take it out of service, but I knew it was going to be a whole lot harder for Carlton and the team in the Ops Center to understand what was happening on the ground now.

However, Mitchell's camera was able to track the threesome as they made their way down the pier together. Then, near the place where Hernando had bought the beers when he'd first arrived, the men disappeared around a corner and were out of sight.

Bledsoe said, "I have a bad feeling about this. I'm going after him."

"We came here in my Jeep. I'll go." Mitchell said.

"No, I'm going. Give me your keys."

Carlton quickly intervened.

"Could one of you focus the camera back on the yacht? We need to see what's happening on the boat."

The camera made a dizzying sweep back down to where the yacht was berthed, and I heard the sound of a door opening and closing.

I was betting Bledsoe had followed Hernando.

Mitchell confirmed this. "Toby is following The Messenger.

Carlton muttered, "He doesn't have adequate backup."

No one disputed that.

♦♦♦♦

As the camera focused back on the main deck of the yacht, several lights on the lower deck were extinguished.

A few minutes later, the lights in the pilothouse came on.

Mitchell said, "Three males are approaching the yacht. They're about halfway down the pier now. Shall I move the camera again?"

"Affirmative."

Mitchell zoomed in on the pier.

The camera showed two men coming toward the yacht carrying duffel bags in their hands. A third man, walking between them, appeared to be barely out of his teens and had a knapsack slung on his back. He also had a mobile phone or an iPod in his hand and ear buds in each ear.

As they neared the boat, the camera zoomed in on their faces.

Although I'd just assumed the two men with the duffel bags were the crewmen who'd left the boat a few minutes earlier with Hernando, as soon as I saw their faces, I realized I was wrong. The men approaching the yacht were much older.

I studied the face of the younger guy with the knapsack. For a split second, I thought he looked slightly familiar, but before I could decide if I'd seen him somewhere before, the camera pulled away.

After they boarded the boat, the iPod guy immediately disappeared below deck. Then, within a couple of minutes, there was a shout from the pilothouse, and one of the older men began retracting the gangplank from the dock, while the other one took the two duffel bags and went below deck.

Mitchell said, "I believe they're making preparations to leave the dock."

A few seconds later, Carlton asked Mitchell, "Didn't Toby say the yacht had a five-member crew?"

Mitchell quickly replied, "Yes, sir. That's what we were told."

At that moment, I realized the two older men who'd just boarded the yacht had to be members of the crew, and the men who'd left with Hernando must have been serving as Ahmed's bodyguards and had been there to deal with any threats to Ahmed's safety.

This revelation made me uneasy, and by the urgency in Carlton's voice, I thought he must have felt the same way.

He said, "Ben, leave the camera and go after Toby. I believe he's in big trouble."

Within a few seconds, the computer screen went blank.

♦♦♦♦

For the next several hours, I sat in the hotel room waiting to hear from Carlton.

Although he had his own unique set of quirks, and he occasionally interfered with my personal life, Douglas Carlton was the only operations officer I trusted, especially if things went sideways during a mission.

Right now, things appeared to be going sideways in Costa Rica.

While I knew Carlton was monitoring communications and trying to locate additional resources for Bledsoe—maybe even alerting the embassy—I was also certain he would get back to me eventually.

While I waited, I watched the local news.

Then, a late-night talk show came on.

After that, I turned the television off and grabbed my computer.

After logging back into the Agency archives, I began trolling through the NSA cable traffic from Costa Rica.

There was nothing of interest there.

Finally, at around four o'clock in the morning, my phone vibrated.

Carlton asked, "Are you clear?"

"Yes."

His voice was raspy, and he sounded exhausted. "This is strictly off the record."

"What happened?"

"We lost Toby Bledsoe."

"Lost him? Lost him as in you can't locate him right now or—"

"He's dead, Titus."

As I listened to Carlton giving me a description of what had happened to Bledsoe, I paced in front of the king-sized bed like a caged tiger.

"About an hour ago, Toby and Hernando were found in a motel room outside of Limón. They had both been shot. We believe Toby followed Hernando to the motel, and when he tried to rescue Hernando from Ahmed's men, they were both killed."

"Did Ben have any contact with Toby after he left the observation post?"

"He got him on his cell phone a few minutes after he left the pier. Toby told Ben he was following Hernando and the two men, and they were traveling south along the coastal road near the Cahuita rainforest. By the time Ben got a taxi, Toby was at least thirty minutes ahead. When he entered the Cahuita National Park, his phone service dropped off."

"Couldn't something be done from the Ops Center?"

Carlton sighed. "Toby was Salazar's man. That meant I had to step aside and let him run the show after the yacht left the harbor with Ahmed. Salazar contacted the embassy in San José and told them to inform the local authorities one of our embassy personnel had gone missing in the Cahuita National Park.

"It took them a couple of hours, but they located the car in the parking lot of a resort. When Ben arrived, the police had already entered the room and found the bodies. He said Toby had managed to kill one of the men, but the other one had gotten away. The men had strapped Hernando to a chair and from all indications, they had already started torturing him by the time Toby arrived on the scene."

Carlton's voice trailed off as he ended his narrative, "Who knows what Hernando gave them before Toby got there."

Toby Bledsoe hadn't been one of Carlton's operatives; he wasn't running him, but, even so, I had to believe his death was as difficult on Carlton as if Bledsoe had been one of his own.

I tried to think of something to say.

Nothing came to mind, so I went into an operational mindset.

"I'm absolutely certain Toby never mentioned anything about me to Hernando," I said. "He couldn't have given me up to his interrogators, because he knew nothing about me."

"That's also my assumption."

"Ben Mitchell is another matter, though. He's been burned, Douglas. He can't stay in Costa Rica after this."

"I've already arranged for him to be at Langley by the end of the day."

It briefly crossed my mind to let Carlton know how Mitchell had reacted to Ernesto's murder. I even thought about suggesting someone keep a close eye on him when he arrived back at the Agency. However, I wasn't sure that was necessary, and I didn't want Mitchell subjected to a bunch of psychiatrists, so I decided to keep quiet.

I asked, "What's your assessment? Were those men working for the cartel?"

"Salazar thinks so, but coming from him, I guess that's not surprising."

"No, it isn't, but I'm inclined to side with him on this one."

“We’re analyzing the video from last night and running the photos through the database. If those men were working for the cartel, we should get a positive identification soon.”

“Maybe they were already acquainted with Hernando, and that’s why he agreed to go with them. They looked very friendly with each other from the moment he stepped on the boat.”

“I agree. They could have suspected Hernando was a snitch and the whole thing was just a setup. Or, if Hernando was asking too many questions, Ahmed could have told the men to get rid of him. We may never know until we grab Ahmed.”

“I don’t believe Toby ever expected Hernando to act so foolishly, otherwise, he would have been better prepared. Toby’s always been the cautious type.”

“There are some here in the Ops Center who are taking Toby’s death pretty hard. It’s particularly tragic because Toby was going to retire next year.”

“I talked with him for several hours the other night, and he never mentioned retirement.”

“So you were able to patch things up with him then?”

“Pretty much.”

“Toby’s death must also be hard on you.”

Carlton didn’t know the half of it.

The other night, after I’d pulled away from Bledsoe’s upscale house, I’d suddenly realized I should have told him about the decision I’d made in Tehran, the decision that had changed my life. He might have laughed at me, but at least he would have heard the truth.

Now, he was gone forever.

“It’s hard on me for several reasons, Douglas.”

“We’re tracking the yacht by satellite now, but, it may be a few days before we’re able to determine Ahmed’s destination. What’s your gut feeling? Where do you think Ahmed is headed?”

“Take a look at Roberto Montilla. Find out what’s on the Trade Minister’s agenda for next week. After reading Sam Wylie’s field reports, I’m convinced Hezbollah is making Venezuela its home in Latin America, and Montilla may be facilitating those efforts. Have Katherine examine the connections between Ahmed and Montilla.”

"We can get Montilla's schedule easily enough. In the meantime, you need to concentrate on your family."

"When will I be briefed in on the revised operation?"

"We'll do it here at Langley in a couple of days. Probably on Saturday. Do you want Travel to book your flight on Friday after your mother's funeral or would you prefer to wait until Saturday morning to leave?"

That was an easy choice.

"Make it Friday."

While that was an easy decision, my next one was a little harder. In the end, though, I didn't feel I had any choice.

"When Ben arrives at Langley, assess him for Level 1 status. If he makes it through the vetting process, consider assigning him as my second on this Venezuelan assignment. After Toby's death, he needs to get back in the field immediately, and I don't think this operation is going to be a one-man job."

"You've never voluntarily accepted additional personnel for an operation before. Is there something you're not telling me?"

"No. Ben needs the experience, and I need Ben. That's it."

"Well, that's a first."

Chapter 20

Thursday, June 7

After sleeping fitfully for about three hours, I awoke the next morning to the sound of thunder.

The sky from outside my window was overcast, and I saw rain coming in from the southwest. Although I wasn't prone to moodiness or depression, I felt shrouded in a gray fog.

I realized the weather and my lack of sleep had to be contributing to my mood, but I also knew I had to go to the funeral home in a few hours to view my mother's body.

Then, of course, there was the death of Toby Bledsoe.

I kept wondering if I'd stayed in San José, if Bledsoe would have even traveled to Limón in the first place.

My self-analysis did little to lighten my mood, so I opened the drawer of the nightstand and pulled out the hotel's Bible. It fell open to Psalm 42.

After reading a few verses, I realized whoever had written the psalm had experienced the same emotions I was having.

He said his soul was downcast, and that's exactly how I felt.

Unlike me, though, he had the solution.

He advised, "Put your hope in God."

Feeling foolish because I hadn't considered this, I bowed my head.

After praying about what was bothering me and explaining the kind of day I was anticipating, I went on to talk about the anger and resentment I had toward my father.

In the midst of this conversation, I found myself weeping.

Then, as if nature were at one with my soul, I heard the rain outside brushing softly against the windowpanes, and I found its melancholy whisper strangely soothing.

Once my prayer was ended, I felt cleansed, with the prospects of the day not quite so dim. I even smiled when I thought about going downstairs and having a couple of cinnamon rolls for breakfast.

But, an hour later, when I sat down to breakfast, I wasn't thinking about cinnamon rolls.

♦♦♦♦

After getting dressed, I headed downstairs to get some breakfast. The moment I opened the door, though, I couldn't believe who was standing on the other side about to knock.

"Nikki?"

"Hi, Titus, may I come in?"

Seeing Nikki Saxon standing in the hallway outside my hotel room left me speechless, and all I could do was motion her inside. When she brushed past me, I could tell she was amused by my reaction.

Finally, I found my voice. "What are you doing here?"

She dropped her purse on top of the desk and turned to face me.

"On the phone yesterday, you sounded like you might need a friend."

She looked at me expectantly, as if she wanted me to react to this statement, but I was still in shock and didn't say anything.

She hurried on. "I just wanted to be that friend."

Standing there across from her, I had a flashback to the first time I'd met her in Oklahoma when she'd arrived at a crime scene and was about to interrogate me. At the time, I was so distracted by her beauty, I wasn't able to answer her questions.

I felt the same way now.

She usually wore her dark brown hair pulled away from her face, but now it was loose and falling down around her shoulders. There were wispy, shorter strands of hair across her forehead, which seemed to accent her almond-shaped eyes. I noticed she wasn't wearing any lipstick.

"I don't know what to say, Nikki. I think I must be in shock."

She smiled. "You're not alone. I surprised myself."

"How did you find me? I know I didn't mention where I was staying."

She tilted her head and gave me a you've-got-to-be-kidding-me look. "I'm a detective, remember?"

"Oh, yeah, that."

She pushed up the sleeves of her dark turquoise shirt and gave me a smug look. "You made it easy, though. You told me you were staying in Grand Blanc, and you're registered here under your own name."

"You're right, Detective. I probably need to work on my clandestine tradecraft."

We smiled at each other.

I wanted to give her a hug.

But, I didn't.

I said, "Thank you for coming, Nikki. I can't tell you how happy I am to see you."

"And thank you for not throwing me out. I wasn't sure how you'd feel if I just showed up here unannounced."

"You're not out of the woods yet. Unless you're able to answer a couple of very important questions to my satisfaction, I might have to send you packing."

"Oh, really? Well, now I'm scared. What's your first question?"

"Who's taking care of Stormy?"

She laughed.

It was a melodic sound, and days later, I was able to recall it perfectly.

"Don't worry. When I told my captain I was taking a few days off, he volunteered to take care of Stormy. He owns a farm south of Norman and has two labs of his own. I imagine Stormy is having a blast right now."

I nodded. "Okay, you aced the first question. Now here's the second, would you like to have breakfast with me?"

She grabbed her purse from the desk. "Are you kidding? It was too late to eat when I got in last night, so now I'm famished."

As we headed down the hallway toward the elevator, she asked, "When am I going to meet your family?"

"Ah . . . probably this afternoon. We're supposed to be at the funeral home around two."

As we took the elevator down to the first floor, I considered how I was going to explain Nikki's presence to my family.

Was she my girlfriend? Nothing of a romantic nature had ever happened between us.

Was she a colleague? Although we'd worked together on a murder case, I could hardly tell my family that story.

I still hadn't made up my mind what to tell them, when I spotted Uncle Harold speaking to the desk clerk in the hotel lobby. Without thinking, I put my arm around Nikki's waist and quickly pulled her around the corner to the breakfast room.

"What was that all about?"

"I'm sorry, I know that was rude of me, but I saw my uncle in the lobby, and I didn't want to share you with anyone right now."

When she looked up at me and smiled, I decided that, although it was difficult to define my relationship with Nikki, it was easy to identify my feelings at that moment.

I felt happy. Really, really happy.

♦♦♦♦

During breakfast, Nikki never asked me where my assignment had taken me since I'd left Norman. Instead, we talked about her life, the robbery case she was working on, and Stormy's funny antics when she took him to a dog park one day.

After we'd met in Norman, although I'd revealed my true identity to Nikki, I'd only given her the minimal details of my work for the CIA; I was a covert officer. I worked in the Middle East.

That was the extent of it.

At first, she didn't believe me. But after verifying my Agency status with a former operative, now employed by the Oklahoma State Bureau of Investigation, she appeared to accept my job and didn't inquire any further into my professional life.

However, if my past relationships with women were any indicator, I knew this kind of lopsided arrangement couldn't last. In fact, the secrecy involved with being an employee of the CIA was the main reason there were so many in-house romances at the Agency. Couples who had the same security clearances could tell each other everything, whereas, those who couldn't share their lives with each other, always had to settle for a more superficial relationship.

Now, sitting across the table from Nikki, I found it difficult not to tell her about the murder of Toby Bledsoe. While doing so might have lessened my burden, it would also have betrayed the oath I'd taken when I joined the Agency.

That was never going to happen—at least not voluntarily.

To keep up my side of the conversation, I told her about my visit to my sister's house the day before, and I followed that with my decision to let Uncle Harold bring a short eulogy at the funeral service.

"Why does your uncle's eulogy have to be short?"

"Well, aside from the fact I'm afraid his early stages of senility might interfere with what he wants to say, I've asked a local minister to speak at the service."

"A minister? You told me your parents never went to church."

Interrogating people was one of Nikki's specialties, and she was used to asking probing questions and remembering insignificant details. It didn't surprise me she'd remembered my religious upbringing.

I nodded. "Yes, it was my idea, but I believe my mother had developed some sort of spiritual relationship before she died. In fact, my sister told me she'd been attending a Bible class at the nursing home. I've asked the minister who taught the class to do the service tomorrow."

Nikki reached over and squeezed my hand.

"That's so wonderful, Titus."

I closed my hand over hers, holding onto it for a few minutes, and then I slowly intertwined my fingers with hers.

When I looked up, it was difficult for me to read the expression on her face. I finally let go of her hand and pushed my plate aside.

"I have an appointment with the minister at eleven o'clock this morning to discuss the service. Would you like to come with me?"

"Oh, definitely," she said.

But then, she immediately looked concerned. "You may not realize this Titus, but there are all kinds of people calling themselves ministers these days. Do you know anything about this guy's church or what kind of minister he is?"

"The name of his church is Living Word Community Church, but I don't have a clue as to what kind of minister he is. Is that important?"

"Probably not. I'll just ask him about it. It's something he shouldn't mind telling us."

"Come to think of it, Detective Saxon, you'd better let me do the talking. I don't want this meeting to be turned into an interrogation."

This remark elicited more laughter from her, and I suddenly realized what a complete turnaround my day had taken since Nikki's arrival.

Then, just when I thought my day couldn't get any better, it did.

Chapter 21

As Nikki and I drove over to meet with the minister, I mulled over my options of how to introduce her to everyone, and when I finally decided to bring up the subject with her, I began by explaining my family's perspective on my employment history.

"My family thinks I've always been employed by the Consortium for International Studies. To them, I'm a Senior Fellow in Middle Eastern Programs at CIS. It's basically the same legend I was living under in Norman when I met you."

"You told me CIS had sent you to Norman to coauthor a book with a professor at The University of Oklahoma."

"That's right, so I'm thinking we should stick to that story. You're certainly familiar with it, and it's a plausible explanation of how I met you."

I stopped at a traffic light and glanced over at her.

She looked at me with a mischievous smile. "We might need to change the circumstances up a bit, though. I don't think I should say you were being considered as a possible suspect in a murder case when we met."

"That's probably not a good idea, although a few people around here might actually believe it."

"Really? I never pictured you as a law-breaking teenager."

I nodded. "Believe me. My temper used to get me in a lot of trouble as a teenager."

As I parked the car at the Living Word church, I said, "Why don't we say we met at church? Technically, that's the truth."

She nodded in agreement. "Stay as close to the truth as possible. That's how the best criminals stay out of trouble."

Criminals and spooks.

♦♦♦♦

John Townsend, the minister I'd spoken to the previous day, had instructed me to enter the building from the west parking lot and follow the signs for the church office.

We followed the signs to a reception area, where a secretary led us down a long corridor to the minister's office.

However, the secretary referred to it as the pastor's study.

Once she had ushered us inside, I understood why it was called a study and not just an office, because, in some ways, it resembled a small library. Bookshelves covered every wall, and the desk in the center of the room was covered in books.

Even the man behind the desk had a book in his hand, but the moment he saw us, he laid the book aside and walked across the room to greet us.

"Hi, I'm John Townsend. People around here call me Pastor John."

Pastor John was in his early fifties and had a tanned, outdoorsy look about him. That feature, along with his athletic build, seemed to suggest he might play some type of outdoor sport. The pencil holder on his desk was shaped like a golf bag, so I was betting golf was his recreation of choice.

His blond hair was thick and wavy and accented his deep blue eyes. The wide curve of his mouth made him appear slightly amused, even when he wasn't smiling.

While I agreed his broad shoulders and slim physique would certainly qualify him as good-looking, I didn't find him as handsome as my sister had suggested.

"I'm Titus Ray, and we spoke on the phone yesterday. This is my friend, Nikki Saxon."

He shook hands with both of us, and then he gestured toward a seating area on the other side of the room.

"Let's sit down over here. Could I get either of you some coffee or maybe a soft drink?"

Both Nikki and I declined his offer, and then we took a seat together on a maroon couch, while Pastor John sat in a cushioned armchair. There was a reading lamp behind it, and I imagined him spending several hours a day there reading books from his ample library.

"You have quite a book collection," I said.

"Yes, I'm an obsessive reader, and although I love technology, I don't enjoy reading books on a mobile device. You'll notice that most of these books," he gestured at the bookshelves around the room, "are really trying to explain what's in this one book." He took a Bible from a small table located next to his chair and held it up in the air for a minute.

I said, "Sometimes when I'm reading the Bible, I feel like I need a library this big to understand what it says."

"Well, at least you're reading it," he said, setting the Bible aside. "I'm afraid I can't say the same for everyone in my church."

Even though I wasn't sure if I'd engaged in the proper amount of social chitchat before steering the conversation over to the purpose of our meeting, I couldn't think of anything else to say, so I got to the topic at hand.

"I realize my mother wasn't a member of your church, Pastor John, so I appreciate your willingness to conduct her funeral service."

"Oh, I'm happy to do it. I saw your mother once a week for a number of years, and that meant I knew her as well as I do some of my own church members." He felt inside his sports coat and pulled out a notebook. "Now, Titus, when we talked on the phone yesterday, you said you would leave it up to me to plan the service. However, I thought you might like to choose some songs or Bible verses that were especially meaningful to your mother."

I wasn't sure what to say.

A few seconds of silence ticked by, and then my training kicked in, and I came up with a plausible lie in response to his question. Although understandable in my line of work, I felt completely ashamed of my reaction.

Nikki must have sensed my discomfort, because she asked him,

"Are there some songs or Scriptures you would recommend for the kind of service you—"

"To be honest, Pastor John," I said, interrupting her, "I never knew anything about my mother's spiritual condition. I've only been a believer for a few months, and when we were growing up, our family never went to church. I seldom heard my parents talk about God—except to use his name in a curse word—and I can't tell you for sure if my mother even believed in God."

"Really?" he said, looking genuinely surprised. "I'm amazed to hear you say that, because Sharon seemed to enjoy our Bible studies so much. She hardly ever missed a session, and although it was difficult for me to follow her train of thought sometimes, whenever I spoke to her, she definitely talked about God. In her own way, she seemed to be participating in worship, and from observing her responses, I know for sure there were some songs that really touched her."

"So you think she was a believer?"

He thought about my question for a moment.

"I don't really know the answer to that question, Titus. Only God knows who belongs to him. But, if it's any comfort to you, I know God always does the right thing."

"I'm not sure I know what you mean by that."

He nodded. "I think you're probably looking for assurance your mother is in heaven right now. So here's what I know. No matter how mentally confused she was, if she responded in faith to the voice of God, then he'll do the right thing and welcome her to his home, because God knows his own children."

He looked at me and smiled. "Does that make sense?"

I nodded. "She tried to talk to me about God once, but that was before I became a believer."

The pastor made a couple of notes in his notebook, and then he asked Nikki and me to tell him how we became believers, although he called it being born again.

Nikki spoke first and told him the story of her childhood conversion. Then, I briefly summarized my own experience, mentioning how I'd met a Christian couple who'd helped me take the first step in my journey of faith.

He asked us both a few more questions, and before I knew it, we had talked for over an hour.

"We've taken up enough of your time," I said.

"It's been a pleasure talking with both of you," he said, shaking our hands, "and Titus, I'll look forward to meeting the rest of your family tomorrow."

As I got up from the sofa, I said, "I've asked an uncle who was close to my mother to give a brief eulogy at the funeral tomorrow. He's supposed to keep it under five minutes. I hope that won't be a problem."

"Oh, no, not at all. I'll make sure the music is something I think your mother would have liked, and then I'll bring a short gospel message."

I nodded. "Thanks for your help."

"Thank you, pastor," Nikki said. "We'll see you tomorrow."

"Let's have a word of prayer before you go," he said, holding out his hands to both of us.

Nikki and I held hands with Pastor John while he prayed for us, and I found myself moved by his words.

Not only did he pray for my family, he also prayed for Nikki and me. And, although he had no way of knowing what I was facing in the days ahead, he asked for my safety and success as I endeavored to carry out the tasks God had given me to do.

Safety and success in capturing Ahmed; I liked the thought of that.

As we walked back to my rental car, I reached out and took Nikki's hand.

"Thank you for coming with me."

She tightened her grip. "You're welcome. I enjoyed meeting Pastor John."

"You forgot to ask him about his church affiliation."

"As soon as he started talking, I decided it didn't really matter."

"He's certainly easy to talk to."

"And a very handsome guy!"

"Really? You didn't think his nose was too big?"

♦♦♦♦

As we drove away from the church, Nikki got a phone call from another detective in the Norman Police Department.

When I heard her discussing a homicide case they were working on, it occurred to me she might be able to give me some advice about Ernesto's murder. With that in mind, when we stopped for lunch at a sandwich shop, I chose a booth at the back of the restaurant where we could talk without being overheard.

After she'd taken a few bites of her tuna sandwich, I said, "I've got a hypothetical case for you to unravel, Detective Saxon."

She wiped her mouth with the edge of her napkin. "What kind of case?"

"It's a homicide."

"My favorite." She quickly made a dismissive motion with her hand. "Don't get me wrong. I'm always sorry when someone gets murdered."

"Of course, I knew that."

"Now that we've established I'm not a hard-hearted detective, what is your hypothetical case?"

When she said the word hypothetical, she used her fingers as quotation marks.

Even though I realized she knew I was picking her brain about my mission, I still fictionalized the homicide for her.

"A couple of guys were traveling together under the same last name, and they were carrying false identities. However, earlier in their travels, the younger of the two had used his real identity to purchase a vehicle. Let's say they stop off in . . . oh, I don't know . . . perhaps, Norman, where they stay in a short-term apartment. This is where things get ugly."

Nikki grabbed some potato chips off my plate. "I can guess what's coming next."

I gently slapped her hand away. "As you've anticipated, a murder takes place. In fact, the older guy murders the younger one. There's no question he did it, so this isn't a murder for you to solve."

"You want me to figure out his motive?"

"No, that's not necessary. His motive is obvious."

"You're not leaving me much of a case to solve."

"Hang on, let me finish. The murderer locks the door behind him and flees the scene, confident he'll be far away before his deed is discovered. However, you, Madam Detective, find out about the murder and visit the scene of the crime. You discover the murderer left behind the false identities they were using. There's no cash around, so you assume he took it all with him. However, he also took the identification item the younger guy had used to purchase the car. Now, what's your best guess as to—"

"Wait a minute. I'm sorry for interrupting, but I have to ask. What do you mean by the identification item? Do you mean a driver's license or something else?"

I shook my finger at her. "This is hypothetical, Nikki. It might have been a driver's license. It could also have been a passport. It doesn't matter what type of identification it was."

"Oh, I see. Okay, go ahead."

"If you had been assigned this case, and you were trying to locate the murderer or guess what his next move might be, how significant would it be that he took the younger man's identification?"

"Hmmm," she said, considering my question. "I need some time to think about this."

"No first impressions?"

"Not really. Since it's only hypothetical, you're not in any rush to hear my answer, are you?"

"Whenever you're ready."

She glanced down at her watch, "Speaking of being ready, I'd like to go back to the hotel and change my clothes before we go over to the funeral home."

"If you're thinking of putting on some fancy clothes in order to impress my family, don't bother. You'll impress them no matter what you're wearing."

Not surprisingly, my opinion didn't seem to make a difference, and she put on some fancy clothes.

Chapter 22

When Nikki and I walked in the front door of the funeral home, I waved at Carla, who was standing in the foyer with the funeral director. She seemed very surprised when she realized the beautiful woman walking in with me was someone I actually knew.

And, I have to admit, I enjoyed her reaction.

"Carla, Mr. Brown, I'd like you to meet my friend, Nikki Saxon. She flew in yesterday from Oklahoma."

Carla, who still looked baffled by Nikki's presence, accepted Nikki's condolences, but then she turned to me and said, "Titus, I thought we might have a few minutes alone in the viewing room before anyone else arrives. Eddie will be here with the kids soon, and I'm sure Uncle Harold and Dorothy are right behind them."

Nikki gestured toward the lobby's seating area. "Go ahead. I'll wait for you over there."

Carla and I followed the funeral director down to the viewing room. Once we arrived at the entrance, though, he stopped at the threshold and motioned us inside.

Carla grabbed my hand as we entered the softly lit room, and the moment the casket came into view, I heard her take a couple of deep breaths.

I wondered if it was a shock for her to realize it was our mother in the casket.

I know it was for me.

As we approached the coffin, I could see Carla's knees buckle.

Thinking she was about to collapse, I put my arm around her waist and held her up as we stood there together looking down at our mother's peaceful countenance.

At that moment, I felt as if someone were holding onto me as well. Tears welled up behind my eyes, but it wasn't sadness I felt. It was joy, because I knew everything was perfect in my mother's world now.

Carla, though, was weeping uncontrollably, and I helped her over to a small sofa in a corner of the room.

I spoke quietly to her, trying to offer her what comfort I could. However, her tears continued to flow. As she began frantically searching around inside her purse for a tissue, I stepped out of the room and walked down the hallway toward the lobby.

As soon as I saw Nikki, I motioned for her to follow me.

When we arrived back at the viewing room, Nikki sat down on the sofa beside Carla. The moment she put her arm around Carla, my sister turned toward Nikki and gave her a weak smile.

And then, a moment later, the two women were embracing.

Once that happened, I returned to the lobby.

It was deserted now.

I was all alone.

♦♦♦♦

Twenty minutes later, Eddie and the kids arrived.

After chatting with him for a few minutes, I saw Nikki and Carla walking down the hall toward us, looking as if they'd been best friends for years.

Carla gestured toward Eddie and the kids. "Nikki, this is my husband, Eddie, and these are my kids, Brian and Kayla."

After Nikki had shaken hands with them, Carla said, "Nikki is Titus' friend from Oklahoma. She and Titus met while he was down there working on a book project with a university professor."

Carla glanced over at me and gave me an approving smile, causing me to wonder if my friendship with Nikki might be as special to her as building a rocket ship to fly us to Mars.

For the rest of the afternoon, a variety of people paraded in and out of the funeral home. They were mostly friends and relatives, but some of my mother's former students also showed up.

After exhausting my meager inventory of social politeness, I was finally able to be alone with Nikki by following her over to a small reception area off the lobby, where refreshments had been laid out for the mourners. A few other people were also in the room, but I steered Nikki over to a coffee urn in a corner of the room, where we could have some privacy.

"Thanks for taking care of Carla," I said. "You two obviously hit it off."

"Even though I hardly knew my own mother, I still remember grieving over her death. Of course, in my line of work, I deal with death a lot."

"You treated Carla like you were her sister. You didn't treat her like a police officer would."

"Women always bond with each other after they've cried together. Didn't you know that?"

"No. My knowledge of women is sadly lacking."

At that moment, Uncle Harold stepped inside the reception area and scanned the room as if he were searching for someone. The moment he spotted me, he raised his voice and said, "I hear there's a beautiful woman in here."

As he quickly made a beeline for Nikki, every head in the room turned in our direction.

"Hi, I'm Harold Ray," he said, extending his hand toward Nikki. Then, he gestured back at me. "I'm this guy's uncle."

Nikki smiled and shook his hand.

Without taking his eyes off Nikki, he asked me, "Where have you been hiding this gorgeous creature, Titus?"

Nikki kept smiling. "It's a pleasure to meet you. Titus has told me all about you."

"He's an excellent liar. Don't believe a word he says."

Nikki laughed and then asked him a few questions—without sounding like an interrogator. However, her inquiries sent him off on a rambling discourse about his sales position at Knoll.

I stepped out of Harold's sightline and silently mouthed to Nikki, "I'm sorry."

Then, I left the room in search of Carla.

I found her talking to some of my mother's former students. When she saw me, though, she excused herself and walked over to where I was standing.

"How are you?" I asked.

"Oh, I'm fine now," she said, twisting a tissue in her hands. "Nikki is wonderful. I really like her."

"She enjoyed meeting you too."

"How long have you two been seeing each other?"

"We're not dating," I said. "She's just a good friend."

Carla sounded exasperated with me. "Titus, a woman doesn't fly across the country to attend the funeral of someone she doesn't know if she just thinks of herself as a friend. Haven't you learned anything about women yet?"

Apparently not.

♦♦♦♦

When the viewing ended, Nikki said she needed to go back to the hotel because she'd promised to check in with her partner about the robbery they were working.

As soon as we were alone in the car, she said. "I've been thinking about your hypothetical case."

"How could you possibly be thinking about my case in the midst of all those people?"

"I do my best work in the middle of chaos. Unlike you federal types who have fancy offices, my fellow detectives and I are stuffed inside our tiny little cubicles like sardines in a can. Somebody's always yapping, and you just have to learn to live with it."

"Sounds a little fishy to me."

"A joke? You actually made a joke?"

"I can be a fun guy sometimes."

I don't think she believed me.

She said, "Here's what I know. Murderers take things from their victims for several reasons. Sometimes they want a souvenir. It's even part of their motivation for killing the person. However, since you said you already knew the killer's motive, I'm assuming this particular reason doesn't apply."

"It doesn't."

"Sometimes a murderer takes something from the scene in order to destroy damaging evidence. He may have wanted to get rid of the younger man's identification because he thought there was something there that could incriminate him."

I thought about the possibility Ernesto's passport could be used to implicate Ahmed in some way, but, since he'd left the false passports behind, I wasn't sure this made sense.

"I'll give that some thought."

"The last reason the guy may have taken the identification was to use it for himself. You didn't give me a description of the two men—other than the fact one was older than the other—so I don't know if that's a possibility or not. Could the older man pass himself off as the younger man? Is there any reason he would want to do that?"

I pulled in the hotel's parking lot and thought about the viability of Ahmed trying to use Ernesto's passport.

Since Ahmed had been waiting on a new passport, this concept didn't seem to fit either, but I didn't discard the theory entirely, especially since his new Venezuelan passport was also in the name of Montilla.

"That's something to consider. Thanks. You've been a big help to me, Detective."

"You mean I've been a big help in a hypothetical sense, don't you?"

I turned sideways in the driver's seat and faced her. "You've been a big help to me all day, Nikki."

She smiled. "This may sound strange under these circumstances, but I've had a really good time today."

She unbuckled her seatbelt and added, "Despite the bad joke."

As she took hold of the door handle, I impulsively grabbed her hand. "Would you go out to dinner with me tonight?"

My question seemed to amuse her.

"Of course," she said. "We've already eaten breakfast and lunch together, why not dinner?"

"No, I want to take you someplace special. I want it to be our first date."

For a split second, I thought she might say she was too tired or she couldn't stand to be around men who told bad jokes, or she never went on dates with men who had uncles who talked too much.

Instead, she said, "A first date sounds wonderful. I can't think of anything I'd like better."

"I'll knock on your door at seven."

"That sounds perfect."

It did.

Chapter 23

When I arrived back in my hotel room, I sat down on the king-sized bed and waited. I knew Carlton would call me. I just didn't know when.

In the meantime, I thought about Ernesto's passport, and the points Nikki had outlined in the phony homicide scenario I'd given her.

My best guess was that Ahmed had originally planned to travel to Venezuela in the company of Ernesto. If he hadn't found it necessary to get rid of Ernesto, then, presumably, the two of them would have cleared Venezuelan customs together. Ernesto would have used his own passport, and Ahmed, using the new passport provided by the cartel in Costa Rica, would have come into the country as Alberto Estéban Montilla.

That situation brought up several questions.

Now that Ernesto was dead, did Ahmed still plan to use Ernesto's passport in some way? How did Ernesto's father, Roberto, fit into this picture? Did he know his son was coming to Venezuela in the company of Ahmed? Was Roberto himself the person responsible for supplying the false passport to Ahmed?

Suddenly, I saw an image of Ahmed's face on the deck of *El Mano Fierro.* I knew this must have something to do with Ernesto's passport, but I couldn't quite make it fit into the puzzle.

I asked myself why an image of Ahmed had come to mind when I'd been thinking about Ernesto's passport, but the more I thought about it, the less sense it made.

Finally, I tried dismissing it entirely, hoping my brain would just arrange everything for me in a neat little package; the neurons coming together, the connection sparking across the plasma membrane, and suddenly, right there, the answer would pop in my mind.

Sometimes it happened that way for me.

However, this time, when I tried thinking about something else, I got nothing—a great big fat zero.

Once Carlton called me, though, everything came together.

♦♦♦♦

"Are you free this evening?" he asked.

"No, I have a dinner engagement."

For the first time in my career, I found myself hoping Carlton wasn't about to tell me the operation had split wide open, and I was about to have to cancel those plans.

"That's fine. I don't want to take you away from your family at a time like this."

Could Nikki be considered family?

I tried prodding him into giving me a progress report on events transpiring in the Operations Center by telling him I still had some time left before I had to leave.

"I don't have anything to discuss with you that can't wait until your briefing on Saturday. Speaking of which, Travel has you booked on a Delta flight at 3:47 tomorrow afternoon. They're sending you the details by email. I'm assuming that time works for you?"

"That's perfect. I'll be finished here by then."

"Ben Mitchell arrived at Langley this afternoon."

"How was he?"

"As to be expected. He was definitely worked up about losing Toby."

"Will you have him vetted for Level 1 status?"

"Yes, I'll be doing that tomorrow. When I told him about your request to have him assigned to the operation, he seemed very surprised to hear you'd asked for him."

"Did he refuse?"

"No, he agreed to do it."

"Good."

He cleared his throat. "Titus, if there's something going on between the two of you, I need to know about it."

If I'd been looking for an opportunity to tell him about Mitchell's breach of security with Sonya, this was definitely it.

"Understood," I said.

"If there's something there, I'll need those details soon."

"Understood."

"Nothing can compromise this mission."

"Got it."

I thought I heard him tapping his cherished Classic Century Cross pen on the edge of his clutter-free desk.

"One other thing," he said. "Our analysts have been able to identify all the men we saw on the yacht yesterday. As we suspected, they're members of the Zeta cartel."

"So Toby was killed by the cartel."

"That seems obvious now." He paused. "I should have said we were able to identify all but one of them."

"Which one wasn't in the database?"

"The younger guy, the one who came aboard with the crewmen after Hernando had left. He was wearing a backpack and listening to his iPod."

Finally, the synapses fired, and it wasn't Ahmed's face I saw, but the iPod guy.

I thought he looked familiar when I'd first seen him on the dock.

Now, I realized he looked a lot like Ernesto. He certainly wasn't an exact match, but, depending on Ernesto's passport photo, he might look enough like him to enter Venezuela on his passport.

"Could that guy be a stand-in for Ernesto?" I asked Carlton. "I just now realized how much he resembled him."

"Is this your explanation of why Ahmed took Ernesto's passport? You think he's going to pass this kid off as Ernesto?"

"It's a possibility."

"For what reason?"

"I'm not sure yet."

"I'll discuss this with Salazar and get back to you. Let me know the minute you come up with something."

"Wait a minute. Why are you conferring with C. J. Salazar about our operation?"

He groaned. "Salazar and I are a duo on this one. It's my operation, but since it's taking place in his territory, the DDO wants us to work together. There's even a possibility the DDO will send his own man to the briefing."

"So what happens when I'm in country? Who will be running me then?"

"I'm not sure, but you don't need to be concerned about that right now. Go to your dinner engagement. Let me worry about Salazar."

"If Salazar worries you, then I'm in trouble."

"I have this under control, Titus, and I know how difficult this may be for you in your circumstances right now, but try and have a good time this evening."

"As hard as that may be, I plan to enjoy myself."

♦♦♦♦

I went up to the third floor and knocked on Nikki's door. It was precisely seven o'clock.

"My kind of date," she said. "You're right on time."

I tried to look her over without being too obvious about it. "You look absolutely stunning."

She had on a slender black skirt with a long-sleeved white blouse, and when the light caught the blouse just right, it seemed to shimmer. Her hair was piled on top of her head, exposing her slender neck and showing off a set of long, silver earrings.

She picked up an envelope-size purse from the dresser.

"Thank you. I wasn't sure what to wear, but I assumed you weren't taking me bowling."

"You assumed correctly."

"One look at you and that's obvious."

I was wearing a gray suit with a navy pinstripe, a white shirt, and a solid navy tie. I'd never set eyes on the suit before. It was one of two included in the suitcase provided by Chuck, and as expected, it was a perfect fit.

When we got in my car, I asked her about her robbery case. Unlike my mission, she was able to describe in detail exactly how her case was proceeding and what she and her partner had done to find their suspect.

Twenty minutes later, we were on the outskirts of Flint at a restaurant called D'Amico's Italian Steakhouse. It was nestled in a wooded area with a curved roadway leading up to the front entrance. The outside of the red-roofed building resembled an Italian villa with overflowing urns of flowering plants and Italian marble statuary anchoring the front doors. The melodic strains of piano music met us as we approached the hostess desk.

Since I'd called and made a reservation earlier in the evening, we were seated immediately.

The table I'd requested was positioned in front of a set of windows overlooking a river. The trees lining the pathway down to the water had been strung with tiny white lights, and as the sun descended over the horizon, the combination of lights and water created a magical glow.

"What a romantic place," Nikki said. "Did you take all your dates here when you were in high school?"

"Only on Prom Night."

"Seriously? You came here on Prom Night?"

I nodded. "My date and I weren't alone, though. Six of us came here, plus our dates, so the waiter put us in a back room in another section of the restaurant. It didn't have a view. I don't believe it even had a window. It was nothing like this."

She looked thoughtful. "When the waiter seated us, he said this was the table you'd requested. How did you know about this room, if you hadn't been in here before?"

I smiled at her. "Even on a night off, Detective, you remain observant."

She shook her finger at me. "Huh uh. You're not getting out of answering my question by that diversionary tactic."

I shrugged. "Okay. Here's the story. The evening of the Senior Prom, I got mad at one of the guys. I can't remember why, but I decided to go outside and cool off. That's when I took a wrong turn and ended up in here."

I paused and looked out the window.

Nikki's face was reflected in the glass.

"A man and a woman were seated right here where we are now, and they were holding hands across the table and laughing together. I remember wondering what it must be like to be that happy."

I turned and looked at her. "But, right now, sitting here with you, I believe I'm much happier than that man could ever dream of being."

As it turned out, dinner was also delicious.

♦♦♦♦

On our way back to the hotel, I brought up the subject neither one of us wanted to discuss.

"What time is your flight tomorrow?" I asked.

"Tomorrow night at nine. What about you? Are you staying over for the weekend?"

"No, I have to be at the airport tomorrow by two."

We both fell silent as the reality of our lives confronted us.

A few minutes went by, and then she asked, "Is it okay for me to know where you're going tomorrow?"

I considered that for about two seconds.

"I'm flying into D. C. tomorrow, and I have to be at a briefing at Langley on Saturday."

I pulled into a parking spot at the hotel.

"Then, I'll probably be on an international flight sometime on Sunday."

We walked into the hotel lobby in silence, and Nikki didn't say anything until we were waiting for the elevator.

"I don't suppose you know when you'll be back in Norman, do you?"

Once we were alone in the elevator, I told her. "To be honest, Nikki, I have no idea. I could be gone for two days, two months, or even two years."

She stared at the floor. "I understand."

I couldn't read the emotional tenor of her voice. She sounded either very sad or very angry.

I placed my hands on her shoulders and turned her towards me. tilting her face so I could look directly into her eyes.

"However, here's what I do know. I *will* be coming back to Norman, and when I do, I want to spend as much time with you as I possibly can."

She nodded.

I added, "That is, if you want me around."

Just as she was about to respond, the elevator doors opened on her floor. Three giggling teenage girls were standing there waiting to get on the elevator.

We got off and walked down the hallway toward her room, but neither one of us spoke until we got to her door.

Nikki said, "Come inside. I'd like to finish this conversation."

I didn't object.

As soon as she used her key card to enter the room, she walked over to the bed and flung her purse on it.

Then, she whirled around and started jabbing me in the chest with her finger.

I finally decided what I heard in her voice earlier was more anger than sadness.

"Of course, I want you around, Titus Ray. Why do you think I came all the way up here to Michigan to see you? It wasn't because I—"

I bent down and kissed her.

As I wrapped my arms around her, her soft lips responded to mine. Our kisses grew more passionate, and I reached a point where I knew I had to stop or I never would.

She must have thought the same thing, because, as I let go of her, she stepped away from me.

I said, "I ought to go now."

She nodded.

I headed toward the door, but then she called my name.

"Titus."

When I turned around, she walked over and kissed me gently on the cheek.

"I couldn't ask for a better first date. It's been wonderful."

Wonderful was hardly the word for it, but I couldn't think of a better one.

Chapter 24

Friday, June 8

The moment I arrived at the funeral chapel and heard the music playing in the background, I knew Pastor John had arranged my mother's funeral service exactly the way I'd envisioned it.

A few minutes after Nikki and I were seated, a female soloist stood to her feet and sang "Amazing Grace." I'd heard the song before, but, for the first time in my life, the words finally made sense to me, because I knew what it meant to be a recipient of God's amazing grace.

Following her song, Pastor John read the obituary, and then Uncle Harold did his eulogy.

Although he took about fifteen minutes longer than the five I'd allotted him, he did an excellent job. In fact, when we all got together for lunch afterward, no one could stop talking about it.

Later, I realized Uncle Harold had done so well because, although the stories happened fifty years ago, his recollections made them sound as if they'd just happened yesterday.

For Pastor John's message, he related several conversations he'd had with my mother. Then, he used those encounters to present the message of the gospel, ending with Jesus' words from John 14:6, "I am the way and the truth and the life. No one comes to the Father except through me."

As we prepared to leave the chapel, Carla whispered to me, "The service was wonderful, Titus. I'm sure Mother would have been pleased."

Once the graveside service at Sunset Memorial Park was over, I told Nikki I'd like to stay at the cemetery a little longer, and she took the hint and rode with Carla back to her house, so I could have some time alone.

A few minutes later, the funeral hearse pulled away, and I walked back over to my parents' burial plots. After lingering at my mother's grave for several minutes, I moved over a few feet and stared down at my father's headstone.

Then, dropping to my knees, I placed my hand on top of the cold granite and whispered, "I wish you were here to hear the words I'm about to say, Dad, because I never thought a time would come when I could say them. But now, because I've been forgiven, I forgive you. I forgive you, Dad. I really forgive you."

Suddenly, I felt as though my legs were being held in place by a steel trap, and I couldn't move. Earlier, a brisk breeze had gusted up, causing the canvas tent covering my mother's gravesite to whip back and forth.

Now, the air was completely calm.

I wasn't calm, though. Inside of me, there was a ferocious battle going on. I wasn't exactly sure what was happening, but, after a few minutes, an incredible peace descended, and I knew what I needed to do next.

Placing my hand back on top of the granite headstone, I said, "If you were here, Dad, I would also ask you to forgive me. I know I never treated you with any kind of respect. I'm sorry for that. I'm so sorry."

Tears began flowing down my cheeks and onto my father's gravestone. My sobs sounded foreign to me; I couldn't remember the last time I'd wept.

"When you were alive, I never once expressed gratitude for the home you gave me or the sacrifice you made for our country. And, most of all, I never tried to understand the kind of pain you suffered that made you want to drown yourself in booze. Please forgive me. Please forgive me for all of that."

The wind suddenly whipped up again, causing the dozens of red rose petals left behind on my mother's grave to swirl around in a tiny vortex. A few seconds later, I watched in awe as they lifted up to heaven and disappeared from sight.

Free now, I stood to my feet and walked away.

♦♦♦♦

By the time I got to Carla's house, the funeral mourners were piling their plates with food from the buffet table in Carla's dining room.

I filled a plate for myself and wandered around the house until I found Nikki. She was in the den and engaged in a serious discussion with Carla's daughter, so I decided to keep on wandering.

When I arrived back in the kitchen, I spotted Carla out on the deck and waved to her. When she saw me, she opened the sliding doors and asked, "Would you mind coming out here and meeting some of my friends?"

I stepped out on the deck and Carla introduced me to several of her neighbors who'd gathered around the picnic table. After I made appropriate answers to their condolence remarks, Carla picked up her glass of ice tea and gestured toward a massive oak tree in the backyard. Underneath the tree was a heavy wooden swing.

She said, "Let's walk over to the swing so we can talk."

The swing was an antique, acquired by my grandparents and then handed down to each generation since. A set of rusty chains attached the dark wooden boards to the frame, and as Carla and I put our weight on it, the swing creaked and groaned.

The sound reminded me of all those summer nights as a teenager I'd spent swinging back and forth in it and gazing up at the stars. I remembered trying to recall that sound, while I was hunkered down underneath the stars in Afghanistan, doing recon on a Taliban camp.

Carla said, "Nikki told me you have to be at the airport in a couple of hours."

I gave the swing a push with my foot and said, "I'm sorry it has to be so soon."

"I've really enjoyed having you here, Titus. You've been a stranger for so long now."

I didn't say anything.

"I guess what I'm trying to say is . . . we'd like to see more of you.

And, of course, you can always bring Nikki whenever you come this way."

As soon as she mentioned Nikki's name, she raised her eyebrows and grinned at me, the way she used to do when we were kids, and we were trying to keep a secret from our parents.

"I promise you, Carla, I'll do my best to come back here more often. As for Nikki, I'm not sure where our relationship is headed right now."

She shook her head. "I can't believe you're still single. You'd be a great catch for any woman."

"You're joking, right? Didn't you once tell me my behavior would drive any woman crazy? And what kind of catch would I be when I have to travel all the time?"

"I just think Nikki might be the kind of woman who could put up with you. That's all I'm saying."

"Well, thanks for that affirmation, Sis."

She laughed, but then she turned serious when she saw me glance at my watch. "Before you go, I wanted you to know I spoke with Rev. Townsend after the—"

"He goes by Pastor John."

"Okay, Pastor John. Anyway, I told him after the funeral service I'd like to talk to him soon. His sermon raised a lot of questions for me."

I smiled at her. "I hope you follow up on those feelings."

She cocked her head to one side and looked at me. "Where's the guy who couldn't care less about anybody but himself? Whatever happened to that kid who used to lose his temper at the slightest provocation?"

She pretended to rap on my head with her knuckles. "Is he still in there?"

"He's still in *here*," I said, pointing at my heart. "I'm fighting him all the time."

♦♦♦♦

Nikki rode back to the hotel with me, so she could pick up her rental car. She told me she planned to spend the rest of the afternoon with Carla before catching her flight back to Oklahoma City.

When we got back to the hotel, I invited her to come up to my room to keep me company while I finished packing. Mostly though, I just wanted to say goodbye to her in private.

As soon as we got up to my room, I started gathering my toiletry items from the bathroom, and she went over and took a seat in the recliner. When I walked back in the room, I saw her staring at the Agency computer I'd placed on top of my suitcase.

She asked, "If your bosses at the CIA knew you'd told me about your job, how much trouble would you be in?

I tucked my shaving kit in a side compartment of the suitcase. "It would depend."

"On what?"

"On whether I voluntarily disclosed the information to them or it came out in a polygraph."

"I see."

I sat down on the bed across from her. "Why? Do you plan on becoming a snitch?"

She leaned in toward me as if to emphasize her words. "You know I would never do that."

"No," I said, holding her gaze, "I don't think you would."

For a brief moment, a look of sadness clouded her face.

"Don't worry about me," I said, getting up from the bed. "I'll tell my boss at an appropriate time before my next polygraph."

She didn't respond.

I snapped the lid down on my suitcase. "But, I hardly think it matters that much. You're law enforcement, and when I told you I worked for the CIA, I had a lot of good reasons for doing so."

Nikki shook her head. "I don't believe the reasons you gave me were the real reasons you wanted to help me with the investigation."

I looked over at her.

She was right, of course. She was too good a detective not to have figured there were things I hadn't told her. I'd never told her an assassin was looking for me. I'd never told her I thought an assassin was responsible for the murder we were investigating. At the time, I suspected she knew I wasn't telling her the whole truth, but this was the first time she'd ever brought it up.

"Listen, Nikki, maybe we need to talk about this before our

relationship goes any further."

I walked across the room and sat down beside her once again. Her hands were resting in her lap, and I picked them up and held them tightly in my own.

"My life is a secret, Nikki. I've sworn to keep it a secret. I go places and do things, and then I lie about them in order for them to remain a secret. That may be hard for you to accept. I know it would be hard for me to accept if our situations were reversed. I honestly wish I could tell you where I'm going next and what I'm going to be doing when I get there. But that's never going to happen. You need to tell me *now* if you think that's going to be a problem later."

She pulled away from me, got up from the chair, and walked over to the window. After staring outside for several seconds, she turned around and faced me.

"I don't know, Titus. I just don't know."

For a few seconds, I simply stared at her; surprised at myself for the anger I felt building up inside of me.

Finally, I said, "In my book, that's a yes. You obviously think my career is going to come between us. If you thought my lifestyle wasn't going to be a problem for you, then you would have said so."

For the first time since meeting her, I heard her raise her voice. "You could be gone for months, Titus. That's a huge obstacle in a relationship."

"You've got that right."

I got up and grabbed my suitcase.

She quickly walked over and stood in front of me. "Don't be angry with me," she said, touching my arm. "Believe me; I really want this relationship to work. I'm not closing the door; I'm doing everything I can to keep it open."

As I looked down on her beautiful face, now clouded over with sadness, I finally managed to get my anger under control.

I dropped the suitcase and took her in my arms.

"I apologize, Nikki. Getting mad at you isn't going to solve anything."

When I let go of her, she looked up at me and smiled, "We'll have a lot to talk about when we see each other again."

I leaned down and gave her a very long, very slow, very satisfying kiss.

Then, without looking back, I headed out the door for Langley.

PART THREE

Chapter 25

As soon as my flight to Langley was airborne, I decided to concentrate on Ahmed Al-Amin. I wanted to focus in on his possible target once he arrived in Venezuela.

Even though I knew my mental exercise was an effort to direct my thoughts away from Nikki, I did it anyway.

It worked pretty well—for about fifteen minutes.

Then, I gave up entirely and replayed our last conversation at slow speed.

While I was sorry I'd gotten angry with Nikki, I didn't regret making her acknowledge the barriers we'd have to overcome if we decided to pursue our feelings for each other.

Although I'd had many relationships with women through the years, for the most part, they'd been temporary and superficial. For the first time in my life, I longed for someone with whom I could share my life forever.

Someone who was tough, but vulnerable; highly intelligent, but down to earth; beautiful, but not conceited.

Someone exactly like Nikki.

In the last analysis, though, I knew Nikki was right.

My career was a big obstacle to any kind of relationship.

Still, I wondered if we couldn't make it work—somehow.

I'm not closing the door; I'm doing everything I can to keep it open.

♦♦♦♦

My flight was long and boring, and when I landed, I realized I was facing an equally long and tedious evening in my hotel room before Carlton's briefing the next morning.

All that changed, however, when my Agency driver announced he'd been instructed to drop me off at one of the CIA's safe houses near Langley.

I asked, "Which one?"

"The Gray. Lucky you."

Beginning in the 90's, the Agency had started identifying their safe houses with a color code. I'd been housed in The Red and The Green before.

However, following my return from Iran, my debriefing had taken place in the Agency's newest acquisition—The Gray, a 10,000-square-foot monstrosity in a gated community. It was completely self-sufficient and had its own mini-hospital and library.

The Gray had been an obvious choice for me when I had returned to the States from Tehran because, not only had my debriefing been expected to go on for several days, I had also needed extensive rehab on my leg during that time.

Now, however, my stay in the area was scheduled to be brief, and I was mystified as to why Carlton had assigned me to The Gray.

A short time after my arrival, though, that mystery was solved.

♦♦♦♦

Greg, the resident manager of The Gray, greeted me as soon as I stepped inside the enormous foyer.

"Hi, Titus, it's nice to have you back."

Greg, and his wife, Martha, were responsible for the overall management of The Gray. To their neighbors, they were the homeowners, but, in reality, the real property owners were the U.S. taxpayers.

Greg pointed at my leg. "I see you've lost your limp. No more problems?"

"Not a bit."

Greg was probably in his late fifties and had short gray hair. While I wouldn't describe him as fat, his midsection was beginning to droop over his belt. However, it was easy for me to understand his thickening middle, because I'd been the recipient of Martha's incredible cooking during my two-week stay at the residence.

"Hi, Titus."

When I heard my name, I glanced up and saw Martha peering down at me over the wooden balustrade of the winding staircase. She wasn't alone, however. She was accompanied by another guest of the house, and at that moment, I understood why Carlton had assigned me to the safe house, instead of putting me up at a hotel.

When Martha and her guest reached the bottom of the stairs, she shook my hand and said, "We weren't expecting you back so soon, but it's certainly nice to see you again."

Martha was an attractive woman with bright blue eyes and a heart-shaped face. Her jet-black hair made her look several years younger than her husband. However, her looks totally belied the drill-sergeant mentality she used when running the household.

"I just couldn't stay away from your cooking, Martha."

She smiled at my compliment and then turned to the man standing next to her. "I believe the two of you know each other already."

I nodded at Mitchell. "How are you, Ben?"

"I'm fine. Nice to see you again."

As Greg and Martha headed toward the kitchen, Martha looked back at us and said, "I'll be serving dinner at seven. Don't be late."

"Yes, ma'am," we both said.

♦♦♦♦

Once Mitchell and I were alone, I glanced up at a camera in the corner of the ceiling. I did this several times. Then I asked, "You feel like taking a walk before dinner?"

He got my hint. "That might be a good idea."

For security purposes, The Gray was monitored 24/7 by a system of closed-circuit cameras. Except for the staff members' personal living quarters, there were cameras in every room of the house.

To most covert operatives, this aspect of living at The Gray for a few weeks might seem comforting, especially if he or she had been living in a stressful situation while they were in the field. However, to someone like me—who valued privacy more than being comforted—the thought of having my face displayed across a security officer's computer screen 24/7 was disconcerting, if not downright irritating.

In order to escape Big Brother's clutches, whenever I was assigned to a safe house, I usually spent most of my time outdoors. Although there were still hidden cameras monitoring the grounds, there were no microphones, and I could always find dozens of blind spots the cameras couldn't penetrate.

Now, I led Mitchell down a path toward a group of yellow forsythia bushes, where we skirted around a large elm tree. From there, Mitchell followed me off the walkway, down around a marshy area close to the lake, until we finally ended up on the high ground beneath a couple of spreading oak trees.

I plopped myself down on the grass. "We should be fine here."

Mitchell lowered himself to the ground a few feet away from me and said, "It's definitely quiet here."

"Quiet with no cameras," I said. "The best place in the world."

Mitchell surveyed the area, craning his neck around so he could look back down the path we'd taken.

"How long before someone comes looking for us?" he asked.

"Maybe thirty minutes."

I took a look at Mitchell's face.

He looked different.

I decided it must be the sadness I saw there.

It hadn't been there the last time I'd seen him, but I realized his melancholy was probably the result of seeing three people brutally murdered within a short amount of time. Although he hadn't really known Ernesto and Hernando, I had the sense he and Bledsoe had developed a father/son relationship, and his death had shocked his system.

"I'm not very good at finessing a subject, Ben, so I'm just going to ask you this outright. Is Toby's death messing with you?"

He cleared his throat and said, "I'm not sure I know what you mean."

"I mean are you seeing bogey men around every corner, are you jumpy, are you constantly thinking you're going to be the next one to go?"

He shook his head. "No. Of course not. Toby's death had nothing to do with me."

"Is that right?"

He yanked a clump of grass out of the ground. "Well, I guess in a way it had something to do with me. I mean, I wish I could have gone after him, provided him backup . . . or . . . or . . . something."

I quickly assured him. "Toby knew he wasn't going to have backup when he went after Hernando. Langley ordered you to remain in place, and you followed orders. You did the right thing."

He looked at me. "Really? Is that what you would have done?"

His question surprised me, and I hesitated before replying. "Ah . . . yeah . . . yeah . . . that's exactly what I would have done."

I continued lying. "The truth is, the Ops Center can see the big picture, and you're better off trusting their judgment in such matters rather than your own."

He gave me a disbelieving look. "You're kidding me, right? I believe you would have figured out a way to go after Toby. In fact, I'm certain of it."

"Well, pardon me if I'm not as sure of my actions as you seem to be."

Mitchell took the clump of grass he'd been holding in his hand and flung it aside. "Well, I didn't go after Toby, and I'm not apologizing for that. Yeah, I was following orders, but I thought staying at the pier was the right thing to do. It was Toby who told me to stay there in the first place."

The muscles in his lower jaw had started to twitch.

Now, it wasn't sadness I saw in his eyes but anger.

"Don't get me wrong," he said. "I'm sorry we lost Toby and Hernando too, for that matter. You can even throw in Ernesto for all I care. But those are the breaks. You lose people in this game."

I didn't say anything. I wanted to see how far down the anger demon had penetrated.

He stared off in the distance for a few seconds. Then he said, "I survived; they didn't."

Suddenly, in one fluid motion, he rose to his feet. "End of story,"

"Yeah," I said, looking up at him, "end of story."

"Did I pass your little test?"

I got to my feet. "My question wasn't a test, Ben. There wasn't any right or wrong answer to it. I was simply trying to gauge whether your anger over Toby's death was going to work for you or whether it was going to work against you."

A look of disgust passed over his face, but I couldn't figure out what I'd done to merit that look. Sure, I'd suggested he stop seeing Sonya, but it was hard to believe his contemptuous look was the result of that bit of advice. He knew he shouldn't have been seeing her in the first place.

Then, I wondered if something else was going on with him.

Before I had a chance to ask him, he turned his back on me and walked away.

I yelled after him, "If it means anything, your anger is definitely going to work for you."

He didn't look back, and seconds later, he disappeared from view.

Yeah, that anger was definitely going to work for him all right—unless it ended up getting us both killed.

Chapter 26

When I returned to The Gray, although it was almost time for dinner, I took a quick trip upstairs before entering the dining room.

As expected, while Mitchell and I had been out playing hide and seek with the cameras, someone had left the Chuck suitcase in the room I'd been assigned. I was still wearing my funeral clothes, so I quickly changed into something more casual and then went downstairs to join everyone else for dinner.

As I sat down at the table, I had the feeling my world was slightly off kilter. Things just didn't seem quite right to me.

However, I'd just buried my mother—and on an emotional level, my father—less than twelve hours before, and during that same time, I'd also had a fight with Nikki, and then I'd angered the one person who was going to be watching my back when I went up against a dangerous Jihadi assassin in Venezuela.

Although I knew my feelings were understandable, they still bothered me, and I didn't say much during the meal. No one at the table seemed to notice my lack of participation in the dinner conversation.

Mitchell, in particular, completely ignored me and talked exclusively with Greg the whole time.

I was beginning to question whether I should have requested that Mitchell be assigned to partner up with me for my run into Venezuela. For that reason, immediately after dinner, I decided to touch base with

Jim Grover, the person responsible for security at The Gray.

Jim and I had met during my previous stay at the house, forming a kind of friendship—or at least a connection—due to our similar backgrounds.

Jim was a former operative who'd been transferred to Support Services following his involvement in a coup attempt in Libya, an operation resulting in the disfigurement of the whole left side of his face. Unfortunately, his memorable features disqualified him from further clandestine work.

After such an occurrence, a covert officer was usually given the opportunity to take a desk job or was asked to provide security at an Agency safe house.

Jim had opted to provide security at The Gray. His responsibilities consisted of keeping the perimeter secure, checking into the backgrounds of every guest at The Gray, recording the debriefing sessions, and a dozen or so other security-related tasks.

When I'd appeared at The Gray's doorstep several months before, my confidence was at an all-time low, and Jim's quiet manner and his I-know-where-you're-coming-from attitude had helped me get over a rough patch in my life.

Jim had also put his own job in jeopardy by giving me some valuable intel on an Agency employee. That intel could have gotten him fired if anyone had found out he was the source of such information.

Now, since I didn't want to draw any undue attention to the conversation I intended having with him, I used a slightly unconventional means to lure him out of his hidden communications room, where I knew he was monitoring the video feed from the grounds.

After dinner, I wandered around the walking trails for a while, and then I took a seat on one of the wrought-iron benches alongside the Olympic-sized swimming pool. The bench I'd chosen was in front of a group of neatly trimmed hedges at the side of the house away from the kitchen, but I knew it was easily visible on the security feed being monitored by Jim in the communications room.

As soon as I sat down, I located one of the cameras mounted on the patio's south-facing walls. Then, while staring directly at the lens, I made a quick circling motion with my forefinger.

A few minutes later, after hearing a noise in the bushes directly behind me, I heard Jim say, "I'll meet you at the boathouse in ten minutes."

I gave him five minutes before I got up from the bench and wandered down a cobblestone path leading over to the lake, which bordered The Gray's property on the south side.

Morningstar Lake was shared by all the homeowners in the luxurious Morningstar Gated Community and each residence had its own dock and access to the waterway. Many of the estates, including The Gray, had elaborate boathouses for their expensive water toys.

The day after I'd made my escape from Iran and landed at Andrews Air Force Base, the person responsible for delivering me to The Gray had told me the Agency had acquired the property during the housing bust in '08. The CIA had remodeled the house shortly after that, equipping it with several unique and one-of-a-kind additions, including a tunnel running underneath Jim's communications room right down to the boat dock.

Each safe house owned by the Agency had some sort of concealed exit, and in the event of a security breach, this feature made it possible for those inside the house to get out safely and make their way to a predetermined rendezvous point.

Since Agency safe houses were not only used for Level 1 operatives returning from the field, but also for high profile defectors and valuable foreign assets, this emergency exit was a necessity.

I'd only used a secret exit at a safe house one time—but not for reasons involving security.

♦♦♦♦

The Gray's boathouse matched the architectural design of the main residence and the portion containing the lift and the boat slip was almost indistinguishable from the building itself—at least from the viewpoint of the main house.

Inside the glorified shed were seating areas, a fully furnished kitchen, and an entertainment/media room. However, the centerpiece of the structure was the luxurious boat parked in the middle of the large room. A brass guardrail separated the entertainment portion of the house from the boat slip and also prevented a careless guest from falling into the water below.

Scattered among the furnishings were gigantic metal sculptures made out of old boat parts. The largest piece of artwork, located near the main entrance, almost reached the ceiling.

To me, it resembled some sort of sea monster. Whether that was the artist's intention or not, I couldn't say, but the other pieces around the room depicted mythical sea creatures, so I didn't think I was too far off the mark.

Personally, the boathouse had no appeal to me.

Most likely, the whole designer showcase appearance of the place was entirely lost on me because, as soon as I stepped inside it, I was almost overcome by nausea. I realized my reaction could have been caused by the gasoline fumes coming off the lake from all the passing motorboats, or the unavoidable pungent fishy odor of the place.

But, I knew that wasn't it.

It was a phobia I experienced whenever I had to be near the water and the accompanying feeling of disorientation that went along with it.

I'd never told anyone at the Agency about my problem, and I didn't plan to do so.

I had it under control.

♦♦♦♦

Seconds after walking in the door, I spotted Jim standing next to a well-stocked bar. He was helping himself to a drink.

When he saw me, he lifted his glass in a mocking salute. "Welcome back. Nice to see you again."

"Thanks."

"Help yourself to a beverage," he said, gesturing toward the bar.

There was a Keurig coffeemaker on the counter, and I chose a K-cup from an assortment of coffee pods. By the time the hot water had finished spurting into the mug, Jim had walked over and sat down on a couch a few feet away from the bar.

The couch faced an enormous oil painting of an ocean scene. When I walked by, I noticed the painter had entitled his masterpiece *Danger On The High Seas.* As I studied the painting, I saw the artist had depicted a fishing vessel being buffeted by an enormous storm, and it looked as if the high wind and waves were putting the sailors aboard her in imminent danger of losing their lives.

I sat down in the armchair next to Jim, and he motioned toward the painting. "Not the most comforting image to have in a boathouse, is it?"

"Maybe it's supposed to serve as a warning. It could be a cautionary tale about what could happen if you take your vessel out on the high seas."

He stared at the painting again. "Could be."

"I think the artist was trying to say if the ocean doesn't get you, then the hurricane might."

He chuckled. "Or your engine might fail."

I nodded. "One never knows what awaits one out there on the high seas."

Jim smiled. "That's the reason we do what we do, isn't it, Titus? We get a thrill out of not knowing. It's the not knowing that keeps us going. At least, when I was in the game that's the way it was for me."

I shook my head. "Not for me. I get pumped up whenever I know things. The more I know, the more excited I become. The more I know, the better I like the game."

"I enjoyed being surprised by the unexpected. Knowing something ahead of time didn't give me that rush, and I really loved that rush."

He looked away, as if remembering something from his past, and I took the opportunity to study the scar running from Jim's eye socket to his ear.

Yes, Jim, you loved the rush of not planning ahead. And where did that get you?

Jim would have been better off clawing around in the dirt for some tiny scrap of information left behind by a bunch of disgruntled Libyan rebels, rather than getting pumped up at the thought of rushing into a rendezvous without a backup.

Had I been in Libya, I would have been down there in the dirt clawing away.

In other words, I would have been doing exactly what I was about to do by asking Jim a few questions.

♦♦♦♦

"Speaking of knowing things, Jim, I need some information."

He studied the ice floating around in the bottom of his glass for a few seconds. Then, he looked up and asked, "Such as?"

Although it wasn't easy to read Jim, he didn't seem apprehensive I'd asked for this meeting. His calm demeanor was one of the reasons I'd sought him out when I'd returned from Iran. Now, though, I could see why a calm guy like Jim might need the thrill of the unexpected in order to experience any real excitement in his life.

"I know you've seen the PDS on Ben Mitchell. He wouldn't be here if the Agency hadn't sent it over. So, what's in his closet? What turns him on?"

A Personal Data Sheet (PDS) was the biographical summary on an Agency employee. It included background, operative status, postings, and any potential security risks posed by the person involved. A station chief received a PDS on any incoming Agency personnel, as did the chief security officer in a hot zone or, in Jim's case, the security officer in a safe house.

Jim put his empty glass down on a side table and leaned forward, rubbing his hands together as if he might need to get his blood flowing.

"Sure, I've seen his PDS, and I'd be happy to tell you what's in it. That's not a problem. Most of it is public knowledge anyway."

I didn't hide my surprise. "Public knowledge? Why would Ben's private data sheet be public knowledge?"

Jim sat back on the couch and smiled. "Don't you know who Ben Mitchell's father is?"

"How would I know who Ben's father is? I just met Ben a couple of days ago."

"Ben Mitchell is the son of *the* Senator."

I mentally flipped through my rolodex of senators, stopping at the only possible choice.

"You mean Elijah Mitchell?"

Jim burst into laughter. "You really didn't know, did you?"

"I had no idea."

♦♦♦♦

Elijah Mitchell was the senior senator from Ohio and a member of the Senate Armed Services Committee. More importantly—at least to me—he was also the Chairman of the Senate Select Committee on Intelligence. A leading news magazine had recently named him one of the three most powerful senators in Congress.

If the son had inherited his father's personality, then it didn't surprise me I'd seen flashes of anger and ill temper in the younger Mitchell.

The older Mitchell was known for his offensive remarks and his impatience. The adjectives most often used to describe him were "abrasive" and "brutal," and those comments usually came from his friends.

However, the Senator appeared to be an equal-opportunity offender, angering both sides of the Senate floor and holding both Democratic and Republican presidents alike to his unyielding standards, especially when it came to any legislation involving the intelligence community.

I had the privilege—or misfortune—of meeting the man once.

My encounter with the Senator had come in the Situation Room of the White House following the 2008 terrorist attack in Mumbai, India.

For three days, extremists, who had been trained in Pakistan, had carried out attacks on two luxury hotels. When it was all over, 170 people had been killed.

After it was determined the terrorists were members of the Lashkar-e-Taiba or the LeT group, an offshoot of Al-Qaeda operating out of Pakistan, I was brought into the White House as part of a CIA crisis management team.

The reason I was asked—or ordered—to join the DOD's crisis team in the Situation Room was because I'd just returned from a deep-cover operation into Pakistan.

But, my presence at the White House was simply window dressing.

My Pakistani mission had not involved LeT, nor was I acquainted with any of its members. However, since the Congressmen were notorious for wanting to speak face-to-face with a covert operative who had been in country, the DOD and Carlton had grabbed me and headed over to the White House for a briefing with members of the House and Senate Intelligence Committees on events happening in Mumbai.

On our way over, Carlton had told me what I should say if anyone decided to ask me any questions.

Senator Mitchell was the only senator to do so.

Before entering the Situation Room, I was told to sit along the perimeter wall, an area dubbed The North Pole.

The North Pole was so named because those seated at the rectangular table in the center of the room were essentially giving the cold shoulder to anyone seated away from it. Those occupying the North Pole were also expected to keep their mouths shut, frozen shut so to speak, unless they were asked to speak by those in the inner circle.

I planned on meeting everyone's expectations and keeping my mouth shut. However, Senator Mitchell had other ideas.

After patiently listening to several lawmakers pontificate on what they thought was going on in India, I'd grown bored with all the bloviating.

Really bored.

And, I wasn't the only person feeling that way.

In the midst of another nonsensical speech, Senator Elijah Mitchell suddenly interrupted his colleague's one-way dialogue.

"This is getting us nowhere," he said. "It's time we heard from someone who should know the motivations behind these attacks, and I'd much rather hear from them than from a bunch of guys sitting around a table running their mouths."

Senator Mitchell pointed over to the North Pole and asked, "Have any of you spooks ever been to Pakistan? Anyone?"

Carlton, in his impeccably tailored suit, rose to his feet.

"Well, Senator, we have one of our finest intelligence officers with us today," he gestured toward me, "and he has just returned from Pakistan. I'm sure he'd be happy to answer any questions you may have."

The Senator looked pleased and pointed at me.

I stood to my feet.

"I'm not going to ask you your name," he said, "because, unlike some of my esteemed colleagues here, I value your service to this country, and I don't want your covert status to be put in any kind of jeopardy."

There were a few groans of protests in response to the Senator's statement, but he ignored them. Then, as if he expected me to respond in some way, he peered over his bifocals at me without saying a word.

I waited a beat or two, and then I said, "Thank you, sir."

He picked up a bunch of papers from the table in front of him. "I'm Elijah Mitchell, by the way."

"Nice to meet you, sir."

"Likewise." He glanced at the papers in his hand. "If you don't mind, just for the record here, I'll address you as Agent A."

"Actually, sir, I'm an intelligence *officer*. For the record, Officer A would be more accurate."

The people around the table snickered, and I heard Carlton draw a deep breath.

The Senator, though, gave no indication he'd heard me.

He slapped the papers down on the table. "Tell me, what's the mindset of these LeT terrorists? What do they hope to gain by their actions?"

I proceeded to give the spoon-fed answers I'd been handed by the Agency, and Senator Mitchell appeared satisfied by my recitation.

However, as I was about to walk out the door after the meeting, he pulled me aside.

Leaning so close to me I could smell the stale coffee on his breath, he said, "I know you were only spouting off what the DOD wanted us to hear. But let me give you a piece of advice. The next time you have an opportunity to speak to me, give me your own opinion. If I'm not mistaken, you appear to be someone who wouldn't mind doing so."

"In that respect, sir, I guess I'm a lot like you."

There was a barely perceptible pause, and then he burst out laughing.

The noise reverberated throughout the room.

A few seconds later, he put his arm around my shoulder and said, "Officer A, I'm going to give you the same advice I often give my son, 'Never mind what people want you to say, tell them what they need to hear. If you do, you'll both be better off for it.'"

♦♦♦♦

Now, as I sat in the boathouse digesting Jim's revelation, I considered how Ben Mitchell's pedigree might affect the mission.

I contemplated every possible angle.

All I could see were sharp edges everywhere.

Jim said. "Since you and Ben are here at The Gray together, then I have to assume you're also headed out to the field together, and according to his PDS, this will be his first run."

"You've got that right."

"If anything goes wrong, it won't be Junior who gets blamed for the failure of your mission."

"Unfortunately, I think you've also got that right. If this mission goes south, I'll be in the Senator's crosshairs."

He shook his head. "I wouldn't want to be in your shoes."

"Yeah, they're beginning to feel a little tight right now." I drained the last drops of coffee from my mug. "What else can you tell me about Ben? Anything in his PDS jump out at you? What kind of student was he?"

"Why don't you ask me yourself?"

Like a creature from out of the deep, Ben Mitchell emerged from behind the shadows of the gigantic metal sea monster in the building's entryway.

He stood there, staring at me.

Without saying a word, Jim got to his feet and slipped out a hidden panel in the wall. The secret door was located a few feet from *Danger*

On The High Seas and led down to the tunnel connecting the boathouse to the main house.

As I watched Jim go, I glanced over at the sailors in the painting. Along with them, I felt as if a gigantic wave might suck me under.

I wasn't going down without a fight, though.

"Ben," I said, "I've been expecting you. Have a seat."

Chapter 27

Mitchell walked over and took the seat just vacated by Jim. "So you were expecting me?" he said. "It certainly didn't look that way to me. In fact, as pale as you are right now, I'd say you were pretty shocked to see me."

Even though I was still fighting back the nausea I'd experienced when I'd entered the boathouse, I said, "I'm fine. Listen, Ben, I don't know what you think you overheard, but I was just—"

"I heard you mention my PDS to Jim, and I know it's a breach of security for him to reveal what's in there. He could be fired for telling you, and you could be disciplined for asking him about it."

Once again, I sensed an anger in him that seemed totally out of proportion to our circumstances.

I said, "I'm sure you're right about that."

"Why were you asking him about my PDS? Don't you know everything about me already? Didn't my father brief you?"

It took me a moment, but then it dawned on me what he was implying. "I have no idea what you're talking about. Until five minutes ago, I didn't have a clue about your genealogy, nor did I particularly care about your parentage."

Mitchell's face registered disbelief. "You're lying."

"And you're being a Class A jerk."

Mitchell looked confused. "I know my father must have pulled some strings to get my Level 2 status changed and have me reassigned to your operation. I've been at the Agency long enough to know all that couldn't have happened without someone's direct intervention. Are you telling me you knew nothing about it?"

The sound of water lapping up against the side of the boathouse suddenly increased in intensity as a large motorboat made a turn in front of the property. When it neared the boathouse, its headlights flooded the windows, casting shadows everywhere.

Mitchell and I stopped talking and gave it our full attention for several minutes. After it made a sweeping turn, spraying water in its wake, the motorboat disappeared into the night.

Although I knew it couldn't be true, as the boat sped away, I felt as if I were being tossed to and fro just like the fishing vessel in *Danger On The High Seas.*

My stomach lurched; I felt bile welling up in my throat.

I said, "No, Ben, I'm not saying I don't know anything about that."

"That's what I—"

"I know exactly why you were vetted for Level 1 status and why you've been reassigned to this operation."

I got out of my chair and quickly walked over to the safety railing surrounding the luxurious boat. The gleaming vessel was resting in the boat slip just above the water line.

I looked at Mitchell. "I'm the one who intervened on your behalf," I said. "I'm the person who asked Carlton to have you vetted for Level 1 status."

Seconds later, I turned and emptied the contents of my stomach into the water below, barely missing the yacht's deck beneath my feet.

♦♦♦♦

"Whoa," Mitchell said, rushing over to the railing. "You okay?"

"Just something I ate."

I walked over and grabbed a towel from the bar. After I wiped the spittle from my face, I said, "I'm fine."

"We ate the same thing at dinner. I don't feel sick."

"Maybe I've caught some kind of bug, or maybe it was the food at the airport."

Mitchell laughed. "Or maybe you're one of those landlubber types and get seasick whenever you're around water."

"I'll be right back," I said and headed over to the bathroom.

Once inside, I doused my face with cold water and vigorously rubbed it dry with a hand towel. When the color finally returned to my face, I told myself I was feeling much better and started to leave.

Then, I paused at the door and wondered if God would mind hearing about my problem?

It wasn't a big deal, but I decided to say a short prayer anyway.

♦♦♦♦

When I came out of the bathroom, Mitchell said, "Give me a heads up the next time you're planning to do that."

"There won't be a next time."

Before I sat back down in the armchair, I angled it away from the oil painting. Now, I was no longer able to see the intensity of the storm or the distressed look on the sailors' faces.

"We'd better wrap this conversation up before someone up at the big house comes looking for us," I said. "Greg is a nervous kind of guy, and Jim can't cover for us indefinitely."

Mitchell ran his fingers through his hair, a gesture I'd seen him make back at the embassy when Bledsoe had dismissed him from the room. He'd also made it at the airport when I'd called him out about dating Sonya.

I thought it might indicate his lack of enthusiasm about doing something.

His next statement bore that out.

"I think I owe you an apology," he said. "For the past two days, I've been under the assumption the Senator called in some favors at the Agency, and that's why I was suddenly vetted for this operation. I thought he'd also exerted his influence over you in some way, and that's why you were being so solicitous toward me this afternoon."

He shrugged. "To some people, that way of thinking might have been a stretch. But I know how much my father loves to control people, and he's certainly capable of doing what I've just described. I've seen him do it hundreds of times."

"I don't doubt that." I waited a couple of beats, and then I added, "Apology accepted."

Mitchell nodded and pointed toward the bar. "Can I get you something to drink?"

I shook my head, and he walked over to the bar and grabbed a Diet Coke out of the refrigerator.

After he'd resumed his seat on the couch, I said, "I had a father who barely paid any attention to me at all. Until a short time ago, I wasn't able to forgive him for that."

He looked surprised at my admission.

It surprised me as well.

"But you forgave him?"

"I did."

He shook his head. "The Senator and I aren't close—at least not in the way I imagine most fathers and sons are—but he's always been interested in everything going on in my life. I'm pretty sure that's the reason I decided to join the Agency."

Mitchell took a swig of his soda, and when he didn't elaborate on his statement, I asked, "Would you care to expand on that?"

Mitchell smiled, and I realized it was the first time I'd seen him do so all day.

He said, "I knew if I became involved in clandestine work, he wouldn't—at least theoretically—be able to control me. I would be beyond his reach. It would be illegal for him to know everything I was doing. That's the reason I lost it when Salazar told me I was being bumped to Level 1 status. I figured my dear old dad had finally found a way into the Agency, and I thought he'd done so because he was trying to help me out after Toby's death."

When Mitchell spoke Bledsoe's name, there was a slight catch to his voice, and I realized the old station chief had probably been more of a father to him than his own father had.

"Have you spoken to your father lately?"

"He called me in Costa Rica shortly after he was briefed on Toby's murder. He told me he was going to insist the DDO bring me back to the States immediately."

"Yeah," I said, shaking my head at the man's arrogance, "well, the

DDO was going to bring you home with or without the Senator's intervention. That's normal operating procedure after losing a station chief in the field."

"I knew that," Mitchell said, "but I didn't tell him. Crossing the Senator usually brings unpleasant consequences."

He slouched down on the couch, resting his head on the back of the cushions and letting out a heavy sigh, as if discussing his father had completely drained him.

Seconds later, though, he raised his head and said, "By the way, you'll be happy to know I broke it off with Sonya."

He chunked his Diet Coke can toward a nearby wastebasket. "Of course, I was leaving the country anyway, but you may have been right about her. She didn't seem too brokenhearted to see me go."

"I was right about her. That relationship was going nowhere."

I'm not closing the door; I'm doing everything I can to keep it open.

Chapter 28

Saturday, June 9

The next morning, Mitchell drove us over to Langley in an Agency vehicle reserved for guests of The Gray. Along the way, I quizzed him about the maps I'd left with him back in San José.

"Did you find anything on those maps I grabbed out of the Durango?"

My question seemed to amuse him. "Trying to get a jump on our briefing this morning?"

"Of course I am, and after you've worked with Carlton for a few days, you'll understand why. He expects his operatives to know more about an operation than he does. And, if they don't, he expects them to make something up. To say he's a driven man is an understatement."

"Salazar's personality is completely the opposite of Carlton's. He's so laid back he drives me crazy." Mitchell shook his head. "But, if he's targeting one of the head honchos in a drug gang, then he's a slave driver."

Because Salazar and Carlton were working together on Operation Clear Signal, I suddenly realized Salazar's operational persona might become a problem, especially since my mission centered on stopping an assassin and not on obliterating some drug lord.

If my prayers were answered though, my field operations handler—the person on the ground in Venezuela running the operation—would be Carlton and not Salazar.

I said, "Carlton told me the two of them were acting as a duo on this one."

"Salazar told me the same thing, and he didn't seem too happy about it." He glanced over at me. "I don't think he likes you very much."

I chuckled. "We had a slight disagreement during that last conference call back at the embassy. I suggested Ernesto could have become radicalized by Islamic jihadists during a visit to Syria, and that was why he was helping Ahmed. On the other hand, Salazar kept insisting the drug cartels had something on Ernesto's father, and they were threatening him in some way. He thought that was the reason Ernesto was traveling with Ahmed."

"I'm not sure I'd describe that conversation as a slight disagreement."

I steered the conversation back to the maps I'd discovered in the glove compartment. Mitchell told me he'd found markings on a street map of Caracas.

"What kind of markings?"

"There were X's on some of the streets. I'm sure the Agency has the specifics pinpointed by now, but, to me, the marks were tagging residential locations."

Mitchell drove up to the security gate at Agency headquarters. Although it was Saturday, the line of cars waiting to get in was long. Checking individual identities and license plates made for a slow crawl through the gate.

Very few Agency employees ever complained about this.

While we waited, Mitchell said, "On another map, I found X's marking two cities. They were both port cities, but that's the only thing I saw they had in common."

"Let me guess. The cities were Maracaibo and Cumaná."

He looked surprised. "You're right. Did you notice the X's before you gave me the maps?"

"No, I was just taking an educated guess. A few days ago, Carlton shared some intel about a couple of buildings under construction in Maracaibo and Cumaná."

"What kind of intel?"

I waited while we cleared the second checkpoint to answer him.

Once we were through, I said, "According to the chief of station in Venezuela, the buildings could be facilities capable of housing chemical weapons."

Mitchell shook his head. "That doesn't surprise me. Toby said he thought Venezuela was involved in chemical weapons research."

"While that may be true, the buildings appear to be storage facilities only. Carlton said our analysts thought Venezuela may have agreed to accept chemical weapons from another country."

"Iran or Syria?"

"My guess is Syria, because the international community has been pressuring them to get rid of their chemical weapons."

Mitchell pulled into a parking spot on the west side of the Old Headquarters Building where the Operations Center was housed.

He turned off the engine. "Why would a Hezbollah assassin be carrying around maps with those construction sites marked on them?"

"Let's hope our briefers know the answer to that one, because I don't have a clue."

♦♦♦♦

After clearing security in the lobby, Mitchell and I parted ways. He headed over to C. J. Salazar's office on the third floor of the east wing, while I took the elevator up to Carlton's office on the fourth floor.

We were due to meet again in one hour for a briefing session in one of the Operations Center's conference rooms.

On my way up to Carlton's office, I thought about the briefing and tried to anticipate what might happen, since I knew Carlton wasn't going to be conducting the briefing by himself.

An operational briefing could take many forms, but, at its most basic level, it involved a division head and some analysts. However, I didn't expect this to be the case with Operation Clear Signal, because the operation now encompassed both the Middle Eastern and Latin American desks.

To complicate matters even further, since the death of two Agency operatives had initiated the operation in the first place, the big guns from the DDO's office would want to be represented. That meant the DDO would probably send the Admiral, his right-hand man, along with a bunch of analysts from Katherine's office.

No matter how many people were present, the only role Mitchell and I would play in the briefing would be to keep our mouths shut and listen.

Protocol dictated covert field officers keep their thoughts to themselves, while the higher-ups imparted their considered opinion, research, and analysis on the Plan of Action, the POA.

Once everyone in the briefing room had been able to have their say, then Mitchell and I would be invited to speak.

When I entered the reception area outside of Carlton's office, Sally Jo Hartford, Carlton's secretary, looked up from her computer.

"Good morning, Sally Jo. You're looking gorgeous as always."

She beamed at me and pushed aside a few wisps of gray hair from her forehead. "Titus Ray, you know flattery won't get you any special favors in this office."

"Can't blame a guy for trying, can you?"

Sally Jo—or Mrs. Hartford as Carlton insisted she be called—was a few years past retirement age but looked at least ten years younger. She had a soft Southern accent and resembled a slightly slimmer version of Mrs. Claus, the wife of the famous man who lived at the North Pole.

Her organizational skills and ability to anticipate Carlton's every move had probably secured her employment at the Agency for as long as she wanted.

I gestured toward Carlton's office. "Is he ready for me?"

"I'm sure he is, but he's not in his office. He's over at the Ops Center. You're supposed to meet him in Conference Room B in one hour."

"He told me to meet him up here so we could prep for the briefing."

She smiled sweetly. "Plans are always subject to change, Titus. You know that."

"What's going on, Sally Jo?"

She wagged a finger at me. "I know you don't really expect me to answer that."

"Could you at least give me a hint?"

"Well," she said, motioning for me to lean in toward her as if there were a roomful of people, and she didn't want them to hear our secret, "remember, not all change is bad. You might decide you like this change. Just keep an open mind."

I tried keeping an open mind as I headed downstairs for the briefing.

It wasn't easy.

♦♦♦♦

The Ops Center was located in the basement of the Old Headquarters Building. It consisted of a labyrinth of conference rooms, offices, and Real Time Management (RTM) Centers where the Agency's day-to-day operations took place.

Ordinarily, I was on the receiving end of intel coming out of an RTM Center; I was seldom part of a team running an operation.

However, one time, when Barnabas Chandler, an operative in Yemen, had to hand over a bundle of cash to a Pakistani military officer through a Spanish-speaking intermediary, I was called in to translate for the Spanish-speaking embassy official who couldn't speak a word of Arabic.

When I'd first entered one of the RTM Centers back then, I'd found myself mesmerized by the wall of video screens encircling the room. The numerous screens seemed to cast a bluish hue, which reflected off the faces of the men and women working at their computer consoles in the center of the room.

Unlike Hollywood depictions of the Agency's Operations Center, it was not a hustling, bustling kind of place. Although telephones occasionally rang and voices sometimes grew loud, overall, there was an air of professionalism and calmness throughout the facility, even though Agency employees were fulfilling urgent requests for information and analyzing mounds of data coming in from around the world.

Now, as I entered Corridor B, I decided to peek inside the RTM Center located across the hallway from Conference Room B. Strictly speaking, it was against RTM procedures for a covert intelligence officer to be present in an RTM Center, unless he or she were accompanied by a division head.

However, since Carlton had been willing to have one of the tech officers in the room send me the video feed of Hernando's meeting with Ahmed in Limón, I thought the rules wouldn't matter. Still, I made sure the lanyard attached to my shirt—indicating my Level 1 security clearance—was clearly displayed.

Then, I slipped inside RTM Center—Room B.

I did so as quietly as possible, and no heads turned in my direction when I shut the door behind me.

Instead, all eyes were on a gigantic multi-screen video monitor encircling the room, and I immediately recognized the image being displayed there.

It was *El Mano Fierro.*

As indicated by the time stamp in the left corner of the screen, the video was in real time, and everyone in the room had a bird's eye view of the yacht's deck. It was literally a bird's eye view because the picture appeared to be coming from a UAV flying overhead.

A smartly dressed woman, standing in the shadows to my left and wearing a headset, was quietly whispering orders to an unseen drone operator located halfway across the United States. She asked for a clear shot of a certain passenger, who, at that moment, was leaning over the starboard bow.

A few seconds later, the young man's face suddenly filled up the entire screen as he turned his head toward the sky and squinted up at the sun.

I recognized him as the iPod guy from Limón who had reminded me of Ernesto. Now that I could see a close up of his face, the resemblance was even more striking, and I doubted he would have any trouble using Ernesto's passport to enter Venezuela.

The camera quickly pulled away as the iPod guy ripped off the shirt he was wearing and flung it aside. The moment he lowered himself into the Jacuzzi, another figure appeared on deck.

For the second time in three days, I found myself staring at a real-time image of Ahmed Al-Amin.

Ahmed walked across the deck to the spot previously occupied by the iPod guy. The moment he reached the railing, he began moving his head from left to right, almost as if were searching for something on the distant horizon.

Seconds later, he turned and disappeared below deck. The whole episode lasted less than a minute.

The RTM manager, who was giving orders to the drone operator, sounded frustrated. "We didn't get a close-up shot. That might have been our one chance, and we didn't get it."

Although it had been ten years since I'd heard it, I suddenly realized the voice belonged to Olivia McConnell, a woman who had once told me she never wanted to see me again.

I turned to leave the room.

The moment I headed toward the door, she called out, "Titus?"

I turned around.

"Hi, Olivia."

She strolled over to where I was standing.

As soon as I saw her emerge from the shadows, I was surprised at how little she'd changed since the last time I'd seen her. Her porcelain skin was still smooth and wrinkle free, and she wore her coal black hair in the same short, boyish hairstyle as when we'd first met as new recruits at Camp Peary years ago.

She was a tall woman, almost as tall as I was, with the body of a fashion model. Her slender frame didn't surprise me, because I'd seldom seen her eat anything except an occasional omelet and maybe a slice of pizza every now and then.

She lived on coffee.

There was a look of astonishment on her face. "What are you doing in here?"

I gestured toward the screens. "Have you figured out where the yacht is headed yet?"

Olivia sounded surprised. "What's your interest in the yacht?"

I glanced over her shoulder at the room full of people who, though seemingly occupied at their consoles, were now fully aware of my presence in the Ops Center. Being noticed made me nervous, and I was hoping she hadn't forgotten that.

Olivia quickly removed her headset. "Let's take this discussion outside."

I opened the door and allowed her to exit first, and then I followed her down the corridor into an employee break room.

There was no one there.

"Now," she said, "explain what you were doing in my Ops Center, and what you know about *El Mano Fierro*."

I gestured toward a coffee machine. "I need some caffeine. Do you want some?"

"You know I do."

Olivia sat down on an uncomfortable-looking sofa, while I filled two Styrofoam cups with coffee. It smelled strong; exactly the way I knew she liked it.

After handing her one of the cups, I said, "First of all, I didn't know it was *your* Ops Center. The last I heard you were handling political footballs for the DDO's office."

She shook her head. "That was three years ago, and I hated every minute of it."

"Yeah, that doesn't surprise me. I can't see you working for Robert Ira."

She smiled. "We had our differences, but I also understand you had your own troubles with Robert."

"That's putting it mildly."

"In fact, there was a rumor going around that he forced you to go on medical leave for a year."

"Unfortunately, that's true."

"So, once again I'm asking you. What were you doing in the Ops Center? I know you're aware this is a restricted area, especially for an officer on medical leave."

"I recently got reinstated for a special ops assignment, and since I was on my way over to a mission briefing, I dropped in to the RTM Center to see if I could pick up some additional intel. You know me, Olivia, always out for that extra bit of intel."

She didn't say anything for a couple of seconds. When she finally spoke, her speech pattern was hesitant, as if she might be reluctant to ask me something.

"So . . . ah . . . let's go back to the yacht. Are you . . . ah . . . interested in the yacht as part of your briefing?"

While she was asking the question, I noticed she was pulling on her earlobe—a nervous gesture I'd seen her make before when she was making an effort to mask her true feelings.

I found both her nervous tic and the way she'd asked her question very disturbing, but I couldn't decide whether to respond to her question or to ask her what was making her so jittery.

However, as it turned out, I didn't have to make that decision because her beeper went off, and she started moving toward the doorway almost immediately.

"Look, Titus, I'm sorry about all this. I had no idea."

Seconds later, she was out the door, and I was left standing there with only her apology to keep me company.

I had no idea.

No idea about what?

Chapter 29

Even though I was a few minutes early, I headed down the hallway to Conference Room B. I thought Carlton might give me a few extra points for being on time, and now that I'd seen Olivia, I had a few questions for him before the briefing began.

However, when I entered the room, it looked as if everyone, except Carlton and Salazar, had already arrived.

Mitchell was seated at the far end of a long conference table all by himself. He looked up from his iPad as I entered the room and nodded at me.

On the right side of the table was Paul Grogan. He was in the center seat—the power seat—studying a thick blue briefing binder. However, when he saw me, he looked up long enough to give me a quick salute.

Before coming to the Agency, Grogan had been with the Department of the Navy, and his staff sometimes referred to him as the Admiral. However, he didn't seem to mind the nickname. In fact, I'd often heard him joke about it, which made me wonder if he'd encouraged them to call him that in the first place.

Representatives from Support Services and the Agency's Legal Services were along the outer wall directly behind Grogan.

Legal was responsible for providing covert operatives mounds of paperwork to sign before they embarked on an operation. Support Services covered all the physical elements required of the mission, including an operative's legend.

I much preferred dealing with Support Services rather than Legal Services' mumbo jumbo, probably because Support Services tried to make sure I stayed alive on the field, whereas Legal Services tried to make sure all the documents were filled out correctly in case I died on the field.

Huddled around a computer screen at the end of the conference table were three intelligence collection analysts. The group consisted of two women and one man—all members of Katherine Broward's team. Katherine was seated at her own computer away from the group, but, as soon as she saw me enter the room, she got up and walked over to greet me.

She squeezed my arm and said, "We were sorry to hear about your mother's passing. Did the funeral go okay?"

"Yes, and thanks for asking."

She gestured toward the analysts. "We sent flowers. I hope they arrived in time."

I remembered seeing baskets of flowers at the funeral home, but I hadn't taken note of where they'd come from or who'd sent them.

Was I supposed to do that?

"The flowers were perfect. Thanks so much."

Having successfully maneuvered my way through yet another awkward social situation, I gestured toward a beverage table at the end of the room. "Could I get you something to drink before the Admiral gets us underway?"

She shook her head. "No, thanks." She glanced at her watch. "He needs to get started. My analysts have given him a ton of data, and we uncovered a—"

"Ms. Broward," Grogan called from across the room, "could I have a moment of your time?"

When she excused herself, I grabbed a bottle of water and sat down next to Mitchell.

"Any idea what's keeping Douglas and Cartel Carlos?" I asked. "It's not like Douglas to be late."

"No idea. I spoke briefly with C. J., and then he told me to meet him down here."

"I don't have a good feeling about this."

Mitchell didn't respond, because he was giving his full attention to the conversation going on between Grogan and Katherine—not necessarily to the conversation itself, just to Katherine herself.

So much for the heartache I thought he felt over his break-up with Sonya.

Katherine returned to her computer and another fifteen minutes passed. Mitchell and I spent the time speculating about what was causing the delay. Our guesses ranged from a crisis erupting in another part of the world to Salazar and Carlton having it out in the courtyard outside the cafeteria.

As it turned out, we weren't too far off the mark on that last one.

♦♦♦♦

After Grogan received a message on his phone, he stood to his feet and said, "We'll begin with the preliminaries now. The other parties will be joining us shortly."

The preliminaries consisted of several legal forms Mitchell and I were required to sign. The documents indicated both of us fully understood the dire consequences of revealing any classified material related to Operation Clear Signal to anyone outside the Agency. In addition, there were forms for us to sign absolving the Agency of any legal responsibility regarding our own personal injury, disease, or death as a consequence of our mission.

Reading such documents was always sobering.

However, I'd been over the identical paperwork many times before, so I quickly signed my name at the bottom of each page. Mitchell, though, took his time and read the legalese before taking a pen and scribbling his own consent on the signature line.

Once these preliminaries were taken care of, and Legal had gathered up all the signed documents, Grogan cued up a set of PowerPoint slides from his laptop, projecting them on the screen at the end of the room.

The title slide had the words, **Plan of Operation (POA)—Operation Clear Signal,** in bold type in the middle of the page. Below this title were three bullet points: **Players, Places, Protocols**.

Grogan followed this same basic outline for each briefing; only the mission title changed. As to why he began each point with the letter P, no one knew for sure, although someone once told me his four children all had names beginning with the letter P.

Even though I knew who the Players were, I was anxious to get to the Places and Protocols of the mission.

However, I was reluctant for Grogan to proceed without knowing what had happened to Carlton. With that in mind, when he clicked over to the Players slide to begin the briefing, I interrupted him.

"Just a quick question before you begin, Admiral."

At that moment, the door to the conference room swung open and Carlton and Salazar walked in.

They were not alone.

Trailing in their wake was Olivia McConnell.

◆◆◆◆

It took the latecomers a few minutes to be seated at the table.

Salazar and Carlton sat down beside Grogan, one on the left side of him and one on the right, while Olivia chose a spot next to Katherine at the end of the table. As Olivia was removing an iPad from her briefcase, she glanced up at me, but, when she noticed I was observing her, she quickly looked away.

After everyone was seated, Grogan said, "What was your question, Titus."

"Never mind," I said, looking directly at Carlton, "it can wait."

Carlton gave me an almost imperceptible nod.

"Let's proceed then."

When Grogan clicked his remote presenter, a photograph of Ahmed filled the screen.

It wasn't necessary for me to see a photograph of Ahmed. His image was seared on the frontal lobe of my brain forever.

"Our number one player in Operation Clear Signal is Ahmed Al-Amin. Since we identified him as the shooter in the Simon Wassermann murder, the Agency has received a Presidential Directive authorizing his apprehension."

Grogan recited Ahmed's resume. It included all known assassinations, plus his affiliation with Iran and Hezbollah as a contract killer. Then, he gave a brief biographical sketch of Ahmed, noting he grew up in Damascus and had worked for the Assad regime at one point in his not so illustrious career.

"We have to assume when Al-Amin arrives in Venezuela, he will be identifying himself as Alberto Estéban Montilla, the name on the Venezuelan passport he picked up during his stopover in San José."

Grogan looked down at his blue binder for a moment. "Here's our second player."

A composite of three different shots was projected up on the screen. All three were pictures of the iPod guy either on the dock in Limón or on the yacht itself. The largest image was the one I'd just seen of him in the RTM Center.

"An hour ago, we identified this man as Javier Flores. He's a resident of Costa Rica. Katherine's people are still pulling the threads on this one, but he seems to have some connection to the Zeta cartel. Presently, he's on his way to Venezuela in the company of Ahmed. More on that in just a moment."

A photo of Ernesto Montilla was displayed next to Javier Flores.

"As you can see from this photograph, there's a strong resemblance between Ernesto Montilla on the right and Javier Flores on the left. We believe Flores will use Ernesto's passport to enter Venezuela as Ernesto Montilla."

Grogan turned to his left and addressed Carlton, "You wanted to speak to the issue of Javier impersonating Ernesto?"

Carlton nodded. "Yes, but I'll wait until you get to the intel section to do that."

"Right."

Grogan pointed his remote mouse at the screen. "Our last player is Roberto Montilla, the father of Ernesto and the assistant secretary in Venezuela's Ministry of Trade and Commerce."

Montilla's photograph was a headshot, the type of image usually included in a press packet. Along with the photograph, there was a newspaper clipping showing Montilla receiving a commendation from the Venezuelan president. It was the same newspaper article Mitchell and I had discovered in Ernesto's belongings.

Roberto Montilla appeared somber in both photographs and looked to be in his early fifties. In the publicity shot, he was modestly dressed and had a drooping moustache and graying sideburns. Judging by the size of the Venezuelan president standing next to him, Ernesto's father was of average height.

"Although we believe Ahmed has now assumed the name of Alberto Montilla, there's no record of an Alberto Montilla in Roberto's family history." Grogan paused and looked over at Katherine. "Ms. Broward will be briefing us about the senior Montilla later."

Katherine nodded at him, and then she looked over at me and smiled.

It was a nice smile.

I smiled back.

Olivia was not smiling.

♦♦♦♦

Grogan clicked on a slide showing the outline of a human figure. The figure had no discernible features, but underneath the icon were the initials UAT.

"I would be remiss if I failed to mention this player. He or she is the Unidentified Assassination Target, our UAT."

Grogan addressed me. "Douglas tells me you've never had any doubt Ahmed was on his way to Venezuela to carry out a hit. The rest of our operations team concurs with your assessment. However, at this moment, the UAT remains just that, an unknown. I believe C. J. will give us the assessment about Ahmed's target as we get deeper into the briefing today."

Salazar gave an affirmative nod.

Grogan displayed the words Data Analysis on the screen.

Grogan turned to Katherine. "Ms. Broward, please proceed with your data analysis of these players."

The moment he sat down, Katherine stood to her feet.

"When my analysts studied these four players, several questions emerged." She looked around the room slowly, as if she wanted to make sure she had everyone's full attention.

She did.

She continued, "Do these players know each other? If so, how did they become acquainted in the first place?" She intertwined her fingers in front of her. "How are they connected with each other at this very moment?"

Katherine touched her keypad and an airline passenger list appeared on the screen in front of us.

"According to these airline records, four years ago, Roberto Montilla, accompanied by his son, Ernesto, arrived in Damascus to meet with various officials in the Syrian government. This meeting was in conjunction with his trade ministry position, and the visit was widely reported in both the Venezuelan and Syrian newspapers."

She showed excerpts from the newspapers with headlines touting the benefits of a trade agreement between the two countries.

"As you can see from these photographs, during his time in Syria, Montilla's translator and escort was this man, Marwan Farage, a known Hezbollah operative."

Katherine picked up a laser pointer and pointed it at Marwan Farage. A red dot appeared on his forehead.

When she continued, there was a note of excitement in her voice. "What we discovered was that Marwan Farage is the cousin of Ahmed Al-Amin."

While I managed to stifle the exhilaration I felt at hearing this news, Mitchell reacted with a loud "Yeah," and I saw the female analysts at the other end of the room giggling.

Katherine pulled up the next slide.

It was a grainy photograph, probably shot with a long-distance camera, of a slightly younger Ahmed and his cousin, Marwan. They were exiting a mosque with two other unidentified Arabic men.

"Ahmed was also present in Damascus during the time of Montilla's visit. That's when this photograph was taken."

The next shot was of Ernesto and Ahmed Al-Amin in front of the same mosque. In this photograph, Ernesto appeared to be carrying a prayer rug.

"Furthermore," she said, "when the older Montilla was making the rounds with Syrian trade officials during the day, the younger Montilla was being entertained by members of the Farage family at the same time."

Mitchell leaned over and whispered, "Nice call."

I looked over at C. J., because I thought he also might like to acknowledge I'd been correct in my assumption that Ernesto had become radicalized while in Syria with his father.

However, Salazar's eyes remained glued to the screen. Obviously, unlike Mitchell, he preferred not to compliment me on my astute observation.

Following her display of photographs, Katherine presented financial records revealing how Montilla had begun receiving substantial amounts of money when he returned home from his visit to Syria.

"We believe these funds either came directly from Hezbollah or from someone in the Syrian government as a way of rewarding Montilla for his help in facilitating the construction of two storage facilities at Maracaibo and Cumaná. We'll be discussing the technical aspects of these construction sites later. However, it would appear the money he received has been used by Montilla to finance Ernesto's education in the States and to pay for his daughter's private schooling in Venezuela."

Katherine smiled. "As this data indicates, we found the connection between Ahmed and the Montillas. They became acquainted with Ahmed Al-Amin while in Damascus, and the older Montilla has been on Hezbollah's payroll ever since."

She nodded at Grogan and sat back down.

"Excellent work, Ms. Broward," Grogan said. "Now, we'll get the intel assessment on these players from C. J. and Douglas."

Even before Carlton stood to his feet, I knew he wouldn't be using the remote presenter, nor would he have any slides to present. When it came to an intelligence briefing, he did it the old-fashioned way, he relied on documents with the word CLASSIFIED stamped across them.

Now, he picked one up from the pile in front of him.

"After being notified of the Presidential Directive, the National Security Agency expedited my request for Roberto's digital communications for the past year. What proved most interesting was a series of recent emails between Roberto and Ahmed. In them, Roberto referred to Ahmed as his brother and addressed him as Alberto. The subject of their emails was Alberto's upcoming visit to Venezuela in the company of Ernesto."

Carlton placed the document back down on his stack of classified materials and carefully aligned the edges of the pile before continuing.

"It's evident from these emails Roberto expects Ahmed and Ernesto to arrive in Venezuela together. Thus, it's my opinion that Roberto has an asset in Passport Control who will clear Javier Flores and Ahmed through customs."

Carlton nodded in my direction. "As you suggested, Titus, we believe Ahmed is bringing Javier as Ernesto's doppelganger in order to deceive Roberto into believing his son is still alive and well."

As Carlton resumed his seat, I muttered, "And what happens to Javier Flores after he's no longer useful to Ahmed's plan?"

Grogan acted as if he hadn't heard me and motioned for Salazar to give his assessment.

I saw no blue binder for Salazar to consult, nor were there any documents stamped CLASSIFIED in front of him.

I didn't take that as a good sign.

Salazar stood to his feet and pointed toward Mitchell. "As I told Ben this morning, I've instructed my people in Venezuela to leave no stone unturned when it comes to digging up intel on Roberto Montilla. Right now, Wylie is reasonably certain it was someone in Montilla's office who obtained the false passport recently delivered to Ahmed in Costa Rica. He gave me a list of possible names, but . . ." Salazar spread his hands out in front of him in an apologetic gesture, "I'm sorry; I must have left that document on my desk."

With a bit of fanfare, Carlton lifted up his stack of documents and pulled out a sheet of paper. Then, he slid it across the table toward Salazar, who quickly picked it up.

"Oh, yes. Here it is." Salazar looked over at Carlton. "Thank you, Douglas."

Carlton nodded, and Salazar proceeded to read off a list of names—all of which meant nothing to anyone in the room—and then he went on to give his own opinion about what Javier Flores might be doing once he showed up in Venezuela.

Since Flores' background indicated some connection to the Zeta drug cartel, Salazar focused in on those connections. However, the details of Salazar's presentation ended up dissolving into an oozy mass of unintelligible speculations.

By the time he'd finished spouting off, I was thinking about telling the DDO I wouldn't work with Salazar, especially if he named him as the field officer for the mission.

However, a few minutes later, after Paul Grogan had revealed the details of his next presentation point, I changed my mind and decided that even if Cartel Carlos ended up being my handler in Venezuela, I would have to see the operation through to the end.

Chapter 30

Grogan clicked forward to the second point in his presentation, but, before calling attention to it, he glanced down at a message on his mobile phone. Then he took a large gulp of water from the bottle in front of him.

Finally, he said, "The next briefing point is **Places** and our first stop will be Margarita Island."

He projected an aerial shot of *Isla de Margarita* on the screen.

Margarita Island, off the northeastern coast of Venezuela, was about an hour's flight from Caracas. I'd never visited the island before, but I knew it was one of Venezuela's top tourist attractions because it had miles and miles of white sand beaches.

"A few hours ago, the operational team in the RTM Center determined *El Mano Fierro* was on course for Margarita Island, and I've just received confirmation the yacht's captain has requested berthing privileges at Porlamar on the island's eastern coast. The yacht should be arriving at the Concorde Marina in Porlamar by five o'clock tomorrow evening."

My heart rate increased momentarily.

Unless something changed in the next twenty-four hours, Mitchell and I were headed to Margarita Island.

The next slide showed a modern, Caribbean-style hotel completely surrounded by palm trees and situated on a promontory overlooking an endless horizon of blue ocean and stark white sand.

"This is the Wyndham Hotel and Conference Center, located a few miles from downtown Porlamar, and one of the most luxurious hotels on the island. It will also be the site of the Caribbean States International Trade Conference due to begin on Monday morning."

Grogan turned from the screen and addressed Katherine.

"Ms. Broward, since the identities of the conference attendees are relevant to the rest of this briefing, would you tell us what your analysts have uncovered about those scheduled to attend these meetings?"

Katherine remained seated at her computer and read off the names of those who would be attending the conference. The list included at least ten heads of state from the Americas and the Caribbean Basin, along with a dozen other foreign dignitaries from around the world. She also noted an unknown number of advisers, banking officials, economic officers, and embassy personnel were expected to attend.

She glanced over at Mitchell and me. "What may interest the two of you is that Roberto Montilla, in his position as a trade minister for the Venezuelan government, is a member of the steering committee and is responsible for organizing this conference. Of course, that means he'll be attending the meetings. He's also scheduled to speak at one of the seminars on Monday."

She leaned in toward her laptop, typed in some keystrokes, and said, "Roberto will arrive at Del Caribe Airport in Porlamar around ten o'clock tomorrow morning, just a few hours before Ahmed arrives in port. We have no idea where Ahmed will be staying, but Roberto is booked into a suite at the Wyndham."

Grogan turned and addressed Mitchell and me. "Before I have the division heads discuss the intelligence implications of this information, I want to call your attention to some other locations pertinent to this briefing."

He replaced the Margarita Island slide with a collage of photographs.

"First, we'll look at the storage facilities being constructed by a Syrian holding company in Maracaibo and Cumaná. Ms. Broward referred to them in her data analysis because Roberto Montilla is facilitating all the documentation involved in getting them built in Venezuela."

This was my first chance to study the buildings Carlton had mentioned to me a couple of days ago, but there wasn't much to see. The photographs could just as well have been taken of any large construction project anywhere in the world. The only anomaly was the high concrete wall—at least twelve feet tall—around the perimeter of the property.

Grogan pointed out some features inside the warehouses that Agency analysts indicated were consistent with a chemical weapons storage facility.

He said, "There's been a slowdown at both construction sites recently, but no one's sure what to make of that. Since work stoppages are a fairly common event in Venezuela, it might not mean anything. At any rate, we've estimated these units are only a few weeks away from completion."

Grogan went on to explain that Ahmed had marked the two construction sites on one of the maps found inside the Durango with an X. Then, Grogan put up the map of Caracas I'd removed from the car's glove box.

"Besides locating Maracaibo and Cumaná on a map of Venezuela," he said, "Ahmed also placed these X's on a Caracas street map."

Grogan circled one of Ahmed's X's with his laser pointer. "This is the *Avenida Francisco* district. It's mostly apartments, with a few restaurants and small retail shops nearby. Wylie says it's a high traffic area because of all the high-rise apartment buildings in the area."

Pointing to the second X, he said, "On the other hand next door to the *Avenida Francisco* district is the *Sabana Grande* addition, which you see here. These are high-dollar, single-family residences. Some of our embassy personnel live in this area, as well as government officials from Venezuela."

Grogan asked Katherine to give us a few more details on both the construction sites in Maracaibo and Cumaná and the residential neighborhoods.

However, after listening to Katherine for a few minutes, I tuned her out.

I knew Mitchell would probably remember the important stuff—he appeared to be giving her his full attention—and I wanted to consider the areas Grogan had pinpointed on Ahmed's map.

I needed to put myself in Ahmed's shoes.

I needed to consider why a shooter would draw X's on a map.

Of course, the most obvious answer was to designate the location of a target, or to note where a target was scheduled to appear sometime in the future.

I knew that sounded logical, but I couldn't picture Ahmed being so careless as to mark a map indicating his next hit and then leave the map inside the glove box of the Durango. He hadn't even bothered to take it inside the safe house where he and Ernesto were staying in San José.

As I thought about the concrete block house in San José, an alert fired across the synapses of my cerebral cortex, but the thought quickly disappeared when I heard Katherine say something about our embassy personnel in Caracas.

"While it will take a little longer to obtain the names of all the occupants of these apartments," she said, "we know most of the identities of those who live in the *Sabana Grande* district. Of particular interest to us is that Roberto Montilla lives there, along with several prominent Venezuelan businessmen and the Peruvian ambassador. More importantly, our embassy's Head of Mission, John Luckenbill, has a residence in this area."

The Venezuelan president had recently expelled the U.S. Ambassador to Venezuela, leaving Luckenbill to direct the affairs of the American Embassy in his stead. Ostensibly, the Ambassador's expulsion had come about as a show of solidarity between the Venezuela president and the Bolivian president. The latter had initiated a dispute with the U.S. over phone calls being monitored by the NSA in Bolivia.

However, most people in the State Department recognized the Venezuelan president was simply looking for an opportunity to tweak Uncle Sam's nose; no one believed anyone in the Venezuelan government really cared about the sensibilities of the Bolivian president.

Grogan said, "Douglas, we're ready for your intel assessment on these locations now."

Carlton nodded but remained quiet for a few seconds.

Then, he gestured toward Salazar and said, "Sam Wylie's your man in Caracas. Why don't you go first? I'll tie up the loose ends when you're finished."

Salazar looked pleased at Carlton's gesture and immediately launched into his analysis. He noted that Sam Wylie had been developing assets in anticipation of the Caribbean States International Trade Conference. In fact, Wylie was already on Margarita Island making preparations to monitor both the CSIT meetings and the foreign diplomats at the conference.

"I'm going to concur with Sam's opinion. He believes Ahmed is planning to assassinate a high-profile diplomat at the trade conference. If that's true, most likely Montilla will be helping him. In what form that help will come is anybody's guess, but Montilla is in charge of the security arrangements for the attendees, so his assistance will probably come in that way. If so, he'll be invaluable to Ahmed."

As Salazar continued speaking, he fleshed out the details of his assessment. Unfortunately, his assessment had nothing to do with uncovering Ahmed's intended target or stopping a Hezbollah assassin from placing a bullet in the UAT's skull.

Salazar finished up by saying, "Once Ahmed has made the hit, I'm certain the cartel will be responsible for getting him out of the country. Without the cartel's help, Ahmed wouldn't have made it to Venezuela in the first place, and he'll probably use them to get back to Syria. Therefore, if we don't want to lose Ahmed once he's made the hit, we should be monitoring his cartel connections right now."

Salazar's assessment was followed by an awkward moment of silence.

Finally, it dawned on Grogan that Salazar had ended his intel analysis. This time, though, he refused to let Salazar off the hook and grilled him about identifying the UAT. Salazar wouldn't commit to anything, though. He said his division was still monitoring sources on the ground.

Grogan, who appeared notably frustrated at Salazar, asked him, "Could you at least make some determination about the chemical storage sites or the residential areas Ahmed marked on the maps?"

When Salazar spoke, the tenor of his voice made it sound like Grogan's question was a nuisance. "Most likely, those sites are part of his backup plan or something like that. If Ahmed can't manage the hit on the island, then he might try and complete his assignment on the mainland. That's probably why Ahmed marked those X's on the maps."

That was the last straw for me.

"It wasn't Ahmed who marked the X's on the maps."

As soon as I spoke up, I saw Carlton purse his lips, an expression I'd seen him make several times before, but its meaning was still unclear to me.

It could mean approval. It could mean disapproval.

Take your pick.

However, it was clear the Admiral disapproved of my comment.

"Titus," he said, "you're allowed to express an opinion at the end of this briefing, but, for now, hold your—"

Salazar cut him off. "No, let him speak. I want to hear what he has to say."

Grogan gestured toward me, "In that case, you have the floor."

When I got to my feet, I pointed to the map of Caracas on the screen. "The maps I found in the glove box of the Durango weren't important to Ahmed. He's a professional. He isn't a careless man. If he had planned to use those maps in some professional capacity, then leaving them in a parked car was a careless act. And, I repeat, Ahmed is not a careless man."

Salazar spoke up. "You could be right. Maybe those maps have nothing whatsoever to do with his hit. The cartel probably gave him those maps for an entirely different purpose."

"If it wasn't Ahmed, who was it then?"

Olivia's question surprised me. I'd almost forgotten she was in the room.

Almost.

I looked at her. "I believe it was Ernesto."

She rolled her eyes and looked up at the ceiling. "And, pray tell, why would you think that?"

"Yeah," Salazar chimed in, "why would you think that?"

I was hoping Carlton might jump into the discussion, but he had his eyes firmly fixed on the map of Caracas.

"Because, as I said, it doesn't make any sense for Ahmed to put X's on a map. On the other hand, Ernesto had a habit of—"

"—marking things with an X," Carlton said, taking his eyes off the map and looking over at me.

"Exactly," I said.

Carlton addressed the group. "There were menus in Ernesto's duffel bag from restaurants in the Austin area. He had marked a few of the entrees with an X. It's logical to assume those items were ones Ernesto either liked or wanted to try. That's what he must have been doing with the maps; he was marking places he wanted to visit or places he liked."

Salazar sounded skeptical. "But that would mean he marked his own neighborhood."

Olivia spoke up, "That actually makes sense, though. He was homesick. He was looking forward to being home again. The same thing could be true of the construction sites. He'd heard his father talk about them; he wanted to see them for himself."

Katherine got the Admiral's attention.

"Yes, Ms. Broward?"

She pointed toward the screen. "See for yourself."

During our discussion, Katherine had pulled up one of the menus Mitchell and I had discovered in Ernesto's duffel bag. It was from a Chinese restaurant called The Flying Dragon. Ernesto had marked an X next to Marpoo Dofu and an X next to something called Ants Climbing Hill."

Mitchell leaned over and whispered, "I could go for some Ants Climbing Hill right now."

Grogan squinted at the screen. "I could be wrong, but it looks like the X's on this menu were made by the same person who made the X's on the maps. There's that same flourish on the upturn at the bottom of the X."

He turned to Katherine. "See if you can get someone to verify that."

Katherine nodded. "I'll get Faulkner to take a look at it."

Carlton said, "Could I see the map again, please?"

Grogan clicked back to the Caracas street map.

I thought I knew why he wanted to see the map again, but I didn't say anything. I'd learned never to steal my boss' thunder. Otherwise, he might rain on my parade one day.

When Carlton asked Grogan to zoom in on the X in the *Avenida Francisco* district, I was happy to see Mitchell studying the map with the same intensity I'd previously seen him studying Katherine.

After a few seconds, I heard him take a deep breath.

I was betting he'd seen it too.

Look for those all-important details, Mitchell. They might save your life one day.

Carlton said, "Did anyone else notice that the X in the *Avenida Francisco* district is a lowercase X, whereas the X in Ernesto's own neighborhood is an uppercase X?"

I said, "Yes, and if I remember correctly, the two construction sites were also marked with a lowercase X."

Mitchell said, "I bet it's some kind of code."

Olivia and I both said, "The menu was—"

She gave me a half-smile. "Go ahead, Titus."

"Ladies first," I said, knowing she would hate that.

She frowned, but she didn't argue with me. "I was about to say he marked the two items on the menu with lowercase X's."

Carlton said, "But we have no way of knowing whether the smaller X meant he liked that item or simply wanted to try it."

Mitchell asked, "Wouldn't his girlfriend know his code?"

What followed next was a long—and to my mind—unnecessary discussion about Ernesto's girlfriend, Charlotte "Charlie" Tedesco. Everyone in the room seemed to have an opinion about what she might or might not know about him.

In the end, Grogan adjourned the briefing for lunch while his office contacted the two FBI agents who'd interviewed Charlie following Simon Wassermann's killing.

The discussion about the relationship between Ernesto and Charlie made me realize I'd gone almost four hours without thinking about Nikki Saxon and our relationship.

I couldn't decide if that was a good thing or a bad thing.

Chapter 31

I tried to catch Carlton before he slipped out of the conference room, but, as I headed out the door, one of the female analysts on Katherine's team stopped me.

"Were the flowers lilies or gladioli?" she asked.

"What?"

"The flowers we sent to your mother's funeral," she said. "Were they lilies or gladioli?"

I mumbled something that probably sounded rude and rushed out the door after Carlton.

However, the hallway was empty.

I considered trying to locate him, but I decided if he had wanted to speak with me privately, he would have stuck around, so I made my way up to the first floor where the cafeteria was located.

The Agency had modernized the cafeteria setup several years ago, and now, the whole area resembled the food court at a mall. When I got there, I spotted Mitchell standing in line at a Burger King.

I strolled over to the Chick-fil-A line, where I purchased a chicken sandwich, waffle fries, and a large lemonade. Originally, I'd planned to eat with Mitchell, but, after paying for my meal, I noticed he was already seated with one of Salazar's secretaries.

Solitude seemed a better choice for me, and I headed in the direction of a small table in a corner of the room with a view of the atrium.

The landscaped atrium in the cafeteria courtyard was filled with a variety of trees and plants, and some of the Agency employees—at least those who didn't mind the heat and humidity of Langley in the summertime—were sitting outside on stone benches dining *al fresco*.

That had no appeal to me, because I knew in just a few hours I would be taking in plenty of sunshine on Margarita Island.

While I ate lunch, I tried to map out the mission protocols, but, for some reason, all I could think about was Nikki. I finally put my sandwich down and pulled out my phone to call her.

At the last minute, I stopped myself.

Why, all of a sudden, did I want to hear her laugh?

After thinking about it, I realized my feelings were triggered by seeing Olivia McConnell, and I was feeling unsettled after spending the last couple of hours in the same room with her.

My relationship with Olivia had never been a smooth ride. In fact, from the very beginning, back at Camp Peary when we'd first met on the Drivers' Obstacle Training course, she'd treated me with disdain. Her attitude back then surprised me because, until the instructor had paired us together on the DOT course, I'd never met her.

When the instructor had called out our names, Olivia had immediately walked over to me and said, "I'm sure you'll insist on being in the driver's seat."

"What makes you think that?"

"You're a man, aren't you?"

"Obviously."

"Well, I'm a woman. Do you have a problem with that?"

And so it went.

After that, I tried to stay as far away from her as possible. However, one day, about six months after we'd finished our training, I was attending a seminar at Langley, and I needed to cool off after having an intense argument on Central American politics. Back then, I was jogging regularly, so I started jogging around the outer perimeter of the Agency's parking lot to let off some steam.

That was when I had encountered Olivia.

She was sitting in her car in the far west parking lot. Although she appeared to be asleep, I could tell something was off.

I rapped on the window, but she didn't stir.

After breaking the glass, I did everything I could to revive her, but when I spotted the empty medicine bottle in the passenger's seat, I finally stopped trying.

Without thinking too much about it, I grabbed her keys out of her purse and drove her over to a nearby hospital.

However, I didn't contact anyone at the Agency.

The full story of why she'd taken the sleeping pills was a long time in coming, and when she finally started talking about it, I didn't really believe her.

We were both excellent liars.

The part I did believe was that she'd gotten involved with the wrong guy, and if that wasn't enough, she'd lost both her mother and sister to breast cancer within a six-month period.

Olivia had no friends.

She said women bored her, and she didn't hold men in very high esteem either.

However, because I'd saved her life, plus allowed her to stay employed by the CIA, she decided to put me in a different category, the I'm-going-to-give-you-a-chance-to-be-my-friend category.

For several years after that, whenever we were in town at the same time, we tried to get together for dinner, or go to the gun range together, or just hang out with each other.

There was nothing romantic about our relationship.

However, the more time I spent with Olivia, the more interesting I found her, and the more I realized I was beginning to care about her.

Olivia was blunt, very sharp-tongued, and occasionally caustic in her sarcasm, but she was also insightful and an excellent sounding board—when I needed that sort of thing. I discovered she was also incredibly good at helping me see things from a different perspective.

About a year after the sleeping pill incident, it was evident the Agency's executives had decided Olivia was someone they wanted to advance up the administrative hierarchy.

They began grooming her by giving her a variety of assignments within the different divisions of Intelligence. After that, they started moving her around the Agency's organizational chart like some CEO's incompetent nephew.

But Olivia was not incompetent.

She had the ability to seize a crisis, look at it in a slightly different way, and facilitate a quick solution. Not surprisingly, because of her skills in risk assessment and pattern analysis, she spent most of her time behind a desk and very little time in the field running an operation.

However, around the time I was sent to Iraq, she was yanked from her desk job in Intelligence and assigned to Operations, specifically to Douglas Carlton in the Middle Eastern division.

As her first assignment, Carlton had sent her over to Camp Beuhring in Kuwait to facilitate a simple weapons transfer. This was during the early days of the first Gulf War. By handing her such an easy task, Carlton had pretty much assured her success.

Later on, someone had told me Olivia had done a superb job managing the logistics at Camp Beuhring, and that she'd also devised a unique plan for keeping track of the weapons she was handing over to the rebels.

However, when I showed up at Camp Beuhring—accompanied by a high profile Iraqi general—things didn't go all that smoothly. That's because, the moment I realized Olivia was going to be responsible for protecting the Iraqi general I'd recruited, I'd completely lost it.

Later, I realized my actions were the result of being afraid she could be killed, or even worse, captured by some of Hussein's elite soldiers, who were still controlling parts of Bagdad.

"I'm contacting Carlton," I told her. "He needs to send me an experienced handler to manage this operation."

"So you don't think I'm capable of being your handler?"

"I didn't say that."

"That's what you're thinking though."

"Don't tell me what I'm thinking."

We went back and forth for a few minutes, and then, I committed the ultimate sin—at least in Olivia's way of thinking.

I said, "You shouldn't be in Kuwait in the first place, Olivia. And, you certainly shouldn't be planning to head up the road to Bagdad to run the general from there."

"And why not?"

"You're a woman, that's why."

From that point on, the argument deteriorated into several inappropriate words that never should have been uttered by either one of us.

Finally, she ended the disagreement by saying she never wanted to see me again. However, she didn't stop there. She went on to say she was going to contact Carlton and have me reassigned.

The next day, when I was told to head back to the States, I thought Olivia had followed through on her threat. But once I was airborne, I was notified that my father had passed away, and I was being sent back to the States to attend his funeral.

Later, Saddam Hussein put the Iraqi general in front of a firing squad and shot him for treason.

I blamed Olivia for that.

I guess I still did.

♦♦♦♦

I picked up my phone to call Nikki. Whether I did so to get Olivia out of my mind, or whether I just wanted to hear her voice, I wasn't sure.

"Hi, Titus, mind if I join you?"

I looked up to see Dr. Terry Howard staring down at me. He was balancing a dinner tray in one hand and holding onto a small medical bag with the other.

I put my phone back in my pocket and pointed over to a bench opposite me. "Have a seat."

When Howard sat down, he said, "What are you doing here? I know the DDO put you on medical leave because I signed the papers myself." He tore open a paper wrapping containing some plastic utensils. "In my medical opinion, you don't need to be on medical leave, but since I'm about to retire, I do what I'm told."

Terry Howard was the in-house physician at The Gray and had given me a physical a few days after I'd made my escape from Iran. The two of us had known each other for years, but we weren't really friends. He had a youthful face and a well-toned body and certainly didn't appear old enough to be near retirement.

"Ira temporarily reinstated me."

"He must have needed someone to do a dirty job for him."

"I wanted this assignment."

"Maybe Ira just made you think you did."

Howard was an old grouch, always had been. He wallowed in negativity; then he wrapped it around himself and wore it everywhere.

We chatted a few minutes about the weather—too hot. Then he shared some tantalizing gossip about someone on the seventh floor—too immoral. He finally ended his grievances by talking about how the prisoners at Gitmo were being treated—too well.

Howard had been one of five physicians assigned to Gitmo before he was transferred to The Gray, and I agreed with him about the place. I also agreed with him about the weather, but I knew nothing about the seventh-floor gossip, so I kept my mouth shut on that one.

After he took a bite of his sandwich, he asked, "Do you remember the question you asked me when we saw each other at The Gray?"

I thought for a second. "I believe I asked you if you'd ever considered becoming a follower of Christ."

He nodded. "That's right."

Howard pushed his food off to the side.

Since he'd barely eaten anything, I wondered if he'd chosen to sit at my table because he wanted to talk with me about my experience of faith in Tehran. However, when I'd shared the story with him before, he'd laughed at me and joked about prescribing me some medication for the types of hallucinations I was having.

Now, as he looked down at the drinking straw he was twisting around his index finger, he said, "I haven't been able to get that question out of my mind. It's been haunting me ever since."

After he admitted this, he looked up at me, but I found it difficult to label the raw emotion I saw written across his face. The only word that came to mind was troubled, but that wasn't it exactly.

Because of the way he'd treated me before, for one brief moment, I thought about saying, "Well then, why don't you take some medication for what's bothering you."

A year ago, I wouldn't have hesitated to deliver such a retort.

Instead, I said, "I asked you that question because some Iranian Christians asked me that same question, and since I'd never considered becoming a follower of Christ before, I decided it was time I did."

As Howard continued staring at me, I finally identified the emotion I saw there. I decided it was fear. Howard looked frightened and unsure of himself—something I'd never seen in him before.

He said, "That's exactly what I've been doing; I've been considering this. I've researched the subject by reading from my wife's Bible, and I've occasionally watched some of those religious programs on cable."

I affirmed him for looking for answers in the Bible, and I told him the first book of the Bible I'd read all the way through was the gospel of John. I suggested he do the same.

That's when he remembered a verse he'd read in John, and he asked me a few questions about what I thought Jesus meant when he said he had come to bring joy to his followers.

It wasn't long before I'd exhausted my meager knowledge of how to be a follower of Christ, so I suggested he find a pastor in the area and make an appointment. I even pulled out my cell phone and gave him Pastor John's phone number.

After he'd finished putting the number on his contacts list, I decided to ask him a question.

"Terry, what's the one thing you need in this world in order to be happy?"

He gave me a strange look. "Is that a religious question?"

"No, it's just a question someone recently asked me. How would you answer that?"

"Well, that's easy. Being healthy makes me happy. The one thing I need most in this world is to be healthy."

Because of Howard's obsession with diet and exercise, I realized I should have known Howard would think his greatest need was his health.

After answering my question, Howard picked up his black bag and said he was late for an appointment.

Before walking away, however, he bent down and whispered in my ear. "Watch your back, Titus. In case you didn't know it, your old nemesis, Olivia McConnell, is working for the DDO now."

Chapter 32

Mitchell was waiting for me when I got off the elevator in the lobby of the Operations Center. As we headed toward Corridor B and the conference room, he began telling me about the conversation he'd had with the secretary in Salazar's office.

"She said Douglas and C. J. got into a heated argument in the cafeteria this morning. One of the other secretaries told her it was about which one of them was going to lead the operation. She doesn't know what was decided, but once they left the cafeteria, they went straight to the DDO's office."

"So you weren't just flirting during lunch? You were actually gathering intel?"

He frowned at me. "I thought you'd be interested in this."

"I don't care who's running the show while we're in country. I'm only interested in identifying Ahmed's target and shipping this murderer off to Gitmo."

I would later regret those words.

♦♦♦♦

When Grogan resumed the briefing, he immediately played the audio of the FBI agent who had contacted Ernesto's girlfriend during our lunch break.

In the recording, the agent described the questions he'd asked Charlie and the responses he'd received.

When Grogan turned off the conversation, he said, "So, as you heard, Ernesto used a lowercase X for something he hadn't tried yet, and that's what he was doing when he marked the Chinese menu. Charlie also said Ernesto used that same method to pick out his classes. He used an uppercase X to designate classes he'd already taken and a lowercase X to mark those he planned to investigate further."

Grogan flipped back to the screen showing X's on the map of Caracas, and then he asked Katherine about the handwriting report. She said Faulkner was ninety percent certain Ernesto had made the X's on all the maps.

"Well, gentlemen," Grogan said, turning first to Carlton and then to Salazar, "anything you want to add before I move on to the operation's protocols? Since Ahmed never made those X's in the first place, it seems pretty obvious the maps are irrelevant when it comes to determining his target."

Salazar nodded. "I agree."

Carlton looked off in the distance a moment, and then he shook his head. "I think it's strange that Ernesto marked the *Avenida Francisco* district. According to his girlfriend, the manner in which he tagged this area meant this was a place he wanted to visit or that he hadn't visited yet. But that doesn't make sense. He just lived a block from this location. Surely he'd been in the *Avenida Francisco* district before."

Carlton glanced down at the other end of the table. "Olivia, what are your thoughts on this?"

Olivia didn't seem surprised by the question and responded decisively. "The X's mark a couple of high-rise apartment buildings. Ernesto might know—or I should say he might have known—someone who lived there and planned to visit them when he returned to Caracas."

Carlton nodded. "I concur."

The Admiral couldn't keep the irritation out of his voice. "Pursue that rabbit, if you must, Douglas, but to my mind, marking those apartment buildings appears to be a very minor detail in the overall picture of this operation."

Carlton didn't reply; instead, he immediately went to work

straightening up his pile of papers.

Then, as Grogan clicked over to the final slide in his briefing and the word **Protocols** appeared on the screen, Carlton looked over at me and smiled.

He'd obviously won some kind of victory. I had no idea what it was.

♦♦♦♦

The **Protocols** slide introduced the final section of the briefing. It outlined the mission's objectives and the means to achieve those objectives.

Grogan said, "There are three interconnected objectives to the mission."

He projected each one in a bulleted format on the screen, and then he addressed Mitchell and me.

"Your first and primary objective is to confirm the identity of the UAT. You'll achieve this objective with the help of Sam Wylie and the team he's assembled on Margarita Island."

Grogan turned to Salazar. "Is Sam available for the conference call yet?"

He shook his head. "I still haven't heard back from him. He must be running late."

Evidently, Sam Wylie hadn't changed. When we'd worked together in Nicaragua, he was notorious for being late.

"Give me a heads up as soon as he's connected," Grogan said, and then he quickly went on to his next point. "Your second objective is to determine Roberto Montilla's role in Ahmed's plans."

Suddenly, I remembered standing in the rental house in San José and unfolding the newspaper clipping, which Ernesto had been carrying around in his wallet. For the very first time, I considered the tribute Ernesto had shown to his father by having this keepsake with him wherever he went.

As I thought about their relationship, an idea came to me.

But, like a tiny seedling when it takes root in fertile soil, it still needed time to germinate, so I left it alone, hoping it might become a full-blown plant or, better still, a plan.

"The mission's third objective is to stop Ahmed from carrying out the hit on the UAT and then take Ahmed into custody for the murder of Simon Wassermann."

Grogan glanced over at Mitchell and me again. "The Presidential Directive authorizes you to take whatever measures are necessary to achieve these objectives. However, please keep in mind our counter-intelligence guys would welcome the opportunity to conduct a thorough and long-termed session with Ahmed Al-Amin before he's turned over to the Attorney General."

I would indeed keep that in mind. It wouldn't be at the forefront of my mind, though. It would be relegated to its proper place at the back.

Grogan closed his laptop and stood to his feet. Now that his role in the briefing had been concluded, it was time for him to turn the briefing over to the operation's field officer.

Would it be Carlton or Salazar?

He said, "Now, I want to address the unusual nature of this mission, specifically, the extraordinary circumstances of having both the Middle Eastern desk and the Latin American desk working together on the same operation."

The Admiral widened his stance slightly, giving me the distinct impression he might be remembering a time when he was standing on the deck of a ship addressing the crew.

"Because of these circumstances, the Deputy Director has made the decision to name an independent field operations officer, one who will be on the ground directing the operation, while coordinating with both division heads back in the Operations Center."

At that moment, in one split second of crystal clear lucidity, everything came together.

Things change.

Keep an open mind.

I had no idea.

"The person he's named as field officer for this operation is Olivia McConnell. She'll be directing the in-country aspects of Operation Clear Signal on the ground in Venezuela, while Douglas and C. J. will be coordinating the operational phases of the mission back here at Langley."

Suddenly, having Salazar as my field officer didn't seem like such a nightmare.

In fact, now that Olivia was my FO, it was more like a cherished dream that hadn't come true.

♦♦♦♦

After Grogan made his announcement, events in the room accelerated. The slow methodical briefing led by the Admiral was soon replaced by The Olivia McConnell Show.

First, the long-awaited hookup with Sam Wylie was initiated. Then, Olivia and Grogan got into a brief skirmish over who would conduct the conference call with him. However, when Olivia pointed out that Wylie would be under her jurisdiction when she was running the operation on site in Venezuela, Grogan relented and allowed her to direct the conversation.

After Wylie had signed off, Olivia announced the schedule for the following day, and then she outlined how she saw the operation playing out once the yacht arrived in Porlamar.

When she concluded the briefing, she addressed Mitchell and me. "It's your turn now. Do either of you want to comment on Paul's briefing or the operational game plan I've laid out?"

Mitchell, who had been subdued ever since Olivia's role in the operation had been announced, suddenly found his voice. "Sam mentioned his team had been able to wire Montilla's suite at the hotel. Is there any chance hotel security might discover those listening devices?"

To Olivia's credit, she didn't ridicule his inexperience in the field. Instead, she went into an explanation about backup contingencies, couching her doubletalk in the aura of newly developed technologies. However, in her closing remark, she managed to sound condescending.

"If you're still unclear on this, Support Services can supply you with some manuals on the subject. Reading those should get you up to speed."

She turned to me and asked, "Any thoughts, Titus?"

"Just one."

My tiny seedling of an idea had now blossomed into a full-blown plan ripe for the plucking.

"The floor's all your's." Olivia said.

As if to demonstrate she was sincere, Olivia resumed her seat beside Katherine.

"I think we need to shake things up in Ahmed's world," I said. "Create a little chaos. Rock his boat, so to speak."

Olivia raised her eyebrows, but she looked more intrigued than surprised by my suggestion. "Sounds interesting. Did you have something specific in mind?"

I nodded. "I believe it's time for the American Embassy in San José to contact Roberto Montilla and inform him his son has been found murdered. Instruct them to keep the report vague. They should say Ernesto's death is under investigation by the Costa Rican authorities, but they should also hint there's every indication his death was a homicide. Let Roberto know it was Ernesto's girlfriend who contacted the embassy after she hadn't heard from him in several days."

Salazar looked as if he wanted to say something, but Olivia raised her hand like a traffic cop and stopped him.

He remained quiet after that.

Olivia contemplated my proposal for a moment. "As soon as Roberto sees Javier, he'll know this kid isn't his son, so how does telling him about Ernesto's death beforehand prove beneficial to us? Wouldn't it make more sense to hear how Ahmed is going to explain Ernesto's death to his father? Hearing his explanation might give us some insight into what his plans are."

I shook my head. "No, I disagree. No matter how Ahmed decides to spin the story to Roberto, we'll just end up playing defense. The best way for us to identify the UAT is to play offense and take the initiative. Roberto Montilla is the unknown here. We have no idea if he's simply a puppet in Ahmed's game or if he's the one pulling the strings. Let's find out which one he is by letting him know his son is dead, and then we can observe how he reacts to that information."

Olivia looked thoughtful. "If Roberto thinks Ahmed is responsible for his son's death, he might never let him off the island alive."

"Ahmed's too smart and well-trained to let that happen. However, I'm confident once Roberto hears about his son's death, things will start to get confusing. And whenever there's confusion, people start making mistakes. I want to create an environment where Ahmed will start making mistakes. Otherwise, we might never identify his target until it's too late."

Olivia surprised me by actually smiling. "I like this idea, Titus, and you're right; whenever there's confusion, people start making mistakes."

Having Olivia agree with me was unsettling, to say the least.

PART FOUR

Chapter 33

Sunday, June 10

The moment I stepped off the plane in Porlamar, I felt a twinge of anxiety. Such worry was unfamiliar to me, so I wondered if it was because Mitchell was my partner on this run.

However, part of me wasn't buying that explanation because Olivia and Mitchell had taken a later flight, and when I disembarked from the plane onto the tarmac at Del Caribe International Airport, I was all by my lonesome.

If having Mitchell along as my partner wasn't the reason for my apprehension, then having Olivia as my handler might have been the cause of it. The two of us hadn't talked since the briefing, but I expected we'd have an opportunity for a one-on-one in the days ahead, and I wasn't looking forward to it.

For one thing, I knew I needed to ask her forgiveness for the things I'd said to her in the past, and I wasn't sure how I was going to do that. Praying about it seemed like a good idea, but I suddenly found myself hesitant to ask for guidance on the issue.

That feeling of reluctance bothered me.

The second reason I was experiencing uneasiness about Olivia was that I wasn't sure she could handle being the field operations officer, the FO, for this mission. However, it had nothing to do with the fact that she was a woman, even though she would probably think so. On the other hand, it had everything to do with her inexperience in the field and her bulldozer attitude.

Sometimes, in order to unearth a solution to a problem, it's more appropriate to use a shovel than it is to use a bulldozer.

I'd never seen any evidence Olivia understood that.

♦♦♦♦

Although the island's main airport had a modern-looking terminal, passengers still had to deplane onto the tarmac and make their way inside on their own. The plane had been full, and I'd chosen to disembark last, so that meant I was slow getting into the building.

Once inside, though, I quickly cleared through customs posing as David Awerbuch, a prestigious member of the U.S. Trade Delegation, who, along with his staff, was attending the Caribbean States International Trade Conference.

My business card didn't actually say I was prestigious. However, that's the way Arnold, a member of Support Services, had described my persona when he had briefed us on the phony identities we'd be using while we were in Venezuela.

I was the prestigious one in the bunch and Olivia and Mitchell were my lackeys. In reality, Arnold had described Olivia and Mitchell as my assistants, but the meaning was the same.

At least to me.

I could tell Olivia was not pleased by the role Legends had fashioned for her. She loved authority and couldn't stand the thought of acting as if she didn't have any—even temporarily.

As I wandered through the terminal, I was tempted to remain at the airport until ten o'clock when Roberto Montilla was due to arrive on his flight from Caracas. I was anxious to get a firsthand look at the man and to get a feel for his personality.

However, there was a real possibility he could be one of those people who could sense he was under surveillance, so I decided against it. Besides that, Sam Wylie had already arranged for a couple of Agency people to be with him on the plane.

As I scanned the crowds looking for the driver I'd been promised, I also kept my eye out for any Arabic-looking faces among the government officials arriving for the trade conference.

My last refresher course at Camp Peary had emphasized a little known or simply overlooked consequence of working as a long-term covert intelligence officer—the possibility of being recognized from a previous mission.

My trainers had warned me that since I'd been working in the Middle East for so long, there existed the real possibility I could run into someone who knew me when I was wearing a different skin. I knew I needed to be especially wary of any government officials from Syria, because I'd once posed as an arms dealer working out of Damascus, and in that role, I'd mingled regularly with ministry staff.

I saw a few Middle Eastern faces in the crowd, but, as far as I could tell, no one looked familiar to me. However, in the midst of my scrutiny, I spotted a driver holding up a placard with the name David Awerbuch on it.

I waved him over.

A few minutes later, I was in the backseat of a late model Cadillac traveling down *Avenida Juan Bautista* toward the world-renowned Wyndham Hotel. The Agency had booked David Awerbuch, along with his two lackeys, into a suite of rooms there, and I was sure such lodgings would be luxurious and well-appointed surroundings that befitted a prestigious member of the U.S. Trade Delegation.

It was a beautiful day on Margarita Island. The temperature was a perfect seventy-four degrees, the skies were clear, and the sun was shining. To top it off, I was being taken to a plush five-star hotel, and outside my car window, I had an incredible view of the blue waters of the Caribbean.

What more could a man want?

A little peace of mind would do.

♦♦♦♦

The Wyndham Hotel managed to live up to its reputation. It was an upscale hotel with deluxe accommodations, and the Agency had booked the three of us into one of their executive suites.

As soon as I entered the room on the seventeenth floor, I understood why the desk clerk had used the word "exclusive" to describe its features. The view of the ocean from the balcony was breathtaking, like a priceless piece of artwork.

The suite consisted of three bedrooms and a living area, with a tiny alcove kitchen at the end of the living room opposite the balcony. The eager bellhop pointed out all the amenities, every last one of them, including the limited-edition apple-scented shampoo in the bathroom.

I tipped him generously with Uncle Sam's money, and that was when he mentioned he'd recently applied for a visa to enter the United States. Any help I might give him would be appreciated.

His name was Mateo Santiago.

I had him write it down for me.

I took the largest bedroom, the one with the king-sized bed, because the prestigious David Awerbuch would have been expected to do so.

And, just in case someone might be tempted to think the room belonged to them, I took some clothes out of my suitcase and placed them on the bed. As I did so, I realized Uncle Harold would have preferred for me to hang them in the closet instead.

As soon I opened the refrigerator door to get a can of soda, there was a knock at the door.

Three short raps. Pause. One rap. Pause. One rap.

Since I didn't have a weapon at my disposal, and I certainly wasn't about to look through the peephole—Neal Fredrick had lost an eye in Budapest doing that—I slid open the glass door leading out to the balcony.

If push came to shove—so to speak—I could at least give an unwelcomed guest a quick exit from the seventeenth floor.

However, as expected, when I opened the door, Sam Wylie was there.

"Hey, Cowboy," I said. "Come on in. Put your feet up."

"Cut the cowboy talk, Titus. It ain't you."

Wylie sauntered into the room carrying a worn messenger bag in the shape of a saddlebag and sat down on one of the modern Danish sofas. Once he'd laid aside the messenger bag, he promptly put his feet up on the glass-topped coffee table. I wasn't surprised to see he was wearing a pair of scuffed leather cowboy boots.

Sam Wylie was a Texan, and although he'd been living in Latin America for many years, he still refused to let anyone forget he was from the great state of Texas. Indeed, he looked the part of a native son from the Lone Star state.

He was a couple of inches over six feet tall, broad-shouldered with a narrow waist and hands as big as baseball gloves. His long, dirty blond hair was tied back in a ponytail.

Evidently, he'd left his cowboy hat in his room.

Today, he was wearing a pair of sharply creased, starched jeans, cinched at the waist by an expensive-looking leather belt—with a buckle made in the shape of Texas—and a short-sleeved dark blue cotton shirt. Attached to his belt was a gun holster.

I had no doubt the pistol inside it was fully loaded, meticulously maintained, and easily retrievable.

Although Wylie was the Agency's chief of station in Venezuela, his position at the American Embassy in Caracas was listed as Embassy Security Chief. Because of this title, he was able to carry the loaded pistol wherever he went.

Wylie pointed at my drink. "Got another one of those?"

I retrieved another can of soda from the kitchen and sat down opposite him on a matching sofa.

He popped the lid on the can, took a swig, and said, "Nice digs you got here. It's me and two other guys in a room half this size down on the tenth floor overlooking the cooling unit."

"It can't be as bad as that flea-infested hotel back in Managua. I stayed in that hole for over a year."

He nodded. "Yeah. Yeah, I remember that place. You forgot to mention the rats, though. Don't forget those rats. Those rats were as big as cats."

I hated small talk. Always had.

It just never made any sense to me.

I decided not to do any more back and forth with him, hoping he'd get the hint and just give me the operational update. We could reminisce some other time.

If at all.

Wylie and I didn't have much to talk about when it came to reminiscing about Nicaragua. I'd worked with Toby Bledsoe when I'd been in Managua years ago, and Wylie had been paired up with Colin Standsford. Since then, we'd occasionally run into each other at Agency headquarters whenever our down times had coincided, but we'd never worked together on the same mission since our time in Nicaragua.

However, I liked Wylie—despite his weird Texas talk—and I'd found his field reports in the Agency archives to be insightful. I wasn't exactly sure what he thought about me, but someone once told me he sometimes referred to me as "that Yankee dude from Michigan."

I'd always preferred to think of myself as someone from America's Heartland.

And never as a dude.

I didn't reply to Wylie's comment about the rats, and after a few moments of silence, he picked up the messenger bag he'd brought in with him.

"First things first," he said, reaching inside the bag and pulling out a Glock pistol. "If you'd prefer something else, let me know."

He handed the weapon over to me, and then he watched as I did a quick inspection.

"I'm not picky," I said. "This will do."

"The rest of your gear is inside the bag."

He tossed it over to me, and I took a quick peek inside. "I presume you've got a similar delivery for Mitchell?"

"Yeah, I'll bring it up when he gets here. Your FO also requested a weapon."

"Olivia? She's strictly the handler for our mission; not really active operational."

He quickly dismissed my remark. "She said she wanted a weapons package, and I got her one. She was pretty insistent about it."

While most handlers preferred to run an operation from a command and control location away from the action, I'd known a few who wanted a more hands-on approach. Evidently, Olivia was of the latter persuasion.

I decided I might try and persuade her otherwise.

Wylie began his operational update by describing the surveillance he'd put in place at the Concorde Marina where *El Mano Fierro* would be berthed. After that, he gave me the names and phone numbers of the watchers he had on site at the dock and told me they were prepared to follow Ahmed and Flores once the yacht made port. He also mentioned the address of the operation's safe house on the island where the communications equipment had been installed.

He said, "If you should need any extra weapons, you can pick them up at that location."

Wylie was a veteran of the game. Only an operative who had been burned before would have realized the importance of disseminating every tidbit about the operation's setup to an incoming principal. Now, should something unforeseen happen to Wylie, I'd have all the info I needed to complete the mission without him.

"It's a good protocol, Sam, and I appreciate the fact you've covered all the bases with me. I usually have to ask for this stuff."

"Yeah, well, I remembered what a stickler you were for details."

"Funny, I remember the same thing about you. We're both still alive, so that must mean something."

As soon as the remark was out of my mouth, I thought of Toby Bledsoe. Then, I saw Wylie's face, and I realized both of us had been thinking the same thing.

"Sorry to hear about Toby," he said, shaking his head. "We lost a good man there."

I agreed with him, and then I filled him in on the details of how Bledsoe had met his untimely death. These were details I knew he hadn't received in the Agency's daily COS briefing. When I finished, we sat there without saying a word, caught up in our own personal grief over Bledsoe's murder.

It was Wylie who broke the silence.

"There's one more thing I should mention."

Wylie's cell phone started to vibrate.

"The training camp—"

Suddenly, he cut himself off in mid-sentence when he glanced down at the caller ID.

"Wylie here. What's up?"

After listening to the caller for a few minutes, he got up and walked out to the balcony. During the conversation, I noticed he was flexing his free hand, and I tensed up just watching him.

However, as he walked back inside, he sounded calm. "Keep the team in place. I'll get back to you."

"Trouble?" I asked, when he ended the conversation.

"Roberto Montilla didn't make his flight from Caracas."

Before I could respond, there was a knock at the door.

I grabbed the Glock from the couch and stuck it in the back of my pants.

"Who is it?" I yelled.

"El botones Mateo."

"It's just the bellhop," I said to Wylie.

When I opened the door, I found Mateo Santiago in the hallway, along with Olivia McConnell and Ben Mitchell.

♦♦♦♦

After reassuring Mateo I'd be happy to explain the room's amenities to my colleagues, I quickly ushered him out of the room.

As soon as I closed the door, Wylie started telling Olivia about Roberto's disappearance. However, instead of having him immediately give her the full details of the report, she told him to wait until she'd brewed herself a cup of coffee.

Wylie shrugged and resumed his place on the sofa, putting his cell phone directly in front of him on the coffee table. A few seconds later, I saw him pick it up again, as if keeping tabs on it would help him discover Roberto's whereabouts.

Meanwhile, I took a seat in a corner of the room, because the spot offered me a full view of the room and the people in it, while Mitchell pulled out his iPad and sat down on the sofa opposite Wylie.

Olivia was in the kitchen filling the coffee pot with water, and for some reason, this struck me as ironic.

Here she was—a woman who absolutely despised being treated

differently than a man—puttering around in the kitchen, while the men sat around doing nothing.

I wanted to point this out to her.

I decided not to do so.

When the coffee was ready, she took her mug over to a bar, which separated the kitchen from the living area. Placing her mug on the countertop, she pulled out a leather barstool and perched herself on it like a judge at a tennis match.

"Okay, Sam," she said, sipping her coffee, "tell me about Roberto."

Wylie laid his cell phone back down on the coffee table and looked up at her.

"As I said before, the surveillance team outside the Montilla residence saw Roberto, along with his wife and daughter, put their luggage in a taxi and head for the airport around seven o'clock this morning. About twenty minutes later, they lost them in heavy traffic, but, since they thought he was headed for the airport, they simply notified the team at the terminal to keep an eye out for his arrival."

Olivia looked down at her watch. "That was nearly three hours ago. Why wasn't I told about this sooner?"

Wylie clenched his jaw. "Well, ma'am, I didn't get this information myself until a few minutes ago."

Olivia's face registered disapproval.

However, I couldn't tell if she disliked Wylie's answer or just his way of addressing her.

She waved her hand at him. "Go on."

He sighed. "It's pretty simple. Montilla never arrived at the airport and the plane took off without him."

"That's unacceptable. Someone from your surveillance crew should have called you as soon as Roberto was out of sight."

"I'm not one of those . . . what do you call them? . . . micro managers. The boys thought they had it covered."

"Well, the boys—"

"Maybe he just got stuck in traffic," Mitchell said. He pointed down at his iPad. "This map shows it's over an hour's drive from Roberto's house out to the airport. With heavy traffic, it could take even longer. Maybe he simply got stuck in traffic and missed his flight."

Wylie shook his head. "There are flights to Porlamar every hour. It's been over three hours now and he still hasn't checked in. That scenario doesn't seem likely."

I spoke up, "Roberto's wife and daughter weren't scheduled to come with him. He was attending the conference alone."

Wylie looked surprised. "Is that right?"

Olivia jumped in before I had a chance to answer. "That's right. He only reserved a room for one person."

"So you think he's skedaddled?" Wylie asked.

Olivia and I looked at each other, but neither of us said a word.

Wylie asked, "What's going on?"

Although she addressed Wylie's question, Olivia kept her eyes on me the whole time. "Well, Sam, the reason he's gone missing is that we rocked his boat. We created confusion in his world."

It was hard for me to read how Olivia felt about Montilla not showing up in Porlamar, but I was happy at this turn of events.

If Roberto Montilla weren't around to help Ahmed carry out his contract, then Ahmed would have to do the footwork himself.

While Ahmed Al-Amin was at the trade conference making those preparations, I planned to be behind him every step of the way, discovering his target and preventing him from fulfilling his contract.

My plan proved to be naive at best.

Chapter 34

While Olivia was getting out her laptop to contact Langley, I filled Wylie in on the details of the call Roberto had received from the American Embassy in Costa Rica notifying him of his son's death.

When I'd finished updating him, he said, "Ahmed just might need to rustle him up some different kind of help once he gets here."

Although I wouldn't have phrased it that way, I agreed with him. "My thoughts exactly."

Olivia said, "I just sent the Ops Center a flash priority on Roberto's missing status. Once they acknowledge it, I'll do an uplink and discuss how we'll proceed with this development."

A few minutes later, she closed her computer and set it aside. "Now," she said, "give me your assessment. What's going on with Roberto? Why did he miss his flight?"

Mitchell seemed surprised at the question. "Isn't it obvious? He's grieving over his son's death and wants to be left alone."

Olivia shook her head. "Don't be foolish, Ben. This conference could make or break his career. Despite Ernesto's death, he wouldn't miss it."

I saw Mitchell's face turned rigid at Olivia's dismissive tone. For a moment, I thought he was going to say something. Instead, he turned his attention to his iPad and kept quiet.

Wylie said, "I believe you're right, ma'am. The Venezuelan president believes this trade conference will raise his stature in the world. If Roberto wants to keep his job, he'll be at the conference."

"There could be any number of reasons Roberto missed his flight this morning," I said. "Maybe Ben's right, and he needed a few more hours with his family before flying to the conference."

I saw Mitchell glance up from his iPad.

I thought he looked surprised at my affirmation.

"Or maybe," I continued, "Roberto put his wife and daughter on a flight to Costa Rica so they could be near Ernesto. He may plan to catch a flight to Margarita later this afternoon."

Olivia said, "I asked the Agency to check on all the airlines. We'll know soon enough if anyone in the Montilla family was booked on a flight out of Caracas today."

"I could have had my people check on the airlines for you," Wylie said.

The moment Olivia raised her eyebrows, I knew he was about to receive a lecture from her on her expertise at running an operation. Before she had chance to do that, I started peppering Wylie with questions.

"Do you have any sources at the Trade Ministry you could use to locate Roberto? Or what about his wife? Could you call her employer and find out if she told them she wasn't coming in to work today?"

Wylie scrolled through his phone. "Wait a minute. I jotted down a few notes about Roberto's family on my phone."

"His wife's name is Marianna and she isn't employed," Olivia said, "but she does do some charity work with *La Fundana,* the children's rights organization. They may know something."

Although I would have expected Carlton to have these facts at his fingertips, I was surprised to hear Olivia recite Roberto's bio from memory.

Wylie typed some notes on his phone. "I'll see what I can find out."

Olivia said, "You should also check on their daughter, Emma. She attends school at *Instituto Educacionale de La Salle*. Find out if her parents called them about her absence from school today."

Wylie stood to his feet, adjusted his belt buckle, and said, "I'll go contact some of my sources. If I hear anything from my boys in Caracas, I'll let you know."

"See that you do," Olivia said.

"Oh, you bet."

♦♦♦♦

When Wylie left the suite, Olivia announced she needed to establish an uplink with the Operations Center at Langley and confer with Carlton and Salazar about events on the ground.

"I saw a desk in here," she said, wheeling her suitcase toward the master bedroom. "That's where I'll do my setup. I'll brief you as soon as I'm done."

As she started to close the door behind her, she said, "And, Titus, you'll need to get your stuff out of here when I'm done. I'm taking this room."

The prestigious David Awerbuch had just been jettisoned from his bedroom by one of his lackeys.

Mitchell closed his iPad and walked out on the balcony. "Man, this view is something else."

I followed him out to the balcony. However, it wasn't because I was interested in the landscape.

"How was your flight?" I asked. "Did you and Olivia manage to bond with each other?"

He laughed. "Would you believe she asked me the same question about you?"

"Is that so?"

Mitchell turned around and faced me. "She asked me how you and I were getting along."

I was hoping he'd elaborate on his answer without any prodding from me, so I didn't say anything.

"Would you like to know what I said to her?"

"Only if you want to tell me."

"I told her I get along with you about as well as I get along with the Senator."

"Ouch."

He smiled. "Since she knows him pretty well herself, she completely understood."

"Olivia knows your father?"

He nodded. "She was the DDO's congressional liaison for a couple of years. She worked closely with some of my father's staff from the Senate Intelligence Committee. That's how I met her."

Another surprise.

Surprises seemed to be occurring on a regular basis with this guy.

"I didn't realize you knew Olivia before she was introduced at the briefing yesterday."

"I was only around her a couple of times. The first time was when I was visiting my father's office. Believe me, it wasn't a pleasant experience."

"Were you Agency then?"

"Barely. I'd been out of Camp Peary for a couple of months, but I was still awaiting assignment. However, she treated me as if I were just out of high school. What made it worse, the Senator never mentioned anything about our family relationship to her. Later, she saw me at headquarters and seemed genuinely surprised when she found out I was working for the CIA. That's when I told her my father was Senator Mitchell."

I didn't ask him if Olivia had apologized for her mistake.

I knew she hadn't done so.

Neither one of us was very good at apologies.

♦♦♦♦

About the time Olivia came out of the bedroom, Wylie arrived back in the suite. He was carrying his messenger bag, and it looked a lot heavier than when he'd left. When he began distributing the goodies inside, I understood why.

First, he handed Mitchell a handgun. It was a Glock, like the one he'd given me, and then he took out a smaller pistol and presented it to Olivia. It was a sub-compact Kimber, something a woman might carry, and I immediately wondered if she would protest his choice of firearm for her.

However, following her conversation with the Ops Center, Olivia appeared distracted, and when she took the weapon from Wylie, she barely looked at it before slipping it inside her purse.

"Any news from your team in Caracas?" she asked Wylie.

"They haven't found Roberto or his family yet, if that's what you're asking. However, I did get in touch with a source in Traffic Control who said they would get me the CCTV feed from this morning's rush hour. I figure it might take some time for my computer guys to study the videos and determine where Roberto was headed when we lost him. But, if we get lucky, we might know something in a few hours."

"And your other phone calls?"

"Well, ma'am, they were all a dead end. No one from *La Fundana* had heard from Marianna Montilla this morning. And no one at the kid's school had heard from the parents. My sources at the Trade Ministry seemed surprised I was even asking about Roberto, because they said he should be on the island by now."

"So, Roberto didn't contact anyone at the Ministry this morning?"

"Not the people I called."

"Interesting."

"I also found it interesting that none of his co-workers knew anything about Ernesto's death. As far as I can tell, Roberto hasn't told anyone about the death of his son."

"That's odd," I said. "I would have expected him to share his grief with at least some of his colleagues."

Wylie agreed. "The whole thing's beginning to seem a little twisted."

Olivia walked over to the bar stool and swiveled it around so that she could face the three of us. When she took her seat, she said, "The Ops Center couldn't find any airline reservations for the Montillas. Wherever the three of them were going this morning, it wasn't to the airport, or, if it was, they didn't book a flight under their own name."

I said, "If the news about Ernesto's murder caused Roberto to take his family and go into hiding, we need to figure out why, and we need to do it soon."

Olivia showed no sign of agreeing with me, so I continued to press my point. "His behavior runs counter to the role we assumed he would play in Ahmed's mission, and it's time we reassess how Ahmed may be planning to use Roberto once he arrives on the island."

Mitchell spoke up. "Roberto's disappearance could be something he was planning all along; it could even be connected to Ahmed's target."

Wylie said. "I'm betting Ahmed's target is John Luckenbill."

Olivia said, "I was told Luckenbill hasn't changed his mind about having extra security. He's your charge, Sam. Can't you convince him he needs to add some extra security?"

Wylie shook his head. "John's an ex-Marine. He says he's been in far more dangerous situations than this, and it's impossible to convince him to take extra precautions. He just doesn't believe there's enough evidence to prove he's in any kind of danger. That's why we need to concentrate on finding Roberto. I agree with Titus. We need to know where all the players are."

Olivia shook her head. "No, we can't be concerned about Roberto's disappearance right now."

I started to protest, but then she hurried on. "His disappearance has to be put on hold because the timetable for the yacht's arrival in Porlamar has just been revised."

"Why?" I asked.

"*El Mano Fierro* will make port around three o'clock today instead of five."

"So what happens when she docks?"

"Under ordinary circumstances, a Customs and Immigration official from the Port Authority's office would board her. The Ops Center has been monitoring communications between the ship's captain and the Port Authority, and in this instance, the port captain himself will be the one coming onboard the yacht to clear her passengers through customs."

"That explains a lot," I said.

Wylie said, "Yeah, the port captain must be on someone's payroll."

Olivia nodded. "C. J. seems to believe the head of Porlamar's Port Authority is being bankrolled by the Zeta cartel, and that's why he'll be the one processing the passengers' passports and clearing Javier Flores through immigration, when he uses Ernesto's passport."

I said, "He's probably right."

"The port captain won't be the only person boarding the yacht, though," Olivia said. "The captain has arranged for a fuel delivery immediately upon arrival, and Carlton believes this is a unique opportunity for us."

"What kind of opportunity?" Mitchell asked.

Knowing Carlton as I did, I ventured a guess. "It's an opportunity for the two of us to board *El Mano Fierro* and plant some listening devices."

Olivia nodded. "That's right. Since Ahmed hasn't made any hotel reservations on the island, Douglas believes he'll be using the yacht as his base of operations. The best way for us to monitor his activities—short of having human intel on the boat—is to put some listening ears onboard."

Olivia explained the plan for boarding the yacht and planting the audio devices—a plan with Carlton's fingerprints all over it. Even so, as she outlined the procedure, I could tell she'd scrutinized the possibilities from every angle and tried to anticipate some scenarios Mitchell and I might encounter.

I made a few minor adjustments to the plan, just refinements really, and then I pointed out the type of clothing we'd need for us to get on the yacht without arousing suspicion.

In different circumstances, I would have picked up the items myself. However, if the prestigious David Awerbuch were seen traipsing around the budget shops of Porlamar looking for cheap, discounted clothing, it might look suspicious.

To Olivia's credit, she agreed with my assessment and volunteered to go with Mitchell to pick up the items for our yachting adventure.

As the two of them were about to leave, I said, "Could you pick us up something to eat on your way back?"

Mitchell asked, "Pizza sound okay with everybody?"

"Yeah, but have them hold—"

"The pepperoni," Olivia said. "I'm not likely to forget that."

Olivia's response caused Mitchell to raise his eyebrows at me, but I ignored him.

♦♦♦♦

When I returned to the living room, Wylie had just finished pouring himself a cup of Olivia's coffee.

He raised his mug in the air when he saw me. "You don't think she'd mind, do you?"

"Are you kidding, Sam? She wouldn't give it a second thought."

He shook his head as if he didn't believe me.

Just to make him feel better, I poured myself a cup.

"Why don't you finish telling me about the other thing?" I said.

He looked puzzled. "The other thing?"

"Before you got the phone call about Montilla, you said you needed to tell me one other thing, something about training."

"Oh, yeah," he said, "I wanted to tell you about the Hezbollah training camp here. I don't know whether you know it or not, but members of Hezbollah have been invading Venezuela like ants at a Texas picnic for more than ten years now."

"I saw your field reports in the archives a few days ago," I said. "It sounds like the Venezuelan government has been encouraging Islamists to immigrate to this country. It's no wonder they've been arriving in droves."

Wylie nodded. "Muslims are coming here because they're getting tax breaks for their businesses. The government is also making it possible for them to build mosques, hospitals, Islamic schools, or just about anything else the local Imam says will benefit the Islamic community."

"We both know this is problematic for the U.S. The more Hispanics they recruit, the easier it will be for their members to arrive in the States as simple laborers in search of jobs."

"I think it's already a problem. That's why I've been warning the Agency about a Hezbollah youth camp right here on the island. You probably saw that in my field reports too."

"Yeah, that youth camp didn't sound like a place I'd send my kid.

"They call it a camp for youth, but after I asked Salazar to have the NSA shoot some satellite images of the place, the Agency analysts agreed it's a militant training camp, and it's being run by some top-notch Hezbollah instructors. Don't get me wrong. I'm not saying Ahmed will have any contact with the camp once he arrives here, but I wanted you to be aware of its location anyway."

"Salazar didn't even mention it during the briefing."

"Since the training camp isn't connected to the cartel, that doesn't surprise me. When I learned Ahmed was coming here to the island, I brought it up with Salazar, but he said there wasn't much chance Ahmed would go near the camp. He's probably right. Most likely, once Ahmed fulfils his contract, he'll leave Margarita Island pronto."

Wylie pulled out a small military-grade laptop from a side pocket of his messenger bag. "The camp is called *Campamento de la Juventud Laguna*, and it's west of Porlamar on the other side of the island. As you might expect, the location is pretty remote."

Wylie opened up his laptop and clicked on a file. "Take a look."

I studied the map for a few minutes, and although I hated to admit it, I had to agree with Salazar that the chances of Ahmed hooking up with some militants at a jihadist's training camp several miles from Porlamar were pretty slim.

"The instructors come and go on a rotating basis," Wylie explained. "Most of them don't stay on the island except for a few weeks at a time."

"So who's in charge?"

Wylie displayed a couple of photographs on the screen. "The day-to-day operations are handled by this guy, Salvador Rascon. He's a Venezuelan who converted to Islam several years ago. He lives at the camp, takes care of maintenance, and manages the instructors. On the surface, he appears to be the camp commander."

Wylie pointed to a second photo. "But it's this man, Rehman Zaidi, who's really in charge of *Campamento Laguna*."

I studied the photo of Zaidi.

The camera had caught him disembarking from a plane at El Caribe airport. He was squinting into the sun, about to put on a pair of dark glasses. Although his eyes were half-closed, I could see they were blue—unlike most men of Arabic descent—and that his nose wasn't as sharply pointed or as long as a typical Arab male.

Although his facial characteristics were noteworthy, what drew my attention was his missing limb. His left arm had either been severed or surgically removed at the elbow.

"What can you tell me about Zaidi?"

"I know what you're thinking. He could be a bomb maker."

I nodded. "It's a fairly typical injury in that line of work and might explain why he's been banished to South America to run a militant training camp."

"I agree, but so far, our analysts haven't been able to come up with very much on his background. He came here from Syria about three years ago. He lives in Caracas and makes his living teaching mathematics in a secondary Islamic school run by Imam Wajdi Raza. He's the highest-ranking Imam in Venezuela. Nothing in the Venezuelan Islamic community gets done without his approval."

I took one last look at the photographs. "Would you mind doing me a favor?" I asked. "Copy all your files on Rehman Zaidi and *Campamento Laguna* and put them in an encrypted email to Douglas Carlton. Use this address."

I quickly scribbled down an email address Carlton and I had used before to bypass internal security.

As I handed it over to Wylie, I said, "If there's any other information you think Douglas should know about Hezbollah's activities in Venezuela, write it up as a separate document."

Wylie slipped the piece of paper in his jeans pocket. "Douglas is a division head. He has access to all my field reports. Why would he need to see what's in these files?"

"I once promised him that if I ever came across intel I knew he didn't have, I'd let him know immediately. Those photographs weren't in the Agency archives. Maybe that's the result of a backlog or a simple oversight on someone's part, but, since I know my Ops Officer is missing intel, I'm keeping that promise."

"Okay, sure, I'll get it to him immediately. Technically, though, Douglas isn't your Operational Officer for this mission. Olivia McConnell is."

"Douglas Carlton may not be in country, Sam, but believe me, he's my handler for this mission. Otherwise, I wouldn't be in Venezuela."

Chapter 35

After Mitchell and I arrived at Concorde Marina on the east side of Porlamar Bay around three o'clock, we stayed hunkered down inside our rented Nissan for over an hour.

The whole time, though, we had our eyes on *El Mano Fierro.* It had anchored in Porlamar Bay along the sea wall approximately two hundred yards away from our location.

We were waiting for the arrival of the port captain, a man named Miguel Cobos. As soon as Cobos arrived and boarded *El Mano Fierro,* Mitchell and I would get on a fuel boat and make our way over to the yacht to begin the task of refueling—not to mention the task of leaving behind some electronic listening devices.

Earlier, Wylie had made arrangements with Juan Ortiz, the owner of one of the refueling stations, to use his boat and deliver fuel to the yacht. I wasn't sure what kind of story Wylie had told Juan, but I knew it involved a great deal of cash—American dollars, not bolivares.

As we sat there observing the yacht, I told Mitchell about watching Hernando come aboard *El Mano Fierro* in Limón while I was at the Holiday Inn Express in Grand Blanc, Michigan.

Mitchell made a joke about my lounging around a hotel room in my pajamas while he was out doing all the work. I smiled, but all I could think about was saying goodbye to Nikki Saxon in that same hotel room.

I'm not closing the door; I'm doing everything I can to keep it open.

"Does it make you sick?"

For a split second, I thought Mitchell had asked me a question about my relationship with Nikki.

I tried to refocus. "Does what make me sick?"

"Being so near the water; seeing those boats bobbing around out there on the waves like that."

"No, it doesn't make me sick. I got sick at the boathouse that night because of something I ate on the plane."

"It's nothing to be ashamed of you know. A college buddy of mine had the same condition. He got sick every time he got near the water. In fact, he always took a Dramamine whenever he went to the beach."

Even if a pill would take care of my nausea, I wouldn't take anything that would make me drowsy—especially when I was about to be in the same neighborhood as Ahmed.

Once again, I told Mitchell I didn't have a problem.

I don't think he bought it, and I felt sure, when we took the fuel boat out to the yacht, he'd be watching me for any sign I might be ready to empty the contents of my stomach into the waters of the Caribbean.

That wasn't going to happen, though, because I'd found a way to deal with my situation.

Earlier in the day, when Olivia had first announced Carlton's plan to use the fuel boat to get aboard the yacht, I'd experienced a few moments of panic at the thought of being out on the water. But then, I tried what Javad had once told me he did whenever he thought the Iranian secret police had him under surveillance.

"I breathe a prayer and keep on walking," he said.

When I'd questioned him about how that worked, he said, "You just ask God to help you. With every breath, you ask God to help. Focus on breathing and asking. Just breathe and ask. Breathe and ask and keep on walking."

Since I was up on the seventeenth floor of the Wyndham hotel when I'd remembered this, I kept my seat and didn't walk anywhere.

But, I did take a deep breath and ask God for help.

Then, I did it again.

And again.

Within minutes, it felt as if my heart rate had returned to normal, and my nausea had disappeared.

Would breathing a prayer work when I was on the fuel boat and headed out to a rendezvous with Ahmed's yacht?

"There he is," Mitchell said, pointing to a car pulling up to the pier.

It was time to find out.

♦♦♦♦

The government lettering on the side of the late model vehicle indicated it belonged to Customs and Immigration.

The person getting out of the car, who I assumed to be Miguel Cobos, looked like a typical Latin American bureaucrat. He was wearing a light green guayabera shirt, wrinkled brown khakis, and a pair of slip-on loafers. In his hand was a battered brown satchel.

I said, "We'll stay in place until he goes aboard the yacht."

"Works for me."

Cobos didn't appear to be in any hurry. As he made his way along the pier, he stopped and greeted several people, and then he had an extended conversation with some men working on a fishing boat.

A few minutes later, he walked over to a soft drink machine. Before depositing his money, though, he turned his head in the direction of *El Mano Fierro*. Then, as if he'd changed his mind, he put the coins back in his pocket and continued making his way down the boardwalk toward the yacht.

Mitchell said, "What was that all about? Couldn't he afford a soda?"

"Maybe he decided to keep his hard-earned cash, since someone will probably offer him a free drink on the boat."

As Cobos approached the yacht, a man suddenly emerged from the shadows of a bait shack on the other side of the boardwalk. Carrying what appeared to be a large black golf bag, the man quickly crossed the short distance to the boat and followed Cobos up the gangway and onto the bridge of *El Mano Fierro*.

I said, "Or maybe he was just killing time until his golf buddy showed up."

When they arrived on the bridge, a man in a red ball cap greeted the two men. Then, the three of them walked past the Jacuzzi and under a white awning near the pilothouse. Seconds later, they disappeared from sight.

"What just happened?" Mitchell asked. "Who was the guy with the golf bag?

"Let's go find out."

♦♦♦♦

Earlier in the day, when we'd been at the hotel mapping out how to get on the yacht, Mitchell had volunteered to pilot the fuel boat out to the yacht. He said he knew his way around boats because of the summers he'd spent on Martha's Vineyard.

I had voiced no objections to his wearing the captain's hat. Better him than me.

The moment we boarded the rickety old vessel at the refueling station, Mitchell immediately went inside the pilothouse and started fooling around with the instruments.

Whether or not he knew what he was doing was yet to be determined.

Meanwhile, I checked out the two large diesel storage tanks at the back of the boat. The dials and hoses looked exactly like the photographs Wylie had shown me back at the hotel.

As I inspected the boat, the phrase "old rust bucket" came to mind. The odd-looking vessel resembled a cross between a small barge and a medium-sized houseboat and was in need of a good paint job, not to mention a few structural repairs.

When Mitchell powered up the motor, the noises from the engine made me wonder if the thing was even capable of pulling away from the dock. Within seconds, though, we were moving out across the water with the smell of diesel fuel trailing in our wake.

Suddenly, the disturbing scene from *Danger On The High Seas* fired across my neurons, and a familiar feeling threatened to engulf me.

I tried breathing a prayer.

Breathe and ask.

I glanced up and saw Mitchell watching me from the pilothouse.

I gave him a thumbs up.

Breathe and ask and keep on walking.

The boat picked up speed and rapidly closed in on *El Mano Fierro*.

Breathe and ask.

When we were within a hundred yards of the yacht, a man wearing a Boston Red Sox cap, lifted a pair of binoculars to his eyes and watched our approach from the bridge.

His actions didn't surprise me.

Ahmed was a cautious man.

As soon as Mitchell started maneuvering the fuel boat alongside the yacht, the Red Sox fan lowered the binoculars and yelled at us.

"*Cuidado. Cuidado,*" he cautioned, warning us not to allow the diesel-laden boat to ram the expensive yacht.

Mitchell handled the cumbersome boat like an expert, and within five minutes or so, I was attaching the hose from the 20,000-gallon tank to the yacht so the refueling process could begin.

The Operations Center had told Olivia if the pump gauges were set at the lowest possible setting, then refueling the yacht should take at least an hour. I followed her instructions and adjusted the pump speed and the flow rate. Then, I calculated I had just enough time to plant the listening devices before the yacht's fuel tanks were topped off.

As soon as I gave Mitchell a nod, he came out of the pilothouse and handed the crewman an invoice, joking with him about the island's nightlife. Once the two of them had started exchanging stories, I announced I was headed inside the pilothouse to take a snooze.

I made sure the Red Sox fan had his eyes on me the whole time.

While waiting inside the cramped quarters, I listened for Mitchell's pre-arranged code that would let me know the guy had turned away from the pilothouse and was no longer interested in my whereabouts. Once I heard the words we'd agreed on, I grabbed the toolkit supplied by Wylie, slipped out the door, and scampered up the yacht's side ladder.

After determining no other crewmen were on the bridge, I made my way over to the stairs leading down to the lower deck and the crew's quarters.

From there, I'd planned to access the rest of the ship and plant the devices.

Within minutes, though, my plans were a distant memory.

♦♦♦♦

When I reached the lower deck, I inserted an earpiece from my toolkit and activated the wireless communication feed between Olivia and me.

She and Wylie had left the hotel and gone to a safe house on the island in order to establish a direct hookup with the Ops Center back at Langley.

Olivia said, "We have you on the grid."

"Copy that."

"Are you a go?"

"Affirmative."

As I moved down the passageway toward the guest suites, I told Olivia about the man who'd boarded the yacht with Cobos. She sounded dissatisfied because of my sketchy description of the man, but I didn't respond because I'd reached the first guest room by then.

I listened outside the door for a few seconds.

Nothing.

I went in, attached a bug to the lamp on the bedside table, and I was out of there in ten seconds. I did the same to the second guest room.

The hard part came next.

"On my way up to the main deck now."

"Copy."

As I got near the stairwell leading up to the main deck, I could hear someone coming down the stairs toward me. I quickly moved over to a tiny lavatory near the crew's quarters and squeezed inside.

I clicked my comms unit once to let Olivia know I was going silent. Moments later, I heard the voices of two men in the hallway outside the lavatory.

As they passed by the door, I heard them arguing. At that moment, I realized I'd either hit the jackpot or been dealt a losing hand because they were communicating with each other in Arabic.

I opened the door a crack.

Down the hallway, about thirty feet away, I saw Ahmed Al-Amin approaching the guest suites where I'd just finished planting the bugs.

Following closely behind him was the guy who'd come onboard with Cobos. He still had the black golf bag over his shoulder.

But now, as I saw Ahmed reach inside the bag, I realized it didn't just contain a set of golf clubs. There was a high-powered rifle in there as well. And, what I hadn't been able to see before was clear to me now. The man's upper arm, which he'd placed against the outer strap of the bag, had been severed at the elbow.

Rehman Zaidi, the Hezbollah commander of *Campamento Laguna,* had come aboard the yacht to deliver weapons to Ahmed.

As the two men entered the guest suite, Ahmed asked Zaidi, "Why hasn't he checked in yet?"

He shut the door before Zaidi answered him.

"Activate number two," I whispered, "and send me the feed."

"Copy."

Seconds later, I was able to hear Zaidi's reply being transmitted by the bug I'd just planted inside the guest suite.

"He hasn't cancelled the reservation. He may still show up tomorrow."

"No, if he's not taking your calls, then something must have happened."

"He could have been in an accident."

"Wouldn't that be ironic?"

"I have men in place. We'll find him."

"There are only two days left on the timetable. If it's not done by then, I won't get paid. It's imperative I get to Caracas and find him immediately."

"The last flight to Caracas has left for the day."

"Then book me on the first flight in the morning."

"Will you still need the rifle?"

"Once I've assessed the situation, I'll let you know my requirements. Take the weapon with you, though. Don't leave it here."

"Of course."

"You understand I must get to Caracas in the morning?"

"I will arrange it. I would be most honored if you would stay at my apartment while you're in Caracas."

"Of course, but you must book separate flights for us. I'll take a taxi

from the airport and meet you there."

"I'll write down the address for you. It's apartment 1705."

"There's no need to write it down. I know the address."

While the conversation between Ahmed and Zaidi was taking place, I was fighting an overwhelming urge to enter the guest suite and deliver the kind of justice I knew Ahmed deserved, not only for the murder of Simon Wassermann, but also for the horrible atrocities he'd committed against Ernesto Montilla.

That desire had become almost overwhelming to me.

The moment I realized I'd removed the Glock from my holster and chambered a round, I decided it was time to abandon ship.

I quickly put away my gun.

Then, I retraced my steps up the stairwell and back across the bridge, making it inside the pilothouse without being seen by the Red Sox fan, who was still engaged in a conversation with Mitchell.

A few minutes later, I came out of the pilothouse.

As I made my way over to the storage tanks, I stretched my limbs and rubbed my eyes as if I'd just been awakened from a nap. The look on Mitchell's face told me I might have been overdoing the drama a little bit.

Once I'd disconnected the fuel hoses from the yacht, Mitchell waved goodbye to the Red Sox fan and fired up the engines, navigating us away from the ship and back toward the refueling station.

The moment we were out over the open water, Mitchell turned and yelled at me, trying to make himself heard above the racket of the engine.

"Did you have any trouble?" he shouted.

I shook my head. "Not a bit."

"Good. Maybe now we'll know where Ahmed's headed when he leaves the yacht."

"He's headed to Caracas."

Mitchell cupped his hand to his ear. "What?"

"We're on our way to Caracas."

Chapter 36

Once Mitchell and I returned to the pier, Olivia instructed us to head over to the Agency's safe house, which was located on the outskirts of Porlamar. Along the way, I filled Mitchell in on the conversation I'd heard between Ahmed and Rehman Zaidi.

As he maneuvered the Nissan up a narrow mountainous road, he said, "They had to be talking about Roberto Montilla. If Ahmed is so desperate to find him, he must be more important to Ahmed's mission than we first thought."

"Or maybe Roberto *is* the mission," I said.

Before Mitchell had a chance to respond, he pulled in the driveway of a sprawling Caribbean style villa with a magnificent view of the ocean.

"Impressive," he said.

It wasn't the three-bedroom bungalow I'd pictured when Wylie had first mentioned a safe house on the island, and its open landscaping and access to the ocean made me wonder how secure it was. However, I couldn't deny it was a beautiful piece of property.

One of Wylie's surveillance guys met us at the door. "They're in the dining room," he said, pointing down a long hallway.

We found Olivia at the head of a rectangular wooden table that could seat at least sixteen people. She had a yellow highlighter in her hand, and she was scrutinizing some documents.

Wylie was standing by the windows at the other end of the room. Behind him was a spectacular view of an infinity pool surrounded by a terraced garden, and on the horizon, just beyond the pool, I could see sailboats skimming across the water.

As soon as we entered the room, Olivia picked up one of the documents and waved it in the air. "I just received the English translation of Ahmed's conversation. There's a lot for us to talk about here."

"Ben and I made it back safely, Olivia. Thank you for your concern."

She appeared unfazed by my sarcasm. "I never doubted it for a moment." She pointed down at the laptop in front of her "I'm expecting an update from the Ops Center any minute. As soon as it comes in, we'll get started."

I said, "I need to get something to drink first."

She pointed off to her left. "Help yourself. The kitchen's that way."

When I entered the kitchen, I saw some lemons in a fruit bowl on the countertop and grabbed one. After removing a knife from the butcher block, I sliced it in half and squeezed the juicy pulp inside a tall glass. Once I'd filled it with cold water and thrown in a few ice cubes, I dropped the lemon halves on top of the ice and gave it a stir.

After taking several big gulps, I stepped out on the patio and called Carlton.

♦♦♦♦

He answered on the first ring.

"Make it quick," he said.

"What's your assessment?"

"You're on the ground, what's yours?"

"Ahmed didn't travel to Venezuela to take out a president or Luckenbill or some foreign dignitary attending the trade conference. He came here to kill Roberto Montilla, and I believe Roberto knows that now. That's why he's on the run or gone to ground somewhere. When he got the news about Ernesto, he must have realized his son died by Ahmed's hand, and he knew he and his family could be next."

"Interesting theory."

"What's yours?"

"I concur with your assessment."

"So why did you call it a theory?"

"While the conversation between Ahmed and Zaidi seemed to indicate Roberto could be Ahmed's target, that's not certain. Hence, it's just a theory. But, if Ahmed has traveled to Venezuela to take out a trade minister, then you need to find out why someone would want him eliminated. Personally, I believe it has something to do with those storage facilities."

"But you agree with my theory?"

"Yes. I'm operating on the assumption Ahmed is in Venezuela to fulfill a contract to assassinate Roberto Montilla. That's why your priority must be to get to Roberto before Ahmed does and determine what's going on with him. You also need to find out more about those storage facilities. When you meet up with Roberto, you should leverage your ability to protect him from Ahmed as a means of obtaining information on those sites."

"We need to find Roberto first."

"The last I heard, the analysts were getting very close to sending Olivia an address on his location. She may have it already."

"She said she was expecting some updates from the Ops Center. Maybe she's got it by now. As to Rehman Zaidi's apartment in Caracas—"

"I just sent her the address of Zaidi's apartment in Caracas."

I decided not to ask him how he found the address, because I thought I already knew the answer to that question. Instead, I asked him something far more important.

"Do you trust her, Douglas? Do you trust Olivia?"

I heard him take a deep breath before answering me.

"Yes, Titus, I trust her completely. I know you still have your doubts, but, in the long run, you'd be better off if you kept an open mind about her."

When we ended the call, I went back inside wondering what I'd done to make both Carlton and Sally Jo think I was such a closed-minded person.

♦♦♦♦

Olivia looked up as I entered the dining room, and when she noticed my lemon water, a smile flickered across her face. "I see you still haven't lost your taste for that stuff."

I raised my glass as if offering her a toast. "Easy to make and available anywhere in the world."

She picked up her coffee mug and took a sip. "Sounds like you're describing coffee to me."

When she set the mug back down, she gave me a why-don't-you-challenge-me-on-that-statement kind of look. But, since I was trying to keep an open mind about her, I told myself I was probably wrong about what her defiant look actually meant.

I asked her, "What's the update from the Ops Center? Have they located Roberto yet?"

"I'll get to that in a moment."

She raised her voice and addressed Mitchell and Wylie, who were standing by the windows at the far end of the room. "Gentlemen," she said, "let's get started."

As soon as Mitchell and Wylie sat down, Olivia handed out a transcript of the conversation between Ahmed and Zaidi. I knew the English translation had come from an Arabic speaker at Langley, because Olivia didn't speak a word of Arabic.

I glanced at it for a few seconds. Then, I laid it aside and said, "There's nothing in this translation about what Ahmed and Zaidi said after I left the yacht."

Olivia said, "That's because the conversation ended when Ahmed thought he heard someone in the passageway. I'm guessing that noise was you making your getaway."

Wylie laughed. "Next time, partner, try removing your spurs. They cause an awful racket on a boat."

Mitchell snickered.

I nodded. "I appreciate the tip, Sam."

Olivia glanced down at her notes and said, "First things first. What seems apparent from this conversation is that someone has hired Ahmed Al-Amin to assassinate Roberto Montilla. You'll be interested to know both Douglas and C. J. agree with me. If anyone here disagrees with this assessment, speak up. Otherwise, the rest of this operation will be built on that assumption."

She looked around the table.

No one said anything.

"Fine. Anyone want to comment about the time crunch Ahmed says he's under?"

She studied the transcript for a second. "He says, 'There are only two days left on the timetable. If it's not done by then, I won't get paid.'"

I said, "Ahmed was delayed several days in Costa Rica while waiting for his passport to arrive, but anyone who's willing to hire a man like Ahmed isn't someone who's willing to listen to that kind of excuse, so Ahmed is probably worried he won't get paid. He may have accepted a certain portion of his fee upfront, and the rest of it is contingent upon his fulfilling the contract by a certain deadline. That deadline must be two days from now."

Olivia turned to Wylie. "Sam, tell Titus and Ben what you told me about Rehman Zaidi."

Wylie recited the same information he'd given me earlier about Zaidi and the *Campamento Laguna* training camp.

He said, "I'm not surprised Zaidi is the person responsible for supplying Ahmed with a weapon. What surprises me is his relationship with Ahmed."

Olivia nodded. "He seems to be Ahmed's subordinate. Is that what you mean?"

"Yes, ma'am. To me he sounded deferential toward Ahmed."

Wylie read from the transcript. "Zaidi says to Ahmed, 'I would be most honored if you would stay at my apartment while you're in Caracas.'"

Wylie shook his head. "He'd be honored. It's as if Ahmed is some kind of holy man to Zaidi."

I said, "That's because he is. To a jihadist like Rehman Zaidi, anyone who has Ahmed's reputation as a killing machine is considered someone to be revered."

Olivia said, "Speaking of Zaidi's apartment; you may remember Douglas was looking into the occupants of that apartment complex Ernesto had marked on the map. Once he heard Ahmed say he knew where Apartment 1705 was located, Douglas checked the residents' roster and found Apartment 1705 is occupied by Rehman Zaidi."

Although I had also wondered if there was a tie-in with Zaidi's apartment and the *Avenida Francisco* address, I kept quiet about it and let Carlton get the credit for this observation.

I said, "I suspect Ernesto could have met Zaidi during his first visit to Damascus at the same time he became acquainted with Ahmed. Maybe he marked Zaidi's apartment because the two of them planned to get together when he came home."

Olivia nodded. "I've instructed the Agency analysts to begin mining the data stream for that information. We also need to understand why someone would want Roberto Montilla dead. Whether it was the Revolutionary Guard in Iran or Assad in Syria, whoever hired Ahmed must have considered Roberto a threat of some nature, and it may be in America's interests to find out why."

Olivia gestured toward me. "Titus, you made a good call when you said the embassy should inform Roberto of his son's death. When he heard about Ernesto this morning, he probably suspected Ahmed was responsible and realized he and his family could be next. Now, his actions have caused Ahmed to panic, and that means when Ahmed goes after Roberto, we should be able to nab him before he makes the hit."

I was surprised at Olivia's compliment, but I tried not to show it.

Mitchell asked, "Has Langley located Roberto yet?"

Wylie said, "My boys found Montilla's vehicle on three traffic videos. It shows Roberto was headed to the *Campo Alegre* area of Caracas."

Olivia nodded. "Right. We have an address now. We believe Roberto is at his sister-in-law's house. Her name is Roxanna Palacio. This is Marianna's sister, and we discovered Marianna made some calls from her cell phone this morning from that address. Those calls, along with the traffic videos, made it possible for the Ops Center to triangulate her location."

Olivia hit some keystrokes on her laptop and then gestured at Wylie. "I've just sent you the address. We need twenty-four-hour surveillance at that location immediately."

Wylie got up from the table. "If you'll excuse me, ma'am, I'll go make those arrangements."

I shook my head as Wylie left the room. "This isn't good. If we can find Roberto, then so can Zaidi. He told Ahmed he has plenty of sources he can use to locate him."

Mitchell asked, "Are you sure Roberto is even at this location? He could have dropped off his wife and daughter and gone somewhere else."

That's good, Ben. Look for the loopholes. Consider the possibilities.

Olivia was preoccupied by something on her computer, and when she answered Mitchell's question, she sounded dismissive. "Nothing's certain at this point, Ben."

Mitchell looked over at me and shrugged.

"Olivia," I said, trying to keep the anger out of my voice, "Ben has a valid point."

Olivia tore herself away from her computer and looked over at me. "I never said he didn't have a valid point."

I said, "So Roberto's wife made some phone calls from her sister's house. That doesn't mean Roberto is staying there. We need something more concrete than suppositions."

"I agree," she said. "That's why I was just requisitioning a UAV to be positioned over that location. It should be in place within the hour. If nothing else, the drone will at least give us the heat signatures from everyone inside that house."

Her response took me by surprise.

"I had no idea you were ordering up a drone."

Olivia smiled at my admission—a really big smile—and said, "This isn't my first rodeo, you know."

At that moment, Wylie walked back in the room. "Did someone mention a rodeo?"

♦♦♦♦

After Wylie resumed his seat, he told Olivia he'd ordered a surveillance crew over to the address on *Avenida Los Jardines* to keep an eye on Roxanna Palacio's residence. He assured Olivia she'd be the first to know the moment he heard back from his boys.

Just as Wylie was finishing up his report, Olivia's cell phone rang.

After a brief conversation, she hung up and announced she'd chartered a plane to fly us from Margarita Island to Caracas in a few hours.

"Once we arrive in Caracas," Olivia said, "we'll be taken to the embassy where I'll contact the Ops Center and get an update on Roberto. By that time, we should know whether he's staying at his sister-in-law's house or not."

She nodded at me. "Titus, if Roberto is at the house on *Los Jardines*, then you and Ben will pay him a visit." Olivia looked over at Wylie, "Sam, you'll take care of Ahmed. The moment he—"

"Just to clarify," I said, interrupting her. "What exactly does take care of Ahmed mean?"

"It means Sam will be part of the surveillance team outside Zaidi's apartment, and he'll let you know if your conversation with Roberto is about to be interrupted by Ahmed."

"Don't worry," Wylie said to me. "I won't lay a finger on Ahmed. When that time comes, he's all yours."

"Or mine," Mitchell muttered under his breath.

Olivia gave no indication she'd heard Mitchell's remark. "Sam," she said, "as soon as you're on site, you should have someone from your team get inside Zaidi's apartment and plant the listening devices. We need to know what Zaidi and Ahmed are discussing, and how close they are to locating Roberto."

"Won't be a problem," Wylie said. "The two guys keeping an eye on the yacht tonight will be on the plane with Ahmed tomorrow, and they'll let me know the minute he lands. As long as no one's in the apartment, we should have plenty of time to wire the place before Ahmed gets there."

I said, "We'll need to make arrangements to remove Roberto from his sister-in-law's house. I want him isolated when I question him tomorrow. His wife, his daughter, or any other family members shouldn't be around when I do that."

"I'll work out the logistics once the surveillance team is in place, and we start receiving images from the drone."

Olivia glanced down at her watch. "We have three hours before we need to be at the airport for our eleven o'clock flight. I've already informed the desk clerk at the Wyndham that Mr. Awerbuch and his party will be flying to Caracas this evening to pay a visit to the embassy, but we still need to return to the hotel and change clothes. Why don't the three of you go back there now, and I'll wrap things up here."

I walked with Mitchell and Wylie to the front door, but, when Wylie went to grab his messenger bag out of the hall closet, I said to Mitchell, "I need to clarify some things with Olivia, so why don't you ride back to the hotel with Sam, and I'll meet you there later."

Mitchell handed me the keys to the rental car. "Are you sure you and Olivia don't need a referee?"

I was hoping an intercessor would be sufficient.

Chapter 37

I walked back down the hallway to the dining room and found Olivia still sitting at the table, but she wasn't working on anything. She had her head down, massaging the back of her neck, as if she might be nursing a sick headache.

She didn't react when I came in, so I stood there a moment and tried to decide whether I should disturb her or not.

Seconds later, she sensed my presence.

"You startled me," she said, suddenly looking up at me. "I thought you'd left with the others."

"I told them I'd meet them back at the hotel later."

"Why?"

Although I knew talking to Olivia was going to be hard, I didn't realize how hard it was going to be until I finally found myself alone with her.

I froze for a moment.

"Are you hungry?" I asked. "I saw some eggs in the kitchen. I could make us an omelet."

She looked surprised. "You stayed here to cook for me?"

I shook my head. "No, not really. I stayed here so I could talk to you about something, but I think both of us need to eat something first. You used to love my omelets."

"They were okay I guess." She nodded. "Sure, go fix us something to eat. Don't put too much butter in mine, though. I won't eat it if you do."

When I started out the door, she called after me. "I'm glad you stayed. I also need to talk to you about something."

I tried to keep an open mind about what that might be.

♦♦♦♦

Once I'd prepared the omelets, I took the plates outside and placed them on a glass-topped table beside the swimming pool. As I turned to go back inside, I spotted Olivia watching me from the window in the dining room.

I motioned for her to come outside.

She disappeared from view and reappeared on the patio a few minutes later with a fresh cup of coffee in her hand.

She walked over and looked down at her plate. "I'll never be able to eat all of that."

"I see your eating habits haven't changed. Just leave it. I'll eat what you don't want."

"Your eating habits haven't changed either."

She sat down and took a small bite. "Not bad. A little salty, though."

"I didn't add any extra salt."

We ate in silence for a few minutes, and then I said, "I just remembered. Toby Bledsoe fixed me an omelet the night before he died."

"I never knew Toby."

"He was a good man."

"That's what everyone says when someone dies, especially a station chief who's been killed in action."

"In Toby's case, it was true, and I believe Ben really cared about him."

Olivia pushed her plate aside, and said, "Let's talk now."

I shoved one last bite in my mouth. "Um . . . sure, but I'd like to go first."

"No, I want to go first. And, since you brought him up, I'll start with Ben."

"You wanted to discuss Ben with me?"

She nodded. "He's the reason I'm in country with you. He's the reason I got assigned as the FO for this mission."

After Olivia made this statement, she sat back in her chair and looked at me.

For some reason, I had the feeling she was enjoying my confusion.

I said, "I assume you're about to explain yourself."

"You sound angry."

"I'm not angry with you. I'm angry with myself. I was preoccupied with someone . . . I should say some family matters, when I got back to Langley, and if I hadn't been distracted, I might have questioned Douglas about your role in the operation."

"I'm not sure he would have told you. He plays his cards pretty close to the vest sometimes."

"That's putting it mildly."

"It might make you feel better to know it was Douglas who recommended me to be the Director of the RTM Centers after the DDO wanted to fire me."

"I know Douglas trusts you, if that's what you're implying."

She waited a beat, and then she asked, "Aren't you curious about why the DDO wanted to fire me?"

"Not really. He wants to fire anyone who crosses him, and I can't imagine you didn't cross him a time or two. What I'm curious about is Ben. What role did he play in the DDO designating you as the handler for this mission?"

"He didn't play any role, at least not directly. It was his father, Senator Mitchell. I guess you know Elijah Mitchell is Ben's father?"

"Of course."

"Last Friday morning, I was told to report to the DDO's office to brief some senators on the Senate Intelligence Committee. When I arrived in his office, aside from the DDO, Senator Mitchell was the only person there."

"That was a couple of days after Toby's death. I think I know where this is headed."

"Don't be so sure. Just when you think you've got the Senator figured out, he does something to blow your mind. I worked with him a few years ago when I was the DDO's congressional liaison."

"I had heard that."

"Believe me, working with the Senator was never easy. On the other hand, I know I'm not the easiest person to work with either. Later, I realized my personality might have been the reason he wanted me to be Ben's handler. The bottom line is, I believe the Senator hates the idea of his son being a covert officer, and he's hoping this operation will discourage him so much he'll get out of the CIA, or, at the very least, accept an administrative desk job somewhere."

"Wait a minute. Let me see if I've got this straight. The Senator went to the DDO and asked for you to be assigned to this operation because he thought the sheer force of your personality would make his son want to quit the Agency?"

"No, you're over simplifying it. That's not what happened."

"So complicate things for me. What happened?"

"The DDO called me up to his office to brief the Senator on the operations running inside the RTM Centers. This wasn't the first time he'd done this, but all the other times, there were several other senators in attendance. When I explained the status of Operation Clear Signal to the Senator and told him we were tracking *El Mano Fierro*, he asked me if I knew his son had recently been assigned to that operation."

"Did you?"

"No, not until he told me. And, until I saw you yesterday in the Ops Center, I had no idea you were one of the principals of Operation Clear Signal either. Working with the principals of an operation is not my responsibility. I work on the logistics of an operation. That's the part I love. Handling personalities is not my thing."

I was tempted to make a sarcastic observation regarding the truth of her statement.

However, because I wanted to move the story along and not precipitate an argument with her, I said, "Was he asking you to give him the operation's risk assessment, or was there some other reason he wanted to make sure you knew of his son's involvement?"

"At first, I thought it was only because he was worried about Ben, and he thought if I knew his son was one of the principals, I might give him more details about the operation. But then, he went into a rant about his son's weaknesses. To sum it up, he said Ben would be better off as an analyst sitting at a desk, rather than an operative trying to catch the bad guys."

"That's absolutely not true. Ben's a good operative, and he has the potential to become an even better one."

"I'm going to take your word for that, because I haven't seen any evidence of it so far, at least not from my end."

"What about his performance this afternoon? He got us out to the yacht and back, didn't he?"

"Anybody can steer a boat."

In my case, that wasn't necessarily true, but I didn't contradict her.

"Okay, go ahead with your story. So the Senator made it clear he wasn't happy about his son's career choice. What happened next?"

"He thanked me for my time, and the DDO dismissed me. Then, yesterday morning, the DDO called me back up to his office and informed me I would be the FO for Operation Clear Signal. He hinted my appointment was at the Senator's request, and that I should keep the conversation about his son in mind as I planned the mission."

I picked up our plates. "Let's go inside. It's getting dark, and I can't see beyond the tree line anymore."

She turned around and looked out toward the ocean. Then she nodded, "You've always been nervous around the water."

"I'm nervous because these grounds aren't secure. They weren't secure in the daytime, and they're even more insecure now that it's getting dark."

"If you say so."

"I say so."

♦♦♦♦

While I rinsed off our plates, Olivia went in the den and made herself comfortable.

When I joined her a few minutes later, I noticed she had taken her shoes off and was rubbing her feet. I sat down at the opposite end of the sofa from her.

"Frankly, Olivia, I'm just not buying your story."

She bristled at my statement. "You think I'm lying?"

"It's just hard for me to believe you would go along with the

Senator's conspiracy against his son without putting up a fight with the DDO. You'll fight with anyone. Why wouldn't you fight the DDO on this, especially since you don't enjoy managing people in the field?"

"I love my job in the Ops Center, and I want to keep it. Ira almost got me fired once, and I knew if I gave him any excuse at all, he'd get it done this time. Besides, if Ben Mitchell is such a pushover that he can't put up with me, then maybe his father is right, and he shouldn't be in this business in the first place."

"Ben isn't a pushover, and I know firsthand he has some of his old man's temperament. Right now, though, he seems intimidated by you. If you tried, Olivia, you could change that."

She studied me a moment. "Your eating habits may not have changed, but something has definitely changed about you. What's happened to you? People in our line of work usually get more calloused as the years go by. Not you, though. You seem to be a kinder, gentler version of the old you. Where's all that anger I used to see? Why won't you fight with me anymore?"

"You really see a difference in me?"

She hesitated before answering. "Well, not a lot, but some. It's mainly that anger thing."

At that moment, I realized I was seeing an answer to prayer. I'd prayed for an opportunity to tell Olivia about my newfound faith, and she'd just opened the door for me to do so.

Now, though, all I could think about were all the ways she could take my words and twist them around. To make matters worse, I wasn't sure I had enough confidence in my beliefs to counter her inevitable barbs.

Since I didn't feel comfortable telling her about my conversion experience, I said, "That anger thing is exactly what I wanted to discuss with you. I need to apologize for what happened in Kuwait at Camp Beuhring. I never should have called you those names or said the things I said."

"After all this time, you want—"

"No, let me finish. I'm asking for your forgiveness, Olivia. Will you forgive me?"

She shifted her weight around on the sofa as if she couldn't get comfortable.

"Oh, sure, Titus. I forgive you. It wasn't a big deal to me."

"I also wanted to say I'm sorry I didn't stay in touch with you. When I heard about Saddam killing the general . . . well, to be truthful, I blamed you for that."

She nodded. "It was partly my fault. I can't deny that."

"Still, I should have been willing to talk with you about it."

She used her fingernail to pick at a soiled spot on the sofa. Then, she looked up and said, "We used to be able to talk about anything."

"That's true."

After a few seconds of awkward silence passed between us, I started to get up and leave. As I did so, Olivia reached out and grabbed my arm.

"Wait a minute."

I sat back down.

"I have breast cancer."

Her words didn't register with me immediately.

But when they did, I found myself searching for the correct way to respond to her.

"Ah . . . I'm so sorry, Olivia."

"I don't want your pity. I just wanted to tell someone."

"Okay, I get that."

"Both my mother and sister died of breast cancer."

"I remember."

She turned away from me and stared out the window at the ocean view.

I'd never seen her look more vulnerable.

She finally said, "All my life, I've done everything the doctors told me to do—eat healthy, get regular checkups, have mammograms, but—"

"When were you diagnosed?"

"Five years ago. That was when I had a lumpectomy and some chemo. After that, I was pronounced cancer free. A few weeks ago, though, I was told the cancer was back, and now, the doctors want to schedule me for a mastectomy."

"Want to schedule you? They haven't done it yet?"

"I'm not sure I'm going to have a mastectomy. This cancer is eventually going to kill me, and I just don't want to put myself through that kind of surgery."

"You can't give up, Olivia. You're still young. Women beat this stuff all the time."

"To be truthful, I don't have much to live for these days." She shook her head. "I guess I never did."

Hearing her say that, I found it impossible to keep quiet about my faith. I told her what had happened to me in Tehran, and how I'd made a decision to commit my life to Christ.

Afterward, I sat back and waited for her reaction.

She slipped her shoes back on and stood to her feet.

"See?" she said. "I knew something had happened to you. You've found religion."

"No, Olivia, I haven't found religion, I've begun a relationship."

She brushed my explanation aside. "Semantics."

"That's not it. It's a way—"

"I will say this, Titus. If you hadn't asked me to forgive you, I wouldn't have listened to what you had to say. Now, though, I may have to give this faith thing a little more thought."

"Here's something else for you to think about. Consider letting me contact the DDO and tell him I can't work with you anymore; that I want another handler. If I were to protest loudly enough, he might assign someone as your replacement. That way, you'll be able to get back to the States and have your surgery immediately."

She shook her head. "Are you serious? Who do you think he'd send down here as the FO?"

"Probably C. J. Salazar, but that doesn't matter."

"I'm not about to turn this operation over to Cartel Carlos, not when we're this close to grabbing Ahmed."

"What if I—"

Olivia's phone rang.

After she took the call, she said, "That was Sam. We may not need the drone now. His surveillance team spotted Roberto at the *Los Jardines* residence a few minutes ago."

"That's good news."

"Time for you to go do your thing now."

"You mean work my incredible powers of persuasion on Roberto the way I've done on you?"

Chapter 38

Monday, June 11

I couldn't get the coffeepot to work. It was the old-fashioned kind, a percolator, where you put the coffee grounds in a basket on the top, fill it up with water, and plug it in.

Right now, I needed coffee.

The whole team—Olivia, Wylie, Mitchell and I—had arrived in Caracas around midnight, and an embassy driver had taken everyone, except Wylie, directly to the American Embassy. Wylie had gone off with a member of his security team to supervise the wiring of Zaidi's apartment before Ahmed showed up.

At the embassy, Olivia had immediately gone into The Bubble to conduct a video conference call with the Ops Center back at Langley. Afterward, she'd briefed Mitchell and me on the logistics of questioning Roberto Montilla.

The interrogation was to take place away from Roberto's hideout, because—according to Olivia—Carlton agreed with me that there were too many risk factors involved in conducting it there. Although snatching Roberto from the house—essentially kidnapping him—also carried risks, those risks were far less dangerous than having a neighbor show up in the middle of the chat Roberto and I were going to have.

Ideally, the kidnapping of Roberto Montilla should take place when he was alone in the house, and shortly after Olivia's video call, she received confirmation there would be a window of opportunity at one o'clock in the afternoon, just a few hours from now.

She'd received this information from the National Security Agency, after they'd been authorized to record all cell phone communications coming from the residence on *Avenida Los Jardines*.

In order to get this authorization, the Agency had been required to show a FISA court judge that Roberto Montilla had been in contact with a known terrorist, one who'd recently murdered an American intelligence officer. I was guessing it was Carlton who'd insisted on going before the FISA courts to get the authorization, because he was always adamant about observing the Foreign Intelligence Services Agreement right down to the letter of the law.

The phone conversations had revealed Roberto's sister-in-law, Roxanna Palacio, had made an appointment with a hair and nail salon for three individuals. It was assumed the other two ladies were Marianna and Emma Montilla. Their appointment was scheduled for one o'clock.

It was now six-thirty in the morning, and since Mitchell and I had been up all night, I desperately needed a caffeine fix.

Although it took me a few minutes to figure it out, I finally realized I didn't have the electrical cord from the percolator to the wall socket plugged in correctly. Once I'd remedied that small detail, the machine immediately began to gurgle.

Along with Mitchell, I was inside a safe house about five miles from Roberto's location.

It wasn't an Agency-owned safe house. It was a residence the Agency had reserved for special occasions, occasions when a homey atmosphere might be more conducive to getting an asset to talk than would a sterile environment, like an office or warehouse setting.

The house itself was owned by a religious organization, which was headquartered in the States. It was usually occupied by one of their missionary families. However, every two years, the family returned to the States for a six-month furlough. Whenever that happened, the embassy paid a rental fee to have full use of the house—identified by Wylie as The Missy Hacienda—and this was done with the understanding that temporary embassy personnel would be staying in the missionaries' residence while they were away.

Today, Mitchell and I were the temporary personnel in residence.

If things went as planned, around two o'clock, there would be one additional occupant—Roberto Montilla.

The Ops Center had decided a four-person team of Level 2 operatives would do a snatch and grab of Roberto from the *Los Jardines* residence and bring him to the safe house.

I wasn't sure whether the person responsible for coming up with the plan was Carlton or Salazar, but when Olivia told Mitchell and me about it, I'd tried to convince her to change it.

"This is all wrong, Olivia. Ben and I should be the ones initiating this action. Those guys won't know how to finesse this. They'll traumatize Roberto, and it may take me hours to gain back his confidence."

"Even though Sam Wylie calls them his boys, one member of the team doing the snatch and grab today is a woman."

"It doesn't matter. The end result will be the same."

"That could be," she said, "but most likely, when they put Roberto in that van, he'll think some of Ahmed's men have taken him. Then, when they bring him to the safe house and he finds sweet, lovable you there, he'll be so grateful it wasn't Ahmed who kidnapped him, he'll start jabbering away."

I quickly realized there was no dissuading her from the plan, and in the end, I admitted the psychology behind the decision to traumatize him might prove beneficial.

Unfortunately, it didn't.

♦♦♦♦

Earlier, when Mitchell and I had arrived at the safe house, I'd suggested he get some sleep. He hadn't protested too much, and now he was snoring away in a back bedroom. I noticed the bedroom was decorated in posters depicting male rock stars, so I was guessing it belonged to the missionaries' teenage daughter.

The room also contained an assortment of musical instruments, including a guitar. Oddly enough, I'd heard Mitchell strumming on the guitar when he'd first gone back to the room to take a snooze.

After drinking several cups of coffee, I walked down the hallway and checked out the electronic equipment Wylie's specialists had set up in the master bedroom. The equipment would be used to record my upcoming conversation with Roberto and to keep in touch with Olivia, who was back at the embassy monitoring the situation at Roberto's hideout and Zaidi's apartment.

For a few brief seconds, I was tempted to check in with Olivia, but then I decided not to bother her.

Or be bothered by her.

On the charter flight from the island to Caracas, she'd kept her distance from me, and I had the distinct feeling she was embarrassed she'd been so open with me about her cancer. I wasn't sure how that might affect our future relationship, but I doubted it would change it much.

Once I'd checked out the communications equipment, I went back to the living room and made some changes to the layout of the room in preparation for Roberto's visit.

First, I removed all the family photos of the missionaries and stored them in an empty drawer in the dining room—I didn't want Roberto to be thinking about any family but his own during our talk. After that, I lowered the blinds and turned on a couple of lamps. Finally, I went around the living room and tested out all the chairs, trying to decide which one of them was the most uncomfortable. It turned out to be a high-backed armchair, and I set that chair aside for me to use.

I planned to give Roberto his choice of the other three, including the sofa, because I wanted him to be as comfortable as possible during our little visit.

However, since I knew he wouldn't be in any kind of shape to make such choices immediately, I removed a straight-backed chair from the kitchen table and placed it in the middle of the room. The last thing I did was make sure all the breakables were moved out of the way.

Mitchell would be in the living room with me during the interrogation, but I had already made sure he understood he wouldn't be the one questioning Roberto.

That would be my job.

Around eleven o'clock, I went down the hall to the girl's bedroom to let Mitchell know his naptime was over. When I looked inside the room, I noticed his head was resting on a pillow with a pink floral pillowcase and teddy bears were sharing the bed with him. That picture made the semi-automatic pistol at his side look out of place—like Carlton sitting at a messy desk.

When I walked in the room, Mitchell opened his eyes and grabbed for the gun. When he recognized I wasn't a threat, he holstered the weapon and asked, "What time is it?"

"Time to get to work."

"Did you get the coffeepot fixed?"

"Yeah, it was complicated, but I finally got it working."

I walked over to a corner of the room and picked up the guitar. "Did I hear you playing this earlier?"

He nodded. "I took some lessons when I was in high school." He pointed toward the posters. "I thought I might become a rock star and embarrass the Senator."

"What stopped you?"

"For one thing, I had no talent. Secondly, I realized I didn't really want to embarrass the Senator as much as I wanted to belong to something he couldn't control. I figured the CIA fit the bill, because as much power as he wields on the Intelligence Committee, he can't govern what I do during an operation."

"Never mind what the Senator wants from you, Ben; do what's best for yourself. You'll both be better off for it."

He laughed. "Would you believe the Senator used to tell me almost the same thing about being honest with people? 'Ben,' he'd say, 'Never mind what people want you to say, tell them what they need to hear. If you do, you'll both be better off for it.'"

Yes, I believe the Senator used to say that, Ben, because he told me so himself.

"It sounds like the kind of advice we both need to remember."

♦♦♦♦

The Agency van rolled inside the garage at 1:48 p.m. with Roberto Montilla in the rear cargo compartment.

Previously, I'd instructed Olivia to inform the operatives they should maintain complete silence from the moment they grabbed Roberto to when I told them otherwise. I also told her to tell them I'd be communicating with them through hand signals once they brought Roberto into the house.

This was a standard disorientation technique, which, in Roberto's case, meant he would not be hearing any voices from the moment he was whisked out of his house until he heard my voice approximately one hour later.

I had no way of knowing whether they'd followed my instructions on their way over to the safe house, but, when they opened the van's cargo doors and pulled Roberto out, none of them uttered a word.

Roberto, on the other hand, was anything but quiet.

Despite the gag in his mouth and the hood over his face, he managed to make enough noise to let it be known he didn't like what was being done to him. Then, when they brought him through the utility room, he struggled against his constraints and ended up kicking the washing machine so forcefully, he was able to send it crashing into the wall behind it.

At that point, the two guys on either side of him picked him up, brought him into the living room, and deposited him on the chair I'd placed in the middle of the room. Afterward, one of them pulled a piece of cord from his back pocket and secured his legs to the chair.

That done, they checked his hands—already bound together by zip ties—and once they'd determined he was still securely cuffed, they gave me a thumbs-up and left the room.

The moment his legs were tied to the chair, Roberto stopped struggling. I saw this as an indication he'd moved from the first tier of responses experienced by a hostage—fighting against a captor—into the second tier—trying to figure out how to survive the ordeal.

As I stood there observing him, I decided he looked heavier than he did in the professional photograph I'd seen of him—the one where he was wearing a suit. Today, he was dressed in jeans and a shirt and had on a pair of jogging shoes.

I slowly walked around his chair a couple of times and looked at him from every angle.

Finally, I stopped and stood in front of him, waiting to see if he would utter some protest, even attempt a word or two—despite the gag inside his mouth.

He didn't.

I signaled for Mitchell to keep an eye on him, and then I walked in the kitchen where Roberto's kidnappers had congregated. The team leader introduced himself as Buck, but he didn't bother introducing the rest of the team to me.

"Any problems?" I asked.

The beefy guy in the group spoke up. "Nothing we couldn't handle."

"Did you have to—"

"We never laid a hand on him," Buck said, giving Mr. Beefcakes a harsh look. "He was more or less cooperative until we drove inside the garage."

The youngest team member, the guy who'd been driving the van, said, "He was packing a suitcase when we showed up at the house. There were several passports, a wad of cash, and some airline tickets in there. We brought those with us; plus, we grabbed his cell phone."

I said, "I'd like to have his cell phone, the passports, and the airline tickets."

He nodded. "They're in the van. I'll get them."

When he went back out to the garage, I asked, "Anything else I need to know?"

The only woman on the team spoke up. "Before we gagged him, he kept saying, 'Don't hurt my family.' He repeated it several times."

After the driver came back in and dropped off the backpack full of the stuff they'd retrieved from Roberto's hideout, he and Mr. Beefcakes left the house and moved the van down the street where they could maintain surveillance on the neighborhood.

Once they were gone, Buck and the woman walked down the hallway to the master bedroom, where they could monitor the recording devices and maintain communications with Olivia back at the embassy.

Even though Olivia was connected via video to the Ops Center at Langley, I'd informed her I didn't want to be micro-managed, and unless there was an emergency, I didn't want to speak to her until I'd finished interrogating Roberto.

She'd agreed.

She hadn't liked it, but she'd agreed.

After a quick examination of the passports and the airline tickets, I picked up Roberto's cell phone and returned to the living room. Mitchell was leaning against the wall about ten feet away from Roberto's chair, and when he saw me, he shook his head.

Roberto hadn't given him any trouble.

In fact, it looked as if all the fight had completely gone out of the man now. He was slumped down in his chair with his chin resting on his chest, and his breathing was slow and steady.

I gestured at Mitchell, who immediately stepped over and pulled the black hood off Roberto's head.

When that happened, Roberto's head jerked up, and even though I'd dimmed the lights, he blinked several times at the sudden brightness. A few seconds later, his eyes darted about the room as if he were trying to memorize his surroundings.

When he turned and looked at me, I saw a mixture of fear and defiance there.

Although I knew I might hear a barrage of expletives, I motioned for Mitchell to remove the gag from his mouth. However, once Mitchell did so, Roberto didn't utter a word.

I said, "I know this may be very hard for you to believe right now, Roberto, but we're here to help you. We brought you here to save your life."

He leaned forward as far as he could and spat in my face.

Chapter 39

Even after I repeated my assertion I was there to help him, Roberto didn't say a word. I offered him something to drink, but he acted as if he hadn't heard me.

Finally, in an effort to demonstrate my good will toward him, I removed the zip ties from around his hands. However, this gesture also proved ineffective in getting him to talk.

Just when I'd made up my mind to wait him out, Mitchell—without asking my permission to do so—walked over and knelt down beside him.

"I was with Ernesto when he died," he said. "I was with your son when he took his last breath."

Roberto gasped in astonishment, and tears suddenly filled his eyes. "There was no need to kill him. He wasn't a threat to you."

Mitchell shook his head. "I didn't kill Ernesto." He pointed over at me. "Neither did he. Both of us tried to save your son from Ahmed Al-Amin. It was Ahmed who killed your son, not us. That's why we're here. We want to make sure it doesn't happen to you or to your family."

Roberto's face softened. "What did my son say before he died?"

I wasn't sure Mitchell could answer that question, but he did.

"Ernesto talked about fishing," Mitchell said. "He wanted to go fishing with you."

Roberto looked grief-stricken when he heard those words, and the tears behind his eyes immediately started flowing down his cheeks.

"Why did Ahmed kill Ernesto?" he asked. "Ernesto was a good boy. He never harmed anyone."

As Roberto continued describing his son, the intensity of his sobs made it impossible to understand what he was saying.

I noticed Mitchell was moved by the man's anguish, and I was not unaffected by it myself.

I motioned for Mitchell to untie Roberto's legs, and as soon as Roberto became aware of what Mitchell was doing, he tried to regain his composure.

Once he was freed, he looked over at Mitchell and said, "We were planning a fishing trip this month to Cumaná or Maracaibo. Ernesto had studied the tide charts and told me June was the best month to book a charter."

I asked, "Were you planning to take him with you the next time you visited those chemical storage units in Cumaná or Maracaibo?"

My question seemed to take him by surprise, and his eyes narrowed as he looked at me. "Who are you?" he asked. "What do you want from me?"

I pointed toward the sofa. "Make yourself comfortable first. Then, I'll answer your questions."

I kept my eye on him when he got up and walked over to the sofa, but he gave no outward indication he might make a mad dash for the front door or do something equally as foolish.

After Roberto sat down on the sofa, Mitchell took the chair Roberto had just vacated and placed it beside the chair I was occupying. When he sat down next to me, I knew it might appear to Roberto that Mitchell and I were equal partners in his interrogation.

After his success in getting Roberto to talk, I decided I was okay with that.

Olivia was sure to voice a different opinion, however.

♦♦♦♦

My conversation with Roberto began when I gave him a couple of phony names for Mitchell and me—Mark and Timothy. Then, I told him we were employed by the American government—I didn't say which branch or organization. After that, I gave him the semi-truthful details of how and when we'd discovered his son had been killed by Ahmed.

First, I outlined how American law enforcement agencies had discovered Ahmed Al-Amin had been working with a Mexican drug cartel to provide left-wing guerillas in Colombia with sophisticated weapons. After that, I explained the State Department had decided arming the Colombian rebels wasn't in America's interests, and a joint US/Colombia operation was underway to find Ahmed and turn him over to the Colombian government.

For my purposes, these facts were close enough to the truth to make our presence in Caracas credible. I wasn't about to tell him Ahmed was responsible for the deaths of two CIA officers.

"Last week," I said, "we located Ahmed in Costa Rica. He was staying in a house in San José owned by one of the drug cartels. But, when we forced our way inside, Ernesto was the only person there. We found him dying from a knife wound to his stomach, and on our way to the hospital, he told us Ahmed had stabbed him. When we—"

"Did he say why Ahmed had stabbed him?" Roberto asked.

"No," Mitchell said, "but it's possible Ernesto had been texting his girlfriend back in Texas. Ahmed probably told him not to use his cell phone, because he knew Ernesto's texts could alert the authorities to his whereabouts. We believe that's why he killed him."

Roberto said, "Ernesto said he was in love with this girl and wanted Marianna and me to meet her. I would never have imagined Ahmed would have killed him for texting her." He shook his head. "I thought Ahmed had killed him for another reason."

"What other reason?"

In what seemed an obvious attempt to look in control of the situation, Roberto threw his arm across the back of the sofa and leaned backed against the cushions. After doing so, he said, "I'm not answering any of your questions until you tell me how you're going to protect my wife and daughter."

When I didn't answer him immediately, he leaned forward and asked, "Did you kidnap them also?"

"Your wife and daughter are with your sister-in-law getting their nails done. When they return home, there's a note at the house explaining your absence, and it's written in what appears to be your handwriting."

Mitchell added, "You can relax, Roberto. We have your family under surveillance. I promise you they're safe—at least for now."

He nodded when he heard Mitchell's answer. Then he asked me, "Are you going to answer my question? How will you protect my family from Ahmed?"

"If I knew what was going on with you, it would be easier for me to protect them. When you heard Ernesto was dead, why did you think Ahmed had killed him? And why does Ahmed want you dead? When you answer those questions, I'll tell you how we plan to keep you and your family safe."

Roberto shook his head and looked away a moment.

When he finally looked me in the eye again, his anguished expression was one I'd seen in other assets. It was a look of resignation brought on by desperation.

It meant Roberto was ready to tell me everything.

◆◆◆◆

Roberto began by explaining how he'd met Ahmed in Syria. Much of what he said was information Katherine and her analysts had already retrieved from the data stream.

I didn't tell him that, though, because I wanted him to open up and start talking to us, and I was hoping Mitchell would take his cue from me and not interrupt Roberto's flow of thought by asking him too many questions.

"About four years ago," Roberto said, "I went to Damascus to finalize a trade agreement between Venezuela and the Syrian government. The talks between our two countries had been going on for several years, and the president of Venezuela sent me there to formalize the deal. At that time, Ernesto was in his last semester of high school, and I received permission for him to accompany me to Damascus.

"I did this because I wanted Ernesto to have a much broader view of the world than the one I'd been given. When I mentioned the trip to him, I was surprised by how excited he was about traveling there. Later, I learned he'd become friends with several Middle Eastern boys in his high school, and that was why he was so interested in the trip. Until we got over to Syria, though, I didn't realize he'd also become very interested in the Muslim faith."

Roberto paused and rubbed his eyes, and I wondered if he was trying to keep himself from breaking down again.

A few moments later, he continued. "The trip was a huge success, and the deal I brokered greatly benefitted Venezuela, particularly our mining industries. The talks, though, were pretty boring for a teenager, so my interpreter arranged for Ernesto to be entertained by some of his family members during the day. That's how we met Ahmed Al-Amin.

"Ahmed was my interpreter's cousin. He was also connected to Hezbollah and the Syrian government in some capacity, but that was never made clear to me. What did become clear to me, however, was that Ernesto had developed a great admiration for Ahmed after spending just a few days with him. I believe he did so because he saw how devoted Ahmed was to Islam, and how many of the men around Ahmed looked up to him.

"At the end of our visit, Ahmed took me aside and told me he saw great potential in my son and suggested I consider sending him to a university in the United States for his college education. When I mentioned I couldn't afford that kind of education for Ernesto, he assured me he knew people in Hezbollah who would be willing to help pay for Ernesto's education in exchange for my help in developing some of their members' business interests in Venezuela.

"Since such ventures were part of my portfolio in the Venezuelan government, I assured him I would be happy to help Hezbollah in any way I could. Before Ernesto and I left for Caracas, Ahmed introduced me to Rehman Zaidi, a mathematics instructor, who was scheduled to join the faculty at a new Muslim school run by Imam Raza here in Caracas. Ahmed said he would be communicating with me about Ernesto's education through Zaidi. When I arrived—"

"Describe Rehman Zaidi for me," I said.

He looked puzzled at my interest in Zaidi, but he said, "I believe he's originally from Syria. He doesn't look Syrian, though, because he has blue eyes and fair skin. He's of average build, but he has only one arm. He said he lost it in a boating accident when he was a teenager."

I nodded. "So what happened when you returned to Venezuela? Did Zaidi get in touch with you?"

"No, not immediately. Six months went by, and I didn't hear anything. Then one day, about the time Ernesto graduated, Zaidi showed up at my house. That's a day I will always remember. It was Saturday, and my son and I were watching a soccer match on TV. Zaidi rang the doorbell, and when I went to answer it, there he was.

"When I invited him in, I was surprised by how happy Ernesto was to see him. It was obvious they'd been communicating, and I later learned they'd been emailing each other regularly. Zaidi said he'd come to the house to invite Ernesto to attend a summer youth camp Hezbollah was sponsoring on Margarita Island. After we talked for awhile, he sent Ernesto out to buy him some cigarettes, and the moment we were alone, Zaidi told me the real reason for his visit."

I asked, "Did it have anything to do with some construction sites?"

Roberto nodded, but then he asked, "How do you know about the construction sites? I don't understand how the sites could be connected to locating Ahmed and turning him over to the Columbian government."

"You don't need to be concerned about that right now, Roberto. Just tell us what Zaidi said to you about the real reason for his visit."

Roberto didn't appear to be satisfied by my answer, but he continued his story anyway. "He said he knew Ahmed Al-Amin had talked to me about helping a consortium of Syrian businessmen develop an import/export business in Venezuela. I told him Ahmed hadn't mentioned what kind of business it was, but I'd be happy to do all I could to facilitate any red tape involved in helping their business get established here in Venezuela. He said—"

"Do you remember any of their names? Could you identify any of the Syrians who wanted your help?" I asked.

Before Roberto had a chance to answer my questions, Buck walked in the room. He stood quietly in the doorway between the kitchen and living room for a few minutes, and since Roberto had his back to him, he didn't realize Buck was even there.

When Buck saw he had my attention, he motioned for me to meet him in the back bedroom. I gave him a brief nod, and he turned and left the room.

Mitchell, who also saw Buck, tried to distract Roberto.

"Roberto, would you like to take a break before answering those questions? I know I could go for something cold to drink right now."

Roberto shrugged. "I'm not in charge here."

I said, "I'll meet you in the kitchen in a few minutes."

After Roberto and Mitchell left the room, I walked down the hallway to the master bedroom, where Buck handed me an Agency sat phone.

"This better be good, Olivia. I was making progress with Roberto."

"That makes two of you. Ahmed's made a lot of progress trying to locate Roberto."

"You've got my attention."

♦♦♦♦

Olivia quickly updated me on Ahmed's status by explaining how the surveillance crew outside of Zaidi's apartment had observed Ahmed entering the apartment building about the time Roberto had arrived at my location.

She said Ahmed was in the apartment by himself for over an hour, but during that time, the bugs hadn't picked up anything besides the sound of a teakettle whistling on the stove.

The situation had changed when Zaidi arrived.

"As soon as Zaidi walked in the door, he told Ahmed he had a good idea where Roberto might have gone. He remembered Roberto's wife had a sister in Caracas, and on his way in from the airport, he had called someone and told them to locate an address for her."

"Where are the ladies now?"

"They're finishing up at the salon. I'm considering grabbing them before they get back to Roxanna's house. If I don't, Zaidi's men might already be there."

"Do it."

"You mean you and I finally agree on something?"

"See? Miracles do happen to you."

It was faint, but I thought I heard her laugh.

She ordered me to stay on the line while she gave Wylie some instructions about where to take the three women.

When she came back on, she said, "I've arranged a safe house for Roberto's family near you, so when you want to question Marianna, she won't be that far away."

"I may not need to question her. Roberto is singing like a bird now." Then I added, "It was Ben who got him to talk. Since Ben was with Ernesto when he died, I think Roberto can tell Ernesto's death affected him."

"Becoming emotionally involved in a case doesn't usually make for a good intelligence officer."

"In this instance, it worked in our favor."

"Roberto may not be willing to keep talking once he knows his family is safe and out of Ahmed's reach."

"Who says I'm sharing that information with him?"

Chapter 40

After I hung up with Olivia, I gave Buck instructions about the role I wanted him to play when my interrogation of Roberto resumed. Basically, I told him to listen for a certain key phrase, and then I asked him to do a bit of play-acting.

When I entered the kitchen, I found both Roberto and Mitchell eating a sandwich, and after I wolfed down something stuck between two slices of bread, the three of us returned to the living room.

As soon as Roberto was seated on the sofa again, I repeated the last question I'd asked him. "When Zaidi approached you about the possibility of helping the Syrians with this business enterprise, did he give you the names of those associated with this project?"

Roberto shook his head. "No. I only dealt with Rehman Zaidi. The consortium's business in Venezuela has always been handled by a lawyer in Caracas."

"So what did they want you to do for them?"

"At first, Zaidi told me the group planned to build two large warehouses in Cumaná and Maracaibo. They were to serve as distribution centers for the goods they were importing from the Middle East. It made perfect sense for the centers to be located near these two port cities, since all their goods would be arriving in cargo ships. However, the task of getting them built quickly—which they insisted was a necessity—required a massive amount of documentation.

"What they needed for me to do for them was cut through all the red tape involved with getting the warehouses built. They wanted me to run interference for them, and I was to make sure all their permits were expedited. I was also to collaborate with the contractors to prevent any work stoppages."

"Is this something you'd ordinarily do in your position as trade minister?"

Roberto shook his head. "No, not really, but . . ." he paused and hung his head, "when Zaidi asked me for this favor, he also gave me a substantial amount of money. He told me it was for Ernesto's college education, but we both knew the cash and the favor he wanted were connected."

"So you used the money to send Ernesto to the University of Texas?"

"Yes, and then the next year, he gave me the same amount of money for Emma's private schooling here in Caracas."

"You've held a government job for most of your life, Roberto, so I'm sure this wasn't the first time you were offered money for expediting someone's paperwork through government channels."

He nodded. "I've done it several times before. As you probably know, that's just the way business is conducted here in Venezuela. But, this time it was different because there was so much money involved and . . ."

He hesitated, and I suspected he'd finally reached the main focus of his story, the real reason Ernesto had been killed.

His hesitancy made me wonder if he felt his behavior was somehow responsible for his son's death.

I prodded him with a question. "And you discovered something about the warehouses?"

He nodded. "When I visited the site in Maracaibo about six months after the construction had gotten underway, I realized the warehouses weren't going to be used for an import business. I came to this conclusion because of the type of security fence being erected around the site. It wasn't the kind of thing usually found at a commercial establishment. I also discovered the storage units had an elaborate climate-controlled environment—something I'd never seen in that type of warehouse before. When I questioned Zaidi about it, he told me the warehouses shouldn't concern me, to forget about what I'd seen, and to concentrate on making sure things ran smoothly.

"I did as I was told, and I tried putting it out of my mind. But a few months ago, I happened to be at a diplomatic reception where I overheard a conversation between a general who was on the National Defense Council and the comptroller general of the National Armed Forces. They were discussing a rumor circulating among the top brass in the military that Syria was disposing of its chemical weapons' stockpile by handing their supplies over to Hezbollah. He'd heard some of those weapons could be headed for either Cuba or Venezuela, maybe even both countries.

"After hearing that, I did some research on the type of storage facilities required to safely handle chemical weapons, and I discovered the buildings being constructed at the two sites met the criteria for storing canisters of sarin gas, exactly the type of chemical Syria was rumored to have turned over to Hezbollah."

Roberto shook his head. "The thought of having weapons of mass destruction in my country was repulsive to me, and I spent many sleepless nights trying to decide what to do about my suspicions. For all I knew, the shipments were coming here with the full knowledge of our president."

I said, "But you didn't really believe that, did you?"

"Not really." He sighed and leaned his head against the sofa for a few moments. "I finally decided to confront Zaidi with this information, and an opportunity presented itself when some of the construction workers initiated a slowdown at the Maracaibo site. I decided not to intervene just to see what would happen. Within a couple of days, Zaidi showed up at my office.

"I knew the only way I could find out what was going on with the warehouses was for me to pretend to be excited about the idea of Venezuela acquiring chemical weapons, so that's exactly what I did. I told him about the rumor I'd heard. I said I hoped he could verify this was true and that the warehouses under construction were going to be used to house Venezuela's first chemical weapons arsenal."

"Did he believe you?"

Roberto nodded. "He totally bought it. This surprised me, but I realized he wanted to believe I didn't have a problem with what Hezbollah was doing. He said the weapons didn't belong to the Venezuelan government, and that no one in the administration knew anything about them.

"He also said the agreement Syrian President Assad had entered into with Sayyed Nasrallah, the Hezbollah leader, meant the weapons were to be held by both the Syrian government and the Iranians, with Hezbollah acting as caretaker. By doing this, Assad was able to retain possession of at least some of his chemical weapons stockpiles, after he was pressured by the international community to destroy them."

I asked, "Did Zaidi tell you where the canisters are being stored while the warehouses are being built? Do you know where these chemical weapons are right now?"

"No, not specifically. He said when Hezbollah was given the pallets of canisters from the storage facilities at Shamat and Furklus, they were placed aboard several ships in an effort to avoid detection by either the Israelis or the Americans."

Mitchell said, "Are you saying there are multiple ships loaded with tons of sarin gas navigating through the ocean's shipping lanes right now?"

Roberto said, "Yes, but the ingredients in the canisters aren't lethal, at least not in their present state. The sarin is stored as two distinct chemicals, and until the two are combined, the canisters pose no danger to anyone. The only way the canisters become weaponized is when they're put in an artillery or rocket shell and fired. Firing the shell mixes the two ingredients, and when it reaches its target, that's when the sarin is released."

Mitchell said, "I guess I should find some comfort in that."

I asked Roberto, "So what changed? You said Zaidi believed you when you said you were okay with the canisters being stored in your country. Now, however, you seem to be on Hezbollah's hit list."

He looked thoughtful for a moment. "Once Zaidi shared this secret with me, he seemed more relaxed around me. I think he enjoys talking, and it wasn't long before I realized he wasn't just Hezbollah's messenger boy; he was actually a member of Hezbollah's leadership council back in Syria. He talked openly with me about the training he'd received in Iran with the Iranian Revolutionary Guard Corps, the IRGC. He also told me the IRGC had instigated a plan to use Hezbollah—particularly their Latin American members—to get back at the United States for boycotting their goods and trying to put an end to their nuclear weapons program."

I asked, "Did he give you any specific details about how Iran plans to use Hezbollah against the U.S.?"

He nodded. "That's why the chemical weapons are being warehoused here. Iran is using Hezbollah to train recruits here, so they can use the chemical weapons against targeted cities in the United States."

"Are you kidding me?" Mitchell said, glancing over at me to gauge my reaction to this news.

I didn't look at him, because I was focused on Roberto's body language. I wanted to see if I could detect any sign the statement he'd just made was a lie.

Unfortunately, I saw nothing to indicate he was lying.

Roberto massaged the bridge of his nose for a second. "No, I'm not kidding."

"Roberto," I said, trying to keep my voice steady, "those canisters are designed to be used in a rocket or an artillery shell. How is Hezbollah planning to target American cities? What mechanism will they use to deliver the gas?"

He shook his head. "He never told me that, and I didn't ask. Since he mentioned dropping the canisters on American cities, I just assumed they were going to use planes to do this, but I don't know that for sure.

"When he told me this, all I could think about was my son in Texas. I asked Zaidi how his plans were going to affect Ernesto, and he said Ernesto had already indicated his willingness to help him advance the cause of Islam. He told me that was the reason Hezbollah was sending students like Ernesto from Venezuela and other Latin American countries to receive their education in the U.S. He said these young people were going to be used to carry out the attacks against the Americans.

"When I realized he was grooming Ernesto to become a terrorist, essentially destroying my son's life, I knew I couldn't stand by and let that happen. I believed the only way I could affect their plans was to slow down the construction of the warehouses, and that's what I did. Although I pretended to be working on the labor problems at the work sites, when construction came to a standstill because of a workers' strike, I did nothing.

"The second thing I did was get in touch with Ernesto. I suggested he leave school a few days early. I even proposed the fishing trip as an incentive for him to do so. I wanted him back here with me, where I knew he'd be safe. I guess he must have told Zaidi I was worried about him, because a few days later, Zaidi questioned me about the slowdown at the work sites. He seemed suspicious of my intentions, and he even grilled me about whether I'd changed my mind about helping Hezbollah store the weapons in Venezuela."

I asked, "So you think he realized you were no longer willing to cooperate with Hezbollah?"

He nodded. "I'm pretty sure that's what happened. I also believe he must have informed his superiors back in Damascus, because a few days later, he told me Ahmed Al-Amin had some business in the States and was planning to get in touch with Ernesto while he was there. He made it sound like a threat of some sort. He also said Ahmed needed my assistance in obtaining a Venezuelan passport. He gave me an email account to use when communicating with Ahmed, and he said I should address him as my brother in the email. He also told me to use the name, Alberto Montilla, on Ahmed's passport."

I said, "Why would Zaidi ask you to get a passport for Ahmed? Issuing passports isn't part of your portfolio at the trade ministry, is it?"

Roberto shook his head, "No, but . . ."

He looked away for a moment, and I thought I knew why. Accepting cash in exchange for cutting through some red tape associated with the warehouses wasn't the only bribe he'd taken from Hezbollah.

Roberto said, "I'd already been working with a friend of mine in Passport Control, and we were obtaining Venezuela passports for some of Zaidi's friends. He was paying both of us very generously for this help."

"Zaidi's friends?" Mitchell said. "Don't you mean Iranians trying to pass themselves off as Hispanics or Arabs claiming to be Venezuelans? Are those the friends you mean?"

I was surprised at the outrage in Mitchell's voice, and Roberto seemed startled by it as well. However, once I realized Mitchell must have been thinking about the cartel members who'd been involved in Bledsoe's murder, then I understood his anger.

Roberto looked over at me, "You said you'd tracked Ahmed to Venezuela because he was selling weapons to the Colombians, but, besides being interested in the construction sites, you also seem to know about the false passports. I'm beginning to wonder if you're really telling me the truth."

Now seemed an appropriate time for Buck to make his acting debut.

I gave him his cue.

I said, "What I'm telling you, Roberto, is that Ahmed Al-Amin is a contract killer hired by Hezbollah to assassinate you. The question is, are you willing to help us capture him before he has a chance to do so?"

Chapter 41

I had barely finished speaking when Buck rushed in the room. He was waving a cell phone in one hand and gesturing at me with the other.

"This phone call's important," he said, attempting to sound excited. "I'm sorry to interrupt you, but you've got to take this call. Ahmed's here in Caracas, and he knows exactly where Roberto is hiding."

When he said this, he looked directly over at Roberto and furrowed his brow. While Buck's expression wasn't exactly the worried look I'd been anticipating, it nevertheless achieved the results I wanted because Roberto immediately jumped to his feet.

"He'll kill my family," he said. "I need to warn them."

I laid my hand on Roberto's shoulder. "We'll talk about this once I've taken the call."

As soon as Buck and I were out of Roberto's sight, I handed him back the phone and congratulated him on his award-winning performance.

He grinned at me.

I think he actually believed me.

When I asked him about the latest update from Olivia, he said everything had gone as planned, and Roberto's family had been safely stashed away at the safe house.

I decided I wouldn't ask him how the ladies were handling their sudden abduction. Grabbing someone off the street and then telling them you have their best interests at heart never goes very smoothly, no matter how well the plan is executed.

♦♦♦♦

When I stepped back in the living room, I noticed Roberto was pacing the floor. He appeared stressed, and I was happy to see Buck's little drama had left a lasting impression on him.

As soon as he saw me, he rushed over and asked, "What's happening with my family?"

"Have a seat, Roberto."

There was a look of frustration on his face, but he walked back over to the sofa and sat down. When I returned to my own seat, I gave Mitchell a quick wink to let him know we were in game mode.

He nodded at me.

The moment I sat down, I pointed my finger at Roberto and said, "Ahmed is in Caracas looking for you, and Rehman Zaidi is helping him. I'm not going to tell you how we came across this information, but Zaidi knows about Roxanna, and he believes you're hiding out at her house."

Roberto's expression was one of pure anguish. "Oh, no."

"I have people ready to take your family to a place of safety, but I need assurances from you that you're willing to do whatever it takes to help us capture Ahmed."

He quickly nodded his assent. "Yes, of course, I'll do whatever you want. Just make sure my family is safe."

I gestured at Mitchell. "Would you let our security team know Roberto is willing to cooperate with us?"

"Sure," he said, getting out of his chair and heading for the door.

Moments before he reached it though, he looked back at Roberto and said, "I just hope they get to your family in time."

The worried look on Mitchell's face was so believable, it even caused me a moment of concern, and that was when I decided Mitchell was a much better actor than Buck was.

♦♦♦♦

As soon as Mitchell returned, Roberto began bombarding him with questions.

"Is my family okay? Are my wife and daughter safe? What about my sister-in-law?"

"Our security team is taking care of your family," Mitchell assured him.

I said, "You'll be able to see them once we're finished here. But first, I want you to tell me about Ahmed's emails."

Roberto took a deep breath. "There were only three emails, but each of them made some kind of reference to Ernesto. In the first one, Ahmed said he and Ernesto were seeing the sights of San Antonio, Texas. In the next one, he said the two of them had decided to drive from Mexico to Costa Rica. Then, in the last one, he said Ernesto had told him he'd never been on a cruise before, so he planned to rent a yacht in Limón, and join me on Margarita Island when I arrived there for the International Trade Conference."

"Did you tell Zaidi about the emails?" I asked.

"I didn't need to tell him. He knew Ahmed was emailing me, and the feeling I got from both of them was that if I didn't cooperate, something would happen to Ernesto. I felt my only leverage with them was Ahmed's passport."

"So you delayed sending it to him?"

He nodded. "I was hoping Ernesto would recognize Ahmed wasn't a friend, and he would try to get away from him. But Ernesto never called or emailed me—not even a text—so I finally made arrangements for Ahmed to get the passport. I felt confident once they arrived in Venezuela, I could get Ernesto alone and explain how dangerous both of these men were."

"And what were you going to do after that?" I asked.

"Leave Venezuela. I'd arranged everything—passports, airline tickets, money—to start a new life in Argentina."

"Argentina? Why not go to America?"

He looked at me as if I'd just proposed doing something completely preposterous.

"Because I wanted my family to have a better life." He paused and shook his head. "Islamic jihadists are planning a sarin gas attack in some of your cities today, but tomorrow they'll be planting dirty bombs in those same cities. The U.S. has too many enemies to survive much longer."

Roberto, like most of America's enemies, believed America was doomed to destruction, but I was ready to give my last breath to prove them wrong.

Mitchell asked, "What made you go into hiding when you heard about Ernesto's death? Why were you so certain it was Ahmed who had taken your son's life?"

"I wasn't all that certain. I just knew something wasn't right, and I needed to act quickly. I guess you could call it my instincts. The moment I got the call, it was clear to me the leadership in Hezbollah didn't want an outsider knowing about their plans to use chemical weapons. I wondered why they didn't just have Zaidi kill me. Why would they go to all the trouble of sending Ahmed to Venezuela? But then, I realized there were too many people who knew Zaidi and I were friends, and they didn't want him coming under suspicion. That's why I didn't go to the trade conference. After hearing about Ernesto's murder, I believed Ahmed was going to kill me too; or even worse, kill my wife and daughter."

I said, "Don't you think you should have given Ahmed the benefit of a doubt? From what you've said, it sounds like both Ahmed and Zaidi have done nothing but treat you and your family with kindness. Maybe you're not thinking straight right now. In fact, with all the long hours you've been working to get ready for the trade conference, plus hearing the news of Ernesto's passing, you've hardly been able to make sense of anything."

Both Mitchell and Roberto looked at me as if I'd just lost my mind.

Roberto said, "Are you crazy? Didn't you just say Ahmed was sent here to kill me?"

I nodded. "I did, and I believe that's true. However, Ahmed needs to be convinced you acted irrationally when you heard about Ernesto's death, and I've just given you some points to remember when you make that argument."

Roberto asked, "When would I need to make that argument?"

"When you invite him over here."

"Over here? You want Ahmed to come here?"

I pulled his cell phone from my pocket. "That's exactly what I want. But first, you need to call Rehman Zaidi and persuade him to let you talk to Ahmed."

♦♦♦♦

Roberto spent the next five minutes arguing with me about calling Zaidi. I kept trying to tell him he wouldn't be present when Ahmed arrived, but he wouldn't shut up long enough to hear me.

Finally, he heard me say I'd be the person confronting the man who'd killed his son, and that's when he agreed to make the call.

However, before I allowed Roberto to use his phone, I took it back to the master bedroom and gave it to Buck. I told him when Roberto made the call to Zaidi, I wanted to be able to monitor everything he said to him.

Buck removed the phone's SIM card and looked it over. Then he said, "Cindy can set up the protocols to make that happen."

The woman sitting at the communications console turned around and lifted one of the earphones away from her ear. Then she said, "Hi, I'm Cindy."

"Nice to meet you."

After listening to Buck's instructions, she said to me, "Olivia said for you to get in touch with her whenever you took a break."

"I'll do that now. Will you be able to have the phone ready when I finish talking to her? I want Roberto to call Rehman Zaidi as soon as possible."

"I can do that," she said. When she handed me an Agency phone, she added, "Oh, and good luck with Olivia. She's sounded a little upset about something."

That didn't sound good.

In order to have some privacy, I walked down the hallway to the guest bedroom. It was larger than the girl's bedroom where Mitchell had taken his nap, and while it had a bed in it, it also contained a desk and some bookshelves.

I sat down at the desk and punched in Olivia's phone number.

When Olivia said hello, I could hear what sounded like several conversations going on in the background.

"Cindy said for me to—"

"Do you think Roberto's telling us everything?"

It was obvious Olivia had been listening to the audio of my interrogation of Roberto. However, she sounded a little too excited for my liking.

"Not everything, but enough. I don't think he's lying about Hezbollah's plan to use the sarin gas, if that's what you mean."

"I believe he knows which American cities they've targeted. You've got to get him to identify them for you."

"Hold on, Olivia. We'll have time for that later. Right now, I need to prep Roberto so he'll sound convincing when he talks to Ahmed. We'll deal with the chemical weapons once we've taken care of Ahmed."

Olivia sounded as if she hadn't heard me. "I've got the analysts working on identifying the ships carrying those weapons. But, for all we know, they could have arrived in port already."

"That's possible, of course, but Roberto seemed pretty certain they were still at sea and wouldn't get here until the warehouses were ready."

"Yes, I heard him say that, but . . ."

I heard her take a deep breath, and then she said, "There's a lot happening right now."

Where was Carlton when I needed him?

I suddenly realized Olivia's greatest strength—her ability to focus on one task and do it well—was also her greatest weakness when it came to handling all the different aspects of being a field officer.

I decided there was only one way to make her refocus and direct her energies toward grabbing Ahmed.

I said, "I could send Ben over to the embassy to help you handle things there. I don't need him here anymore, so he could easily manage the operation from there."

There were several seconds of silence, and then she said. "Contrary to what you might think, Titus, I'm perfectly capable of conducting this operation without Ben's help. If someone needs Ben's help, it's you. From everything I've heard, he has more rapport with Roberto than you do."

She was right about that, so I didn't argue with her. Instead, I changed the subject by asking her what was going on at Zaidi's apartment. Once she started updating me, I was relieved to hear she sounded in control again.

"Zaidi's guys discovered a laptop computer at Roxanna's house, and when they delivered it to the apartment, Zaidi began searching through Roberto's files. He told Ahmed he hoped they would provide a clue to Roberto's whereabouts."

"It sounds like the perfect time for Roberto to call Ahmed and invite him over here."

"Roberto can call and set up the meeting time for tomorrow morning, but I've decided the plan needs tweaking—at least the part about making sure Zaidi doesn't follow Ahmed to your location."

I didn't like last-minute changes when the end game was in sight, but I decided not to say anything. I even gave myself a mental pat on the back for my ability to keep quiet—until Olivia finished telling me about her revised plan.

She said, "Instead of taking Zaidi out of the picture tonight by having him involved in a car accident, I've arranged for a major crisis to erupt at *Campamento Laguna* during the night. That means Zaidi will have to fly back to Margarita Island tomorrow morning to handle it, and then you'll only have to deal with Ahmed when he makes his rendezvous with you tomorrow."

"You call that tweaking, Olivia?" I asked. "You've completely altered the whole plan. We agreed to take Ahmed out tonight, because by tomorrow—"

"The Presidential Directive states—"

"—by tomorrow Roberto's colleagues will notice he's missing from the conference and start making inquiries about him. When the military initiates a search for him, things are going to get awfully dicey for us around here."

Olivia shook her head. "I've decided having Zaidi involved in a car accident tonight has too many variables. The Presidential Directive explicitly states the Agency is only authorized to grab Ahmed. That means Rehman Zaidi shouldn't be touched. Logistically, this is more doable."

I took a deep breath and decided to try another tactic.

"Have you cleared this with the Ops Center yet?"

"Both Douglas and C. J. concur with my assessment."

While I found it hard to believe Carlton had agreed to alter the plan, I didn't have time to contact him, so I made a last-ditch effort to get Olivia to allow everything to go forward as planned.

"There's no way I can let Roberto leave the house and rejoin his family until we're sure Ahmed is on his way over here. Since you've changed the POA, Roberto will have to spend the night here without getting in touch with his family, and I know that's not going to make him happy."

"You're an expert at pushing someone's buttons, Titus, so I'm sure you'll find a way to redirect his attention."

Chapter 42

In an effort to cool down after my confrontation with Olivia, I sat at the desk a moment and perused the titles of the books on the missionaries' bookshelves.

One book caught my attention.

It was entitled *When God Redirects Your Plan*, and I was struck by the irony of the title in light of my present circumstances.

I pulled the book from the shelf.

As I thumbed through some of its pages, I noticed several of the paragraphs had been underlined, and I quickly read through a couple of them.

After a few minutes, I put the book back on the shelf.

The author's folksy style made his insights sound refreshingly down-to-earth, and as I left the room, one of the author's key points lingered with me.

He wrote, *"Nothing takes God by surprise. If your plans get changed, altered, diverted, or simply shot to smithereens, he's still in control. Trust God. He's got your back."*

♦♦♦♦

For the next two hours, I prepped Roberto on what he should say to Zaidi, and how he should approach him in order to set up the meeting with Ahmed. I decided not to tell Roberto how we planned to take Zaidi out of the picture, nor did I divulge what arrangements the

Agency had made to ferret Ahmed out of Caracas and deposit him on a ship in the Caribbean for transport to Gitmo.

What most concerned Roberto was what would happen to his family once we took care of Ahmed. On that score, I assured him if he still wanted to relocate his family to Argentina, then the U.S. government would show its appreciation for his help by facilitating those plans. I also told him we would make sure Ernesto's body was taken to Argentina as well.

After giving him these assurances, he seemed satisfied and ready to make the call to Zaidi. However, at the last minute, he asked for me to put those guarantees in writing. After a quick consultation with Olivia, I provided Roberto with a detailed outline of what the U.S. taxpayers would be willing to do in order to resettle his family in Argentina.

Both of us signed the agreement.

If I had known his true intentions in having me draw up the contract, I would have done things differently.

♦♦♦♦

Around eight o'clock, I announced it was time for Roberto to make the call to Rehman Zaidi. To give him an incentive, I told him he'd be allowed to get in touch with his wife once he'd completed the call.

In order to monitor the conversation with Zaidi, Buck provided both Mitchell and me with our own set of earphones, but, as the three of us sat down together at the table in the dining room, I warned Roberto not to indicate there were other people in the room with him.

Moments later, he pressed a number on his speed dial and Zaidi came on the line.

"Roberto?"

It didn't surprise me to hear a note of skepticism in Zaidi's voice. He had every reason to doubt the call was actually coming from Roberto.

"Yes, it's me."

"Where are you? Why aren't you at the conference? Are you sick?"

"No, I'm not sick. I need to talk to Ahmed. Has he arrived yet?"

"Yes, he's here. We've both been worried about you. Where are you right now?"

"Did Ahmed tell you what happened to Ernesto? Did he tell you my son is dead?"

There was a short pause, and then Zaidi said, "Of course he did. I'm so sorry for your loss, Roberto. We're both very sorry."

"I must talk to Ahmed. I need to know what happened to Ernesto."

"You wish to speak with Ahmed?"

"Yes. I must speak to him."

"Okay, I'll arrange that. I'll have him call you. Where are—"

Before Zaidi could say another word, Roberto hung up.

I congratulated him on a job well done, and he gave me a weak smile. We both knew the hardest part was yet to come.

Twenty minutes later, Ahmed called Roberto.

"It's me, Ahmed."

"I must talk with you about my son's death."

"I don't know what you may have heard, but his death was an accident, and I can explain everything. Where are you?"

"I'm at a friend's house in Caracas. When I heard about Ernesto's death, my wife and I couldn't be alone."

"Give me the address. I'll meet you there."

"You're in Caracas?"

"Yes, I caught the first flight out when Rehman told me you weren't on the island, Where are you?"

"I can't meet with you tonight. My wife is too ill. I'll call you in the morning."

"No, it would be better if we met tonight."

"I can't do that. I'll call you at nine o'clock tomorrow morning. We'll meet then."

As per my directions, once Roberto delivered those instructions, he immediately hung up.

After a few seconds of silence, he looked across the room at me and said, "That man killed my son."

♦♦♦♦

Olivia was right about one thing. I was able to get Roberto refocused on something besides his family.

I didn't do this by pushing his buttons, though. I did it by telling him he wouldn't be able to leave the house the next day until he'd given me a written account of everything he'd told me about Ahmed. I even provided him with a laptop computer to make the task easier for him.

Of course, what I told him was a lie. Every word he'd spoken to me had been recorded and was already in the hands of Katherine's analysts back at Langley.

Roberto immediately agreed to write it all out for me.

I'm a very believable liar.

Sometimes, that's a good thing.

But not always.

♦♦♦♦

Olivia had arranged for several pizzas to be delivered to the house, and once we'd eaten, Roberto took the laptop and went to work typing out the details of his narrative.

While he was pecking away at the keyboard, I had Buck keep an eye on him, and Mitchell and I went back to the master bedroom to have a conference call with Olivia.

Because Olivia had planned Ahmed's extraction down to the smallest detail of the operation, it took the three of us almost an hour to discuss the logistics of the POA.

Mitchell said very little during the call, until Olivia told him how the scenario would play out the next morning.

"Ben," she said, "as soon as Roberto completes the call to Ahmed, I want you to take the van and transport Roberto over to the safe house so he can rejoin his family."

Mitchell immediately protested. "Why should I be the one to take Roberto over there? Why not have Buck or one of Sam's other guys do it? If I leave the house, Titus will have to face Ahmed alone."

While I appreciated his concern, I suspected he was more distressed about missing out on the opportunity to see Ahmed taken down than he was worried about my welfare.

Olivia said, "Titus won't be at the house alone, but even if he were, he would be the first to tell you, he's a big boy and can take care of himself. Sam will have two teams following Ahmed, and once he's inside, Sam will move in with the extraction teams to help Titus secure him."

I said, "Olivia, why don't you have Buck take Roberto over to the safe house instead of Ben taking him?"

"No, that won't work. He and Cindy need to be monitoring communications and recording what Ahmed has to say to you before you call in the troops. And, Titus, don't delay too long in giving them the go-ahead. Just execute the plan."

"Got it."

"No funny stuff and no heroics."

"You know I never make guarantees, Olivia."

Chapter 43

Tuesday, June 12

It was a sleepless night. At least it was for me. I suspected Mitchell rested pretty well. He took the girl's bedroom, while Roberto slept in the guest bedroom, and both of them awoke the next morning looking better than they had when they'd gone to bed.

Not so for me. I spent most of my time in the master bedroom monitoring the listening devices in Zaidi's apartment. I wanted to hear firsthand what was transpiring between Ahmed and Zaidi as they prepared to take out Roberto.

Shortly after midnight, Zaidi received word he needed to catch the first flight to Margarita Island to deal with a full-blown rebellion among his young recruits at *Campamento de la Juventud Laguna*. I wondered how Olivia had been able to precipitate such action at the training camp, but I decided I would wait and ask her once the operation was over.

When Zaidi heard this news, Ahmed assured him he would have no trouble taking care of Roberto by himself. In fact, I thought Ahmed sounded relieved to be rid of Zaidi, and that he was pleased to be left on his own.

I might have been projecting my own feelings onto the situation, however.

A few minutes after receiving the phone call, Ahmed discussed the weapons he planned to use to kill Roberto. It was because of this conversation, I learned Ahmed intended to have two different handguns on him when he met up with Roberto—his extra gun would be strapped inside an ankle holster—and besides the handguns, he also planned to have a high-powered rifle in the car with him.

He told Zaidi he wanted the rifle just in case Roberto suggested meeting him at a location where it would be easier for him to make a long-distance shot rather than engage in close-in action.

Since Ahmed would be meeting Roberto at The Missy Hacienda, I took the rifle out of the equation.

That subtraction meant Ahmed would still have two handguns on him when he arrived, but I could deal with that.

Later, Zaidi told Ahmed he'd made arrangements for one of his men to drive Ahmed to the meeting with Roberto. I wasn't surprised to hear Ahmed remind him that he planned to arrive at the designated location long before Roberto was expecting him.

That meant Ahmed could easily be on my doorstep within thirty minutes of Roberto's call.

I mentioned this to Olivia, and we both agreed Mitchell should get Roberto out of the house immediately after he made his phone call.

I asked her what she planned to do about Ahmed's driver, and she said Wylie had volunteered to take care of him.

She said, "I believe Sam's exact words were, 'Ma'am, leave that stagecoach driver to me,' or something to that effect."

"Very impressive Texas accent, Olivia."

"Oh, please, Titus. Don't patronize me."

Once it was evident Ahmed and Zaidi had gone to bed, I said goodnight to Olivia—but not in a patronizing way—and turned the monitoring equipment back over to Buck and Cindy. Then, I went in search of a place to get a few hours of rest.

Although I tried using the sofa in the living room for a bed, I finally gave up and stretched out on the floor.

When my internal clock went off at six o'clock the next morning, I realized I'd been dreaming about Nikki. In the dream, she was trying to tell me something, but I was refusing to listen to her. As I was processing some of the fuzzy mental images in the dream, I suddenly realized I didn't want to hear what Nikki had to say because I was afraid she was going to tell me she had cancer.

I decided not to spend too much time analyzing that dream.

♦♦♦♦

By the time everyone woke up at seven o'clock, I had scrambled some eggs, fried some bacon, and toasted half a dozen slices of bread. Anyone wandering into the kitchen in search of coffee ended up grabbing a plate and gobbling down a few bites, but no one was in the mood for a sit-down meal.

Mitchell was still fuming about having to deliver Roberto to his family and missing the moment Ahmed was finally captured. But, once I told him I would put in a request for him to accompany me to Gitmo in order to observe Ahmed's interrogation, he seemed to be less agitated.

When Roberto showed up in the kitchen, he barely spoke to anyone, nor did he eat anything. As the minutes ticked down for him to call Ahmed again, he became even more withdrawn. As a diversionary tactic, I suggested he sit down at the dining table and look over the statement he'd typed up for me on the computer.

He did so without protesting.

A few minutes later, I left Mitchell with him and went back to the master bedroom for a last-minute chat with Olivia.

She informed me Wylie and the extraction teams were on standby a few blocks from my location, and the surveillance teams had their eyes on Ahmed, who was already inside a black SUV outside of Zaidi's apartment, waiting for Roberto to call him and give him an address.

Satisfied all the players were in position, I walked back to the dining room and gave Roberto a slip of paper with the address of The Missy Hacienda on it.

"Here's the address you need to give to Ahmed," I said. "You can make the phone call to him now."

Roberto took the piece of paper from me, and then he lowered the lid on the computer. "I've made some corrections and added a few paragraphs to my statement. I believe you'll find everything's complete now."

"I'm sure it's fine, "I said. "I'll take a look at it later."

Roberto looked disappointed at my response, and in retrospect, I should have at least given his statement a cursory glance. In my defense, though, I was focused on capturing Ahmed and not on the details of what he may have revealed in his document.

When I handed Roberto his cell phone, I noticed his fingers were trembling as he punched in the number.

I tried to reassure him. "As soon as you make the call, you'll be on your way to see your family."

"And Ahmed?" Roberto asked. "Where will he be going?"

Before I could respond, Ahmed came on the line.

Once Roberto had given him the address, Ahmed lied and said it would probably take him an hour to get to his location. Then, he immediately hung up.

Roberto's face was ashen and covered in sweat when he handed me back the phone. Seconds later, he bolted from the chair and headed for the bathroom.

"Talking to Ahmed hasn't been easy for him," Mitchell said.

"No, but keeping his family safe provided him with enough motivation to get it done."

"Family connections make great motivators, don't they?"

He had no idea.

♦♦♦♦

While we were waiting for Roberto, Buck came in the living room and handed Mitchell the van keys, along with the directions to the safe house.

A few seconds later, Roberto walked back in the room.

I noticed the color had returned to his face, and he no longer looked like the beaten man I'd interrogated the day before. Instead, there was an air of defiance about him, much like the fighting spirit he'd exhibited when Buck's team had first abducted him.

I handed him back the passports and the airline tickets the team had confiscated from him, and Buck counted out the cash they'd found in his suitcase.

I said, "I'm keeping your cell phone just in case Ahmed tries to call you back."

I thought he was about to protest my decision, but instead, without saying a word, he turned and followed Mitchell out the door.

Buck called out after him, "What? No goodbye hug?"

♦♦♦♦

As soon as Mitchell left the house with Roberto, I walked back to the master bedroom and talked with Buck and Cindy about how I wanted them to proceed once Ahmed showed up at the house.

I gave them explicit instructions not to interrupt the conversation I was planning to have with Ahmed, and I told them not to give Wylie and his extraction teams the go-ahead to enter the house, until I had notified them to do so.

When I returned to the living room, I rearranged the furniture in much the same configuration as when I'd been anticipating Roberto's arrival the day before.

While doing so, I found myself breathing a mini-prayer. It was one I'd read in the Bible a few days earlier.

It mostly consisted of "Help, Lord."

Once everything was in place, I unlocked the front door, left it slightly ajar, and waited for Ahmed Al-Amin to arrive.

My pulse rate was somewhat elevated.

Chapter 44

Buck notified me the moment he received word Ahmed's vehicle had entered the neighborhood. After that, he and Cindy remained out of sight in the master bedroom.

I waited for Ahmed in the shadows of the hallway, just around the corner from the living room. I had my gun trained on the doorway, and the front foyer was in my sightline.

However, I was also aware of an alternative scenario in which Ahmed could skirt around the garage and enter the house from the backyard. There was a back door into the utility room from the patio, and I'd checked it to make sure it was unlocked, but, unlike the front door, I hadn't left it ajar.

It didn't matter to me which door Ahmed decided to use.

He would still have to cross the threshold into the living room, and that's where I planned for us to have our first—and last—encounter.

My theory was that if Ahmed truly believed Roberto simply wanted to meet with him in order to talk about the circumstances of his son's death, then, he would enter the house through the front door. Otherwise, if Ahmed thought he was being set up, he would enter the house through the back door and try to surprise Roberto.

I didn't have long to wait before finding out which door Ahmed had chosen.

Five minutes after I was told Ahmed's vehicle had been seen, the assassin himself was at the front door.

I watched him as he stood there, studying the open door, seemingly uncertain as to his next move.

Finally, he stepped forward and knocked lightly on the doorframe. "Roberto," he said, pushing the door aside slowly, "may I come in?"

He widened the opening until he had a full view of the living room, and as he took a step inside the foyer, he called out again, "Roberto, are you here?"

I was able to observe the exact second Ahmed realized something was off, and moments later, I saw him reaching for his gun.

That's when I stepped out of the shadows and leveled my Glock at him.

"Roberto's not here, Ahmed," I said to him in Arabic.

He froze and stared at me.

"Yeah, you blew it," I said, as he studied my face. "I'm not dead. Unfortunately, you killed my friend instead, and you're going to have to pay for that."

I suddenly realized I'd never seen Ahmed's eyes before. In the videos, he'd always been wearing sunglasses. Now, I saw his eyes were dark brown, almost black, and looked as lifeless as lumps of coal.

I said, "Remove your weapon, do it slowly; then place it on the floor and move away."

He followed my instructions to the letter.

I motioned for him to sit down in the chair in the center of the room.

As he moved towards it, I knew he was trying to figure out the optimum moment to make a grab for the gun in his ankle holster. I could almost see the calculations going on in his head.

However, I decided not to reveal I was aware of the gun—at least not yet.

I realized it was a gamble, but I wanted him to think he had the upper hand. I figured if he thought he was about to kill me, he might be willing to answer my questions truthfully.

I asked him, "Do you still have the knife you used to slice open Ernesto?"

The scornful look on his face was one of pure hatred.

"It was like cutting up a baby goat," he said.

The moment Ahmed opened his mouth, I felt a slight breeze, like a disturbance in the air around me. At first, I thought the sheer evil of the man had caused me to imagine the whiff of air.

Then, I quickly realized someone had opened the back door and entered the house through the utility room.

I looked at Ahmed, but his expression hadn't changed.

Was it Wylie? Had he decided I needed some extra backup?

Was it Ahmed's driver? Had Wylie failed to take him out?

Friend or foe?

Suddenly, Roberto Montilla entered the room, and I knew it was neither friend nor foe.

It was a grieving father who'd lost his son to an assassin, and he had a gun pointed directly at the killer's head.

"You killed my son," he shouted at Ahmed. "You killed Ernesto."

Ahmed used the distraction as the opportunity he'd been waiting for and went for his spare gun. Before he had a chance to retrieve it, Roberto stepped forward, steadied the gun with both hands, and shot Ahmed three times in the torso.

Ahmed's eyes widened when he realized he'd been shot. Then, in a slow-motion dance, he clutched at his chest and fell to the floor. As blood gushed from his wounds, he made a feeble attempt to get at his gun yet again.

I pointed my weapon at Roberto. "Drop the gun, Roberto."

He ignored me and fired two more shots at Ahmed.

Ahmed finally stopped moving.

Seconds later, Wylie came through the front door, closely followed by Buck and Cindy, and all three of them had their weapons trained on Roberto.

He flopped down on the sofa and dropped the gun beside him.

As I picked it up, I immediately recognized it as the gun Mitchell had been carrying, and I leaned over and grabbed Roberto by the collar.

"Roberto, where's . . ." I caught myself before calling him Ben, "Where's Mark?" I asked. "What's happened to him?"

Roberto, who appeared to be in shock, shook his head.

I didn't know what that meant, and I tightened my grip on his throat.

"Hold on, partner," Wylie said, pulling me off Roberto. "We need to talk."

Wylie motioned for me to follow him out to the kitchen, but, before leaving the room, I walked over and looked down at Ahmed's body.

The assassin was dead.

I felt certain his soul would not rest in peace.

♦♦♦♦

In the kitchen, I opened the refrigerator door and pulled out a couple of bottles of water. I tossed one over to Wylie and kept one for myself.

After taking a long swig, I said, "You know what's happened to Ben, don't you? Is he dead? Did Roberto kill him too?"

Wylie shook his head. "He has a bump on his head the size of a goose egg, but otherwise he's fine. At least that's what he said when he called me."

"Thank God," I said, and I meant it. "I couldn't have taken another dead soldier in this operation. So what happened? Where's he now?"

"I just sent one of my boys to pick him up. He's in the *Las Colinas* area. He said when he and Roberto were driving through there, Roberto asked Ben if he would mind stopping by a street vendor's flower stall and buying his wife some flowers. When Ben opened the cargo doors of the van to put the flowers inside, Roberto hit him over the head. He lost consciousness, and when he came to, he was lying in an alleyway behind a bar. That's when he discovered Roberto had taken his gun and left with the van. The kid still had his phone, so he called me to say he thought Roberto might be headed back over here."

"Why didn't he call Olivia?"

Wylie grinned. "Do you really need to ask me that? If she hears Ben let Roberto get to him, she'll put him on a spit and roast him like a pig. She already thinks Ben's not suited for field work as it is."

"You're right."

"So you agree we should keep Olivia in the dark about exactly what went down here with Roberto?"

Wylie took my comment further than I'd intended it, but I considered what he was suggesting.

I made a quick decision.

At the time, it seemed like the right decision, but, later on, I had to do a lot of soul-searching about what we finally agreed to do.

I nodded. "I'm in; otherwise, Ben's days at the Agency are over. And now that our guys have no chance of interrogating Ahmed at Gitmo, I doubt the DDO will honor the agreement I made with Roberto to let him leave Venezuela with his family."

"Yeah, Ira will probably want to punish Roberto by alerting the Venezuelan authorities their trade minister just murdered someone."

"I can't let that happen."

Wylie and I quickly initiated a series of actions to cover up what had gone down with Ahmed, beginning with when he showed up at the front door.

First, Wylie called Buck and Cindy into the kitchen so he could have what he called a "heart-to-heart" talk with them, while I went out to the living room to have my own little chat with Roberto.

He was still sitting on the sofa, but the shock of what he'd done seemed to have worn off.

When he saw me, he got up off the sofa and pointed down at Ahmed's body.

"I did everyone a favor by getting rid of him."

I didn't dispute his sentiment, but I didn't endorse it either.

"I'm about to do you a favor, Roberto. In the next few minutes, someone will drive you over to where your family is staying. Then, they'll return in a few days to take you and your family to the airport, where you'll catch a flight to Argentina."

"You're letting me go?"

"As long as you agree to forget what just happened here."

He thought about my offer for all of two seconds. "Of course. That's not a problem."

He stuck out his hand to seal the deal, as if we'd just negotiated a trade agreement.

After a brief pause, I shook his hand and said, "I'm only doing this because I believe you're genuinely sorry for making decisions that put your family in jeopardy and cost you the life of your son."

He looked me in the eye. "I'll never forgive myself, and I'll never act so foolishly again."

"Here's a little tip for you, Roberto. If you're really interested in turning over a new leaf, try searching for answers in the Bible. There's a lot in there about forgiveness and acting like a fool."

He looked at me as if he couldn't believe what I'd just said.

I was pretty surprised at it myself.

Wylie appeared in the living room with the same beefy looking guy who'd delivered Roberto to me the day before. He indicated Mr. Beefcakes would be taking Roberto to be reunited with his family, and seconds later, Roberto followed him out the door.

Once they were gone, Wylie and I got our stories straight about what we were going to tell Olivia, and when Mitchell arrived a few minutes later, he was the first of many people to hear the tapestry of lies we'd woven together.

"What happened here?" he asked, taking in Ahmed's dead body and the Glock resting at my side.

I said, "He went for his gun, and I had to shoot him."

♦♦♦♦

I told Mitchell when Ahmed showed up, I had immediately disarmed him, but I had continued to pretend ignorance of his spare gun, thinking it might give him the false impression he had the upper hand and would answer my questions.

I admitted this was a miscalculation on my part, because I got distracted, and that's when Ahmed went for his spare gun.

I said, "I shot him before he was able to get to it."

Mitchell walked over and looked down at Ahmed's body.

"It looks like you shot him several times."

I didn't comment.

Mitchell asked, "What distracted you?"

"Now here's the thing," Wylie said. "Titus could have been distracted by any number of things. We'll just have to think of the most plausible one."

A light suddenly went on in Mitchell's eyes, and he turned to me for affirmation.

"Roberto shot Ahmed, didn't he? Why are you covering for him?"

"Look at the alternative."

Mitchell pieced it together. "When the Agency finds out Roberto killed Ahmed, they'll refuse to help him leave Venezuela. They'll throw him under the bus."

"Right."

He said, "It's partly my fault. I let him talk me into getting those flowers. I should have refused, and then none of this would have happened in the first place."

Wylie said, "We're going to make it look like it didn't happen. Or rather, we'll make it look like it happened in a different way."

Mitchell asked, "Where's Roberto now?"

Wylie looked at his watch. "He should be in the arms of his family by now. One of my boys drove him over there after he agreed to keep quiet in exchange for the Agency's help in getting him to Argentina."

Mitchell glanced over at me. "Are you okay with this? If you take the blame for shooting Ahmed, you'll end up being grilled, and as I'm sure you already know, the DDO won't be happy about the way things have turned out here."

"I can handle it."

Wylie said, "Not only is Titus saving Roberto's life, he's also making sure you're not stuck behind a desk shuffling papers in the Agency's archives for the rest of your career."

Mitchell looked at me. "Is that true?"

I nodded. "Olivia will make sure of that. She can be pretty revengeful when someone doesn't follow through on her meticulous plans."

Mitchell said, "So I'm supposed to say I delivered Roberto to his family without incident, and when I came back here, I found you staring down at Ahmed's dead body?"

"That's it," Wylie said, slapping Mitchell on the back. "From the moment I laid eyes on you, I knew you'd be a quick study. Shall I call Olivia and tell her about the shootout now?"

"What about the audio recording?" Mitchell asked. "What happens when Olivia or someone in the Ops Center listens to the tapes?"

Wylie said, "Buck and Cindy already took care of the tapes. For some reason, the recording equipment malfunctioned right before Ahmed showed up here. It went kaput. Happens all the time. Shouldn't be a problem."

"So that's how it's going to be?"

Wylie said. "That's it. Ready for me to make the call to Olivia now?"

Mitchell didn't hesitate. "Let's do it."

And so we did.

♦♦♦♦

A few hours later, Olivia, Mitchell, and I landed at Del Caribe Airport in Porlamar and an hour after that, we boarded a flight for Miami. In Miami, before we got on our plane to Washington, I was able to wander off by myself and call Carlton.

"What went wrong?" he asked.

"Nothing. Everything. But we got Ahmed."

"Olivia said you shot him."

"He went for his gun."

"No chance for you to have a conversation with him?"

"He wasn't much of a conversationalist."

"I was told there was no audio of your encounter."

"I heard there was some kind of equipment malfunction."

"Deputy Ira won't be pleased. With Ahmed dead, he won't be able to crow about snatching up another terrorist and shipping him off to Gitmo."

"The DDO is about to have more pressing matters to deal with than a dead terrorist."

"If you're referring to what Roberto said about Iran using chemical weapons on the homeland, you're right."

"Have you been able to locate any sources in Syria to collaborate Roberto's story?"

"We're working on that, and Katherine's also looking into Rehman Zaidi's connections in Syria."

"That could be my next assignment, Douglas. Once Katherine uncovers Rehman Zaidi's connections, you'll need someone to go to Damascus and penetrate that network. It only makes sense for me to be the one to do that. I know the background, and I'm fully briefed in already."

There was a long pause, and then Carlton said, "As far as I know, Titus, you're still on the Deputy's blacklist. After you've been debriefed, I fully expect him to reinstate your medical leave and send you back to Oklahoma again."

"I haven't redeemed myself by taking care of Ahmed?"

"Probably not."

Chapter 45

Wednesday, June 13

Early the next morning, after Olivia, Mitchell, and I had spent the night in The Gray and were getting ready to be debriefed in the conference room on the lower floor, I invited Olivia to join me on the patio for a cup of coffee.

She sat down next to me in one of the lounge chairs and pointed out toward the horizon where the sun could be seen peeking through a thick grove of trees.

"Remember those beautiful sunrises we used to see when we'd do our morning jog together?"

"If I think back far enough, I can, but I don't ever recall hearing you express any appreciation for them."

"Since there are a limited number of sunrises in my future, I'm just grateful to see another one."

"About your future, Olivia. You should schedule your surg—"

"Don't lecture me, Titus. It won't do any good."

"Would it do any good for me to ask you why you insisted on having Ben drive Roberto to the safe house yesterday?"

She took her eyes off the sunrise and looked at me. "Like I told Ben, he was the logical person to do it."

"No, he wasn't. Sam could have had any of his team members escort Roberto over there. I believe you had another reason for getting Ben out of the house before Ahmed arrived."

"Which was?"

"You were following the DDO's instructions and trying to keep Ben away from the action. You didn't want him exposed to the inevitable adrenaline rush of capturing Ahmed and being hooked forever on the covert life."

She took a sip of her coffee before answering me. "You're right, but I was also trying to protect him in case something went wrong, and the Senator found some reason to blame me."

"Since things turned out the way they did, it appears you made a wise decision. Now, if the Senator's upset because Ahmed wasn't able to give us any good intel, he'll blame me, and Ben shall forever remain guiltless."

"The Senator will be more interested in the intel Roberto gave us about Syria's chemical weapons than with anything Ahmed could have told us."

"Have you read Roberto's statement yet? The one I had him type up on the computer?"

"Not yet. Buck said he was sending it to the Ops Center. Didn't you read it?"

"No, I never got the chance. I presume it's the same stuff he told me verbally."

Being presumptuous in a life-and-death situation is never a good idea.

♦♦♦♦

Following our five-hour debriefing, I asked Greg if he would give me a ride over to Langley to retrieve my Range Rover. When he agreed to do so, I told him I'd meet him in the driveway, and while I was standing there, I noticed Olivia getting in the car with the DDO for the ride back to Langley.

She saw me staring at her as they drove off, and she gave me a brief wave through the tinted glass. Obviously, we weren't going to have a tearful goodbye or it's-been-nice-working-with-you-again moment.

And that was fine with me.

However, had I known the next time I saw her, she would be hooked up to an assortment of machines and surrounded by a bunch of doctors, I might have felt differently.

A few minutes later, Mitchell showed up in the garage looking for me.

"So you're headed back to Oklahoma?" he asked.

"The DDO has reinstated my medical leave."

Mitchell motioned toward the path leading down to the lake. "Let's take a walk. There's something I want to ask you."

"If it's all the same to you, I'd rather not go down to the boathouse."

He laughed. "Okay. Let's walk over here then." He pointed to the other side of the circle drive where the previous owner had erected an elaborate gazebo.

As we walked over there, Mitchell said, "The Deputy has offered me a position on the Latin American counter-intelligence team. I'll be overseeing the Central American group as the top security analyst."

"It sounds like a good opportunity for you," I said, trying to sound sincere. "Are you going to take it?"

"That's what I wanted to ask you. Do you think I should? It would mean getting out of field work, but Olivia told me I wasn't really suited for it anyway."

I decided to tell Mitchell what he needed to hear and not what the Senator or the DDO wanted me to say.

"No, Ben, I don't think you should take it. You're a natural covert operations officer. You've got all the necessary skills to excel at running assets and conducting operations, and I'll prove it to you."

We'd reached the gazebo, and I quickly scanned the structure just to make sure the Agency hadn't decided to install security cameras inside.

Satisfied no one was monitoring our conversation, I sat down on one of the benches and said, "When we were interrogating Roberto and he asked you about Ernesto's last words before he died, I was surprised to hear you say Ernesto had told you about going fishing with his dad. That wasn't true, was it?"

He smiled. "No. I just made that up. Ernesto was mumbling something about fishing before he died, and I just took a wild stab in the dark, hoping that was something they'd done together."

"Okay, that proves my point. You know how to read people and use that knowledge to achieve an objective. An analyst interprets facts and data; a covert operative interprets people and situations. You're still green, but you're better at the latter than the former."

He thought about what I'd said for a moment. "Thanks. I'll keep that in mind when I make my decision."

"The reason Olivia doesn't think you're a good operations officer is that you have a tendency to get emotionally involved with the players. I know firsthand such empathy will get you into a lot of trouble."

He didn't respond, and I thought he looked uncomfortable as he thought about my observation.

I said, "It happened yesterday, didn't it?"

"I'm not sure I know what you mean."

"Sure, you do. You empathized with Roberto's hatred of Ahmed for killing Ernesto, and you despised Ahmed for being responsible for Toby's death. That attitude caused you to be less vigilant about Roberto's intentions in asking you to buy his wife some flowers. Or maybe I'm wrong, and the two of you conspired together to concoct the story about Roberto hitting you over the head and taking your gun. Which was it?"

His facial expression was a mask of contradictions. "I'm standing by the explanation I gave the debriefing committee."

I smiled at him. "Good answer. Exactly what you should have said."

My praise seemed to take him off guard, and he quickly looked away.

After a few seconds of awkward silence, I decided to ask him another question. "Tell me, Ben, what's the one thing you need in this world in order to be happy?"

It only took him a few seconds to respond. "My independence."

"Why does that not surprise me?"

I got up from the bench and offered him my hand. "It's been a pleasure working with you, Ben. I'd advise you to consider learning Arabic and then asking for a transfer to the Middle Eastern desk. No one should have to work with Cartel Carlos for more than five years."

After he shook my hand, he said, "Maybe we'll see each other again soon."

It turned out to be sooner than either one of us could have

anticipated.

♦♦♦♦

Once I'd retrieved my Range Rover from the parking lot at the Agency, I gassed it up and headed for Oklahoma. When I stopped for the night outside of Louisville, Kentucky, I called Nikki.

"Hi, it's me, Titus."

"Well, hi, yourself."

"I was able to wrap things up a little quicker than I'd anticipated. I'm headed back to Norman now, and I should be there around five o'clock tomorrow afternoon."

"Is that when you want me to bring Stormy over to your place?"

"Yes. I'd also like to take you out to dinner then."

"It's a date."

"I'm looking forward to it."

"Me too. See you then."

Before hanging up, she added. "And, Titus, I have some news to share with you."

"Good news or bad news?"

"I'll let you decide that."

Chapter 46

Thursday, June 14

It was late afternoon when I pulled up at the security gate outside my newly acquired residence on East Tecumseh Road in Norman. After I entered my code and the gate swung open, I drove down the long winding road to the ranch-style farmhouse.

Before leaving Norman, I'd left the management of the thirty-acre property in the hands of Eric Hawley, the real estate agent who'd sold me the property in the first place. I was happy to see the acreage had been recently mowed, and some of the dead branches on the trees bordering the lake had been removed. Someone had also planted some flowers at the side of the house, but I suspected Nikki had done that.

After turning on the lights in the house and cranking up the air conditioning, I went back out to the garage to get my stuff out of the Range Rover. That's when I saw a black GMC Terrain coming up the driveway towards the house.

Besides Eric Hawley, only Nikki had the security code to the gate, and since she drove a silver Toyota sedan, I immediately started reaching for my gun. Within seconds, though, I recognized it was Nikki driving the SUV, and Stormy was sitting beside her in the front passenger seat.

He appeared to be grinning from ear to ear.

Nikki had a smile on her face too.

When she opened the car door, Stormy bounded out and immediately headed straight for me. If I hadn't braced myself, the yellow Lab would have bowled me over.

"What have you been feeding this guy? He's twice as big as when I left."

She laughed. "He's certainly happy to see you."

Once his belly had been rubbed to his satisfaction, he rolled over and ran down towards the lake.

I pointed at the Terrain. "Is this yours? Did you buy a new car while I was gone?"

"I just bought it on Monday. I decided my Toyota was too small to haul around such a big dog, so I had to choose whether to get a new vehicle or get rid of your dog."

"You definitely made the better choice."

"I thought you might approve, but it wasn't a very hard decision for me, especially after my partner asked me to pick him up in the car lot at Ferguson's on Monday morning. That's when I saw this beauty and found I just couldn't resist her."

I understood the concept.

I asked, "Was this the news you wanted to share with me?"

"No, I'm saving that for later."

Once we were inside the house, I took Nikki in my arms and kissed her lightly on the lips.

"I've missed you," I said.

She pulled me closer and kissed me back.

When we finally drew apart, she said, "I've missed you too."

For a few short minutes, I didn't think about chemical weapons, Islamic terrorists, or a dead assassin. Instead, I lost myself in the scent of her hair and the smoothness of her skin.

Finally, when it dawned on me Stormy had been barking at the patio doors for several minutes, I let go of her and went out to the kitchen to let him in the house.

After Nikki retrieved Stormy's food and water dishes from her car, I asked her where she'd like to go for dinner. She suggested Charleston's on the west side of Norman, and she insisted on driving me to the restaurant in her new car.

I didn't protest.

Little did she know, at that moment, she could have asked me for anything, and I would have given it to her.

♦♦♦♦

The décor at Charleston's restaurant was all dark wood and ambient lighting and it appeared to be the perfect place to take a beautiful woman for dinner.

Nikki and I were seated in an elevated portion of the restaurant, and when the waitress showed us to our booth, Nikki motioned for me to take the seat with the best view of the dining room.

Even though I wasn't operational, I appreciated the gesture.

Once we'd both ordered the filets—medium rare with burgundy mushrooms on the side—she asked me about my recently completed assignment.

"Was Pastor John's prayer answered?" she asked.

I thought back to the prayer he'd prayed for me. "If I remember correctly, he prayed for my safety and success. As you can see, I came out of the operation unscathed."

"Was the outcome successful?"

"Yes and no. I achieved my objective, but my superiors had a different objective in mind. That's why I'm back in Norman so soon."

She nodded her head but didn't say anything.

Since talking about the mission had brought us right back to the discussion we'd been having in the hotel room in Grand Blanc before I'd left for Langley, I decided I had to address the issue.

"The whole time I was away, I couldn't stop thinking about us. I kept remembering what you said about wanting to make our relationship work, and I realized wanting to make it work is really all it's going to take. We both have to want to make this work. Surely two smart, intelligent people like us can figure out how to do that."

"You forgot bright."

I smiled at her. "Right. Two smart, intelligent, and bright people like us can make this work."

Nikki put her fork down and laid her hand over mine. "I agree. I know we can do this. And that brings me to the news I wanted to tell you."

She pulled a piece of paper out of her purse and handed it to me. It was a letter written on FBI stationery informing Nikki Saxon that she'd been invited to participate in the FBI's sixteen-week Law Enforcement Training School at the FBI National Academy in Quantico, Virginia.

I handed the letter back over to her. "Congratulations, Nikki. This is quite an honor. Are you going to accept the invitation?"

She nodded. "I've already done so. I was afraid if I delayed, they might offer it to someone else. They only invite 200 law enforcement officials a year to take the course."

"Why did you think I might consider this bad news?"

"It means I'll have to be gone from Norman for four months, and if you're called away on an assignment during that period, you'll have to board Stormy. I wasn't sure how you'd feel about putting him in a kennel."

"It doesn't look like I'm going anywhere soon, so I'll be here to see about Stormy while you're up at Quantico. Plus, this could be very good news for us. When you graduate, you'll be part of Homeland Security's terrorism defense team with a top security clearance. While I won't be able to discuss everything with you about my job, I should be able to share more with you than I can right now."

She said, "This isn't happening immediately. I still have two more weeks before I have to leave for Virginia."

"Good. For the next two weeks, I'm counting on being on your schedule as much as possible."

She agreed to fit me in.

A week later, all those plans changed with one phone call.

♦♦♦♦

It came from Carlton.

Someone in the Ops Center had finally gotten around to reading Roberto's statement, the one he'd typed out for me at The Missy Hacienda. In the document, Roberto admitted to lying about Iran's plan to use sarin gas on several American cities. He said they were targeting only one city—Washington, D. C.

Carlton said the DDO wanted me back at Langley immediately.

I left the next day.

Never The End, Always A Beginning

ACKNOWLEDGEMENTS

Although many people have given me support and encouragement in the process of writing *Two Days in Caracas*, first and foremost, I wish to thank my husband, James, and my daughter, Karis, who have never failed to uplift me with their prayers, strengthen me with their love, and bolster me with their confidence.

I also wish to thank Pat Brown and Kheva Kingery, who proofed my early copies, and Becky Miller, who gave me advice on a character's health issue, and Debbie Ratliff, who answered my maritime and boating questions.

A special word of gratitude goes out to photographer and friend, Charles Samples, for my author photos.

Saving the best for last, I wish to thank my faithful readers, many of whom write to me on a weekly basis. Your love of Titus Ray Thrillers keeps me writing past midnight. May you never stop asking, "When is your next book coming out?"

All of you serve as my inspiration.

A NOTE TO MY READERS

Dear Reader,

Thank you for reading *Two Days in Caracas*. If you enjoyed it, you might also enjoy reading the next book in the series, *Three Weeks in Washington,* available on Amazon, along with the other novels in the Titus Ray Thriller Series. My mystery series, Mylas Grey Mysteries, features Mylas Grey, a private investigator. You can learn more about this series at MylasGreyMysteries.com.

I'd love for you to do a review of *Two Days in Caracas* on Amazon. Since word-of-mouth testimonies and written reviews are usually the deciding factor in helping readers pick out a book, they are an author's best friend and much appreciated.

Would you also consider signing up for my newsletter? When you do, I'll send you a FREE Kindle copy of *Titus Ray Thriller Recipes with Short Stories.* You can sign up for my newsletter at www.LuanaEhrlich.com, and you can read more about Titus at www.TitusRayThrillers.com and more about Mylas Grey at www.MylasGreyMysteries.com.

One of my greatest blessings comes from receiving email from my readers. My email address is author@luanaehrlich.com. I would love to hear from you!

Made in the USA
Monee, IL
12 December 2020

52584194R00218